I0825793

THE CHESS SHOP

THE CHESS SHOP

A Bohemian Saga

David Kantey

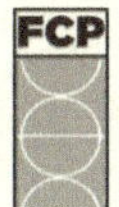

Full Court Press
Englewood Cliffs, New Jersey

First Edition

Published in the United States of America
by Full Court Press, 601 Palisade Avenue,
Englewood Cliffs, NJ 07632
fullcourtpress.com

ISBN 978-1-946989-31-4
Library of Congress Control No. 2021912979

Editing and book design by Barry Sheinkopf

TO MY TWO HEALERS

Richard Hersh, M.D.

and Albert Ellis, Ph.D.

Time: 1990s

Place: New York City

(and Iowa City)

CHAPTER 1

EVERY AFTERNOON AT ONE O'CLOCK, as he crossed Delancey Street, David Rabinowitz took off his *yarmulke* and put it in a plastic bag with his chess books. He had been raised as an Orthodox Jew. For reasons unknown even to himself, he had left the fold. With no experience in the secular world, how was he to fit in? His hobby, chess, provided a tenuous answer. David started spending his afternoons in The Chess Shop, on Tompkins Street in Greenwich Village.

The Chess Shop was founded in 1972 by Marcus Graf, who had immigrated from Germany after the famous Fischer–Spassky world championship match. Graf had been working as an assistant in a shop belonging to Grandmaster Nicholas Rossolimo when the Fischer–Spassky match started grabbing headlines, and he decided to open his own shop. He started buying chess sets from all over the world and displaying them in the windows. Inside The Shop he set up twenty tables, each with a chessboard. As he had anticipated, his business became a big success.

Naomi Hoffman, Marcus' wife, did the books at The Chess Shop and supervised the employees when Marcus was busy playing chess, which he did for hours on end. When she wasn't working, she sat at a table outside The Shop, reading *The New York Times* from cover to cover, underlining or circling items of interest to her. She spoke several languages fluently, and she enjoyed greeting tourists who passed The Shop in their native tongues.

Chess has a venerable tradition in Greenwich Village. The Marshall Chess Club, on West 10th Street, has been frequented by many World Champions. At the southwest corner of Washington Square Park, several chess players come to play every day during the summer months. Some of these "hustlers" make their sole living by playing chess with tourists for five dollars a game.

Many of the chess players in the Village are unusual characters, to say the least. It was in this strange subculture that David Rabinowitz found his new home.

One of the regulars at The Chess Shop, Sam Kanter, took a liking to David. Sam, a chess addict in his thirties, drove a yellow cab at night to support himself. Both he and David were iconoclastic, each in his own way. David, who had dropped out of high school to become a talmudic scholar before becoming disillusioned with Orthodox Judaism, was a highly intelligent young man, but he had very little life experience and very limited social skills. Sam, an assimilated Jew who suffered from bipolar disorder, found in David someone he could confide in and from whom he could learn more about Judaism, albeit from David's unusual perspective.

Sam and David became inseparable. They were very evenly matched as chess players. After fighting ferociously over the chess board, they would go for long walks together, exploring the city and each other's minds.

Although David had little formal education, he was very well read. He focused his unschooled eye on the secular Western tradition from Descartes to Marx, Freud, and Heidegger. He formed his own bold opinions of these writers and bounced them off Sam to see what he thought.

Like many people with a religious upbringing, David had a problem with Darwin. Sam and David argued bitterly about evolution, David claiming that Sam wasn't thinking for himself but blindly parroting the scientific authorities, while Sam claimed that David wasn't really thinking for himself either; according to Sam, it was only because of his religious upbringing that David couldn't countenance the idea of evolution.

David had a highly analytical mind; he enjoyed studying chess positions more than actually playing. He would spend hours looking at a simple endgame where one side had a slight advantage, to see whether it was a draw or a win for the stronger side. Other players called him "The Theoretician."

One of the salespeople in The Chess Shop was a young actress named Carla—the first to call the friends "Sam and Dave," after the pop singers with that appellation. Sam, like most of the men there, had a crush on her. Unfortunately, he had very little in common with her. She was a devotee of the New York club scene, which Sam abhorred. He didn't like the fact that the big nightclubs had bouncers who could decide whom to admit and whom to exclude.

"I always get in," she said.

"I think you're missing the point," he said. "The doormen shouldn't be allowed to decide who gets in and who doesn't. I'm surprised someone hasn't filed a lawsuit!"

They also argued about music. Carla didn't like jazz, and Sam didn't like pop music, especially what was popular in the Nineties.

"When disco first came out in the Seventies, I hated it. Now that they have this horrendous 'house' music, I wish disco would come back."

"You're a fossil!" she said.

Another friend of Sam's was a young Italian named Freddy, an economics major at the New School and one of the best chess players in the Village. Freddy loved to gamble. His favorite opponent was Dr. Li, a middle-aged Chinese-American and his best friend in New York. Freddy referred to many of the chess players by their country of origin—Dr. Li was "The Chinese"; Pavel, a multi-tattooed Russian immigrant, "The Russian"; Costos, a foul-mouthed player who was either in The Shop or in Washington Square Park twelve hours a day, "The Greek"; and Mike, a good-natured buffoon from New Delhi, "The Indian."

Each had his own spiel. Mike called his opponents "donkey" and shouted at them in mock anger. Costos would say, "You're playing like a man repossessed"; and Jim, an odds player who was an out-of-work actor, repeated, "Easy with the whiffle!" after each move his opponent made.

Sam and Freddy frequented a bar in the East Village called The Continental Divide, hoping to meet women. Although Freddy was handsome and had tremendous charm, he knew about nothing besides economics and chess. Sam, on the other hand, was cultured enough to keep a conversation going once the ice had been broken.

One evening at The Shop, Freddy took Sam aside and said, "Let's go to Café Reggio. There's something I want to show you."

In the café on MacDougal Street, Freddy took a backgammon board out of his valise. Along with the board, he had a magnet and a pair of loaded dice. He strapped the magnet to his leg, raised the leg so the magnet was directly under the table, and rolled the dice. They came up double-sixes. He rolled them again—and, again, double-sixes.

"Where did you get these?" Sam asked in astonishment.

"From Lenny," Freddy said. Lenny was a small-time hood who also frequented The Shop.

"We're going to play backgammon with a high-roller for thirty dollars a point."

"Don't do it!" Sam exclaimed. "He'll see that the dice are rolling funny, and you'll be lucky if he doesn't kill you!"

"Maybe you're right."

"Forget about it! Let's go to The Continental Divide."

At the Divide, Sam and Freddy sat at their usual table. At a table by the door, a beautiful brunette was sitting by herself. "I've got to have her," said Freddy. "I'm going to establish eye contact."

Sam laughed. "Stay here," he said. He went up to the girl and asked, "What would you think about someone who cheats at backgammon?"

In a slurred voice, she told him, "I think it would be reprehensible."

"Come with me," Sam said.

He led her over to Freddy and said, "Show her the dice."

Freddy took them out, put the magnet under the table, and rolled. Double-sixes.

"Cool! Let me try," said the girl.

When she awkwardly rolled the dice, they fell off the board and onto the floor.

"Oh no!" Freddy exclaimed. "If I lose these dice, I'll owe the Mafia a thousand bucks!"

All three of them got down on their knees and searched for the dice. The room was crowded and dark; they groped for the dice amid dozens of legs. When they finally found them, Sam excused himself to go to the men's room. While he was gone, Freddy asked the girl, "Would you like to have a drink at the bar?"

When Sam came back, Freddy was at the table sitting alone. "Where's the girl?" Sam asked him.

"She told me she's married."

"So? We could still hang out with her, couldn't we?"

"No cherry, no Freddy," was his response.

When Sam and David had known each other for about six months, Sam invited David for dinner at his mother's apartment in Hackensack, New Jersey. David was excited; he had never been in a secular household before. On the bus from New York, Sam warned David about his sister Eleanor, who was in town on a rare visit from California. "I guarantee that she'll say something negative about Orthodox Jews. When she does, just agree with her, and she'll like you."

Sure enough, within twenty minutes after they sat down to dinner, Eleanor exclaimed, "Orthodox Jews are disgusting."

"I agree with you!" David answered exuberantly.

After he left, Eleanor said, "He's a nice guy."

He also charmed Sam's mother. "Mrs. Kanter," he said, "you've given me a problem with my mother's cooking."

When Sam and Dave were on their afternoon walk that Sunday, David told him that a guy named Mark, one of the salesmen in The Shop, had been fired for stealing.

"Have they hired anyone to take his place yet?" Sam asked.

"No, they're looking for someone."

"Let's go there right now," Sam said excitedly.

Sam immediately approached Mr. Graf and asked him if he could have the job.

"Will you work for me forever?" Marcus asked wryly.

"Until my dying day."

"When can you start?"

"I need to give the taxi company five minutes notice!"

Marcus smiled. "You can start tomorrow at noon," he said.

Sam began his new job with some trepidation; because of his illness, he wasn't very organized. Managing The Shop was not an easy job. He had to keep the books, keep track of the players, serve coffee and snacks, and sell the chess sets.

The most difficult task was remembering where all the sets were stored. They were arranged in an apparently arbitrary fashion in a large closet in the back room. Sometimes Sam had to search for a set for twenty minutes while the customer waited impatiently at the counter.

The managerial style of Marcus and Naomi was very strict; they criticized Sam's every mistake and gave him little encouragement when he got things right. He found them very intimidating; he was nervous when they were there and made more mistakes, especially in keeping the books.

Now that he and Carla were working at the same shop, they began spending more time together. One evening, they went to The Continental Divide with Freddy. Carla and Freddy sat next to each other, across from Sam. As

Sam and Carla chatted, Freddy slipped his hand under Carla's skirt and started caressing her thigh. Carla showed no reaction whatsoever. She nonchalantly continued the conversation while Freddy groped.

Later, after Sam and Freddy walked Carla home, the two of them went to the Café Figaro.

"I'm gonna fuck her," Freddy said. "I have no respect for the little cunt. Did you see the way she let me feel her up, all the way up to her panties? What a fucking cunt."

As the weeks went by, Sam continued to have trouble handling the job at The Shop. Mr. Graf became more and more resentful, complaining bitterly to his wife about Sam's incompetence and glowering fiercely at his employee. Sam hated the job more and more, but he was reluctant to drive a cab again, so he grimly held onto his position.

David Rabinowitz was becoming Sam's favorite confidante. While they were on their walks together, Sam complained about his troubles at work and told him about his misadventures with women.

Sam was thirty-five; he had been single for four years and was desperate to find a girlfriend. After work and on weekends he would go to the jazz clubs on Bleeker Street. He was a regular at the Village Corner and the Village Gate.

One Saturday evening, he approached a young blonde sitting at the bar in the Gate. She was dressed so as to downplay her looks, wearing a long white cotton dress and a blue scarf on her head. Despite her camouflage, Sam could tell that she was stunning. He sat down next to her, and they struck up a conversation. Her name was Bathsheba. They talked about the story of David and Bathsheba in the Old Testament and about the character with that name in Thomas Hardy's *Far from the Madding Crowd*. The conversation flowed effortlessly.

Sam and Bathsheba went bar-hopping, stopping at Bradlee's, Fat Tuesday's, and the Village Corner before finishing at the Blue Note at 3:00 a.m. Sam was irritated that a cup of coffee, which would have cost seventy-five cents at a deli, went for five bucks at the Blue Note. At 3:30, Bathsheba gave him her phone number and hopped into a cab.

As Sam was sitting there, dreamingly finishing his coffee, the bartender approached him and said, "Hey, your friend left her purse."

"I'll take it," Sam replied. "I have her number."

He was inwardly excited, for now he had a pretext by which to see her again the next day. He walked to his apartment on Carmine Street, humming to himself and snapping his fingers.

The next afternoon, when he appeared at The Shop, Carla told him, "A woman just called and hurled a stream of abuse at you. She said you stole her purse last night."

Sam called Bathsheba on the player phone. "I've got your purse," he said.

"You motherfucker!" Bathsheba shouted. "Why the fuck did you take it?"

"I-I thought it would be safer with me than in the bar," he stammered.

"We only knew each other for *four hours!"* she screamed. "I would never take that responsibility!"

"Relax," Sam said.

"Relax? My *keys* were in that fucking bag! I couldn't get in my fucking *apartment!* I went on a fucking wild goose chase, back to the Blue Note and home again! I had to wake the fucking super at five in the morning."

"Relax," Sam repeated in a strained voice. "I'm at The Chess Shop. You can come and get it."

"I can't come now! I have to see my agent!"

"Alright, alright. Give me your address. I'll bring it to you."

Sam took the 1 train up to Bathsheba's building on the Upper West Side. He gave her apartment number to the doorman, who said, "She just stepped out. You can leave her purse with me."

"Okay," Sam said.

When he left the building, he went to the deli next door to buy a Coke. As he approached the cashier, Bathsheba entered the store with her boyfriend, a hefty young man in his twenties.

"What are you doing here?" she shrieked.

"I-I came to return your bag."

"But here? Here?"

"I just came to buy a soda, that's all."

Bathsheba heaved a sigh of relief. "I was *frantic* last night," she said.

"She *waaas*," drawled her boyfriend, rolling his eyes. Sam felt sorry for the young man, who, he realized, must have been the target of most of her hysteria. Bathsheba, who was suddenly as calm as if nothing had happened, said: "I'd like to play chess with you sometime."

"Uh. . .I'll call you," Sam said.

CHAPTER 2

ON ANOTHER OCCASION, SAM ASKED OUT a beautiful New York University exchange student from France named Elaine, who occasionally played chess at The Shop. She had curly light brown hair and striking blue eyes. Sam and Elaine always talked pleasantly when she came to The Chess Shop on his shift. Sam liked to practice his French with her.

"*Tu as des yeux pas possible,*" he told her.

They made a date for dinner on a Friday night. On Wednesday, when Sam returned to his apartment, he found the following message on his answering machine: "Hi, Sam. This is Elaine. I just had dinner last night with a group of Native American women. All the servers were men, which made me feel vindicated. Anyway, I'll meet you at The Shop at 6:00 on Friday."

Sam wondered what that was about. I guess I'll find out on Friday, he told himself.

That Friday night, Sam finished work at 6:00 p.m. Carla replaced him. He was too full of excitement to play, so he watched two masters play speed chess. As was almost obligatory in The Shop, they talked trash to each other as they played:

"You're bothering me. You're bothering me for no reason."

"I'm not bothering anybody. I'm a nice guy."

"You're bothering me. You're bothering me for no good reason."

"I'm not bothering anybody. I'm a very nice guy."

"You're bothering me. . . ."

Elaine wasn't there at 6:00 or 6:30. By 7:00, Sam was getting anxious and couldn't focus on the game he was watching. At 7:30 Elaine finally showed up in blue jeans and a black leather jacket.

"I'm sorry I'm late," she said.

"That's okay," Sam lied. "Let's go have dinner."

"Oh. . .I just had dinner with a friend on Christopher Street."

Sam frowned. "Well, I'm starved," he said. "Do you mind if I just get a burger, and then we can do something later?"

"No problem."

They went to the Waverly Diner. While Sam ate, Elaine showed a side of herself that he had never seen before. "Men are useless, wombless creatures," she said.

"Well, you need them too, don't you?"

"A way will be found to do without them."

Sam was perplexed. He quickly finished the burger and washed it down with a Coke. "Well, what would you like to do?" he asked her. "Do you want to go to a movie?"

"Let's go play chess," she said.

Sam shrugged.

At The Shop, they talked briefly with Carla, and then sat down to play. Sam's mind was elsewhere; he lost to Elaine for the first time.

"Carla's cute," Elaine said after the game. "Is she a lesbian?"

"No. Are you?" he asked, pointedly.

"Anything with an opposable thumb," she said.

AT THE CHESS SHOP, THINGS WEREN'T GETTING ANY BETTER. Marcus and Naomi, afraid to leave The Shop in Sam's hands, canceled a planned trip to Germany. Marcus' resentment was palpable.

Sam complained to David about the Grafs' management style, although he admitted that the main problem was his poor memory and concentration.

Sam's mother, Ruth, asked him to invite David to her apartment for Passover. David couldn't come; he was expected at his own parents' house in Brooklyn.

Sam loved the ritual of the Passover Seder: the four glasses of wine, the Hillel sandwich of matzah and *charoset*, and the story of the Jewish exodus from Egypt. That Sunday, Sam and David compared the Seder in Mrs. Kanter's reform household to David's experience in the traditional home of his parents.

"What part of the Seder did you like the least?" David asked.

"The plagues," Sam replied.

"What part did you like the best?"

"The Passover meal."

Like many Orthodox Jews, David Rabinowitz had a strong dislike of Reform Judaism. When Sam told David that he was considering joining a synagogue, David said, "Don't join a Reform one. I think you'd find Conservative or Modern Orthodox much more interesting."

"Why?" Sam asked.

"I think Reform Judaism is 'make it up as you go along' Judaism. The Jews have always been the people of the book. Reform Judaism rejects the tradition of Jewish law, which goes back thousands of years."

"To me, it's more important to find a rabbi who's very wise than to adhere to one set of religious practices or another," Sam told him.

"If you believe in the God of the Old Testament, then you should abide by his laws," David said emphatically.

"But you told me to join a Modern Orthodox or Conservative synagogue. They don't observe the letter of Jewish Law, do they?"

"Yes, but I think it's better to compromise on tradition than to reject it outright."

Carla, who had been taking acting classes with Uta Hagen at HB Studios, was cast in the title role in Sophocles' *Antigone* in an off-Broadway production, so she cut her schedule at The Chess Shop to two evening shifts in the middle of the week. To cover her vacant shifts, Marcus and Naomi hired Johannah Lawrenson, the widow of Abbie Hoffman. Abbie had committed suicide a few years before, and Johannah's face was still ashen with misery. Marcus and Naomi had sheltered Abbie and Johannah when they were hiding from the authorities because Abbie was wanted on drug charges. They were good friends, though their politics were diametrically opposed. Marcus and Naomi were arch-conservative, while Johannah, like her husband, was a leftist. Naomi and Abbie had had virulent political arguments without damaging their friendship in the slightest. Now that Abbie was deceased, Johannah carried the ideological torch.

"Every country in Europe has socialized medicine and free higher education. We're the most backward country in the West. In another generation, we'll have socialism, you'll see."

"I think socialism is like feudalism," Marcus replied.

"It's worse than feudalism," Naomi said. "You give up your freedom, and in exchange you're taken care of from cradle to grave."

The only periodical Johannah read was *The Nation.*

"People who only read literature that reinforces their beliefs are just brainwashing themselves," Naomi said. "I'm very conservative, but I read *The New York Times* every day."

"*The Nation* is all I have time for," Johannah answered. "I'm too busy with the Abbie Hoffman Foundation to—"

"You're celebrating the legacy of a crackpot!" Naomi snapped.

Johannah winced. If she knew anything, Naomi knew how to push buttons.

Another one of the regulars at The Chess Shop was Raphael D'Lugoff, the manager of the Village Gate. Raphael booked the jazz musicians who played at the Gate. He also played every Monday night with his trio. His bass player, a guy named Ben Woolf, and his drummer, Jimmy Lovelace, were legends in the Greenwich Village jazz scene. Jimmy, a drummer from the old school, would dress up all in white for a year, and then suddenly show up all in black.

Raphael was a fanatical chess enthusiast. In his apartment on Bleecker Street, he had over five hundred chess books, as well as three thousand jazz records.

Rafi was like Rageneau, the pastry chef in *Cyrano de Bergerac* who fed his favorite poets when they came into his shop. When a grandmaster came into the Gate, Raphael would drop everything, buy him drinks, and engage him in a chess game. Raphael wasn't a master, but occasionally he played so well that he would take the scalp of a player two or three classes above him.

Dorian, one of the waitresses at the Gate, was a gorgeous blonde. She worked three nights a week, including Mondays, when Raphael's trio performed. Sam made a point of going to the Gate every Monday, as much to see Dorian as to hear his friend perform. One Monday night, he brought David Rabinowitz to the Gate, and was disappointed to discover that Dorian wasn't there. After the first set, he approached Raphael and said, "You don't play badly, but where's Dorian?"

"The Point!" Rafi said. "I wish I could play as good as she looks."

Raphael had a geeky young friend named Ben. About once a month, Raphael and Ben stayed at the Gate until dawn, playing speed chess. Although the two of them were roughly equal as chess players, Ben, in a state of frenzy, would sometimes win ninety percent of the games.

Although Ben was highly intelligent, he seemed to want everyone to think he was a genius. This had the opposite effect of what he wanted; people thought he was a fool. He was constantly making exaggerated claims about his prowess in a number of areas.

"This summer I'm going to play vibes with a trio in Washington Square," he said.

"I didn't know you played the vibraphone," Raphael replied.

"I'll just pick it up."

"You'll just pick it up?"

"It won't be a problem. The keyboard is exactly the same as the piano."

"You can't just *pick it up*," Raphael said, shaking his head. "Vibes players use two mallets in their left hand to play the chords. That takes some getting used to."

"It won't be a problem," Ben assured him.

On another occasion, Ben said, "I'm about to make a breakthrough in cellular biology."

"How are you going to do that?" Raphael asked incredulously.

"I can use the lab at NYU. My parents are on the faculty."

Raphael rolled his eyes. "Nobody will pay attention to you," he said. "You need a Ph.D., and you need to pass peer review."

"I already have a periodical interested in my work."

"What periodical? *National Lampoon*?"

SAM AND FREDDY WENT TO SEE CARLA IN *ANTIGONE*. Much to their surprise, she gave a stellar performance. After the show, Freddy said to him, "I didn't think a little cunt like her could pull off that kind of part." Then he added, "Leave me alone with her. I'm going to try and get into her pants."

"I'll make myself scarce," Sam said accommodatingly.

Freddy went backstage, complimented her on her performance, and offered to walk her home. The theatre was on West Forty-Second Street. They walked all the way to Carla's apartment in The Village. On the way, Carla did most of the talking; Freddy pretended to be interested in what she said.

Every time he tried to put his arm around her, she squirmed away. When they reached her building, she thanked him for coming to see her, gave him a quick peck on the lips, ducked inside, and closed the door before he had a chance to get in.

"Dammit," he said to himself.

When *Antigone* was over, instead of laying off Johannah, Marcus took away two of Sam's shifts and gave them to Carla. Sam was in no position to argue.

Now that he had just three shifts a week, Sam started going on long walks with David Rabinowitz again. One afternoon, as they were sitting in Bryant Park, David said, "I think I have an edge in our games."

Sam didn't reply, but inwardly he resolved to prove him wrong. The next day, with Freddy watching, David and Sam faced off for a series of speed chess games, each having only five minutes for a whole game. After Sam won the first three games, he said, "So you think you have an edge, huh?"

"I'll show you," David answered.

A crowd of people came over to their table and started watching their games.

When two evenly matched players meet, whoever has more will power usually prevails. On that occasion, Sam had the psychological edge. After he won five more games in a row, Freddy taunted David. "What's the score, Dave?" he asked.

"That's enough for today," David said, sullenly.

Sam and Dave went outside for their walk. When they were out of earshot, David said, "Now I can kill you!"

Sam laughed.

The next day they played again. This time, Sam won nine out of ten.

"What's the score, Dave?" Freddy asked again.

"Freddy, you're being an asshole!" David said. "Get the fuck away from my table."

For the next few days, David stayed away from The Shop. When he returned, he ignored Sam completely. Sam left him alone. *(He'll get over it.)*

Now that he couldn't play his favorite opponent, Sam started playing speed games with Jim Smith for five dollars a game. Jim's usual opponent, Costos, was on vacation in Greece. In these speed games, Sam had three minutes for the entire game while Jim had ten. When Sam won a game, Jim would say, "This is an outrage! *The New York Times* shall hear of this!"

When Jim won, he said, "This is one of the reasons they call me Master Jim!"

One sunny afternoon in June, while Sam was walking along West 4th Street, he saw a cute young bartender sitting by herself in a restaurant called

Karavas Place. She was a gregarious sixteen-year-old charmer named Cindy, with darting brown eyes and an infectious laugh, who got hired by using a fake ID showing she was eighteen. Sam started going to Karavas on his days off, drinking Guinness and munching on *shawarma* sandwiches on pita bread. Sam had never been a barfly before, but the combination of his troubles at work and David's cold shoulder made him feel lonely and depressed. Drinking several pints of Guinness four days a week didn't help.

Sam hadn't played in an official chess tournament since he was in college ten years before. To keep himself busy, he joined the Marshall Chess Club and started playing one tournament game every Thursday night.

At The Shop, Sam had played speed chess almost exclusively. This had made his game very superficial, so that, at first, he played very weakly at the Marshall, where there were slower time limits. When he blundered in a slow game, Sam was very hard on himself, which only exacerbated his depression.

Depression can be a vicious cycle—at work he started making more mistakes, which, in turn, made him more depressed. Marcus took away another of Sam's shifts, so he was down to two shifts a week. He faced a difficult decision: either start driving a cab again or move to a less expensive apartment in one of the outer boroughs or in New Jersey. He started driving again, but on his third day on the road he had an accident; he clipped the side of a car he was passing, and his boss fired him.

So, he decided to move to Brooklyn. As New Yorkers all know, the best way to get an apartment in the five boroughs was to buy the *Village Voice* on Tuesday night and be the first to arrive at the apartment you wanted on Wednesday morning, with a check in your hand. He answered an ad for an apartment in Greenpoint and got there at 8:00 a.m. on Wednesday. The rent was only $450.00 a month. He wrote out a check for $900.00 to cover the first month and security, and signed a lease beginning on August 1, two weeks ahead.

At The Chess Shop the next day, he approached David Rabinowitz and said: "If I offended you in any way, please let me know, so I can make amends."

David was astonished. "You don't know?" he asked, incredulously.

"Maybe I'm obtuse, but I really don't."

David stared at him intently for a few seconds, then said, "I'll tell you what. Forget about it."

"If I did something that upset you, I want to know," Sam said.

"Forget about it," David repeated with finality. Sam shrugged.

After Sam got off work that day, he went to The Waverly Diner for a quick meal, then walked over to the Village Corner to hear Steven Fall play jazz piano. Fall was a talented musician with a master's degree in composition from Columbia University, and he was very left wing politically. He had written a series of songs with Brecht-like lyrics. Sam was a liberal himself, but well within the mainstream. He and Steven constantly argued.

Steven was a big fan of Oliver Stone. He thought that *JFK* told the truth about the Kennedy assassination. Sam told him: "I have no interest in seeing that movie."

"That's because you don't want to know what happened."

"I don't believe in learning about history from a movie," Sam replied.

One of the waitresses at the Village Corner was Jennifer, a blonde with a chunky body but the face of a movie star. Jennifer also worked as a bartender at the Village Idiot, a dive on First Avenue in the East Village. Sam started going there to drink—instead of Guinness, his drink of choice became Johnny Walker Black with one ice cube.

Jennifer was a graduate student of ancient languages at New York University. The Idiot was not a place for intellectual conversation, however. The barmaids were expected to coerce the barflies into buying them drink after drink, so both the barmaids and the customers drank until they were almost comatose.

"How do you say 'sit on my face' in ancient Greek?" asked Reuben, Sam's neighbor at the bar.

"Ancient Greek is too modern," Jennifer told him. "If you want me, you'll have to proposition me in Linear B."

"I'll take a course at Berlitz," Reuben quipped.

Sam was in love. He asked Jennifer if she would like to go with him to the Film Forum, where they were having a John Houston retrospective.

"I'd love to go to a movie with you," Jennifer said. "I don't have my book with me today, but come see me tomorrow night at the Village Corner, and we'll make a date."

That evening, Sam wandered around the Village for hours; he didn't make it to Greenpoint until 3:00 a.m. When he finally went to bed, he couldn't sleep. He lay awake until dawn, when he came into the city and walked over to Washington Square Park.

Some of the hustlers were already there to claim their table for the day. A wizened old man was sweeping up the garbage from the previous day. The drug dealers accosted Sam: "Sess? Sess?"

Michael, the Jamaican preacher, was giving a sermon. "Marijuana is not a drug. It is a plant! Drugs are man-made! Anything with a seed and a flower. . .comes from God! He put it there for us to use! My son got busted in this very park for smoking ganja! Show me a cop who does not do cocaine!" *(Coming from a preacher who also deals drugs, I guess that's perfect logic.)*

At 10:00 a.m., Sam took a two-hour nap on a park bench before heading over to The Shop, where he told David Rabinowitz all about Jennifer.

"She sounds wild," David said. "Just be careful you don't get in over your head."

"I'm already in over my head," Sam replied.

That evening he went to the Village Corner to look for her. He said to Jeff, the manager, "I thought Jennifer was on the schedule for tonight."

Sam had a premonition that something was wrong. *(No, that's just my paranoia.)* He tried to listen to Steven Fall's playing. For the first set, Fall played only Thelonious Monk tunes. Sam closed his eyes and listened.

CHAPTER 3

THE NEXT DAY, WHEN IT WAS TIME FOR SAM to open The Chess Shop, he couldn't find the keys, so he called his boss at home. Marcus came to open The Shop himself and gave Sam an extra set of keys. "Don't let this happen again," he said, fixing Sam with a withering stare.

All day, Sam watched the clock impatiently. As soon as his shift was over, he ran to the Village Idiot. No Jennifer. Out of breath, he jumped in a cab and told the driver to take him to the Village Corner.

"Where's Jennifer?" he asked Valerie, the bartender.

"She's at The Idiot today," she said.

"The Idiot's closed. I just came from there!"

"Hang on, I'll give her a call." She dialed Jennifer's home number; no one answered. "Don't worry," Valerie said. "I'm sure there's an explanation."

Sam tried to hide his anxiety. "Give me a Johnny Walker Black with one ice cube," he said.

While he was sitting at the bar, lost in thought, someone tapped him on the shoulder. He looked up; it was Jennifer.

"Where were you? I was worried about you," Sam said.

"Can we go somewhere and talk?" she asked him.

They went to Café Reggio and sat in a dark corner.

"What's on your mind?" he asked her.

"I don't know why I decided to tell you. . .I hardly know you."

"You can tell me anything you want," he said. "It won't go any farther than here."

"I have a close friend who's a heroin addict," she said. "He's homeless and broke. I can't let him stay with me. The last time I did, he stole my VCR and sold it. I'm beside myself."

"What's his name?" Sam asked.

"Chris."

"Where is he?"

"He's on the sidewalk near the Christopher Street subway station."

"Let's go talk to him," Sam said.

"Could you go by yourself? He won't talk to me." She looked at Sam searchingly.

Sam was out of breath. After a minute, he said, faintly, "Okay."

"Oh thank you," she said, throwing her arms around him. *(What am I getting myself into?)*

Chris was a thin nineteen-year-old with long blonde hair. Sam knew who he was right away. As Sam approached, Chris said, "Help me out, so I don't have to sell my body."

"Can I buy you a coffee?" Sam asked him.

With the instincts of a street person, Chris knew right away that Sam was someone he could trust. They went to the Waverly Diner and ordered two coffees.

"Have you had anything to eat today?" Sam asked.

"A bagel this morning."

"That's all?"

"I can't afford anything else. I need to save enough to get my fix."

"How long have you been an addict?"

"Almost two years."

"Do you have a family?"

"My mother died when I was three. If I go to my father, he'll kill me." Chris said this without showing any emotion.

"Let me buy you a burger, and I'll check on you tomorrow."

"I'm a vegetarian," Chris said. "Why don't you just give me some money and I'll go buy a salad."

"Nice try," Sam said. "I'll buy you another bagel, and I'll check on you tomorrow. Will you be in the same place?"

"Why are you doing this?" Chris asked him.

Sam didn't know if Jennifer wanted him to mention her.

"I don't know," he said with a sigh. Sam walked the kid back to his stoop, then stopped by Karavas Place to see Cindy. The only other customer at the bar was a big, glowering black man seated by the window, eating a shawarma sandwich. Sam sat down at the other end of the bar.

"Where have you been?" Cindy asked cheerfully.

"I've been two-timing you," Sam said.

"Shame on you."

"I'll have a Johnny Walker Black with one ice cube."

"Movin' up in the world."

Her other customer waved to her. He ordered a Brandy Alexander. Cindy came back to Sam and asked under her breath, "He ordered a Brandy Alexander. Do you know what kind of glass this goes in?"

Sam shook his head.

She poured it into a snifter and took it to the customer, then came back to Sam.

"What did he say?" Sam asked.

"He said, 'You're lucky you're cute.'"

WHEN SAM WENT BACK TO THE VILLAGE CORNER, Jennifer was sitting at the bar with a big guy with a Mohawk. Sam chatted with one of the other customers and listened to Steven Fall playing, trying to appear nonchalant.

After an hour he went back to The Chess Shop to look for David Rabinowitz. David was in the middle of an odds game with Jim Smith. When Jim made a mistake, David said, "You're a sick man."

Sam watched for an hour, then gave up and went home.

The next day, Sam went to the Village Idiot to see Jennifer again. After three drinks, he got up the courage to ask her, "So when are you coming to the Forum with me?"

"I can't go with you," she said. "I have a new boyfriend and I think he'd be jealous."

Sam's face fell.

"I'm sorry," she said.

Sam went to see Chris, as he had promised. They went to the Waverly Diner again. Before the coffee arrived, Sam asked, "Did you get your fix?"

"This morning I used my usual line and—"

"Your usual line?"

"Help me out, so I don't have to sell my body."

"And. . . ?"

"And this guy said, 'Let me know when you want to sell your body.' I thought for a second and said, 'Come here.' We went to his apartment on Hudson Street, he put on a rubber, and I went down on him."

"Are you gay or straight?"

"I'm straight."

Sam was astounded. "And you're doing gay prostitution?"

"I think this guy really cares about me. He's going to help me get into a detox. . . ."

Sam felt like he was suffocating. "I can't cope with this," he blurted out, and bolted out of the diner. Sometimes the facts of life are hard to face, especially when your heart is breaking.

TO GET TO GREENWICH VILLAGE FROM GREENPOINT, Sam had to take the G train to Queens Plaza, then switch to the E or F and ride to the West 4th Street station. The G ran very seldom, especially late at night; sometimes it took him almost two hours to get into the city. He spent his travel time browsing through Chess Life magazine, or just looking at people.

The apartment was a four-room railroad flat. The floor was in bad condition; Sam laid down new linoleum tiles. He built new bookshelves and put gates on the windows.

In the 1990s, Greenpoint was still a Polish neighborhood, one of the most homogenous ethnic neighborhoods in the five boroughs. Sam bought a Polish phrasebook and began to teach himself the language, which was still spoken by many of his neighbors. He went to the Polish restaurants, feasting on kielbasa sausage, pierogis, and other hearty Polish dishes.

One of the regulars at The Chess Shop was Pierre, a thin bearded Frenchman with unkempt dirty blonde hair and thick glasses. Like Naomi, Pierre loved to push buttons; he knew how sensitive David was about his decisive losses to Sam. One afternoon he found the two friends seated at a table outside The Shop. He approached them and said, in an exaggerated French accent, "Mr. Sam, I heard that you demolished David—everyone is talking about it. How many games did you win in a row?"

Sam stared at Pierre for a few seconds, then said, "Pierre, there's a circle in hell for sowers of discord."

Sam continued playing one tournament game each week at the Marshall Chess Club. At the end of each month, whoever had the highest score was the winner. In the summer months he had fared badly; in the fall he gradually started regaining his form.

ONE OF THE CHESS PLAYERS AT THE MARSHALL was a sweet-faced Russian girl from Brighton Beach named Antonia. Sam took every opportunity he could find to chat with her. When he had known her for about two months, Sam found the courage to ask her out for dinner and a movie. They went to see The Unbearable Lightness of Being, which was playing at the Film Forum. The movie was a sexy one. As soon as things started heating up on screen, Sam put his arm around Antonia. (Let's see what happens.) To his surprise, she said, "May I?" and snuggled up to him.

After the movie, she was ready to leave, but Sam wanted to see the credits. "Are you looking for something in particular?" she asked him.

"Yes. I want to see who wrote the music."

It was Janacek, the great Czech composer.

"No wonder it was so good," he said.

He invited her to his apartment; she immediately assented. Luckily, she had brought her car with her from Brighton Beach. Although the subway trip to Sam's apartment in Greenpoint sometimes took an hour or more, by car the trip took only fifteen minutes.

As soon as they were in the door, they were all over each other. Sam fumbled with her blouse, her camisole, her skirt. When he tried to take off her pantyhose, she said, "I can't go all the way."

Sam didn't believe her and continued to struggle. After a few more minutes of this, she said, "Maybe I should go."

"You don't have to go," he barely heard himself saying.

She explained that she was a devout follower of the Russian Orthodox Church. For religious reasons, she couldn't lose her virginity before marriage.

"*Oy, gevalt*," Sam droned. He had never been so frustrated in his life. Now that they had come this far, he didn't want to go back, but he couldn't go forward either. They went on several dates together in the next few months. Each time, they went just as far but no further. Sam started becoming abusive: "Grow up!" he said. "This is the twentieth century! Nobody your age is a virgin!"

Her feelings were badly hurt, but she refused to give in.

"You're the Rock of Gibraltar," he said sarcastically.

After four months, she broke up with him. "Obviously you can't accept me as I am," she said.

"I'm sorry, but whatever you do, just don't get in bed with a guy, take off your clothes, and say, 'I can't go all the way.' If you had told me beforehand, I would have understood. We could have become friends first and things might have happened differently. After that first night I couldn't go back and I couldn't go forward. It was like the *Myth of Sisyphus.* Oh well," he sighed. "Maybe you'll meet some Russian guy and. . . whatever."

ALTHOUGH SAM WAS HANDLING THE JOB AT THE CHESS SHOP somewhat better, Marcus finally decided to let him go. He was replaced by Ahmed, a young man from Lebanon who was a Fulbright scholar studying English Literature at New York University. Ahmed had done his undergraduate work in Damascus; he was in a master's program at NYU. When Ahmed learned that he was replacing someone who had been fired, he was alarmed. He told Sam, "In Lebanon, if you take someone's job, they'll kill you!"

"This is America, Ahmed," Sam said. "Nobody's gonna kill you."

After that, Sam, who was somewhat ashamed that he had been fired, stopped coming to The Shop. Three weeks later, David Rabinowitz called him.

"Where have you been?" he asked.

"Uh, I've been kind of busy," Sam said.

"Everyone misses you at The Shop. Why don't you come over and play?"

"I don't know if Marcus is going to want me there."

"Are you kidding? Of course Marcus will take your money."

"That's part of the problem. I don't *have* much money."

"Well, at least come to The Shop and hang out."

Sam reflected for a few seconds. "All right," he said. "I'll be in the city tomorrow, looking for work. I'll come to The Shop after dinner."

When Sam showed up the next evening, Marcus greeted him at the door. "I'm going to let you play for free for a long time," he said.

Sam was taken aback. He was used to Marcus' tough managerial style; he had no idea that he could be so generous.

"Thanks a million," he said.

Later, when the two friends were walking around the East Village, Sam said to David, "He's just doing this because he doesn't want me to collect unemployment."

"Don't be such a fucking cynic!" David said.

CHAPTER 4

SAM FOUND A JOB AT THE DOUBLEDAY BOOKSTORE on Fifth Avenue. In order to get to the store at 8:00 a.m., he had to leave Greenpoint at 6:30. His job at The Chess Shop had started at noon; now Sam had a terrible time getting himself out of bed each morning. When he got to the bookstore, he was still sleepy and depressed, but by the time more customers started coming into the store at about 11:00 a.m., he usually felt somewhat better.

The assistant manager at Doubleday was a spunky young single mother named Megan. After Sam had been working in the store only two weeks, she invited him to go bar-hopping with her and her friends. They went to McSorley's Old Ale House with Megan's roommate Jean and two of their male friends who were illegal immigrants from Ireland.

After about forty minutes in McSorley's, Megan's friends suggested that they go to another bar.

"Go ahead," Megan said. "We'll join you later."

Megan lived on Avenue A in the East Village. After they had downed about six beers each, she told Sam, "You don't have to go back to Brooklyn. You can stay at my place."

Megan had a six-year-old daughter named Chrissy. When they arrived at the apartment, Megan told the babysitter that she could go, checked on her sleeping daughter, and pulled Sam into the room where she and her roommate slept.

"Let's not waste time," she said. "Jean might come in at any minute."

They tore their clothes off and devoured each other.

"Don't you feel lucky?" she asked afterwards.

"I feel like I just won the lottery," he said breathlessly.

When they awoke the next morning, they found Chrissy and Jean playing with their two cats, India and Bangladesh.

"Where did you sleep?" Sam asked Jean.

"On the floor with the cats," Jean said nonchalantly.

Chrissy was a love-child whom Megan had conceived with an Eskimo man on a trip to Alaska. She had beautiful brown creamy skin and slanty eyes. Chrissy had seen many of Megan's boyfriends come and go, and she was jealous when Megan gave Sam her attention. Sam fell in love with the little girl.

Every Friday night after work, Megan and Sam picked up Chrissy at the day care center, ate dinner at The Kiev restaurant, rented a video, and crashed at Megan's place.

The pay at Doubleday was only slightly above minimum wage. Though his rent was only $450.00 a month, Sam needed to take a roommate. He put up a sign at The Chess Shop and at the Marshall.

Many of the chess addicts in the Village have very little money; several of them expressed interest in sharing Sam's apartment.

José Gonzales was a brilliant chess master from Honduras who had only recently arrived in New York City. Sam offered him the room for only $200.00 a month, if he would throw in a few chess lessons.

At The Shop, Ahmed was proving himself the best salesman Marcus had ever hired. He was also very adept at ingratiating himself with everyone in The Shop. He bought Naomi a copy of the discredited book *From Time Immemorial,* which claimed that there was almost no one in Palestine when the Jewish settlers arrived. He pretended to be moderate about Israeli-Palestinian issues; he told Sam that only the Arabs who had left after the six-day war in 1967 were intransigent; the 1948 refugees, he said, accepted Israel. Ahmed asked all the other employees at The Shop out for coffee and insisted on paying. Within three months, Marcus gave Ahmed a raise and made him the manager.

With José's help, Sam's chess improved rapidly. José analyzed his games, pointing out his mistakes and telling him what moves he should have made in the most critical positions. He also told Sam which books to read and helped him with his opening repertoire. They played dozens of speed games; José's tactical talent was so prodigious that he won ninety-five percent of the games.

Since José made his sole living from chess, when he won he paid the rent on time. When he didn't win, sometimes he was late with the rent. Sam, who had always eaten in restaurants when he lived in the Village, reluctantly started teaching himself to cook in order to save money. He bought an Italian cookbook and began learning to prepare various pasta dishes.

On their walks together, Sam told David Rabinowitz all about Megan and Chrissy. "You'll get to meet them sooner or later," Sam said.

David, who had never had a girlfriend, said, "You must sometimes wonder if I'm gay."

"I know you're not gay," Sam replied.

CHAPTER 5

EARLY IN JULY, SAM INVITED MEGAN AND CHRISSY to his mother's apartment in Hackensack. Mrs. Kanter fell in love with the little Eskimo girl and her mom. Afterward, Chrissy and the lovers went back to Megan's place. Megan read Chrissy a story and put her to bed; then Megan and Sam made hungry love.

"Is this what they call happiness?" Sam asked wistfully.

In his apartment in Brooklyn, Sam had hundreds of books, mostly novels and volumes of poetry. When José wasn't playing or studying chess, he delved into Sam's library. One evening, while they were having dinner, José asked him, "So who are the greatest poets?"

Sam said, "Well. . .Homer, Dante, Shakespeare, a few others. . . ."

"They're the grandmasters?" José asked naively.

"No, they're the world champions. The rest are ordinary grandmasters."

ONE SUNDAY NIGHT, MEGAN AND SAM INVITED David Rabinowitz to dinner. David played Go Fish with Chrissy and showed her how to make an origami bird. Megan cooked Chicken Parmigiana, penne arrabiata, and broccoli rabe.

Sam, the novice cook, watched everything she did.

"Wow," David exclaimed. "She cooks as well as your mom."

"With the table between us, she looks just like Venus," Sam said.

Megan shot back, "What do I look like the rest of the time, Medusa?"

Sam changed the subject. "David, I guess if you can eat Chicken Parmigiana, you're not kosher anymore."

"Don't talk," David said. "God might be listening."

"What's 'kosher' mean?" Chrissy asked.

David said, "If you're an Orthodox Jew, there's all kinds of rules about what you can and can't eat."

"What's an Orthodox Jew?"

"A man with long sideburns who dresses all in black because he thinks that's what God wants."

"What about an Orthodox woman?"

"Orthodox women do whatever their husbands and fathers want them to do."

"That's silly," Chrissy concluded.

WHEN THEY HAD BEEN DATING FOR ABOUT four months, Sam finally told Megan about his mental illness.

"Do you take medication?" Megan asked.

"I take Lithium and Prozac."

Megan paused. "Suppose we have children—will they be likely to become ill?"

"That's a distinct possibility."

"You know what?" Megan said. "I don't care."

"Now you're really my girlfriend," Sam said. He hugged her as if his life depended on it.

Freddy had finished his Economics degree in December and planned to return to Italy. He told Sam that his ambition to seduce Carla had remained unfulfilled. "She dresses like a slut, but she's really a prude," Freddy lamented. "And believe me, I'm not the first one she's led on."

The night before he left, Freddy and Sam went to The Continental Divide. They ordered a pitcher of Budweiser and talked about women.

"I'll be coming back at least once a year," Freddy said. "The Chinese is gonna put me up. Last night he took care of me big time. We went to a whorehouse in Queens, and he paid for everything. Girls, drinks, everything."

"A man for all seasons," Sam said.

"Anyway, you gotta come to Milan, dude. My friends and I are gonna go in together for an apartment just to bring girls to, and you can stay there if we're not using it."

"I might just take you up on that."

"*Arriverderci, amico.*"

"*Arriverderci.*"

ONE MORNING IN MARCH, SAM TOOK MEGAN and Chrissy to hear Raphael and his trio at the Village Gate. In between sets, Rafi came over to their table.

"Who are you?" he asked Chrissy with mock suspicion.

"I'm Chrissy."

"Do you like jazz?"

"I hate jazz."

"What *do* you like?"

"I like my cats, and I like my mommy."

"You have good taste," Raphael said, giving Megan the once-over. "Do you have any requests?" he asked Megan.

"How about the *Eroica Symphony*?"

"We'll play that in the last set," Rafi replied.

EVERY THURSDAY NIGHT, JOSÉ PLAYED "ACTION CHESS" at the Marshall Chess club, where each player gets a half hour for the whole game, whereas in typical tournament chess, one game can last five hours or more. Because of his tactical prowess and experience hustling at speed chess, in action chess José was almost grandmaster strength.

In the summer months, José had spent his days playing for money in Washington Square Park. In the fall he studied, gave lessons, and played in tournaments.

José was a "sandbagger"; he kept his rating low so he could win big cash prizes in class tournaments by competing with players much weaker than him. When he came in first, he won thousands of dollars.

On Friday nights, Megan and Sam continued their routine, eating dinner at The Kiev. When he was at Megan's apartment on weeknights, Sam played with Chrissy while Megan cooked. He started giving chess lessons to the little girl, teaching her the four-move checkmate—"Scholar's mate"—how to checkmate with a queen or rook, and the principles of opening play: development, central control, and castling. By the time the lesson was over, dinner was ready. The three of them would dine sitting on the floor, Japanese style; often Megan's roommate Jean would join them. Chrissy was somewhat dyslexic, so after dinner Jean helped her with her homework while Megan practiced guitar and Sam studied chess. At eight o'clock, after everyone had worked for an hour at their various pursuits, it was time for Chrissy to go to bed, so they took turns reading her a bedtime story, then they put in a video from Jean's huge collection. Jean had all the James Bond movies, the *Star Trek* movies, *Terminator 1* and *2*, and so on.

Meanwhile, David Rabinowitz was starting to have trouble with some people in The Shop. He complained that Johannah Lawrenson never said hello to him when he came in on her shift. When Sam repeated this to Johannah, she said, "He comes barreling into The Shop, looking straight ahead. Even if I'm not busy with a customer, he never looks at me. And he's complaining that I don't say hello to him?"

David also had a falling out with some of the players. One of the best in The Shop was James Flateman, a graduate student in Philosophy at the New School. While James was in the middle of a game, David asked him, "Why didn't you check him with your knight on f7?"

Making comments on other people's games is called "kibitzing" in the chess world, and many players consider it very rude. James blew up at David. "You know *nothing* about chess! Why don't you learn how to *play* before you tell me what to do?"

"You're an arrogant motherfucker, Flateman, and you're also a fucking hypocrite! As if you never tell people what moves to make!"

"Yeah, but I'm only three classes better than you. Maybe if you listened to me and stopped acting as if you're a grandmaster, you might learn something."

David and James never spoke again.

LATE IN DECEMBER, JOSÉ SUDDENLY DISAPPEARED. When Sam hadn't seen him in two weeks, he began to worry. He went to José's favorite bars and pool halls to see if he had shown up there. No one had seen him. After another week, Sam called the police and reported him missing. Two officers came to the apartment in Greenpoint and told Sam to come to the precinct house and fill out a missing person report.

When José hadn't shown up by the end of March, Sam reluctantly decided to take another roommate. He chose Bernardo, another Honduran chess master, and a friend of José's. Bernardo assured him, "Don't worry about José. He's disappeared before, and he always shows up eventually."

Bernardo was the quintessential Latin lover. Devastatingly handsome, he had an American girlfriend named Dorothy, whom he cheated on at every opportunity. She was extremely jealous; she had never caught him cheating but was wracked with suspicion. Every night when they were apart, they fought for an hour on the phone; when they were together, her anger melted away, and she was putty in his hands.

Sam found himself in the unenviable position of covering Bernardo's tracks. When Bernardo brought another girl home, Sam lied to Dorothy and said he wasn't there.

AT THE CHESS SHOP, AHMED AND CARLA had a falling out. Carla was rude to a customer; Ahmed, who was polite almost to the point of unctuousness, was offended. He didn't confront her; instead he started ignoring her. She, who knew why he was angry, approached him and said, in a coquettish tone of voice, "Can I apologize?"

He was unmoved. The atmosphere in The Shop when the two of them were there became very uncomfortable, so Carla started looking for another job. When she found a position managing a small theatre in the East Village, Marcus and Naomi hired an art student named Sylvia to replace her.

Sylvia had long dark hair and pale white skin. She wore thick glasses with clunky black frames and loose-fitting black clothes. Ahmed quickly developed a crush on her. Every night after her shift, he walked her back to her home in SoHo. He frequently took her out to dinner or to see an old movie at the Film Forum. She wasn't attracted to him at all, but she loved all the attention he gave her.

Sylvia's abstract metal sculptures were being exhibited in a gallery in Chelsea. Ahmed and Sam went together to see her work.

"I don't understand this," Sam said afterward.

"You should have lived a hundred years ago."

"A hundred years ago I probably would have been an old academic who didn't understand Impressionism," Sam replied.

Now that José was gone, Sam started showing his chess games to Bernardo. Sam entered a weekend tournament at the Marshall Chess Club for players under master strength. He came in tied for second place, beating two experts in the process—his best result ever. Bernardo was an excellent analyst; he even showed Sam how he could have drawn the one game he lost.

Bernardo's younger brother, Miguel, was even stronger than he was; at seventeen, he won the U.S. Junior Championship. Although Miguel lived with his parents in Rhode Island, he frequently came to New York City to compete in tournaments. When he did, he stayed with Bernardo and Sam in Greenpoint.

On Sam's computer he had Fritz, the strongest chess program available at that time. When Miguel was staying with them, he'd play blitz games against the computer, starting with the same position over and over, alternating between the white and black pieces. When he had done this for two hours, he knew all the nuances of the position in question.

Bernardo and Sam brought Miguel to the Village Gate to meet Raphael. Rafi ignored his managerial duties for an hour to play speed chess with the boy. Miguel gave him 5-1—Raphael had five minutes for each game, and Miguel had only one. It's hard to believe, but players of Miguel's strength can play a whole game in one minute.

SAM DECIDED TO HAVE A SMALL DINNER PARTY at his apartment. He invited Megan and Chrissy, Bernardo, Dorothy, Sylvia, and Ahmed. He served linguine with clam sauce, fresh asparagus, and homemade oatmeal raisin cookies for dessert. He had to borrow two bridge tables and seven chairs from his neighbors; the only furniture in the apartment was his sofa bed, Bernardo's futon, a few bookshelves, and a small piano.

After dinner, Bernardo played a blindfold game with Chrissy, announcing his moves with his eyes closed while Sam moved the pieces for him. While they were playing, Sylvia made a quick sketch of Chrissy at the chessboard. After the game (which Bernardo let her win), Chrissy fell asleep on Sam's lap. He carried the little girl to the futon without waking her, then said goodbye to his guests. Bernardo went back to Manhattan to spend the night at Dorothy's place; they shared a cab with Sylvia and Ahmed. Megan went to sleep right away, but Sam lay awake for hours, wistfully wondering how long his new happiness would last.

The weather that spring was magnificent. Sam, Megan, and Chrissy started having picnics every Saturday afternoon at Sheep's Meadow in Central Park. Sam taught the kid how to throw a Frisbee; he had been on the Rutgers Ultimate Frisbee team as an undergraduate. Megan read Sam's Tarot cards and did his astrological chart.

ON SUNDAYS, SAM AND DAVID CONTINUED to explore the city. They walked along the Hudson River, stopping by the boat basin to see how the other half lived, or walked along the East River as far as Carl Shurz Park and Gracie Mansion. When Sam took David to see the Cloisters, the latter exclaimed, "I didn't know a place like this existed in New York City!"

Every weekend when the weather was fine, Bernardo went to Washington Square to play speed chess with Dr. Li, Freddy's old friend. Bernardo was almost as good at speed chess as José; some days he won over $200.00. Dr. Li didn't care; he loved to gamble. Another of Bernardo's opponents was Tommy Starks, an odds player who was a successful painter as well as one of the best poker players in the city. Far from having a poker face, when Tommy gambled his gaze wandered around abstractedly as if he were highly absentminded. Those who knew him well knew that this was only a pose—Tommy knew exactly what was going on around him. Bernardo's games with Tommy always attracted a big crowd of spectators, with several of the gamblers making side bets on the outcome.

Many of the hustlers in the park were gambling addicts who squandered the money they made from chess at the racetrack or in Atlantic City. The most successful hustler in the park was Lovey Jenkins. He always sat at the table closest to the entrance to the park, in order to lure tourists into a game. The other players called Lovey "The Manager": He was at the top of the pecking order in Washington Square Park.

By far the strongest player in the park was Boris, a Grandmaster who was notorious for not paying his debts when he lost. In a speed game Boris could give ordinary masters 7-1; the ideas he could come up with in a minute were truly astonishing.

ONE TUESDAY EARLY IN JULY, José suddenly showed up at The Chess Shop. David called Sam to tell him his old roommate was back. After work Sam went to the Village to look for him; he found him in the park, playing speed chess with Raphael.

"Where have you *been?*" Sam asked him. "I was worried about you."

"I was in Florida, visiting my sister."

"Do you need a place to stay?"

"No—I met a girl down there who lives on the Upper West Side. We're getting married soon."

"You're full of surprises," Sam said.

Raphael took José and Sam to dinner at the Olive Tree on MacDougal

Street. After dinner the three of them went downstairs to the Comedy Cellar. On stage there was a female comedian doing a routine about a visit to the gynecologist. She pantomimed a speculum.

"Do you know what this is?" she asked Raphael.

"No," he said.

"It's a contraption the gynecologist uses to open a woman's pussy."

"Where can I get one?" Rafi asked.

After the show the three of them went to the Village Gate, where they played speed chess until 6:00 a.m., long after the waiters and the bartender had gone home; then they went to the Waverly Diner for breakfast. Sam called in sick, and the three of them crashed at Raphael's apartment above Café Figaro.

That Sunday, Sam and Dave took the 1 train down to Battery Park. The park was full of tourists going to the Statue of Liberty or Ellis Island.

"Let's go to the statue," Sam said.

David shrugged. "I suppose it's something everyone should do once."

They waited in line for two hours before they could get on a boat. Inside the statue, the line moved so slowly, it took them another half an hour before they reached the top. On the way back, David declared, "I have been inside your skull, and it was empty."

Seated behind them was a Southern couple with a fifteen- year-old daughter. The girl asked Sam and Dave, "Ya'll from 'round here?"

"How could you tell?" David asked.

The next weekend, the weather was spectacular, so Sam and Dave went to Central Park to play chess in the sun. Sitting near them were three cute Chinese girls. When it was David's turn to move, Sam flirted with them. David couldn't focus on the game, so he lost pretty badly. Although Sam had an edge in their speed games, David always maintained that, in slow chess, he was at least equal to, or better than, him, so when he lost the game it was a bitter disappointment. He hid his feelings until they had left the park, but later, while they were drinking cappuccino at Café Reggio, he blurted, "That game today was a joke. It wasn't even chess."

"Why, because I was hitting on those girls?"

"No, that's not it," David said irritably.

"Then I have no idea what you mean."

"Forget about it."

Sam remembered another occasion when David had said "forget about it."

"David. . . ."

"Forget it!" he snapped, averting his gaze.

Sam cursed under his breath.

CHAPTER 6

AT THE CHESS SHOP, AHMED AND DAVID were soon becoming good friends. Like many men from the Middle East, Ahmed was an expert backgammon player. David and Ahmed began a friendly barter system: David taught Ahmed how to play chess, and Ahmed taught David to play backgammon.

Ahmed was an exceptionally hard worker. When he wasn't at The Chess Shop, he was a fixture at the NYU library, staying there every night until closing. His apartment was filled with books he had checked out of the library, most of them overdue. Within a year at NYU, he had completed his master's in English Literature.

To celebrate his graduation, he took Sam and David for a late night dinner at Mitali, on East 6th Street. David, who had never eaten Indian food before, loved it so much that he said, "I'm going to come here on a regular basis."

After dinner, they walked together as far as Houston Street, where each went in his own direction—David to the Lower East Side, Ahmed to NYU housing, and Sam back to Brooklyn.

He took the F train to Queens, where he usually switched to the G. That weekend they were doing track work on the G line, so he had to take a shuttle bus. He didn't reach his apartment until 3:30 a.m. on Sunday morning. Even then he couldn't fall asleep; he lay awake until dawn. As he usually did when he was up all night, he decided to go into the city. He was at Washington Square Park at 6:30 a.m., before any of the hustlers showed up. He leaned against the fence on the outside of the park, watching the joggers and the dog walkers, and waiting for someone to play with.

Sometimes when Sam hadn't slept, he still played a reasonable game of speed chess. The first players to arrive that morning were Bill, a big, tough, retired cop with a heart of gold, and Steve, one of the park regulars. The three played three-way speed chess, with the loser of each game getting up and the extra man taking his place.

After they had played for about four hours, Sam went to The Chess Shop and tried to rest in the back room. At 4:30 in the afternoon, he dragged himself up and went back to Brooklyn, where he slept for twelve hours.

Megan knew how much Sam hated the time-consuming commute between Greenpoint and Manhattan. One evening after work she asked him, "Why don't you move in with us?"

"What about Jean?"

"She's a sport," Megan said. "Besides, I think she feels she has too little privacy when you're here in the evening."

"Well, if it's okay with her, I'd love to move in with you and Chrissy."

Even as the words were leaving his lips, he had a premonition that living together might not be the right decision, but he kept it to himself.

Jean had so many friends in the East Village that she had no trouble finding a place to stay. Megan and Sam decided that he would move in on September 1. Bernardo decided to move in with his girlfriend, even though he knew that he would have fewer opportunities for cheating, his favorite activity. He would have preferred to rent his own place, but he couldn't afford it on what he earned as a hustler. Dorothy, needless to say, was glad to have Bernardo at home where she could keep an eye on him.

At The Chess Shop, people occasionally asked about chess lessons. One of the regulars, Tom, taught the beginners, and Richard Kelly, a strong master who was always at The Shop, taught the advanced players. Tom was a history major at NYU as well as a first-rate rock guitarist. As a chess teacher, however, he was somewhat unreliable. He often showed up late for lessons and occasionally missed a lesson without calling The Shop. Marcus asked Sam if he would like to teach.

"Even though I was a failure as a salesman?"

"Teaching is a very different kind of job," Marcus said. "I think you'd be good at it."

The pay at Doubleday was so poor that Sam welcomed the chance to make a few extra bucks. He arranged his schedule so that he could give three or four lessons every Saturday afternoon.

Sam's favorite student was a precocious six-year-old named Adam Silver, who was very talented. Sam taught him the basic theoretical endgames, gave him tactical problems to solve, and helped him with his opening repertoire. After working with him for a month, he came to watch the boy play in a tournament at the Hunter School. Adam's mother, Erica, was somewhat of a stage mother. She took Sam aside and said, "Don't tell the other parents that you're a chess teacher, because if their kids take lessons, they might be able to beat Adam in a game."

Her husband, Noah, said, "You're very silly."

Adam won every game, mowing down four opponents in a row. He was so elated that he asked his parents, "Can I have a chess lesson every day?"

Adam was precocious in other ways as well. Sometimes Sam forgot that he was a child. One Saturday, during a lesson, there was a traffic tie-up outside The Shop on Tompkins Street. One impatient cabdriver was incessantly leaning on his horn. Sam became more and more irritated, and shouted, "Blow it out your ass!"

Adam found that oh-so-funny. He laughed nonstop for twenty seconds. Later in the lesson, he kept remembering what Sam had said and burst out laughing again: "Ha, ha, ha! Blow it out your ass!"

Sam and Adam became very close. Sometimes Sam would babysit for him when his parents were out. On one occasion, when Adam was misbehaving, Sam said: "If you don't cut it out, I'm gonna smack you."

Adam put his hands on his hips and said: "I have the law on my side."

AT SIX, ADAM WAS SAM'S YOUNGEST STUDENT; his oldest was Mary, an eighty-five-year-old novelist who taught writing at New York University. After their first lesson at The Shop, he taught her at her apartment in the NYU housing.

Mary had published six novels, one of which had been translated into German. Even at her advanced age, she still woke up at 6:00 a.m. every morning and wrote for four hours. She gave him two of her novels to read; he thought them brilliant.

As a chess player, however, she was less than brilliant. She found it difficult to solve even the most elementary checkmates. Chess is always a difficult game to learn as an adult, especially for an octogenarian. Sam thought that she was probably just studying chess in order to use the game in one of her novels, although when he asked her whether that was the case, she denied it.

Sam had dabbled in poetry while he was an English major at Rutgers. When he showed Mary some of his poems, she was very encouraging. "You should keep it up," she told him.

"Ever since I started coming to The Chess Shop, I haven't written a single poem."

"Well, chess is a creative endeavor also, isn't it?" Mary asked him.

"That's what I keep telling myself," he said.

AT THE BEGINNING OF SEPTEMBER, SAM MOVED IN with Megan and Chrissy. Megan planned a big party in honor of the occasion. She put all the bedroom furniture in the basement of the building so they could use the room for dancing. All Sam's friends came to the party—Raphael, Ahmed, Sylvia, David, Bernardo and Dorothy, and José and Susan, his fiancé. Megan invited Jean, as well as several of her Irish friends, some of whom Sam had never met. Chrissy danced with all the men; her favorite was José, whom she flirted with until midnight, when she fell asleep on the living room floor.

Sam found Kelly and Aidan, two of Megan's Irish friends, particularly interesting. Aidan was a bartender at Swifts, an Irish bar on East 4th street. Kelly was a fashion designer whose exquisite silver jewelry had been bought by Barbara Streisand and other celebrities. Aidan dressed in East Village style, with a Mohawk haircut and tattoos on his chest and arms. Kelly wore ankle-length black dresses, and black headscarves, to match her waist-length dyed black hair. Kelly was the singer and Aidan the bass player in a rock band called The Bundlers, which performed regularly at CBGB's on the Bowery.

When Kelly learned that Sam was a chess teacher, she said, "I've always wanted to learn."

"Do you know the rules?"

"Yes, but not much more than that."

"Why don't you take some lessons?" he asked her.

"Maybe I will," she replied.

He was intrigued by her exotic good looks and her bold personality. They danced together without making their lovers jealous. Long after all the other guests had left, the two couples sat up chatting until dawn. When Chrissy woke up they all went to the Odessa diner for breakfast. When Sam and Megan finally got home, he said, "They are way cool."

IN MID-SEPTEMBER, JOSÉ AND SUSAN were married in a civil ceremony in downtown Manhattan; Raphael and Sam came as witnesses. Afterward, the four of them went out for a drink in SoHo.

Susan was a remarkable woman—an only child who had grown up in a secluded area in Alaska. Her parents were teachers in a school in a small town. To get to the school, she and her parents had flown in a private airplane. She had spent most of her childhood by herself, exploring the forests and streams near her house, and reading dozens of novels at her favorite spot in the woods. When she came to New York City at age eighteen, she had quickly adapted to her new environment, going to the opera and the ballet and working as an editor for *Dissent*. She even learned to play a reasonable game of chess. She and José had met at a bar where they both played pool in an amateur league.

José and Susan went to Costa Rica for their honeymoon. José was surprised by how quickly Susan picked up Spanish. The two of them moved into an apartment on the Upper West Side. After that, José decided that he wanted to study chess full time in order to become a grandmaster. Susan believed in him completely; she wasn't bothered by the fact that he brought in no income other than what he earned by hustling.

AFTER A WHILE, SAM AND MEGAN DECIDED to take a vacation together. They both took two weeks off from Doubleday in October and booked a flight. Chrissy stayed with Jean. They spent three days in Rome, then took a train to Venice. They enjoyed drinking Chianti and getting lost in the maze of streets and canals. On a gondola in the Grand Canal, Sam proposed. She smiled. "You're so romantic," she said.

"Where does romantic end and corny begin?" he asked.

"Let's do it!" she exclaimed.

Back in New York, Sam told David that he and Megan were engaged. "Good decision," David said. "I wish I had some prospects."

"Would your wife have to be Orthodox?" Sam asked.

"I don't know. . . . If I married someone she'd have to be *Jewish*, but *Orthodox?* I'm not really Orthodox myself anymore."

"What you need is a lapsed Orthodox Jewish chess player."

"There ain't no such animal," David said.

"Well, either you find someone or you'll be alone."

"Is there a third possibility?"

"You could always kill yourself."

Kelly bought a series of five chess lessons from Sam. At their first lesson, he played several games with her and told her what her mistakes were. After the lesson, he said, "I think you have some aptitude."

"I just want to be able to give Aidan a thrashing."

The two went to Reggio for coffee. Sam asked her when their band would be playing. "We'll be at CBGB's at 10:00 p.m. on Saturday night."

"I'll be there for sure."

Kelly noticed that he didn't say "We'll be there."

"Why do you dress all in black?" he asked her.

"I used to dress in sexy clothes, but I was insulted by the comments men made about me."

"Such as. . . ?"

"'Fresh meat! Wash it off!'"

Sam struggled to keep from laughing.

On the stereo at the café, they were playing an opera recording. When *"Quando m'en vo"* came on, Kelly started singing along.

"Wow! A rock singer who knows *La Boheme*. What else can you do?"

"I give great blow jobs."

"Oh! If I weren't engaged. . . ."

"I'm not offering you one, I'm just listing my talents," she told him.

"Is this one on your resume?"

"No, I just use it at interviews."

ONE AFTERNOON, WHEN JOSÉ WAS IN THE SHOP, a young mother named Sarah came in with her seven-year-old daughter, Rachel. José played a game with the young girl, who fell in love with him, as did her mom. When they asked him about lessons, Ahmed interrupted: "We have two teachers on our staff here."

José ignored him. "Here's my card," he said.

Ahmed was very angry, but he kept quiet to avoid making a scene. The next time he saw Sam, he said, "I think you should know that José is stealing your students."

"I don't believe it."

"You'd *better* believe it."

"Well, don't do anything until I talk to him."

Sam called José at home and asked him if Ahmed was telling the truth. "I only have one student," José said.

"Please don't solicit students at The Shop. There aren't enough to go around."

"Not even one?"

"One is a lot," Sam said. "In one month, that could amount to a hundred dollars or more. That's a lot of money for someone who works in a bookstore."

"I understand," José said. "I'll explain it to her mom and send her to you."

The next day, Ahmed came in on Sylvia's shift and found José playing speed chess.

"There's a thief in The Shop," he said, loudly enough so that everyone could hear him.

"Then why don't you call the police?" José shot back.

"Maybe I'll do that."

Ahmed did. When they arrived, he told them that he wanted them to escort José out. "What did he do?" one officer asked.

"He's been stealing students from our teachers and not paying us our share."

"Did he refuse to leave?"

"Well. . .not exactly."

"Did you *ask* him to leave?"

"No, I want *you* to ask him to leave."

The officer in charge became very angry. "Don't call us unless someone *refuses* to leave. We've got better things to do than to come here for no reason."

José laughed mockingly. "Watch me leave on my own volition," he said.

José called Sam and told him what had happened. "He made a total fool of himself," he said. The two of them laughed conspiratorially.

At Kelly's second lesson, Sam taught her the elementary checkmates: checkmate with a queen, a rook, or the two bishops. "How have your games with Aidan been going?" Sam asked her.

"We go back and forth," she said.

They went to Café Reggio again. "When are you and Aidan getting married?" Sam asked.

"I don't want to marry Aidan," she said. "I'm getting tired of him."

"I'm surprised. I thought you were the perfect couple."

"No way. We fight constantly."

"Boy, if I weren't taken, I would move in so fast. . . ."

"If you weren't taken, *I* would move in so fast. . . ."

Sam swallowed hard. "Let's talk about something else," he said.

"Well, what should we talk about?"

"Um. . .how about The Cold War?"

Kelly laughed. "Maybe you could negotiate a détente between Aidan and me."

"I've never been much of a diplomat," Sam said.

On November 1st, Sam and Megan went to CBGB's to hear Kelly and Aidan perform. Kelly was disappointed to see Megan there. Sam wasn't crazy about the band; he thought they were sort of generic punk rockers.

After the show, he said, "I feel like going for a walk."

Megan told him, "I'm really tired. I'm going to go straight home."

Sam walked crosstown to Karavas Place. He was happy to see that Cindy was behind the bar. At the other end of the bar, Cindy's father was seated with Joey, a friend of hers. Cindy came up to Sam and said, "I just cut off my dad."

"Why?" Sam asked.

"He was saying things like 'I remember the day you were born!'"

"Whoa. Maybe you didn't cut him off soon enough."

Sam ordered a Johnny Walker Black with one ice cube.

"I heard through the grapevine that you're engaged," Cindy said. "When are you getting married?"

"I don't even know *if* I'm getting married," Sam said with a sigh. "I've been so happy with Megan, but now someone else is in my head. I've never been so confused in my life."

"My brother once told me that lovers are like Second Avenue buses—you wait forever, then four come at once."

Sam stayed in Karavas Place until the bar closed at 4:00 a.m., then walked around the Village until morning, getting home just in time for breakfast. Megan was used to his nocturnal wanderings; she asked him no questions.

She made French toast with challah bread, and hot Columbian coffee. After breakfast, Sam and Chrissy read the comics in the *Daily News* while Megan cleaned up. *(I'd be such a fool to blow this.)*

CHAPTER 7

UNDER DAVID'S TUTELAGE, AHMED WAS GRADUALLY becoming a strong chess player. Whenever business was slow on his shift, he would play a game with anyone who had no opponent. He started writing down his games, so he could show them to David.

In addition to teaching David backgammon, Ahmed started recommending novels and poems for him to read. They went to poetry readings together; sometimes they even cooked meals together in Ahmed's apartment.

Sam told David about Kelly. "What should I do?" he asked in a pained voice.

"Do you love Kelly, or is it just a physical attraction?"

"I can't always tell the difference."

"Well, I can't tell you what to do. You'll have to decide for yourself."

At their third lesson, Sam started helping her with her opening repertoire. He showed her the Queen's Gambit Declined and the Sicilian defense.

"Is there an Irish defense?" Kelly asked.

"No, not that I know of. There's a French defense, an English opening, and a Scotch game, but no Irish defense."

"The Irish are always left behind."

"So were the Jews, at least until 1948."

"Are you part of the infamous Jewish conspiracy?"

"When I heard that there was a Jewish conspiracy, I tried to join, but they didn't want me."

"Well, I want you."

Sam stared at her silently for a few seconds. With great difficulty, he asked: "Would you. . . ?"

"Would I what?"

"Would you. . .have sex just once?"

"Yes," Kelly said emphatically.

"Where would we. . . ?"

"Anywhere. We could go to a motel in Queens."

"A motel?"

"Sure. I know a place that's cheap and clean. We can go there right now if you want."

"All right. Let's go," Sam said.

They jumped in a cab. On the way, they necked like teenagers. They reserved a room; Kelly paid. Once inside it, Sam hesitated. Kelly backed him against the wall, unzipped his fly and went down on him.

When they were finished Sam asked, "Have you done this before?"

"Once or twice."

"I want you to know. . .this doesn't change the way I feel about Megan," Sam said.

"Don't be a hypocrite," Kelly said with an ironic smile.

HE TOLD DAVID WHAT HAD HAPPENED. "Don't breathe a word of this to anyone," he said.

"Maybe I'll blackmail you," David replied.

Sam shuddered. "Don't even joke about it."

"You need to get your mind off it," David said. "Let's play chess."

They played for two hours. Sam's concentration was so poor that David won every game.

"I can't focus today," Sam said.

"All right. Let's go for a walk."

They went to East River Park, where several Hispanic boys were playing soccer.

"Let's ask them if we can join in," Sam said.

"I've never played soccer," David replied. "But you go ahead. I'll just watch."

Sam wasn't much of an athlete, but he had played soccer on his high school team. He played with the boys for an hour, which temporarily made him feel much better.

At work that week, he had trouble focusing on what he was doing. At night, for the first time in years, he started suffering regularly from insomnia. Sometimes it took him three or four hours to fall asleep. He fantasized about Kelly constantly—and was wracked with guilt about it. For the previous five years he hadn't needed therapy; he had just visited Dr. Berkun, the psychopharmacologist who wrote his prescriptions, every three months.

Now he decided to seek professional help. He asked the manager at Doubleday if he could take one weekday off and work on Sundays instead. Monday was the slowest day at the bookstore; Sam made an appointment to see Dr. Brown, a psychologist Dr. Berkun recommended.

AFTER THEIR FOURTH LESSON, KELLY AND SAM went to Café Reggio as usual, but there were no seats available, so they went to Café La Lanterna on the next block. They sat by the window and watched the passersby. Just for fun, they began rating the appearance of everyone who walked by the window on a scale of one to ten, Sam rating the women and Kelly the men. After ten minutes of this, Kelly turned to Sam and asked: "Well, what do I get?"

"Oh, about an eight," Sam said. "What do I get?"

"About an eight."

"I thought the woman was supposed to be better looking and the man was supposed to have more money."

Kelly narrowed her eyes. "You seven!" she said.

They bought a six-pack of Heineken and went to the motel again. This time Sam took the initiative. He tore off her clothes and threw her on the bed.

"You're promising, for a neophyte," Kelly said afterwards.

AT HIS FIRST SESSION WITH DR. BROWN, SAM ASKED what he could do about his insomnia. The doctor taught him how to hypnotize himself. "Start by visualizing a bucolic scene."

Sam tried to visualize the lake in Central Park, focusing on the lily pads and the ducks floating on the water. He fell asleep for a second, then jolted awake.

"Now focus on relaxing every muscle in your body, starting with the arches in your feet and gradually moving up your body until you reach your neck and facial muscles."

The same thing happened; he fell asleep for a second, then woke up abruptly.

"Now try to empty your mind completely and listen to your breathing."

The same thing happened again; Sam was very frustrated.

"Practice these techniques every night," said the doctor. "Even if you don't fall asleep right away, they should help shorten the time it takes to fall asleep."

ALTHOUGH SAM TOLD MEGAN THAT HE WAS GOING to a therapist, she had no inkling that he had another woman on his mind. She knew that Sam was giving chess lessons to Kelly, but, as Sam himself had at first, she thought that Kelly and Aidan were a perfect couple. Although she sensed that Sam's insomnia wasn't the whole story, she decided not to ask him what was wrong.

Sam had five private students by then—three on Saturday, and two on weekday evenings. His newest student was Charles, a wealthy currency trader who owned a townhouse on the Upper West Side. After their first lesson at The Shop, Sam taught him at his home. Charles worked long hours, sometimes as much as sixteen hours a day. Often, he would wake up in the middle of the night to check currency rates in Japan. When he wasn't working, he pursued various hobbies: squash, fencing, and now chess. In his home there were two Asian women. Sam assumed that one of them was his wife and the other was a maid, but he couldn't tell which was which. There was very little furniture in the house, and no art on the walls. It looked as if Charles had just moved in that week.

Sam told Megan about Charles and the way he lived. "I feel sorry for him," she said. "He's missing out on life."

AFTER THEIR FIFTH AND FINAL LESSON, Sam asked Kelly, "Are you going to start a new series?"

"That's up to you," she replied.

"What do you mean, it's up to me?"

"I want to be more than just your chess student."

"You're already more than—"

"That's not enough."

". . . What are you saying?"

"I want you to decide between Megan and me."

"Oh, God," Sam groaned.

"If you say the word, I'll break up with Aidan and get my own place."

Sam felt as if his head was in a vise.

"You have to face it," she said. "We're in love."

"I need some time to think about it."

"You can have some time, but not a *lot* of time. I can't wait forever."

"Should we—"

"Go to the motel? Not until you make up your mind."

At his next session with Dr. Brown, Sam told him about his dilemma. "I feel so weak," he said.

"I don't think you're weak," Dr. Brown said. "I think you're a powerful person. Two beautiful women are in love with you."

"What I mean is. . .I have no will power. I'm just letting events carry me along."

"I think you're ambivalent. When you're ready to decide, you'll make a definite choice."

"How am I going to do that?"

"Why don't you make a list of the pros and cons of both alternatives? You can bring your list to our next session."

Sam was incredulous. "You want me to make a rational decision, as if I were choosing a car to buy? What about following my heart?"

"What does your heart tell you?"

"My heart. . .my heart is split down the middle."

"Then use your head."

"My head is in a fog."

"Well, then. . . ."

"This isn't helping, damn it!"

"You want me to solve all your problems in one session? Be realistic. You have a difficult decision to make. Take your time, and make up your mind."

Sam shook his head. "Whatever," he said.

ON NOVEMBER 4TH, MEGAN AND JEAN THREW a party for Chrissy's seventh birthday at Jean's apartment. They invited several of Chrissy's friends as well as a few adults, among them Kelly and Aidan. Kelly was one of the best liars Sam had ever seen; she didn't show the slightest sign that anything unusual was going on. Sam, on the other hand, was very agitated. To sedate himself, he drank glass after glass of red wine. At nine o'clock he excused himself, complaining of a bad headache. He told Megan, "I am going to go home, take some Advil, and crash."

To Chrissy he said, "Happy birthday, sweetie. I love you."

That he loved Chrissy, at least, he was sure of.

It had been a while since Sam had been to the Village Corner. On the evening after Chrissy's party, Sam, David, and Ahmed went there to hear Stephen Fall. Sam told them, "This is just what I need—to get away from both women long enough to regain my sanity, even if it's only for one night."

Neither David nor Ahmed had ever had a girlfriend. Ahmed said, "I wish I had two women to choose from."

Sam groaned.

In between sets, Stephen came to their table. He asked them, "Do you have any requests?"

Sam said, "I'd love to hear some soothing bossa nova."

Stephen played three songs by Antonio Carlos Jobim: "One Note Samba," "The Girl from Ipanema," and "Quiet Night of Quiet Stars."

Sam closed his eyes and softly sang along. "I feel so serene," he said afterwards.

Now, in addition to his insomnia and his ambivalence about Kelly, Sam started suffering from depression as well. He had trouble getting out of bed in time to go to work at the bookstore. Megan was very helpful. She did everything she could to get him up. When she was unable to, she enlisted Chrissy to help her. Sam didn't want to appear to be an invalid to the little girl, so he forced himself up. Megan gave him the responsibility of bringing Chrissy to her daycare center. This was an excellent strategy, because Sam cared more about Chrissy's well-being than his own.

At work, Sam was listless and detached. Barbara, the store manager, told him, "You look like you don't want to be here."

"That's not the case," he said. "I'm just having some problems at home, that's all."

"All right," Barbara said cautiously. "Just try not to let it affect your work."

The following Monday, Sam went to see Dr. Brown again. "Things are getting worse and worse," he said.

"Maybe we need to adjust your medication."

Sam was irritated. "I'm taking enough pills already," he snapped.

The doctor waited a few seconds before asking, "What's your thinking about your dilemma?"

Sam told him about his depression and how Megan was helping him fight it. "She's a rock to me," he said. "But my craving for Kelly is becoming overwhelming."

"It's a tough one," the doctor acknowledged.

"What would you do if you were in my place?"

"Honestly, I'd stick with Megan," Dr. Brown said. "Kelly sounds like trouble."

Sam gazed absently out the window.

". . . What are you thinking?" the doctor asked him.

"I'm thinking. . .I guess you're right."

That evening, Sam called Kelly on The Chess Shop phone. "I need to see you," he said.

"Where are you?"

"I'm at The Shop."

"I'll meet you at Café Reggio in an hour," Kelly said.

Sam bought a copy of *The New York Times* and sat at a table near the window, nervously turning the pages.

Kelly arrived right on time. "What's the scoop?" she asked him.

"Kelly. . .I'm losing my mind."

"Come live with me," she said. "I'll make you so happy."

"I can't," he said faintly.

Kelly stared at him silently. "Is that your final decision?" she asked.

"Yes," he said.

Without a word, she stood up and left the cafe. Sam sat for twenty minutes with his head in his hands, then got up and trudged home.

Kelly was not one to give up without a fight. Even as she rode the E train back to Queens, the wheels were turning in her mind. What if Megan found out that Sam was cheating on her? She couldn't tell her herself. She'd have to find a way to leak it to her indirectly.

By the time she reached her stop, she had made up her mind. She would tell Jean about her affair with Sam and pretend that she was torn between Sam and Aidan. She gambled that Jean would spill the beans to Megan without saying anything to Aidan.

When Kelly got home, Aidan was waiting for her.

"You've got to hear this new song I just wrote."

"Sure," she said with a smile.

"It's based on a line from an old *Star Trek* episode."

"Which one?" Kelly asked. "I've seen most of them."

"The women are ruling a planet in another galaxy. They live inside the planet, and the men live outside. The women's computer has broken down, and they want to use Spock's brain to replace it. The men are basically the women's slaves, and they call them "the givers of pleasure and pain." That's what I call my new song: "The Givers of Pleasure and Pain."

She looked at him quizzically. For a split second, she wondered whether he was insinuating something. Then she said, "Let's hear it."

When Sam got home, he gave both Megan and Chrissy a big hug and went right to bed. He fell asleep instantly, for the first time in weeks.

AFTER DINNER THAT FRIDAY, HE WENT STRAIGHT to The Chess Shop. Raphael and Ben were there, playing speed chess. Sam joined in, and they played three-way until The Shop closed at midnight, then went to the Washington Square Diner, where they continued playing until dawn. When they were finished, Sam was ahead by twelve games.

"What drugs are you taking?" Raphael asked him afterwards. "I've never seen you play this well."

Sam told him about the decision he'd made. Ben's reaction was the same as Ahmed's: "I wish *I* had two women to choose from."

"Maybe I should introduce you to Kelly," Sam said.

They put away the chess set and timer and ordered breakfast. Then they went their separate ways. Sam got home just as Chrissy was waking up. While they were waiting for Megan, he read her favorite book, *The Cat in the Hat Comes Back,* by Dr. Seuss. Afterward, he fell asleep on the living room floor.

When he awoke several hours later, he realized that he had missed his first appointment at The Chess Shop. He called and asked Johanna to tell his student to wait, then ran to The Shop as fast as he could, arriving at 2:15, forty-five minutes late. His student, Cliff, was one of the regulars there. Sam promised him a free lesson, then played him a quick game until his next student arrived at 2:30. Cliff was an easy-going guy; he wasn't upset at all. But Marcus, who was as punctilious as anyone, was irritated. "Please be on time for your appointments," he said, fixing Sam with the stare that had intimidated him so much when he was a salesman.

KELLY CALLED JEAN ON SUNDAY AFTERNOON. "What are you doing later?" she asked her.

"You know I have no social life," Jean said. "I'll be at home jerking off as usual."

"Do you want to have a drink with me?"

"I don't want to have a drink, but I wouldn't mind having seven or eight drinks."

Kelly laughed. "Let's meet at the Odessa bar at eight," she said.

When Jean got there, Kelly was seated in a booth, drinking a martini. Jean joined her and ordered a Guinness.

"So," Kelly began. "How's your love life?"

"Nonexistent."

"What about your sex life?"

"That's another story,"

"Is it a good story?"

"It depends how fast you turn the pages."

Kelly paused. "I have a confession to make," she said.

"Spill it."

"I'm having an affair with Sam."

"*Megan's* Sam?"

"Yes."

"Whoa."

"I don't know what to do."

"You already have a good man. Why screw things up?"

"I can't get Sam out of my head."

"Do you love him?"

Kelly thought for a second. "I guess not," she lied.

"Do you love Aidan?"

"Yes," she lied again.

"Then don't blow things. Forget about Sam."

"I want both of them."

"So why are you asking me?"

Kelly paused. Shrewdly, she said, "I just wanted to hear myself say these things."

Jean stared at her angrily. "Frankly, I don't have the slightest sympathy for you," she said. "I think you're the most selfish person I've ever met.".

Kelly got up abruptly, put seven dollars on the table, and stomped out of the room. As she walked back to the F train, she said to herself, "I think I played my cards perfectly."

CHAPTER 8

JEAN IMMEDIATELY CALLED MEGAN AT HOME. "Can you come to the Odessa bar right away?" she asked. "It's very important." "Are you all right?" "I'm fine, but I have something to tell you that I can't say over the phone."

"I'll be right there."

She asked Sam, "Could you put Chrissy to bed? I have to go talk to Jean."

"Sure," he said.

As soon as she saw her, Megan knew that something was wrong. Sitting down across from her, she asked, "What's the matter?"

"There's nothing I can do but tell you directly. Kelly and Sam are having an affair."

"No," Megan said, and stared open-mouthed at her.

"Your good friend Kelly says she wants both Aidan and Sam."

"No," she said again.

"The poor thing came to me looking for sympathy."

As Megan sat there silently, tears started streaming down her face.

"Don't shed a tear over these cheaters," Jean said. "Pull yourself together."

Megan clenched her teeth. "You're right," she said. After a moment, she added, "I'm sure Kelly initiated it."

"It always takes two."

Megan went home and found Sam reading a chess magazine in the living room. He looked up and saw the fury in her face. "What's wrong?" he asked.

"I just heard that you're having an affair with Kelly. Is this true?"

". . . Well, we did have a brief affair, but it's over now."

"You bastard!"

"I'm sorry, Megan."

"How could you do it?"

"I'm really sorry," he repeated.

"Damn it!"

"If you can forgive me, I'll make it up to you."

"You're going to have to move out," Megan said decisively. "I can't cope with this."

"Oh, no," he groaned.

She went into the bedroom and slammed the door.

"What a fool I am," he said out loud. "What a fucking fool."

He went into Chrissy's room and watched her sleep for a few minutes. Then he left the apartment, went outside, and broke into a run. He ran to Broadway, made a left turn, and ran blindly until he was exhausted. He looked around and realized that he had reached Wall Street.

As always, late at night, the financial district was a ghost town. Sam passed the stock exchange and sat on the steps of the Federal Hall National Memorial. The night was cool and clear. He was too restless to spend a lot of time in one place. After sitting for a few minutes, he decided to walk across the Brooklyn Bridge, something he had always wanted to do. As he did, he had a fleeting thought of jumping off. *(No, that's not an option.)* He remembered what Woody Allen had said about suicide: "I'd have to kill my parents first."

When Sam reached Brooklyn, he made his way to the Promenade in Brooklyn Heights. He sat on a bench and looked at the spectacular view of downtown Manhattan. *(Maybe Megan will change her mind.)*

Strangely, he had no thought of Kelly. He tried to empty his mind as Dr. Brown had taught him. This time, it worked. In a few minutes he felt very calm, then he drifted off to sleep.

When he awoke, it was light. He got up, dragged himself to the nearest subway stop, and took the train back to the Village.

By the time he approached Washington Square, it was eight o'clock. He dialed the bookstore on a pay phone and called in sick. Then he played speed chess with Lovey Jenkins for two dollars a game. After three hours, he was down by only $12.00. *(I have to keep myself occupied, or I'll go insane.)* He went to the newsstand by the West 4th Street station, where he bought a copy of *The New York Times*, then went to the Waverly Diner and ordered a Spanish omelet with rye toast and a glass of orange juice.

“Spanish omelet with whiskey down,” the waiter called to the kitchen.

“I love New York,” Sam said to no one in particular.

When The Chess Shop opened at 11:00 a.m., Sam went there to wait for David Rabinowitz. Meanwhile, he watched Costos and Jim Smith play an odds game, bantering back and forth, each hoping to gain the psychological advantage.

“Baboon!” Costos exclaimed.

“Boboonovsky!” Jim countered.

“Baboonovich!”

Richard Kelly said to Sam, “I think this is the real chess right here. Bobby Fisher is boring in comparison.”

David Rabinowitz walked in at one o’clock. “Are you ready for a beating?” he asked Sam.

“I need to talk to you,” Sam said.

David rolled his eyes as if to say, *What is it now?*

They went to Washington Square Park and sat on a bench near the fountain. “So what’s the latest?” David asked.

“Megan found out about Kelly and me. She wants me to move out.”

“Sounds like you blew it, buddy.”

“I’m such a schmuck,” Sam said, shaking his head from side to side.

“Well, there’s always Kelly,” David said.

“I don’t want Kelly. I want to get Megan back if I can.”

“I guess you had to lose her to see how important she is to you.”

“She’s everything to me.”

“Well, give it a little time. Maybe she’ll come around.”

“Let’s go somewhere we’ve never been before,” Sam said suddenly.

“Where, for example?”

“Do you know who Marcel Duchamp was?”

“No.”

“An influential artist who gave up art to become a chess player. They have a lot of his artwork at the Philadelphia Museum.”

“You want to go to Philadelphia?”

“How about it?”

David shrugged. “I guess I don’t see why not,” he agreed.

They went to the Port Authority Bus Terminal and hopped on a Greyhound bus. On the way, they played a game of blindfold chess. After about thirty moves, their game reached a very simplified position, and they agreed to a draw. After they were finished, David asked, "How good a player was Marcel Duchamp?"

"Well, he wasn't a world-class player, but he was definitely master strength. At one point, he was on the French national team. He was also a devotee of hypermodern chess."

"What's hypermodern chess?"

"The hypermoderns were the first players to realize that it's not necessary to occupy the center with pawns. You can control the center with pieces, or even let your opponent have the center and then attack it."

". . .Boy, today everyone knows that. I'd forgotten that those ideas were once in the *avant-garde*."

When they pulled into the Philadelphia bus station, they headed straight for the museum. Sam showed David the urinal signed *R. Mutt*. "This was to make fun of the art establishment and to question what is art."

He also showed David "Nude Descending a Staircase" and the "*Etant Donnes*," Duchamp's final work. David looked through the peephole at the naked woman and said, "I guess pussy is what matters most."

On the way back to New York, Sam fell asleep. When they reached the Port Authority, David had a hard time waking him up.

When Sam got home at 8:00 p.m., he discovered that Megan had changed the locks on their door. He knocked several times, but no one answered, so he went back to The Chess Shop. David was outside, smoking a cigarette.

"It looks like Megan's playing hardball," Sam said to his friend. "She's changed the locks. I thought she'd at least let me stay until the end of the month."

"Where *are* you going to stay?"

"Damned if I know."

"I can't put you up. My studio is barely big enough for me."

"I'll think of something," Sam said. "If I have to, I'll move in with my mom until I find something else. She won't like it, but if my only alternative is sleeping on the subway, I'm sure she'll put me up."

He called his mother on the corner payphone. "I'm in somewhat of a bind," he told her. "Can you put me up tonight?"

"What happened?"

"Megan and I had a fight. I'll tell you more when I arrive."

He took the A train to the Port Authority and caught a bus to Hackensack. When he got there, he told his mother that Megan had thrown him out, but he didn't tell her why.

"Can I stay here until I find a place?"

"If you must," she said. "But try to be out by the first of the month."

That gave him two weeks until December 1. "I don't know if I should go to work tomorrow. The atmosphere is going to be very tense, to say the least."

"It's always better to be busy when you're upset," she said.

"I'll be busy enough looking for a place. I don't think I should see Megan at all until we can talk quietly."

"Well, whatever you do, don't quit. Keep your options open."

"I'll just call in sick tomorrow."

Ms. Kanter shook her head. "Nobody knows the meaning of work today," she said.

Sam slept on the couch in her living room. In the morning, after eating three bowls of Cheerios, he took the bus back into the city. He bought the *Village Voice* at the newsstand on Tompkins Street and sat on a stoop near The Chess Shop and went through the classifieds. There were no apartments he could afford on what he earned at the bookstore, so he decided to look for another job before finding a place. He went to all the used bookstores in Manhattan, correctly assuming that they would pay better than Doubleday. None had anything available immediately, but a few of the owners promised to call him should an opening come up.

MEANWHILE, KELLY WAS GETTING IMPATIENT. She couldn't stand waiting to hear whether her scheme had succeeded. She knew that calling Sam at Megan's place was risky, so she decided to drop by The Chess Shop on Wednesday evening to see what she could find out. She was happy to discover Sam there playing an odds game with Jim Smith.

"Hello," he said when he looked up and saw her watching.

"Finish the game," Kelly said. "Don't let me interrupt you."

Sam always played better when he had an audience. He won decisively, then said to Jim, "I'm going to stop and join my friend. You can pay me tomorrow."

Sam and Kelly walked the two blocks to Café Reggio. On the way, Kelly asked him, "How's everything?"

"Not good."

"What's up?"

"Wait until we're seated. I can't walk and cry at the same time."

They sat at a table in the corner, away from the other customers.

"Megan found out about us," he finally said.

Kelly feigned astonishment. "Who told her?" she asked.

"Apparently, Jean told her. I have no idea how Jean found out."

Kelly quoted the old poem: "Oh what a tangled web we weave when first we practice to deceive."

He had no inkling that she was the spider and he was the fly.

"What are you going to do?" she asked him.

"I don't know," he said, shaking his head slowly from side to side. "She changed the locks on the apartment. I'm staying with my mother until I find a new place."

"I hope you know that you can live with me," she said. "I'm leaving Aidan and finding my own place one way or another." She actually had no intention of leaving Aidan until she had landed Sam.

"I'm not ready to move in," Sam said. "I've got to put myself back together first."

"All right," Kelly agreed. "Call me when you're ready."

They made their way back to the West 4th Street station, where Kelly caught the E train back to Queens.

"Just remember I love you," she said as they parted.

On Thursday morning, Sam called in sick again, then phoned Dr. Brown at his office. "When is your first available appointment?" he asked.

"Can you come at 11:00 a.m. tomorrow?"

"I'll be there."

Sam's mother told him, "If you keep calling in sick, you're going to lose your job."

"I can't see Megan yet."

"Well then, you'd better find another job. You can't stay here indefinitely."

"Mom, I'm losing my mind," he said.

"If you don't keep busy, things will get worse, not better."

"I can't *talk* to you!" he shouted, running out the door.

The next morning, he arrived on time for his appointment. "How are you?" the doctor asked.

"I've never been worse," Sam said. He told him about his situation.

"Never a dull moment," the doctor said.

"What I'd like right now is about ten dull years."

"Well, I don't think you'll get that with Kelly."

"I know that. That's why, if Megan would take me back, I wouldn't even *look* at another woman."

"Well, that's the first thing I'd tell her," the doctor said.

"I'm afraid to approach her until her anger cools down. I don't even want to see her at work."

"I don't think anyone will be interested in you if you're unemployed."

"I'll find a job," Sam said, gritting his teeth.

GRADUALLY, SAM'S DEPRESSION BEGAN TO WORSEN. As always when he was depressed, he had a terrible time getting himself out of bed. His mother began to play the role that Megan had before; she did everything in her power to make sure he was up by noon at the latest. Looking for a job, which is hard work for anyone, was an ordeal for him. He only felt relatively happy on his walks with David. But he knew that harping on his problems would put a strain on the friendship, so he tried to steer the conversation into other directions.

The day before Thanksgiving, they walked all the way from The Chess Shop to Lincoln Center on the Upper West Side. On the way, Sam asked, "Remember that time you stopped talking to me? What was that about?"

"You had beaten me badly at speed chess. I thought it was mean of you to rub it in by bragging to Freddy."

"That's all?"

"I was afraid you would react like that. That's why I told you forget about it."

"I didn't know you were so sensitive."

"Let's change the subject," David said.

"Would you rather hear more about Megan and me?" Sam asked half-jokingly.

David rolled his eyes.

"Well, then, what should we talk about?"

"How about the *Book of Job*?"

At Lincoln Center, Sam showed David around. "Have you ever been to an opera?"

"No."

"We should go when I have some money coming in. Seats are expensive, but you can buy standing room for a reasonable price."

"Which one do you recommend for a beginner?"

"*La Bohème* is the most accessible and one of the best."

La Bohème was playing that winter at the New York City Opera. "It's a date," David said.

ON THANKSGIVING, SAM'S MOTHER WENT for dinner at the home of an old friend of hers. Sam was invited but he decided not to go. He spent the evening lying on the sofa in her apartment, listening to her LP of Glen Gould playing The Goldberg Variations. When the first side of the disc came to an end, he found it an effort just to get off the sofa and turn it over. When she returned at 10:30 p.m., she found him lying on the couch fully clothed.

"You could at least take your shoes off," she said.

"Happy Thanksgiving, Mom," he said faintly, then burst into tears.

"Honey, what's wrong?" she asked him.

"I don't know what to *do*," he said, desperately. "My life is falling apart."

"Take off your shoes and try to get some sleep. You can call Dr. Brown in the morning."

He lay on the sofa, staring at the ceiling. He forced himself to try the doctor's self-hypnosis techniques, to no avail. The hours went by agonizingly slowly. When the sun came up, he was still awake.

His mother arose at 8:00 and went into the living room to talk to him. "Listen, don't worry about finding your own place just yet. You can stay here until you're feeling better."

He sighed deeply.

"What time does Dr. Brown arrive at his office?" she asked.

"I don't know."

"Try calling him at nine. Right now, come into the kitchen and have some hot coffee."

CHAPTER 9

At 9:00, he called Dr. Brown's number and left a message on his answering machine, asking him to call back as soon as possible. The doctor returned his call at 11:00. "Do you have any openings today?" Sam asked him.

"Why don't you come at 4:30 this afternoon?"

Sam took the 2:20 bus from Hackensack to the Port Authority, then the subway to Dr. Brown's office. The doctor could see right away that Sam's mood had worsened. He was unshaven, and his brows were knitted.

"Everything is becoming an effort," Sam said. "I desperately need to find an apartment and a job, but I don't have any energy."

"Keep trying, but don't be hard on yourself if you don't succeed right away," Dr. Brown said. "If you put yourself down, you'll just make yourself more depressed."

After the session ended, Sam went to The Chess Shop to look for David. He was there, analyzing an endgame position with Richard Kelly. Sam didn't want to interrupt their analysis, so he waited outside, hoping David would be finished soon. After twenty minutes, he started getting impatient. He felt like jumping out of his skin. *(What am I going to do with myself?)*

Unable to wait any longer, he started walking at a brisk pace. After fifteen minutes, he looked around in confusion until he realized he was on First Avenue. He decided to drop by the Village Idiot to see if Jennifer was there.

Sure enough, she was behind the bar. When he entered, she gave him a big smile.

"Where you been?" she asked him.

"In the Twilight Zone," he said morosely.

He had thought that he would be happy to see her; instead he felt like he'd been punched in the stomach.

"Do you want a Johnny Walker Black?"

"Give me a double."

He closed his eyes and felt the searing liquid pour down his throat. He went to the jukebox, played five Johnny Cash songs, then sat by himself at the end of the bar. Jennifer, who was familiar with the many moods of her customers, could see he wanted to be left alone.

He downed one scotch after another without noticing the time go by. After two hours he ran out of money.

"Can I have one on credit?" he asked.

"You've had enough," she said.

It didn't occur to Sam to borrow money from Jennifer. When he stopped by The Chess Shop on the way home David was no longer there, so he borrowed five dollars from Ahmed and headed back to Hackensack.

When he walked in the door, his mother had good news for him: "A man called from Mercer Books. He said they had an opening, and he wants you to stop by tomorrow."

"Thank God!" Sam exclaimed. He went into the living room and took a Philip Roth novel off the bookshelf. He had trouble focusing, so after only five pages he turned on the television. *The Simpsons* was playing on Channel 5. *(That's about all I can handle right now.)*

THE NEXT MORNING, HIS MOTHER WOKE HIM UP. After he showered and shaved, he felt an overwhelming desire to get back under the warm blankets. He sat on the living room sofa in his underwear, fighting the impulse to lie down but unable to finish dressing. After a few minutes, she found him sitting there with his head on a cushion and his eyes closed.

"Sam, get up!" she shouted. "You've got to get this job! Don't blow it!"

With a Herculean effort, Sam dressed himself, left the building, and dragged himself to the bus stop. He was the only one there. "Lord help me," he said aloud.

When he was seated on the bus, he promptly fell asleep and only woke up when the bus entered the Lincoln Tunnel. At the terminal, he was the last one to leave his seat. He took the A train to West 4th Street, then walked east until he reached Mercer Street. *(Hide your misery, or they'll never hire you.)*

He entered the store and asked the girl at the desk if he could speak with the manager. She called him in his office on the intercom.

"Someone here who wants to see you," she said.

"Tell them to wait. I'll be out in five minutes."

Sam perused the books in the philosophy section. He was so preoccupied that the titles were a blur to him. *(Pull yourself together!)*

When the manager entered the room, Sam was surprised to see that he was one of the regulars at the Village Corner. "Hi, Dale," Sam said. "I had no idea. . . ."

"I was surprised myself when I saw your application. When can you start?"

Sam was relieved—he'd expected a lengthy interview. "Right away."

"Good. Take a look around and familiarize yourself with where things are. You can start next Monday."

"Great," Sam exclaimed. He was truly excited. *(Thank God.)*

He spent a half hour looking around, then ran to The Chess Shop to tell David the good news. David was playing blitz chess with Marcus. "Do you want to play three way?" Marcus asked him.

"No, I'd rather just watch and learn."

When Marcus was a tournament player, he'd had an expert rating. He was a very creative player; all his openings were homegrown. Although David was fully Marcus' equal at slow chess, he was no match for him at blitz. Marcus was able to steer the games into positions that were unfamiliar to David, who became lost in a sea of variations. After winning the first game Sam watched, David lost six in a row. "I give up," he said.

It was a beautiful fall day. The two friends took the A train to Columbus Circle and entered Central Park. On the way, Sam told David about his new job. Years earlier, he had lived on the Upper West Side, so he knew Central Park like the back of his hand. They walked over to the east side of the park, past the carousel, through the zoo, and up to the pond, where children sailed their toy boats or climbed on the statue of Alice in Wonderland. "Now that I've got a job, all I need to do is find an apartment, then I'll try giving Megan a call," Sam said.

They walked through the Ramble, past Strawberry Fields, and up to Belvedere Castle. Sam took a deep breath, filling his lungs with the crisp fall air. "You're a good friend, David," he said.

On Sunday night, Sam went to bed early, so he could get plenty of rest before starting his new job. After two hours, he was still wide awake, though, so he left the apartment and walked to a twenty-four-hour diner a few blocks away, where he ordered a pizza burger deluxe and a Diet Coke.

The girl at the counter was very flirtatious. "Are you married?" she asked him.

"Not yet," he said.

"Well, what are we waiting for? Let's elope in the morning."

"You're such a shy little wallflower," he told her.

He was surprised that he could still attract a woman in the emotional state he was in. He thought his misery was so palpable that everyone was aware of it.

When he finished eating, he returned to his mother's house, where he had no trouble falling asleep. At 7:30 in the morning, his mother woke him up. "Rise and shine!" she said.

When he arrived at Mercer Books at 10:00 a.m., Dale gave him a cart of used philosophy books and told him to shelve them in alphabetical order according to the author's last names. The work was tedious, but he found it very relaxing. At 2:00, Dale gave him an hour-long lunch break. He walked over to Tre Giovanni, an Italian restaurant he had patronized for years. He ordered lasagna, his favorite meal when he wanted something to stick to his ribs.

After lunch, Dale showed him how to use the register and left him there to check the customers' bags and ring up the sales. Near the register lay a big collection of classical CDs for him to choose from. His first selection was Beethoven's "Kreutzer Sonata," with Yitzhak Perlman on violin and Daniel Barenboim on piano. In this way, his first day at work passed pleasantly.

AFTERWARD, HE STOPPED BY THE CHESS SHOP to see who was there. None of his favorite opponents were in The Shop, so he chatted with Ahmed for half an hour. Before leaving, he asked Marcus if he could put up a sign inquiring whether anyone had a room to offer. Then he headed back to Hackensack.

His days off at Mercer Books were Friday and Sunday, so he made an appointment to see Dr. Brown on Friday afternoon.

When he was there, he asked him the question foremost in his mind: "Do you think I should call Megan, or should I wait until I find a place to live?"

"Do you feel ready?"

"I don't know."

"Well, you'll be taking a big risk. It's hard to predict how she'll react. If she yells at you, you might go into a tailspin."

"I guess I'd better wait," Sam said.

Johanna Lawrenson had been planning a big event to raise money for her Abbie Hoffman foundation. A lot of prominent leftists were there, like William Kunstler and Mark Green. Sam went with Ahmed, Sylvia, and James Flateman. There was live music, speeches by many of Johanna's friends, and a video of Abbie in his heyday.

After the event was over, the four went out for a late dinner. Ahmed fawned over Sylvia, showering her with compliments and insisting that he pay her bill in its entirety. James, who could be very irritable at times, blurted out, "Stop patronizing her!"

Ahmed was so offended that he immediately turned his back on James. After five minutes, James got up and left. Sylvia reprimanded Ahmed: "You behaved much worse than he did."

"He needs to be taught a lesson," Ahmed replied.

When they finished, Ahmed walked Sylvia home as he always did. When Sam went to The Shop to see if anyone had answered his inquiry, Marcus told him that Natan, an Israeli immigrant who occasionally played there, had answered the ad. Excited, Sam immediately called him on the player phone.

"Can I come right up and take a look at the place?" he asked.

"Sure," Natan replied. He gave Sam the address and apartment number. Without waiting a minute, Sam ran over to West 4th and took the A to Washington Heights.

The apartment was a huge three-bedroom that took up half of the third floor in a building on 181st Street. From the living room, there was a spectacular view of the George Washington Bridge and the Palisades on the New Jersey side of the Hudson River. Sam loved the place. He immediately wrote a check for the first month's rent. Then he called Megan on Natan's phone.

"Am I on your shit list?" he asked her.

"You're not on my shit list," she replied warmly.

He still had most of his clothes, his stereo, and his collection of CDs at Megan's place.

"Can I come over on my day off and get my things?" he asked her.

"Sure," she said.

The following Friday he hired a moving van to pick up his belongings at

3:00 p.m. He arrived at Megan's at 1:00 p.m. to pack. He was surprised to see that she had already packed everything in cardboard boxes and put them in the hall. Since they had a couple of hours to kill, they went to Odessa on Avenue A for a cup of coffee.

As soon as they were seated, he asked her, "How are you?"

"I'm all right," she replied.

"Are you. . .seeing someone?"

"I actually have two guys who are interested in me, but I don't know if I want either one of them. I think I'll just be alone for a while."

Sam didn't have the courage to tell her that he desperately wanted her back. *(I'll know when it's time.)*

"How's Chrissy?" he asked.

"She's okay. She misses you a lot."

"I'd love to see her, if you don't mind."

"Let me think about it. So many men have come in and out of her life," she said, shaking her head. "I don't want. . . ." She didn't finish the sentence.

NOW THAT SAM HAD A GOOD JOB AND A NICE PLACE TO LIVE, his depression melted away. When business was slow, he read voraciously. He started going to the Village Gate again. He had friendly arguments with Natan, whose politics were even farther to the left then Steven's or Johanna's.

Little by little, he became friends with Megan again, although he knew that he'd have to be very judicious to win her back as a lover.

Late in February, Sam went skating in Central Park with Megan, Chrissy, and Jean. Afterwards, they all went to an Irish restaurant on the East Side for corned beef and cabbage. Before they went their separate ways, Megan kissed him lightly on the lips.

Since he was now working on Saturdays, he switched his chess lessons to Sunday afternoons. Three of his students were able to make the switch; the others he referred to Richard Kelly. He put up a sign in The Chess Shop in order to drum up more business. He started studying chess for two hours every evening with the goal of attaining an expert rating. He was good in the opening and in middle-game planning; he was weaker in tactics and endgames, so he started by focusing on those. David Rabinowitz, who was almost a Master in the endgame, helped him by analyzing endgame positions with him. To work on his tactics, he bought a book filled with tactical problems in ascending order of difficulty. Little by little, his tactical vision improved, and he threw himself vigorously into his studies. *(Now if I can only win Megan back, I'll feel whole again.)*

The first Sunday in March, Sam and David went to see *La Bohème* at Lincoln Center as they had planned. David was enthralled. "I loved it!" he said afterwards. "I always thought that opera was an acquired taste."

"A lot of it is, but not *La Bohème*."

The two of them went to Café La Fortuna, a favorite hangout for opera buffs. "I guess there's more in this world than chess and Talmud," David said.

OF ALL THE EMPLOYEES AT THE VILLAGE CORNER, Valerie had been there the longest. She was a big voluptuous redhead who had a large cadre of adoring regulars. Sam started coming in on her shift. Since he no longer needed to go to Dr. Brown, Valerie became his unofficial therapist. Together they half-jokingly plotted strategies for the recapture of Megan.

"Women want romance," Valerie said. "You need to take her to Hawaii for a week."

"All the way to Hawaii? The Jersey shore won't suffice?"

"No way! Florida is the minimum."

"I thought Florida was just a big retirement home for aging New Yorkers."

"Precisely. If you take her there, you'll have no competition."

"You might have something there," Sam admitted.

SAM'S NEWEST STUDENT WAS A HANDSOME six-year-old boy named Paul, whose mom, Leslie, was an attractive blonde in her forties. After the first lesson, Leslie invited Sam to dinner with her and her son.

"Have you ever been to So Yen?" she asked him.

"What kind of food do they have there?"

"How you ever tried macrobiotic food?"

"No."

"Really? That's all I eat."

"I guess it won't hurt to try it."

They went to the restaurant in SoHo. When the waiter brought them their menus, Sam asked Leslie what to order. She suggested a half dragon of seaweed, beans, and tofu. When he took a bite, he was revolted. "I can't swallow this," he said, spitting it into his napkin.

"Why don't you try the fish?" Leslie suggested.

Sam tried the salmon. "This has no flavor," he said.

"Really? I think it's delicious."

"Well it's not for me. Go ahead and eat. I'll just have a burger later." While she was eating, Leslie proceeded to tell Sam all about her love life, right in front of her son. She was married to a man she had met at the Harvard Business School. Theirs was a loveless marriage; they only stayed together for financial reasons. They had an open relationship—apparently, both of them had as many affairs as they could.

Sam was extremely disturbed that Leslie would talk like that in front of her child. He changed the subject to engage the young boy.

Paul was a big fan of the Teenage Mutant Ninja Turtles. He also had a big collection of toy musical instruments, which he described in detail. Sam and Paul hit it off.

Leslie decide to buy the boy one lesson a week. "The Chess Shop is a little crowded and noisy," she said. "Is there somewhere quieter we can have the lessons?"

"Sometimes I go to my student's homes."

"What about the Manhattan Chess Club?"

Sam was surprised that Leslie knew about the Manhattan. "You need to be a member," he said.

"Could we buy a family membership for the three of us?"

"I'll call them and find out."

Sam told David about Leslie and Paul.

"He sounds like an adorable kid," David said. "Too bad he's got such a nut for a mother."

"When they're six, they cope. But I think he'll have big problems when he's an adolescent."

Unlike the Marshall, which had been in a brownstone on West 10th Street for decades, the Manhattan Chess Club had moved several times. At the time, the club was located on West 46th, Restaurant Row. After her son's first lesson at the Manhattan, Leslie took Sam and Paul to the Russian Tea Room on West 57th, where Sam and Paul ordered borsht and shashlik. Leslie ate caviar, the only food on the menu allowed on her macrobiotic diet. She told Sam that she'd like to take lessons on her own so she could keep up with her son.

Now Sam taught Paul every Sunday and Leslie on Thursday evenings. After

Leslie's lessons, the conversation invariably turned to the topic of sex. Sam told David, "I get the distinct feeling that she's trying to seduce me."

"Well, why don't you go for it? You're a free man now."

"I think she's gross," Sam said.

Every time Paul came for his lesson, he greeted Sam with a big hug. Sam occasionally gave him little presents—Batman comic books or a toy yellow cab.

After three months, Leslie stopped bringing Paul and just came for her own lesson. "He seems to be losing interest," she said. Sam didn't know whether to believe her. He suspected that Leslie was jealous of the young boy's affection for his chess tutor. He said, "The boy needs more male companionship."

Leslie was angry, which was precisely the reaction Sam was hoping for. "He has plenty of male companionship," she said.

"Well, if he's lost interest in chess, why are you continuing to take lessons?"

"You have a point there," she said, trying to keep her composure. "I'll think about it and give you a call."

Sam was relieved. He told David: "I don't think I'll be hearing from her anytime soon."

"Good," David said. "And now you're a member of the Manhattan Chess Club."

"How about that?" Sam said.

CHAPTER 10

SAM AND MEGAN BECAME GOOD FRIENDS AGAIN. They made a point of going ice-skating together once a week. When the weather got too warm to skate in Central Park, they started going to Chelsea Piers. For Chrissy's birthday, Sam bought her two months of figure-skating lessons.

Sam's longing for Megan's love grew and grew as the months went by. Valerie told him, "You've either got to try to get her back or totally forget about her. You'll never be happy just being friends."

"I'll *never* totally forget about her. Right now I just want to be a good friend to regain her confidence. When I get some encouragement, I'll try to get her back."

"I feel sorry for you," Valerie said.

"Well, don't be. I'm a big boy. I'll survive, Megan or no Megan."

In the spring, Freddy came to New York for a visit. He stayed with Dr. Li, his surrogate father. Freddy and Sam went to The Continental Divide, where they killed off two pitchers of Budweiser. In Washington Square Park, Freddy played rook-odds games with Tommy Starks for six hours straight. Sam, who seldom gambled for more than a dollar a game, bet heavily on Freddy. By the end of the day he was ahead by $95.00.

After the session was over, Sam took Freddy to Karavas Place to see Cindy. Freddy turned on the charm, as only an Italian can. When Cindy's shift was over, Sam made himself scarce, and Freddy and the young girl went to the Limelight. In between steamy dancing sessions, Freddy bought her frozen margaritas and cocaine. After the club closed, he walked her to her apartment on West 4th. On the stoop in front of her building, Cindy kissed him good night. "Aren't you going to invite me in?" Freddy asked her.

"I'm underage," she said.

"Then how can you work as a barmaid?"

"I have a fake ID that shows I'm eighteen."

"Let me stay with you. You can make this such a memorable vacation for me."

"I'm sorry."

"Okay. . .anyway, you gotta come visit me in Italy." He gave her his address and telephone number, and they kissed again and said good night.

When Dr. Li drove Freddy to Kennedy Airport, Sam came along for the ride. On the way, Freddy complained about Cindy. "I hate when these little tarts lead me on like that. I must've spent eighty dollars on her, and what do I get? Nothing!"

"Very few women will sleep with a guy on the first date," Sam said.

"Yeah, but she *knew* I was going back to Italy. We didn't have any time to waste."

"Well, there's always next year."

When Sam and Dr. Li returned to Manhattan, Sam went to Karavas to see Cindy. "I think I broke his heart," she said.

"Well, he'll get over it. Believe me, the girls I loved when I was twenty-two—I wouldn't know them today if they sat on my face."

Cindy and Sam laughed out loud.

ON A BEAUTIFUL DAY IN MAY, SAM, MEGAN, CHRISSY, AND JEAN all went skating together at Chelsea Piers. When they were finished, Sam and Megan decided to walk home, so they gave the keys to Jean, who hopped in a cab with Chrissy. On the way home, Megan told Sam that she was dating a man she had met in Tompkins Square Park.

"Is it serious?" Sam asked.

"Not yet."

Sam bit his lip. "Do you ever. . .think of us getting back together?"

"I'd never forget what you did to me."

"It would never happen again."

"Well, even if I could forgive you on the theoretical level, I don't know if I could be with you again. You've cost me so much grief. . . ."

"It's the only thing I've ever done that I regret."

"I have to be sure that you want *me*, just not someone."

When they arrived at her place, Megan invited him in. Chrissy was sitting on the rug in the living room, playing Go Fish with Jean. When she saw Sam, her face lit up. "Can I take you all out for dinner?" Sam asked them.

"Has your ship come in?" Jean asked him.

"My ship is stranded on a glacier in the Arctic Ocean, but I can do this once in a while."

The four of them went to The Kiev, where they ate hearty Ukrainian food. Sam walked them home, then headed back to Washington Heights.

EARLY IN JUNE, AHMED'S FATHER CAME from Lebanon for a visit. He took Ahmed, Sylvia, Sam, and David for Middle Eastern food at a restaurant on Atlantic Avenue in Brooklyn Heights. The menu was in both Arabic and English. Then they walked to the Promenade to look at the skyline of downtown Manhattan. Ahmed said, "This is my family in New York City."

"I can tell that you're in good hands," his father replied.

After two weeks in New York, Ahmed's father went back to Lebanon. Before he left, he asked his son, "Just how long does it take to get a Ph.D.?"

"I'll be finished in two more years."

Later, when Ahmed repeated this, Sam was astonished that he hadn't told his father that he'd quit his studies. "You lied to your father?" he asked.

"Believe me, if I told him the truth, I'd have nothing but trouble."

"I don't understand you," Sam said.

IN ALL THE DAYS THEY SPENT WALKING TOGETHER, Sam and David had never visited the neighborhood in Brooklyn were David had grown up. After Ahmed, his father, and Sylvia took the train back to Manhattan, David took Sam on a tour of Williamsburg, where most of the followers of the Satmar Rebbe reside. "I'd like to meet your family," Sam said.

"I wouldn't feel comfortable bringing you there. My parents think that Reform Jews are worse than goyim."

"I'm not really even Reform. I'm more secular."

"That's even worse," David said. "Humanism is a secular Jew's religion. It's a religion without God."

"I've never thought about humanism as a religion. All humanism means to me is that I care about people and what they create. What's wrong with that?"

"What's wrong with that is that man becomes the center of the universe, not just part of God's creation."

"I don't think that humanism and belief in God are mutually exclusive. Sometimes I think there's a God."

". . .Do you? Is it a relevant God?'

"I don't know."

"Well then, you're an agnostic."

"I think agnosticism is the most honest approach. What's more honest than saying 'I don't know'?"

SAM TOLD VALERIE THAT MEGAN WAS DATING another guy. Valerie said, "You'd better make your move now, before she gets too involved with the other guy. You have no time to waste."

He called Megan and made a date for Friday night. The night before, he couldn't sleep. Towards morning he started having an anxiety attack, so he took a dose ofThorazine to try to calm his nerves. In the morning he went to Washington Square Park to play speed chess, but he was so nervous that he couldn't focus. He had a premonition that the worst was going to happen.

In the afternoon, he went for a walk with David down to Soho, where they stopped in a café to have cappuccino. "I've never seen you like this," David said. "Your hands are shaking."

"I've got to appear calm when I see her, or I'll blow it."

An hour before his date with Megan, he took another hundred milligrams of Thorazine. When they met, he could tell just by looking at her what she was going to say. "I have something to tell you," she said, as they sat at the Odessa.

"You're in love with your new boyfriend."

"I am. We've been together every night for the last week. He's already asked me to marry him."

"You're fast workers," Sam said.

"Please don't joke about it."

"What's his name?"

"His name is Spencer."

"Well, I hope you're happy together. I'd like to stay friends, if the two of you don't mind."

"Of course," Megan said.

Although Sam had succeeded in appearing calm for Megan, he was extremely agitated after he left her. He went straight home, called Dr. Brown, and left a message on his answering machine. "It's an emergency," he said. "Can I see you tomorrow? Please call me at home as soon as you get this message."

Dr. Brown was very conscientious. He seldom saw patients on Saturday, but he checked his messages twice daily, even on weekends. As soon as he received Sam's message, he called him back and made an appointment for Saturday morning.

"I can't thank you enough," Sam said. He called Mercer Books and told Dale that he had a bad cold and would have to take Saturday off.

That night was one of the worst in his life. Not only could he not sleep; he couldn't lie still. Once again, he took a dose of Thorazine to help him calm down. He was so desperate, he knelt on the floor and prayed, "Oh, God, please make this torment go way. I'll never cheat again. I'll thank you every day of my life. Please, Lord, help me now."

The hours went by with excruciating slowness. He kept looking at his watch every few hours. Finally, he put on a recording of Verdi's *Otello*. He sang along: "*Dio, mi potevi scagliar tutti I mali della miseria, della vergonga. . . .*" The music had a cathartic effect on him. He buried his face under the covers and sobbed convulsively.

Somehow he got through the night alive. His appointment with Dr. Brown was at 10:00 a.m. By 9:00, he was already outside his office. Not knowing what to do, he walked around the neighborhood, oblivious to the people, stores, and apartment buildings he passed. At 9:50, he rang the doorbell, and Dr. Brown let him in.

"What am I going to do?" he asked after relating what had happened. "I don't feel strong enough to fight to get her back, but if I don't make the effort, I don't know if I can live with myself. I'm at my wit's end."

He also told the doctor that he had been taking Thorazine to quell his agitation.

"I thought you were taking only Lithium and Prozac."

"I am, but I used to take Thorazine before Dr. Berkun put me on Lithium, and I still have half a bottle left."

"I think the first thing you should do is make an appointment with Dr. Berkun. He might want to make an adjustment in your medication. As far as

Megan is concerned, I can't tell you what to do—but if she rejects you, your condition may worsen. Sometimes when you're feeling ill, it's best not to take risks."

Sam stared at the doctor silently. "I guess you're right," he said in a weak voice.

Dr. Berkun, Sam's psychopharmacologist, was a resident at the Psychiatric Institute at Columbia Presbyterian Hospital. When Sam first moved to New York City in the '80s, he had been in the clinic there and had been treated by young doctors supervised by some of the most prominent psychiatrists in the city. Although these psychotherapists were highly intelligent, he had found them to be almost useless. Some were younger than he was, and, as he had told Dr. Brown when he first went to him, "You don't learn much about life when you're in medical school."

Fortunately for Sam, Dr. Berkun worked on Sundays at Columbia, at the intensive outpatient clinic. Sam called him early Sunday morning, and the doctor returned his call within the hour. Sam described exactly what was happening, mentioning that he was taking Thorazine to calm himself down. Dr. Berkun told him to come to his office at the clinic at 4:00 p.m. the next day.

The doctor worked very quickly. When he laid eyes on Sam, he sized him up in a few minutes. "Take 300 milligrams of Thorazine at bedtime, continue taking Lithium, and let's cut out the Prozac for now, because it might be contributing to your agitation. Of course, if things take a turn for the worse, call me right away. If you have an emergency, go to the psychiatric emergency room or dial 911."

Sam like the fact that, no matter how ill his patients became, Dr. Berkun remained very calm and professional. "Thank you very much," he said as he was leaving.

He took the A train down to the Village and headed to The Chess Shop to look for David. The two of them went to Café Reggio. When they were seated, David remarked, "You seem much calmer today."

"I am." Sam added that Dr. Brown had counseled him not to take the risk of trying to win Megan back.

"I don't know if I agree," David said. "You said she's everything to you. If that's really the case, then she's worth fighting for."

"Please don't confuse me," Sam said.

"If you don't try to get her back, you'll always regret it. She's only been with this guy for a couple weeks. The two of you were in love for long time."

"Oh, my God. I thought I had made up my mind."

As soon as Sam left the café, his agitation started to return. He ran blindly through the Village for fifteen minutes. When he looked up, he noticed that he was right in front of Megan's building. He considered ringing her doorbell but couldn't muster the courage to do so. He hopped in a cab and went back to The Chess Shop. David was in the middle of a game. Sam couldn't sit still even to watch. He got on the A train and rode to Washington Heights. Natan wasn't at home.

(I can't be alone now.) He called his mother in Hackensack. She wasn't home either. *(Oh, my God.)* He got on the A train again, went back to the Village, and ran to the Village Corner. Valerie was behind the bar. *(Thank God.)*

"How are you?" she asked him.

"I'm bugging out," he said.

"Really? What's wrong?"

"I can't talk about it."

He ordered a shot of Johnny Walker Black and a pint of Budweiser. When he was finished, he went outside and made a collect call to his mom. "I'm in bad shape, Mom," he said. "Can I come stay with you tonight?"

"What time is it?" she asked him. "You woke me up."

Sam looked at his watch. "Oh, it's 11:30. I'm sorry. I didn't realize it was so late."

"Well, if you have to, you can come. Just let yourself in and please don't wake me again."

"I won't."

Sam went to the Port Authority and caught the last bus to Hackensack. He let himself into his mother's apartment and lay down on the living room sofa. Then it dawned on him that he had forgotten to bring his medications with him. *(It's going to be a long night.)*

He went into the kitchen and raided the refrigerator. In the freezer, he found an unopened pint of rum raisin ice cream. He opened the carton and ate all of it. Then he went back into the living room and turned on the TV without the sound. On AMC the Hitchcock film *North by Northwest* was playing. Sam watched the familiar images: Cary Grant on the train with Eva Marie Saint, Cary Grant avoiding the crop duster, Cary Grant and Eva Marie Saint on Mount Rushmore. . . .

When the movie ended, he looked at his watch. It was only 3:30 a.m. As he lay on the sofa, his stomach started to ache. *(What if the ice cream was poisoned? The FBI has ways of doing things like that.)* He went into the bathroom and opened the medicine cabinet. On the top shelf was a box of Alka-Seltzer. *(No, they want me to take that. Am I becoming paranoid? I'd better play it safe and not take any Alka-Seltzer.*} He went into the hall and dropped the box of Alka-Seltzer into the incinerator. Then he realized that he had left his keys inside the apartment. *(Should I knock? She'll kill me if I wake her up again. Well, it's almost 4:00 a.m. She'll be up in three hours.)* He sat down and leaned his back on the apartment door. *(Maybe I'm supposed to guard the apartment. From whom? It isn't clear. Anyway. . . .)* He closed his eyes and tried to sleep. *(To die. . .to sleep. . .perchance to dream. . . . I'm only mad North by Northwest. When the wind is southerly. . . .*} He drifted off to sleep.

When his mother opened the door at 7:30 to pick up her copy of *The New York Times*, she found him lying asleep on the floor in the hall.

"My God," she said. "How long have you been here?"

"Not long," he said.

"Why didn't you knock?"

"I didn't want to wake you again."

"Oh, honey. . . . Come in. I'll make you some breakfast."

"Thanks, but I'd rather go back to sleep."

"Are you all right?"

"I'll tell you later."

"You don't have to sleep on the sofa. You can sleep in my room."

He lay down on his mother's bed and slept like a baby. When he awoke at 11:00, he realized that he had forgotten to call in sick. He called Dale and told him that he still had a high fever.

"I'll probably be out for several days," he said.

"Take care of yourself," Dale replied.

Sam went back to the bedroom and lay down again. He had a vague feeling that there was something incestuous about lying in his mother's bed. *(No, that's just my paranoia again.)*

At 2:30 in the afternoon, his mother woke him up. "If you sleep all day, you'll be up all night."

"I'll get up," Sam said.

"Would you like something to eat?"

"Like what?"

"How about some split pea soup?"

"I'm not in the mood for soup." *(With that green color, split pea would be very easy for the FBI to poison.)*

"How about a tuna salad sandwich?"

(That might be full of mercury.) "I'm not really hungry right now," he said.

"What about some coffee?"

"What brand?"

"What *brand?* How about Chock full o' Nuts?"

(Chock full o' Nuts—that's what The Chess Shop is.) "Brewed or instant?"

"Brewed, of course."

"Are you having a cup yourself?"

She looked at him carefully. "Sam, are you little paranoid?"

"I don't know," he said.

"Maybe you should call Dr. Brown."

He called and left a message on Dr. Brown's answering machine. As always, the doctor returned his call promptly. "How are you?" he asked him.

"I don't know," Sam said. "I'm becoming very fearful, and I don't know if I'm paranoid or if my fears are justified."

"What are you afraid of?"

"I don't want to talk about it over the phone. Can I come see you tomorrow?"

"I have an opening at one in the afternoon."

"I'll be there," Sam said.

He told his mother that he'd forgotten to bring his medication.

"Then you'd better sleep in your apartment tonight," she said.

"I'm afraid of staying in my apartment."

"What are you afraid of?"

"I can't tell you that."

"Well, then stop at home and pick up your medication."

"All right," he said.

CHAPTER 11

He took the 3:00 p.m. bus back to the Port Authority. *(What if they're following me? I'd better take a cab if I want to lose them.)* He hopped into a cab and told the driver to take him to the Metropolitan Museum of Art. When they got there, he ran across the park, exiting at 81st Street and Central Park West. Then he flagged another cab and went to Washington Heights. Before entering his building, he looked around suspiciously. *(I guess the coast is clear.)* He took the elevator to the fifth floor and took the stairs down to the third, where he and Natan lived. He took his pills out of their hiding place in his suit jacket pocket and immediately left. Instead of taking the A train to the Port Authority, as he usually did, he walked to the George Washington Bridge terminal and boarded the first bus to Hackensack.

Although it got to Hackensack much quicker than the one from 42nd Street, the closest stop to his mother's apartment was about a half-mile walk. *(In case they're following me, though, I'll have a better chance of losing them this way.)*

He got off at Passaic Street and Prospect Avenue and walked quickly to his mother's building. He looked carefully around, then let himself in. *{I'd better not take the elevator; I might get stuck between floors.)* He climbed the stairs to the fifth floor and rang his mother's doorbell.

"Just in time for dinner," she said as she let him into the apartment. "I made your favorite—chicken Milanese."

"How do you know that's my favorite?" he asked her suspiciously.

"Sam, I've only known you for thirty-five years," she said with a smile. After dinner, they watched *The News Hour with Jim Lehrer*. *(He's looking straight at me. Did I see him wink at me? What is he trying to tell me?)*

"Do you have a chess set?" he asked his mother.

"I don't think so, but I have a Scrabble set. Do you want to play?"

"Yeah, if you don't mind. If I watch any more television, I'll lose my mind."

His mother had no idea how literally he meant this.

They each picked one letter from a small bag. Sam picked an *S* and his mother picked an *M*. *(Mother and Sam?)* She went first and played "axle". *(Have they tampered with my mother's car?)* Sam played "rabid". *(Could I catch rabies from the chicken Milanese?)* Every word they played was loaded with meaning for him, but she was totally unaware of it. She thought the game was just a pleasant diversion for him.

As the game progressed, he became more and more fearful. *(If I don't get a seven-letter word, I'll die.)* Two-thirds of the way through the game, he played the word "Savior". "What a relief," he said out loud. *(Savior. Maybe Megan's new boyfriend is the Messiah? Well, then, I'd better let him have her, or I'll go to hell.)*

After the game, Sam took his medication, removed his shoes and socks, lay down on the sofa, and started reminiscing about his childhood—how, as a boy, he had been afraid of the dark. *(I could turn on the light. . . . No, that would make it easier for them to watch me.)* He remembered how his mother had washed his hair when he took a bath: "Lean your head back, honey bunny. Look at the butterflies on the ceiling." He remembered how his father had trapped him in between his knees in the evening: "You'll never get away. You'll never get away. You'll never, never, never, never, never get away." He remembered how, when his parents separated the month before his fifteenth birthday, he had thought it was his fault. He remembered his first love, Andrea. *(Why didn't I ever tell her how I felt? If only I were fifteen and know what I know now.)* He continued free-associating in this way for about an hour, then gradually fell asleep.

At 10:00 in the morning, Sam's mother woke him up for breakfast. "What would you like? Eggs or french toast?"

(I'd better make the right decision. Either the eggs or the french toast will be poison.) "I'd love some french toast," he said.

"How many slices?"

(It's crucial that I make the right decision.) "Three slices would be perfect."

"Do you want maple syrup or strawberry jam?"

(Why is she testing me like this?) "Strawberry jam."

After breakfast, Sam shaved and showered. *(Am I going to cut my throat with this razor? Will the liquid in the shower be water or acid?)*

When he got to the city, he called Dr. Brown from a pay phone. "I'm going to have to walk all the way to your office," he said.

"Is that the only way?" the doctor asked.

"I'm afraid so." He walked briskly, avoiding everyone's gaze. By the time he reached Dr. Brown's office, he was twenty minutes late. "I wanted to be on time," he said, "but I was being followed by someone, and I had to lose them."

". . .Who is following you?"

"I can't tell you that, but I'm in grave danger."

"In danger of what?"

"Someone's trying to poison me."

"How would they do that?"

"By putting rat poison in my food."

"Rat poison?"

"Yes, rat poison. Why do I have to repeat myself?"

". . .Sam, I think you should go to the hospital," the doctor said.

"Why?"

"I think you're delusional."

"Well, that's possible, but I doubt it." *(Is Dr. Brown part of the conspiracy?)*

"If you're not sure, I think you should talk to Dr. Berkun. I'm willing to bet that he'll give you the same advice."

"Well, if you both say the same thing. . . ." *(Could they be in this together?)*

"All right. I'll call him."

"Please call me and let me know what he says," the doctor said. "And if you decide not to go in, at least call me every few days and let me know how you're doing."

"Okay."

"Do you want to use my phone to call him?"

"No, thank you." *(Maybe they're in this together. How is that possible?)*

Sam wandered through the city, talking to himself out loud. *(They must be in this together. Remember what Sherlock Holmes said:"When you have eliminated the impossible, whatever remains, however improbable, must be the truth.")*

When Sam finally looked around, he realized that he was near Central Park. He entered, walked to the pond, and sat on a bench watching the children play. A five-year-old girl with long blonde hair, wearing a light blue cotton skirt and a white blouse, came up to him and said, "I have a cat named Cleo."

Sam smiled. "Is she as pretty as you?"

The little girl giggled and ran back to her mother, who was seated by the edge of the pond.

(Maybe I am delusional. After all, Dr. Brown has never lied to me. And Dr. Berkun seems okay, too.) Moments of insight like this had always kept him from going over the deep end in the past. *(I'm just afraid that, if I enter the hospital, they might keep me for a long time.)*

Sam suddenly felt very tired. He closed his eyes and felt the warm afternoon sun on his face. *(I can't let anyone deprive me of my freedom. Who can I talk to? Who can I trust? Valerie? David? None of my friends have the slightest idea what I'm going through. I feel so alone. . . .)*

Forty-five minutes later, he got up and walked back to the bus terminal.

When he reached Hackensack, he found his mother in front of her building, chatting with a neighbor, a Russian woman named Irina. *(Is Irina in the KGB?)*

"Long time no see," Irina said. "How are you?"

(I'd better not let her know that I'm onto her.) "Fine," he said.

"You're a good boy, coming out here to visit your mom."

(Good boy? What am I, a dog?) "Anything for a good meal," he said.

Irina said goodbye.

"How are you?" Mrs. Kanter asked him when they were alone.

"Let's talk inside."

They rode the elevator to her floor, entered the apartment, and sat down at the kitchen table. "What did Dr. Brown say?"

"He thinks I should go into the hospital."

"What do you think?"

"I'm not sure. . . . He said I should call Dr. Berkun." After a long pause, Sam added, "Mom, I'm afraid that, once I go in, they might not let me out."

"Well, when you call Dr. Berkun, you can ask about that."

"Can I trust him?"

"Sam, he's never done you any harm."

(Is she in on this, too? No, don't be ridiculous.) "Let me sleep on it," he said.

"Maybe you should stay up until 10:00 or so. If you go to sleep now, you'll probably wake up in the middle of the night."

"You're probably right."

She smiled. "How about some dinner?"

"Terrific."

She made meatloaf, mashed potatoes, and broccoli, which he ate ravenously.

"Well, whatever's wrong with you, it certainly hasn't affected your appetite."

While his mom was cleaning up, Sam went to the big maple dresser in her bedroom and started looking through the drawers. *(Something tells me I'll find a clue here.)* In the bottom drawer he found a folder where his mother kept everything he had written as a child. There were several little poems, letters from camp, a diary, and some cartoons. *(This is the key to my psyche! Everything that's happening to me now stems from this! I'll have to show this folder to Dr. Brown. . .no, then he'll have conclusive evidence. . . .)*

"Sam, do you want some coffee?" Mrs. Kanter shouted from the kitchen.

"Coming!" *(She can't know that I've been in this drawer.)*

He carefully replaced everything exactly how he found it, silently closed the drawer, and walked back to the kitchen. His mother poured the coffee into a big mug with a picture of Garfield the cat on it. *(Why is she giving me this particular mug?)*

"How about another game of Scrabble?" she asked him.

"No, thanks, I barely survived the last game."

After he finished his coffee, he left a message on Dr. Berkun's answering machine, asking him to call him as soon as possible, then went into the living room, took a book of poetry off a shelf, and lay down on the sofa. He turned to one of his favorite poems by Petrarch: *"Solo e pensoso, I piu deserti campi,"* and read it, both in Italian and English. He read each line of the English version separately, closing his eyes and repeating it silently to himself. In twenty minutes he had the whole thing memorized. He went into the kitchen and recited to his mom.

"He writes for you," she said.

AT 10:00 P.M., SAM TOOK OFF ALL HIS CLOTHES and lay down on the living room floor under a big comforter. He sang a song that had been popular when he was a boy: "They're coming to take me away ha-ha, ho-ho, he-he, to the funny farm. . . ." and burst into laughter.

"What's so funny?" Mrs. Kanter shouted from the kitchen.

"Nothing."

At 11:00 p.m., she said good night and retired to her room. Sam lay awake, staring at the New York skyline. He decided to pass the time by seeing how many buildings he could identify. *(The Empire State building, the World Trade Center, the Chrysler building, the MetLife building. How many composers can I name? How about one for each letter? (Albinoni, Beethoven, Copeland, Dvorzak, Franck, Gershwin, Honneger, Ibert, Joplin, Kodaly, Lalo, Mozart. . . . What about painters?)*

Just before midnight, he noticed the lights on the Empire State building. *(The city is good. New Jersey is evil. What will happen to me if I stay here all night? Maybe I should take a cab back to the city. What if something should happen to my mother? I'd never forgive myself. No, I'd better take the risk and stay here. . . .)* He pulled the covers over his head and shivered with fear.

At 2:30 a.m. he was still awake, so he turned on the TV without the sound. This time, *Birdman of Alcatraz*, with Burt Lancaster, was playing. *(What if they put me on Alcatraz? No, they'd be more likely to put me on Riker's Island. Or Wards Island? If I jump in the East River to escape, I might drown. Who will remember me when I'm a prisoner?)*

He turned off the TV and started taking books off the shelves one by one. *(Are these books in the right order? I'd better put them in the right order, or my mother might die!)* He started by putting all the poetry books in alphabetical order. *(Wait! Fiction comes before poetry.)* He took out all the poetry books and stacked them evenly on the floor, then arranged all the novels in alphabetical order. Then he put all the novels on the floor, replaced them with the poetry books, and put all the novels where the poetry books had been. *(God saw his creation, and it was good.)* He removed all the history books and placed them in reverse order, then put the biographies on top of the TV. *(I can put this on my resumé, along with Mercer Books. Maybe I'll get a job as a librarian.)* He laughed out loud. "Me a librarian! Ha, ha, ha, ha, ha!"

At that moment Mrs. Kanter woke up, put on her bathrobe, and came into the living room. "What on earth are you doing?" she asked him.

"Shhh," Sam whispered. "I'm trying to save your life."

". . .Sam, I think you should go into the hospital."

"No way. Not in the middle of the night."

"All right. But promise to call Dr. Berkun first thing in the morning."

"I already left a message on his machine."

"I know, but he doesn't know how urgent it is. Please call him at 9:00 a.m. "

"Alright, alright, alright!"

"Please don't be angry with me. I'm worried about you."

"I'll be fine," Sam said emphatically. "Go back to bed."

When she was asleep, he silently took her car keys, left the building, and drove to a go-go club on Route 46. In the center of the room, a circular bar surrounded a large stage. He ordered a Budweiser and watched the girls dance on the stage. The man sitting next to him asked him, "Are you following me?"

Sam said "No," and moved to another seat. A girl with a face like a hatchet did a lap dance for him. *(I wish I could find this attractive.)* When the man he had originally been seated next to went to the bathroom, the girl whispered, "He has a gun."

Alarmed, Sam thanked her and left the bar. *(Now I'm sure they're after me.)*

He was afraid to drive to Hackensack by the most direct route. *(I've got to lose them.)* Instead, he drove west to Paterson, drove across the city, then got on Route 4 and drove back to Hackensack. Bob Marley's "I Shot the Sheriff" came on the radio. ". . .If I am guilty I will pay. . . ." *(They're trying to frame me, just like the character in the song.)*

He broke into a sweat and floored the accelerator. By the time he was back at his mother's building, it was already becoming light. After he parked the car, he walked up the stairs to her floor. *(If I get trapped in the elevator, I'll suffocate.)* He sat on a folding chair on the balcony and watched the sunrise.

At 7:30 a.m., she found him sleeping on the balcony. "Rise and shine," she said.

"Hi."

"How did you sleep?"

"I had the strangest dream. I dreamt I was in a go-go bar on Route 46 and the guy sitting next to me had a gun."

"Boy, you're even paranoid when you're asleep."

"Am I?" he asked her.

"Come into the kitchen. I'll make you some breakfast."

She made a Spanish omelet, which he finished in about two minutes, washing it down with a glass of orange juice. Then she turned on the coffee machine, brought *The New York Times* in from the hall, and sat across from him.

"How are you?" she asked.

"I don't know," he said, covering his face with his hands.

"Why don't you keep yourself occupied by reading the newspaper? The coffee will be ready in a few minutes."

On the front page there was a story about ethnic cleansing in Yugoslavia. *(They're killing the Muslims, and the Jews will be next. We won't be safe anywhere, not even in New York. It's going to be another Holocaust. What can I do to prevent it?)*

"Anything interesting on the front page?" she asked.

"No," he said, "just the usual garbage."

At 9:00 a.m., Sam called Dr. Berkun and left another message on his machine. The doctor called him back within the hour. "How's it going?" he asked him.

"I'm very paranoid. Dr. Brown thinks I should go to the hospital."

"Why don't you come to see me at Columbia tomorrow at 10:00 a.m.? Tonight you can take up to 800 mg of Thorazine."

"Okay," Sam said.

"What did he say?" Mrs. Kanter asked after he hung up.

"He said I should come to see him tomorrow morning."

"Can you wait that long?"

"We'll just have to see." Sam had already decided to go into the city. "I'll spend the day playing chess in the Village," he told her.

"Are you sure you'll be alright?"

"I'm not even sure that two plus two makes four."

"Well, please call me when you get to The Chess Shop."

CHAPTER 12

He hopped on the next bus to the Port Authority, took the A train to the Village, and ambled down the block to Washington Square Park. All the hustlers were there: Lovey, Pavel (The Russian), Costos (The Greek), Dr. Li (The Chinese). . . . *(Everyone has a nickname, just like in the Mafia. Maybe this is the Mafia. I'd better get out of here!)*

He walked over to The Chess Shop, hoping to find David Rabinowitz there. *(Should I tell David what I'm going through? No, I'd better not.)*

Neither David nor Ahmed were there, though, so he played a few games with Richard Kelly. Needless to say, in his distracted state, he lost every game. *(Am I the devil? If I am, anyone who loses to me will go to hell.)*

When the session was over, he called his mother as he had planned. "Are you okay?" she asked him.

(I'm certain this phone is tapped, so I'd better watch what I say.) "Never better," he said.

"Will you be home for dinner?"

"Let's play it by ear."

"Well, if you're going to be late, please call me again. I'm worried about you."

"That makes two of us."

"Please try to be back by 10:00 or so. If I don't know where you are, I won't be able to sleep."

"Don't worry. I'll be fine," Sam said.

He went to the McDonald's on West 3rd, where he quickly consumed a Big Mac and a large order of fries, washing them down with a Coke.

He decided to walk to the Port Authority. *(There are spies everywhere. I'd better take a circuitous route if I want to lose them.)* He took Bleecker Street and headed west. When he reached Hudson, he turned right, turned left on West 12th, and headed to the Hudson River. He walked along the waterfront to 42nd, turned right, and went to the Port Authority.

When he got there, he couldn't remember which bus to take. He asked the woman in the information booth.

"Take the 163," she told him.

"Do you need to see my passport?"

She stared at him for a moment. "This isn't an airport."

"I thought they were cracking down on interstate travel."

She frowned. "Buy your ticket from any of the NJ Transit ticket sellers."

There were three NJ Transit windows open, each with a long line. *(Left, right, or center? If I go to the left, they'll think I'm a communist.)*

He waited at the end of the line on the right. There were ten people ahead of him. He began to sing: "A hundred bottles of beer on the wall, a hundred bottles of beer. If one of those bottles should happen to fall—ninety-nine bottles of beer on the wall. Ninety-nine bottles of beer on the wall. . . ."

No one paid any attention. In a few minutes, he was at the front of the line. "One way to Hackensack," he said. "Uh, which. . .which. . . ." He couldn't remember the word "platform." "Where is it?"

"Platform 224."

He had trouble finding it. The signs were confusing. *(Pull yourself together! You've been here hundreds of times!)*

Somehow he found the platform, but there was a long line for the express bus. *(Should I go express or local?)* He asked the man at the end of the line, "Which is faster, the express or the local?"

"Don't bust my chops," the man said. "I've had a long day."

Sam got on the line for the local bus. *(This man's a terrorist. I'd better not ride the same bus with him.)* There were only six people on the local bus. He took the front seat, to the right of the driver.

In the Lincoln Tunnel, the traffic moved very slowly. He was terrified. *(We're all going to suffocate.)*

The driver noticed his agitation. "Are you all right, sir?"

"I'm okay." *(I can't let him know, or he'll panic.)* Sam started to sing the Beatles' You've Got to Hide Your Love Away.

"You have a good voice," the driver said. "You ought to be on Broadway."

"Thank you."

When he got off the bus, Sam hurried to his mother's building, sweating with fear. Once again, afraid to take the elevator, he walked up the stairs. As he climbed, he remembered the scene from Hitchcock's *Vertigo* in which Jimmy Stewart had trouble climbing the stairs. *(I'm going to die!)*

He even forgot which floor his mother lived on. He got off the stairs on the third floor and walked back and forth the length of the hallway. From inside Apartment 3E he heard a recording of Beethoven's *Fifth Symphony*. He knocked in time to the music: Ta-ta-ta-ta. A woman in her forties, wearing a silk nightgown, opened the door.

"Can I help you?" she asked him.

Sam stammered: "I. . .I. . . . Do you know where Mrs. Kanter lives?"

"Of course. She's in 5A. . .but haven't I seen you here before?"

"Possibly," he said.

"Are you all right?"

"I'm fine."

When he found his mother's apartment, he knocked furiously. "Hurry up! They're after me!" he shouted.

Alarmed, Mrs. Kanter quickly opened the door. "Thank God you're all right," she said.

"Believe me, I just got here in the nick of time."

"You'd better take your Thorazine right away."

"Are you sure it's not poisoned?"

". . .Sam, it's not poisoned. You're paranoid."

"Are you sure?"

"I'm certain."

His hands were shaking so much, he had trouble holding onto the pills. *(Lord, save my soul.)* With a supreme effort, he swallowed eight 100-milligram tablets one after the other, washing them down with three glasses of water.

"Now try to get some sleep," his mother said.

"I'm afraid to close my eyes. Please stay in the room with me. I'm afraid to be alone."

"Everything will be all right. The medication will help you, and you'll be safe in the hospital tomorrow."

"I'm still afraid that, if I go in, they might not let me out."

"Sam, that's never happened before, has it?"

"No. But this time the FBI is in on it."

"What would they want with you?"

"I can't tell you. Your apartment is bugged."

"They're not allowed to do that."

"Believe me, they can do whatever they want. I know from experience."

His mother sighed. "What can we do to distract you until the pills take effect? Let's see. . .why don't we look at some of my art books?"

"Yes," he said.

Mrs. Kanter had studied art history during her college days before she went to nursing school. She had over a hundred art books on shelves in her bedroom. "Where should we start?" he asked her.

"What about van Gogh?"

"I *knew* you'd pick him. He's the only one who was as deranged as I am."

She laughed. "I think, if nothing else does, your sense of humor will get you through this."

". . .I wasn't joking," Sam said.

"Let's see. . . . How about Gauguin?"

"That's a better choice."

They leafed through a book of Gauguin's exotic paintings. *(Maybe if I focus enough, I can transport myself to the South Pacific.)*

SAM FORGOT ABOUT HIS APPOINTMENT with Dr. Berkun the next morning. When he didn't show up by 10:30, the doctor called. Sam's mother went into the kitchen and picked up the phone.

"How is he?" Dr. Berkun asked her.

"I think he's very sick."

"If he's not feeling better by tomorrow morning, please bring him to the Leonard Pavilion. I'll make sure they have a bed for him."

"It might not be that easy to get him to come."

"Are you conspiring against me?" Sam shouted from the living room.

"No, honey. Come into the kitchen and talk to Dr. Berkun."

"I have nothing to say to him."

"Tell him you're worried that they might keep you in the hospital for a long time."

"*You* tell him. I'll go to the other phone and listen in." He ran into her bedroom and picked up the extension.

"Dr. Berkun," she said, "Sam is worried that you might keep him in the hospital for a long time."

"Tell him I'll only keep him there for a few weeks, until he's stabilized on medication."

"I'll tell him."

"Please call me at my office tomorrow morning to let me know how he's doing. He can take another 800 mg of Thorazine again tonight. If the medicine kicks in, he might not need to be hospitalized."

"Thank you, Doctor," she said.

Sam lay down on the living room sofa; she sat in an armchair. He closed his eyes. "Tell me a story about my dad, like you did when I was a boy."

"Which story do you want to hear?"

"Tell me once again how you met."

"Well, let's see. We were both volunteers in Israel's War of Independence. He was in the artillery, and I was a nurse. He was badly wounded when a grenade went off a few yards from the armored car he was driving. They brought him to the hospital and put him in the ward that I was supervising. Lights out was at 10:00 p.m. He asked me if he could come into my office after 10:00, so he could read. I said yes. After that he returned to my office every night. Little by little we got to know each other."

"Do you remember what he was reading?"

"Yes, as a matter fact I do. He was reading *USA*, by John Dos Passos."

"I've been meaning to read that myself."

Sam took some more Thorazine, lay down again, and fell asleep with a peaceful smile on his face. His mother watched him silently for a few minutes, then went to bed in her own room.

AT 8:30 THE NEXT MORNING, SAM WOKE UP. His mother was already in the kitchen, making breakfast.

"How about some oatmeal?" she asked.

"Perfect," he said.

"How are you feeling?"

"I don't know yet."

She poured him a big mug of hot coffee.

He took a sip. "This hits the spot," he told her.

"Do you think the Thorazine is helping?"

"Well, it certainly helped me sleep, but I don't think I'm out of the woods yet."

"Why don't you read the newspaper? In an hour you can call Dr. Berkun and tell him exactly how you're feeling."

"Fair enough."

On the front page of *The New York Times*, he found another article about the war in Yugoslavia. Sam had been to Dubrovnik in his twenties. "They're destroying the most beautiful city in the world," he said. "I've got to fly there to save the city."

"Wow," Mrs. Kanter muttered under her breath.

At 9:15 he called Dr. Berkun.

"Tell me how you doing," the doctor asked.

"I don't know," Sam replied. "Sometimes I think that I'm fine, but at other times I think I'm ready for the funny farm."

"Do you think the Thorazine is helping?"

"I don't know."

"Why don't you go to the Leonard Pavilion? I've already reserved a bed for you."

"Please just give me some time to make up my mind. I'll call you in an hour or two."

"Okay," the doctor said.

When Sam hung up, his mother asked, "What did he say?

"He wants me to go to the hospital."

"What do *you* want?"

"I don't know. I don't know. *I don't know!*" Sam burst into tears.

"Don't cry, honey. Everything will be all right."

Sam clenched his teeth. "I'll go to the hospital, but only if you come with me."

"Of course I'll come with you."

"Okay. Call Dr. Berkun and tell him I'll check in this afternoon."

She did so. Afterwards, she told Sam, "I know you're doing the right thing."

"I wish I were as confident as you are."

THE LEONARD PAVILION IS NEAR THE NORTHERNMOST TIP of Manhattan, near Columbia University's playing fields. Mrs. Kanter called a cab, which showed up ten minutes later. When they were seated in it, she said: "We'd better stop at your apartment on the way to pick up enough clothing for a few days."

"I'm going to be there more than a few days," Sam replied.

"I know, but they'll have washing machines there if you need them."

They stopped outside Sam's building, and he went to his room. Natan, who was in the kitchen, asked, "Where have you been?"

"On a sabbatical."

Natan looked at him with a curious expression. "I see," he said.

Sam went into his room, opened his dresser drawers one by one, and threw all his clothes on the floor. Then he took his suit out of the closet, folded it carefully, and hid it under the bed. He put his shoes on the windowsill. *(What else should I do?)* He took out his Nikon camera, took several pictures of his room, then went out in the hall and threw the camera in the incinerator chute. When he went back to his room, he heard the taxi horn blaring from the street below. He leaned his head out the window and shouted, "I'll be right down!" *(It would be so easy to jump. . . .)*

He picked up three pairs of underwear, three pairs of socks, two T-shirts, and one pair of jeans, put them in a plastic bag, and descended the stairs to the street. Before getting back in the cab, he memorized the license plate number. *(I'll need this if I want to prosecute him.)* When he was in the back seat with his mother again, he gave the driver the address of the Leonard Pavilion, then added, "Don't go by the most direct route, or we might be followed."

The driver replied: "Whatever you say, Chief."

"I'm not a chief; I'm only a lieutenant." *(If he thinks I'm a police officer, he'll be less likely to try and cheat us.)*

"Okay, Lieutenant."

When they reached the hospital, she paid the driver, tipping him generously. Sam told him, "Please don't tell anyone about this."

"Okay, Lieutenant. Take care of yourself."

Sam and his mother entered the building through the front door. The receptionist told them to go to admissions in Room 211.

"We'd better use the stairs," Sam said.

They took the stairs to the second floor and followed the signs to 211. In the room, were two young women behind a counter and a bald middle-aged man at a computer desk. Sam's mom approached one of the women and said, "Sam wants to be admitted to psychiatry."

Sam said, "Just remember she said that, and I didn't."

The man at the desk said, "We just need some information."

". . . What information?" Sam demanded.

"Just a few things. What's your name, sir?"

"My name is Sue; how do you do?"

"Stop clowning around, Sam," Mrs. Kanter said.

"All right. My name is Sam Kanter. What's yours?"

"My name is Bill Strauss. I need to put some information in the computer."

"Who's going to have access to this information?"

"Just the hospital and your insurance company."

"Are you sure?"

"Yes."

"Okay. Fire away."

"Please give me your address."

"I live at 200 West 181st St."

"What's your Social Security number?"

"I don't remember."

"Okay, I'll see if I can find it on the computer."

He typed rapidly on the keyboard.

"Boy, I wish I could type that fast."

"What's your phone number?"

Sam gave it to him.

"Date of birth?"

"March 1st, 1955."

"What kind of insurance do you have?"

"Zilch."

"Where do you work?"

Sam gave him the name and address of Mercer Books.

"You're doing great," Mrs. Kanter told him.

"How much do you earn?"

"Why do you need to know that?"

"You may qualify for Medicaid."

"All right. I work full-time, but I earn only ten dollars an hour."

"I need your medical history. When was your first hospitalization?"

Sam had been hospitalized five times since he was eighteen, twice for mania and three times for depression. He spent ten minutes telling Strauss his medical history and all the drugs he had been treated with. Then the man asked him to sign a waiver allowing the hospital to contact all Sam's doctors and therapists, authorizing them to send all his records. Sam became terrified. *(If the government gets hold of these records, I'll be at their mercy.)*

After the interview, Strauss told him to go to the psychiatric ward and report to the nurse's station. An attractive nurse in her forties greeted him there and said, "My name is Isabel. I'll be your nurse today. First let me show you your room and introduce you to your roommate. Then we can have a talk."

At that point, Mrs. Kanter said goodbye. "I'll call you soon," she said, and left.

Isabel said: "Come with me." She showed him his room, which was at the end of the hall. There were two twin beds, two closets, and two small dressers in the room. A large window with iron gates looked out on Broadway.

"You can leave your things here," Isabel said. "Now let's go to the day room, so I can introduce you to your roommate."

In the day room, there were several comfortable chairs, a small piano, two large couches with stained off-white upholstery, and a large bookshelf with about two hundred books on a variety of subjects. There were three patients in the room, all sleeping soundly. Isabel gently woke up Sam's roommate.

"Billy, this is Sam, your new roommate."

Billy was an overweight, red-headed man in his twenties. "Welcome to the monkey house," he said.

"Now," she said to Sam, "let's go back to your room and have a talk."

They did.

CHAPTER 13

"So," Isabel asked. "What brings you here? Have you been taking your medication?" "Yes, but it hasn't been working. Otherwise I wouldn't be here." "What are you taking?"

"I was taking Lithium and Prozac, but my shrink took me off Prozac and added some Thorazine."

"Are you having any problems, or do you think it's just that the medicine isn't working?"

"It's not just the medication—my heart is breaking."

"Do you want to tell me about it?"

"Three steps: one, I cheated on my girlfriend; two, she dumped me; and three, she found a new guy. Tragic, isn't it?"

"You think you can win her back?"

"No. When she makes up her mind, she sticks to it."

"Have you thought of hurting yourself?"

"No."

"Have you thought of hurting her?"

"Of course not."

"Well, you don't seem at all psychotic."

"I have moments of clarity, but believe me, I'm in bad shape."

"What kinds of thoughts have you been having?"

"God, I don't know where to start. Sometimes I think the FBI is trying to entrap me, sometimes I think the TV is sending me signals, and sometimes I feel like I can't trust anyone, not even my mother. But at the same time, I know that I'm very ill, and I came here voluntarily."

"That's good," Isabel said. "Many people who are psychotic don't know that there's anything wrong with them."

"Well, I've been through this before, and sooner or later I've always been able to separate the real from the imaginary."

"I can tell you're very intelligent."

"Thank you," Sam said.

"Make yourself at home. Dinner is at 5:00 p.m., and your doctor will see you tomorrow."

Sam looked at his watch; it was 2:00 p.m. He decided to take a look around. The psychiatric ward was on the sixth floor of the Leonard Pavilion. There were twenty rooms for the patients, sixteen with two beds each; the other four had only one bed. In the center of the hall was the nurses' station, directly across from the elevators, to the right of which was the dining room, which had two large tables with eighteen chairs around each of them, a large refrigerator, a long counter with a sink in the middle, several closets, and a microwave oven. Three women were sleeping with their heads on the table; two others were playing Scrabble, and an Orthodox Jew with a big long beard was seated alone talking to himself. On the other side of the dining room lay the occupational therapy room. There the patients were more animated. They chatted pleasantly while they worked on art projects. Sam noticed a beautiful, elegantly dressed Hispanic woman sitting by herself. *(What's she doing here?)* To the left of the nurses' station was an office where the doctors held consultations with their patients. Next to that was the "quiet room," where they kept patients who acted out excessively. Across from the quiet room was a lounge, where several of the patients and a few aides were listlessly watching a soap opera on an old black-and-white TV. At the very end of the hall was the day room.

After exploring the ward, Sam went to the Occupational Therapy room. The occupational therapist was a cheerful woman in her fifties. "Hi," she said when he walked in. "My name is Edith." She introduced him to everyone there. Seated next to her was a frail-looking middle-aged man with dandruff on his shirt. "This is Frank," she said.

"Nice to meet you," said Frank in a gravelly voice.

Across from Frank was Jill, an emaciated young woman who would have been attractive had she weighed twenty more pounds. Next to Jill sat Rita, a pudgy woman with short hair and razor marks all over her arms. The beautiful Hispanic woman was named Mary. She suffered from chronic depression, which gave her a sultry look. Seated next to her was Peter, a teenage boy wearing headphones who didn't seem to be aware of anyone outside himself.

"Would you like to start a project?" Edith asked Sam.

"I'm not very good with arts and crafts," he confessed.

"Well, we could find something easy to do, or if you prefer, you can just stay here and keep us company."

"I'd rather just sit here. Maybe I'll start a project in a day or two."

"That's fine."

"Who's your doctor?" Jill asked him.

"My psychopharmacologist, Dr. Berkun, signed me in. But I don't know if he'll be my doctor on the ward."

"I've seen Dr. Berkun," she told him. "He seems like a nice guy."

"He *is* a nice guy."

After fifteen minutes in the OT room, Sam thought he'd try to get in touch with David Rabinowitz. He called The Chess Shop from a phone booth in the hall. Richard Kelly answered the phone.

"Is David Rabinowitz there?" Sam asked him.

"Just a second, I'll put him on."

David was in the middle of a speed game. "Take his number," he told Richard. "I'll call him back in five minutes."

Sam waited by the phone until David called him back.

"What's up?" David said.

"Can I rely on your discretion?"

"Of course."

"I'm in a mental hospital."

"My God." David asked him, "What's wrong?"

"I'm flipping out," Sam said. "Are you surprised?"

"Well, I sensed that something was wrong, but I had no idea that you were flipping *out*. I thought it had something to do with Megan."

"That's a big part of it."

"Is there anything I can do?"

"Yes, there is. Can you take over my students until I come back?"

"Certainly."

Sam had his phonebook with him. He gave Dave the names and numbers of all his students.

"Can I come visit you?" David asked.

"That would be great." Sam gave him the address of the place. "You can come between noon and three in the afternoon, or between six and eight in the evening."

"I'll come see you tomorrow."

Next Sam called Mercer Books. Dale picked up the phone. "Hey, stranger," he said. "When are you coming back to work?"

"It might be a long time," Sam said. "I think you'd better hire someone to replace me."

"What's wrong?"

"I'm very sick. I'll call you as soon as I feel better."

"Okay," Dale said.

As soon as he hung up, Sam started having paranoid thoughts again. *(There's a Dragnet closing in on me: David, Dale, Dr. Brown, Dr. Berkun, Mary, maybe even my mother. I'd better keep my thoughts to myself from now on, or they'll have enough on me to put me away forever.)*

He went back to the OT room and sat down next to Mary. "What are you working on?" he asked her.

"I'm making a belt," she said. "This is about the sixth belt I've made."

"Can I ask you what brought you here? You seem so normal."

"I don't want to talk about it in front of everyone, but in a word: D–E–P–R–E–S-S-I-O-N."

"Well, I have to say, your depression certainly hasn't affected your looks."

"Thanks, you're very charming. But my looks have never brought me anything but grief."

"Well, if you get tired of making belts, I can teach you how to play chess." *(She's going to think I'm coming onto her.)*

"I'd love to learn chess."

"It takes some time to learn."

In a throaty voice, she said, "We have all the time in the world."

"Let's go to the nurse's station and see if they have a set."

"Why don't you go by yourself? I'll wait here."

When Sam left the room, Edith said, "*He's* a fast worker."

Everyone laughed.

"I could use a little adventure to break up the monotony here," Mary said.

"Oooh," said everyone in unison.

"No, I'm not totally serious. Actually, I think I like him too much to pursue him, because if I did, my husband would kill him."

"Yipes!" Rita said.

At the nurses' station, Sam found three nurses, all doing some paperwork. "Excuse me," he said. "Do you guys know if there's a chess set on the ward?"

A tall male nurse with a closely cropped beard answered: "In the dining room, to the right of the refrigerator, is a closet with every kind of game imaginable."

"Thank you."

Sam went to the dining room, found the chess set, and returned to the OT room.

"We're in luck," he told Mary. "Where should we play?"

"Let's go to the dining room."

(I'd better be careful what I say to her. She might be a spy.)

In the dining room, they sat by themselves. "Do you know the rules?" he asked her.

"Yes, I do, but not much more."

"Good," he said. "I hate teaching the rules."

They set up the pieces and began to play. Mary had white. For her first move she played 1e4.

"Now, why is that a good move?" he asked her.

"I don't know," she said. "That's what my husband always starts with."

(She's married? Dammit.) "Okay. There are three things you generally want to do in the opening. First, you usually move a center pawn-either e4, as you did, or d4. Both of these control important central squares. Secondly, you want to develop your minor pieces—your knights and bishops. The move you made allows you to develop your King bishop. And third, you want to castle to make your King safe, usually on the King side. So let's play a game and discuss the moves as we play."

They played for an hour, after which Sam said, "That's enough for today. I'll give you another lesson tomorrow."

"Thank you," she said. "That was a lot of fun."

There was still an hour left before dinner time. She went back to OT, and he went to the day room, where he was all by himself. He perused the bookshelf carefully, then picked out a copy of Shakespeare's *King Lear* and began to read. *(Which of these characters would I play? Edmund: "Stand up for bastards," Edgar: "Poor Tom's a cold," or the King: "I am more sinned against than sinning." It would have to be one of these three. . . . Am I a bastard? I must be. And my parents never told me? That explains everything.)*

He started reminiscing about his childhood. He remembered his first date, when he was fifteen. He and his father had taken Petra Samuelson fishing at Lake Tiorati in upstate New York. *(What a beauty she was, and I'm sure she wanted to sleep with me. I was such a wuss.)* He remembered playing Little League baseball. *(When my dad came to watch me play, I hit a double. He was so proud. . . .)*

He dropped the book on the floor, closed his eyes, and began to weep. Mary came into the day room and saw the tears streaming down his face. "Sam! What's the matter?" she asked.

"Oh, nothing," he said.

"It's time for dinner."

"You go ahead. I'll join you in a minute."

He collected himself, looked out in the hall to make sure no one was watching, and then hid the copy of *King Lear* under the sofa. *(If someone finds this before I finish reading it, they'll know I'm a bastard. They might even put me in prison.)*

All twenty-four patients on the ward were seated quietly in the dining room. Sam sat down next to Mary. When the dinner cart arrived, the patients formed a line to wait their turn to take their trays. When Sam uncovered his, he grimaced. Dinner consisted of a grayish piece of meat, a slice of white bread, and overcooked peas and carrots.

"This looks worse than airline food," he said.

Mary laughed. "Just wait until you taste it."

"Here goes."

Sam took a bite and immediately spit the food into his napkin. "I can't eat this," he said.

"Sometimes there's some sandwiches left over from lunch," Mary said. "Check in the refrigerator."

He picked out a tuna sandwich on whole wheat bread.

"Is that better?" she asked him.

"Well, at least it isn't poisoned."

Mary looked alarmed. "Do you think your meal was poisoned?"

"No," he said. "I was just joking." *(I'd better not tell her what I'm really thinking, or it might get back to my doctor.)*

The time between dinner and lights out was the most monotonous part of the day on the ward. The rest of it was boring too, but at least it was broken up by meals, various groups, OT, and doctors' visits. At night the patients were totally on their own. Sam, hoping to continue conversing with Mary, was disappointed when she went to her room. He went back to the day room, retrieved *King Lear* from under the sofa, and began to read, but he had trouble concentrating. After six pages he gave up, put the book back on the shelf, and went to the lounge, where three aides and seven patients were watching a video of the comedy *The Producers*, starring Zero Mostel. After ten minutes he muttered, "This is inane."

One of the aides, a sullen black woman in her fifties, snapped, "Well, you don't have to watch it!"

Sam stared at her silently for a few seconds, then said, "You're right." He went to the dining room, where he found Frank playing solitaire with a worn-out deck of cards.

"Can I join you?" He asked.

"Sure," said Frank. "Just let me finish this hand. By the way," he added, "I have the distinction of being the only person who cheats at solitaire."

Sam laughed. "Can I ask why you're here?"

"Oh, it's a long story," Frank said. "I was evicted from my apartment in SoHo, and after living on the street for six months, I became so depressed that I couldn't even beg for money. I was lying in a doorway, almost in a coma, when the police finally picked me up and took me to Bellevue.

"So how did you end up here?"

"Luckily, I have a relative who's on the research staff at Columbia. She had me transferred."

"How long have you been here?"

"Next week it'll be three months."

"Jesus."

"What about you? Why are you here?"

"Basically, because I'm flipping out."

"Is this the first time you've been hospitalized?"

Sam laughed. "Not by a long shot."

"What you do?"

"I teach chess to children."

"How cool is that? And you're able to make a living doing that?"

"No, I also work in a bookstore."

"Sounds like you have a nice life."

"Considering the fact that I'm miserable seven days a week, I *do* have a nice life."

"Well, misery loves company, as the saying goes. I'm glad to make your acquaintance."

They were joined by Sally, a flirtatious young girl with a bad case of acne.

"Who's the handsome new patient?" she asked them.

Sam looked at her suspiciously. *(Lead him on to pleasures. Glean what afflicts him. Maybe I should be reading* Hamlet *instead of* King Lear.*)*

"Why are you looking at me like that?" Sally asked him.

"My mother told me never to trust a woman," he said.

"In that case, you shouldn't trust your mother."

"I don't."

Unsure whether he was joking or not, she was mute for a few seconds, then laughed uncomfortably. Frank laughed too, then said, "Why don't you find one more patient so we can have a game of bridge?"

"What's bridge?" Sally asked.

At 9:00 p.m., the patients lined up, and the nurses gave them their medication. For Sam, the doctor on call had made no changes in his regimen, prescribing Lithium and 800 mg of Thorazine. He took his pills and went back to the dining room.

"What did they give you?" Frank asked him.

"Enough Thorazine to knock out a horse."

"Ouch."

"Well, if it doesn't make my paranoia go away, maybe it will at least put me to sleep." *(To die, to sleep, to sleep, perchance to dream. . . .)*

"What did they give you?" Sam asked.

"It's a new antidepressant called Wellbutrin."

"Is it helping?"

"I don't know."

Jill, who had overheard their conversation, chimed in, "If it doesn't help, you shouldn't take it. All these drugs have side effects."

"What are you here for?" Sam asked her.

"The doctors think I'm anorexic, but I think they're full of shit."

"You do look very thin," he ventured.

"So what?"

To avoid a confrontation, he said, "I can't diagnose you. I'm not a doctor."

"Well, I don't think the doctors can diagnose me either. I'm pretty sure I'm here just because my parents want me here."

Lights out was at 10:00. When Sam entered his room, he found Billy already there, lying in bed listening to his Discman through a large pair of headphones with the volume turned up so high that it could be heard out in the hall. When Sam asked him to turn it down, Billy ignored him. Sam shrugged and lay down on his bed. His thoughts turned to Megan. *(What's her boyfriend like? Do they live together? Are they making love right now?)*

He shuddered. *(I've got to think about something else.)* He thought about Chrissy. *(Isn't she adorable? I'm going to miss her as much as I miss Megan. What a pity—just as soon as she gets used to me and is beginning to love me, I'm out of her life.)*

He shook his head. *(What a fool I was. What a fucking fool.)*

When Billy turned off his Discman, Sam forced himself to stop crying. After lying awake for about an hour, he gradually became drowsy and drifted off to sleep.

CHAPTER 14

At 8:00 in the morning, one of the nurses woke Sam and Billy and told them to go to the dining room. Sam, who had never been a morning person, had trouble getting out of bed. He had to be reminded three times before he was finally able to leave his room.

In the dining room, aides were taking the patients' blood pressure and temperature. After their vital signs had been taken, the breakfast cart arrived. Sam found breakfast almost as unpalatable as dinner had been—a small portion of scrambled eggs, white toast, and a tiny cup of orange juice. After forcing himself to eat a little bit, he went back to his room and got in bed again.

At 11:00 a.m., a black woman in her thirties woke him up. "I'm Dr. Jackson," she said. I'll be treating you while you're in the Leonard Pavilion."

"Hi."

"I spoke to Dr. Berkun, and he told me that it isn't clear whether the Thorazine is effective. Do you think it helps?"

"Maybe a little bit."

"I have to tell you; I'm concerned about the possibility of your developing tardive dyskinesia."

"What's that?"

"Sometimes Thorazine causes involuntary movements of the hands and mouth, and once it happens, it's irreversible."

"That would be great for my social life."

"I'd like to try you on Zyprexa and see if it's effective."

"What side effects does it have?"

"It occasionally causes akathisia—the inability to sit still—and it can also cause constipation, dizziness, or drowsiness."

"Terrific," Sam said.

"The side effects only occur rarely."

"All right. Let's try it."

"For our next meeting, I want you to come to my office."

"I'll do my best."

After Dr. Jackson left his room, Sam got up and went back to the dining room. On the blackboard on the wall, there was a list of the groups for the day. Dr. Jackson had scheduled him for art therapy at 1:00 and a walk around the grounds at 4:00. Sam looked at his watch. It was 11:30 a.m. He made his way to the OT room to look for Mary. When he entered, she smiled.

"How about a chess game?" he asked her.

"Let's do it."

They went to the dining room, sat in a corner by themselves, and set up the pieces.

"Before we start," Sam asked her, "what are the three things you want to do in the opening?"

"Move a center pawn, develop the minor pieces, and castle safely."

"Good. You take the white pieces."

Mary moved her king pawn, put her knights and bishops on good squares, and castled on the kingside. "Now what I do?" she asked him.

"Now you want to get your queen and rooks in the game. Usually you move your queen close to home and put your rooks on an open file or a file that could be open."

". . . What's an open file?"

"A vertical line with no pawns."

"How do you open a file?"

"You do it by exchanging pawns. Let me show you. . . ." They played until 12:15, when the lunch trays arrived.

After lunch, Sam went to his art therapy group. Margaret, the art therapist, was a beautiful Irish woman with sparkling green eyes. Sam felt like putting an apple on her desk.

"Think about what would make you happy," she said, "and draw it as well as you can. Then we'll take turns talking about your work."

Sam, who had been in art therapy before, had never liked talking about his feelings with strangers. *(I guess if I don't reveal too much, no harm will be done.)* He drew a picture of himself lying on a secluded sandy beach with a beautiful blonde in a bikini next to him, leaning her head on his chest. Billy, his roommate, drew a picture of himself on a big stage, playing an electric guitar in front of an enthusiastic audience. Also in the group were Sally, Rita, and Miles, a taciturn black teenager who looked as though he wished he were a thousand miles away.

After everyone finished their drawings, they took turns discussing what they had drawn. Sam played along although he really thought the whole enterprise was a waste of time. *(I know that if I don't go to the groups, they'll keep me here much longer.)*

When the group concluded, Sam looked at his watch again. It was 2:00 p.m. *(Two more hours before we go on our walk.)* He went back to his room and took a nap. Forty-five minutes later, Mary woke him up and said, "There's a call for you on the patient phone."

Sam yawned. "Thank you." He went out in the hall and picked up the telephone. It was his mother.

"How are you?" she asked.

"Officially, fine."

"And unofficially?"

"I can't tell you right now. I think this phone is bugged."

She shook her head. "I'll come and visit you in a day or two."

The rest of the day passed uneventfully. Walk at 4:00. Dinner at 5:00. Medication at 9:00. Lights out at 10:00.

The first day or two in a mental hospital can be mildly interesting because the patient sees new faces and has new experiences. After that, life on the ward becomes a dreary routine. Sam was hoping that his friendship with Mary would spice things up a bit, but she was so depressed that, aside from their time playing chess together, it was hard to get two words out of her.

When he tried to read, he found that his concentration was so poor that he could only manage a page or two at a time, so he spent a lot of time just walking up and down the hall, daydreaming and reminiscing about his time with Megan, the only time in his life when he had been truly happy.

On his fourth day in the Leonard Pavilion, his mother came to visit as she had promised. Instead of being happy to see her, he became very upset. *(You're the reason I'm in this condition. I don't ever want to see you again!)* He ran to his room, slammed the door, got in bed, and pulled the covers over his head. After asking the nurses how he was doing, his mother went downstairs, took the A train back to the George Washington Bridge bus terminal, and caught the bus back to Hackensack.

The following morning Sam received a call from David Rabinowitz. "Can I visit you this afternoon?"

"Please do. I'm bored to death here."

David appeared a few hours later with a list of Sam's students. "I've taught two of them already, and I have appointments with three more."

"Do you want to meet my newest student?"

"Sure."

Sam found her in the OT room.

"Mary, this is my friend David."

"Any friend of Sam's is a friend of mine."

"With a beautiful student like this, how can you be bored to death?"

"She's the only ray of light in this dungeon."

Sam and Dave went to the dining room, where David noticed the Orthodox Jew talking to himself as he had on Sam's first day on the ward.

"I want to talk to him," David said.

"Give it a try."

David introduced himself. They spoke in Yiddish for a few minutes; then David told Sam to come and join them. "This is Yitzhak," he said. "He'd like to learn to play chess."

"Sure. Maybe you and Mary can play each other."

Yitzhak said something in Yiddish to David.

"What did he say?" Sam asked.

"That women make him uncomfortable."

"Well, then, chess is the perfect game for him. Ninety-five percent of all chess players are men."

The whole staff of the Leonard Pavilion carefully monitored the patients and reported any change to the doctors. When, after about two weeks, the Zyprexa started working, both the nurses and the aides noticed that Sam was doing better. He was more outspoken in the groups, his moods more stable, and he was much more focused and much less turned in on himself. Dr. Jackson was ecstatic. "Let's wait a few more days, and if you keep improving, we'll release you."

When his mother came to visit him again, he didn't act strangely. He introduced her to Frank and Mary and chatted with her pleasantly.

"What a miracle!" she exclaimed.

The day before he was released, Sam gave Mary one last chess lesson. He took white and opened with 1Nf3.

"I thought you were supposed to move a center pawn."

"If you want to play classically, yes, you open with a center pawn, but you can also control the center with pieces if you prefer."

"I can see that I'm still a beginner," she said.

"No, you're far from a beginner."

"What should I do to improve?"

"There's a book I recommend to all my students. It's called *Chess Tactics for Champions*, by Susan Polgar. Solve a page of problems every day, and you'll learn how to calculate."

"Will I see you again?" she asked him.

". . .What would your husband think about that?"

"I don't care what he thinks."

Sam looked at her silently for a few seconds. Then he said, "I don't want to sneak around."

"You're a good person."

"You don't know me very well," he said with a sigh.

SAM WAS RELEASED FROM THE LEONARD PAVILION three weeks after he was admitted. He left the building and headed straight for The Chess Shop, arriving at 2:00 p.m. When he walked in the door, he was greeted by Ahmed. "Where've you been, stranger?"

"I haven't been feeling well."

"What's the matter?"

"I don't want to talk about that right now."

David Rabinowitz wasn't there, so Sam played some blitz games with Jim Smith. They bantered back and forth in the classic Greenwich Village style. When Jim put Sam in check, he delivered his usual line: "This is one of the reasons they call me Master Jim."

"What are the other reasons?"

"The other reasons are. . .the other reasons."

When Jim gained the advantage, he rubbed his hands together gleefully. "And now for the mate."

After they had played for an hour and a half, Sam excused himself. "It's always a pleasure to play a master of your iniquity," he said.

"The pleasure is mine, my dear Master Sam."

Sam walked over to Mercer Books to see Dale. "How are you?" Dale asked.

"Never better," Sam lied.

"I have to tell you—I hired someone to cover your shifts, and I can't really let her go, but I do have an opening on Saturday afternoons. Is that okay?"

"That's fine."

"Okay, why don't you report at 11:00 a.m. next Saturday?"

"See you then."

He took the A train to Washington Heights. When he entered the apartment, he ran into Natan, who was on the way out. "Where've you been?" Natan wanted to know.

"Out of town." Sam said.

"Out of town or not, I need you to pay the rent on time."

He had forgotten about it. He immediately wrote a check and gave it to Natan. "I'm sorry," he said. "It won't happen again."

He found his room exactly as he had left it, with his clothes all over the floor. He covered his face and sat on the edge of the bed. After a few minutes, the phone rang. It was David Rabinowitz. "I heard that you're back in circulation."

"Yes, thank God."

"We need to have a talk about the students."

Sam found that to be a strange remark. What was there to talk about?

"I'll be at The Shop tomorrow afternoon," Sam said.

After he finished putting his clothes away, he put on a recording of Beethoven's *Pastoral Symphony*, lay down on his bed, and drifted off to sleep. When he awoke at 3:00 a.m., he realized that he hadn't taken his medication. He took the Zyprexa, washing it down with a glass of milk, lay back down, and tried to sleep again. When he hadn't fallen asleep by 4:30 a.m., he got dressed and left the building. He started walking down Broadway at a brisk pace, singing the Beatles song on the way: "It's getting better all the time. . . ." *(Am I still a little manic?)*

By the time the sun came up he had reached Columbus Circle, where he hopped on the A train and rode down to the Village. In Washington Square Park, he was happy to find Pavel "The Russian" sitting by himself, waiting for an opponent. Pavel was one of the strongest of the hustlers, and one of the fastest. He gave Sam 5-1 odds, allowing himself only one minute for each game. After they had played for four hours at three dollars a game, Pavel was ahead by $39.00.

Afterwards, Sam went to the Waverly Diner for breakfast. As he ate, he read *The New York Times*. When he was finished, he felt very tired, so he went back to the park, lay down on the grass, and slept soundly until two in the afternoon.

When he awoke, he went back to The Chess Shop to look for David Rabinowitz. He found him sitting on the doorstep outside The Chess Shop, smoking a cigarette.

"Are things back to normal?" David said.

"I'm not sure about that, but they're much better than they were."

"So, about the students. . . . I'm going to keep three of them and give the rest back to you."

Sam was surprised. "I just asked you to *cover* for me, not to keep them for yourself."

"Well, I want to keep them, because Marcus and Naomi will let me play for free if I teach."

"But they're *my students*," Sam said, raising his voice slightly.

"I don't think it's up to you to decide who teaches, I think it's up to Naomi."

Sam didn't feel strong enough to argue just then, but he considered what David was doing to be nothing but stealing. He went into The Shop and called his mother on the player phone. "I have my freedom," he told her. "I'm calling from The Chess Shop."

"That's wonderful," Mrs. Kanter said.

"Now I need to find some way to make a living. I have only one shift at Mercer Books, and David is keeping half my students."

". . . .How can he *do* that?"

Sam bit his lip. "I don't want to talk about that right now."

It was Sunday, so Sam taught his three remaining students, then bought the *Village Voice* and went back to the Waverly diner to read the classifieds. He looked at all the ads in the help wanted section; nothing appealed to him, except for a few jobs he wasn't qualified for. *(If I don't find something soon, I'll have to take a messenger job, or something equally unappetizing.)*

He wasn't in the mood for more chess, so he went to the Strand Bookstore on Broadway and 12th Street. He filled out an application for employment although he knew that the Strand paid its employees very little. Then he went up to the second floor, where he spent an hour looking at art books. Every few minutes, he glanced at his watch. *(What should I do with myself?)* Finally, he ambled over to the Village Corner to see who was bartending. He was surprised to find Kelly there.

"Holy shit!" he exclaimed. "How long have you been working here?"

"Just a week."

"How many shifts do you have?"

"For now, just Saturday and Sunday afternoons."

"Is this your first bartending job?"

"No, I did it when I was much younger."

"Holy shit," he repeated.

"Are you still living with Megan?" she asked, although she knew the answer was no.

"Nope. That's been over for a while now."

"Well, what have you been doing with yourself?"

"You wouldn't believe it if I told you."

In a hushed voice, Kelly said, "I only *took* this job because I know you're regular here."

"I guess that's good to know," he said.

"Can I buy you a drink?"

"Give me a Johnny Walker Black with one ice cube," he said.

"I'm going to ply you with liquor and have my way with you."

Sam laughed. "Same old Kelly."

He stayed in the bar for two hours, getting thoroughly plastered for the first time since the days when he frequented the Village Idiot.

At 6:00, when he was about to leave, she asked him, "Where are you staying tonight?"

Sam lied: "I've got to turn in early tonight. I have some important things to take care of in the morning."

He staggered out, walked down the block to the Village Gate, and sat at a corner table till 7:00, when Raphael was scheduled to play with Ben Woolf and Jimmy Lovelace. When the set began, he closed his eyes and immersed himself in the music, sobering up somewhat in the process. After the set was over, he walked over to The Chess Shop. He was happy to see that Johanna Lawrenson was working.

"Can I talk to you after you get off?" he asked her.

He knew that her husband, Abbie Hoffman, had been mentally ill, so he thought that she would be the best person to talk to. After she closed The Shop a little after midnight, they went to Café Figaro. On the way, Johanna asked him, "You've been drinking, haven't you?"

"Nothing I can't handle." Sam said.

He told her about his illness, his hospital stay, and what had happened with Jean and Kelly.

Johanna was surprised. "From the way you behave, I would never have guessed that you're mentally ill."

"Well, I don't act out like many manic-depressives do, but believe me, since I've been an adult, I've never gone more than five years without being hospitalized."

"I never would've known."

He told her that Kelly was working at the Village Corner and that she seemed to be interested in picking up where they had left off.

"Does she love you?"

"I think so."

"You'd better be pretty sure before you start up with her, because you're very vulnerable now, and I know you're the type that gets involved."

"Instinctively, I think she's okay."

"You might be right, but don't go by instincts alone. Consider things carefully, and make a responsible decision."

"Spoken like a woman," he said.

"What do you mean by that?"

"Men always say that women think with their head, and men with their groin."

"Think with your head," she said. "Decide."

CHAPTER 15

SAM WALKED TO SIXTH AVENUE and took the A train back uptown. Somewhere between 59th and 125th Streets he fell asleep, waking up only when the train reached Dykman Street. On the way, he dreamed that he was giving a chess lesson to Kelly. In the opening, she played a move he'd never seen before.

"Did you figure out that move by yourself?" he asked her.

"No, Aidan showed it to me."

"You might be too good for me to teach," Sam said.

When he opened his eyes and realized where he was, he shrugged and walked back to 181st Street. He took off his clothes, got into bed, and slept soundly for twelve hours.

When he awoke, Sam headed back down to Washington Square Park. He was surprised to see Freddy there, playing speed chess with Dr. Li, his old nemesis and benefactor. His first reaction was suspicion. *(That's two people from my past that I've run into in two days. Is this a coincidence or is this part of the dragnet? I'd better be careful.)*

He waited until they finished the game, then greeted his old friend. "Freddy! How are you?"

"Hey, buddy, I was hoping you'd show up. Let me just play two more games, then we can hang out."

"Dr. Li, can I make a side bet?"

"Who are you betting on?"

"Freddy, of course."

"No, thanks. I don't want any psychological complications."

"Fair enough."

Freddy and Dr. Li split the last two games.

"What's the score?" Sam asked them afterwards.

"I'm up four games," Freddy said. "It's pay time."

Dr. Li coughed up $20.00.

"Better luck next time," Sam said.

"It's not a matter of luck," the doctor replied.

Sam and Freddy strolled to Karavas Place to see Cindy, but she wasn't there. Freddy ordered a Greek salad. "Can I buy you something?" he asked.

"I don't see why not," Sam said, and ordered a chicken souvlaki sandwich.

"How's the pussy situation?" Freddy asked.

"Nothing's going on right now. How about you?"

"I'm seeing three different broads. It's funny—two of them are brunettes, and one's a blonde, but the blond has the only pussy I like to eat. It seems like, whenever I want to go down on a broad, she's always a blonde. Do you think blonde pussy tastes better?"

"You might have something there."

They headed for The Chess Shop to see who was there. Apart from Dr. Li, Freddy's favorite opponent was Jim Smith, whom he could give incredible odds to and still win. In a speed game, Freddy would give him ten minutes to one, in a slow game, rook- odds.

"Welcome back, my dear Freddy," Jim said. "Would you like to sit at the Masters table?"

"I'd be delighted."

They began a series of speed games. Jim used his extra time to carefully check that all his pieces were protected and stop his opponent's immediate threats. Even so, Freddy won the majority of their games.

After watching them play for about forty minutes, Sam challenged David Rabinowitz to a game. Their games had always been a test of wills, with Sam usually coming out on top. Now, however, David beat him mercilessly. "I guess I'm still in a weakened condition after being ill," said Sam under his breath.

"No excuses," David said.

When he finished teaching on Sunday afternoon, Sam returned to the Village Corner to see Kelly. He sat down next to Stephen Fall, who was between sets. As they always did, Sam and Stephen talked politics. When Stephen went back to the piano, Kelly came over. After a brief awkward silence, he asked her, "How are things with Aidan?"

"I'm sick and tired of Aidan. If you say the word, I'll break up with him and we can move in together."

(If you're sick and tired of Aidan, then why are you stringing him along?)

"Kelly," he said, "I. . .I'm not ready to start anything right now. If you knew what I've been going through. . . ."

She hid her disappointment. "We can be friends for now if you want, and if you want to tell me what you're going through, it won't go any further than here."

"You wouldn't believe it if I told you," he said, shaking his head from side to side.

"Tell me when you're ready."

He averted his gaze, then said, "So who's been buying your jewelry lately? Anyone I might know?"

"I sold a brooch to Beverly Sills and a pair of earrings to Robert De Niro's wife."

"That's *wonderful*."

"If you like my jewelry, wait until you see my paintings."

"I'd *love* to see your paintings." *(It's going to be hard to keep this platonic.)*

"Why don't you come to dinner with Aidan and me next week?"

"I'd love to," Sam said.

"You'll see how I paint, and you'll see how I cook."

"I can't wait."

THE FOLLOWING FRIDAY, HE WENT OUT to Kelly and Aidan's place in Astoria. Kelly cooked moussaka.

"This is delicious," Sam said.

After dinner, Kelly brought out several of her paintings for him to look at. He wasn't impressed; he thought they were basically run-of-the-mill abstract expressionism.

"Do you like them?"

"You have potential," he lied.

Aidan brought out his guitar. "Do you like the Beatles?" he asked.

"That's an understatement!" Sam exclaimed.

"Name any Beatles song."

"How about 'Happiness is a Warm Gun'?"

Aidan sang the song in a beautiful baritone voice. On the lyric "She's not a girl who misses much," Sam winked at Kelly, who pretended not to notice.

"What else should I play?"

"How about 'In my life?'"

Aidan played and sang the song, inserting a guitar solo where George Martin had played his Baroque keyboard solo. Afterwards, Aidan brought out a bottle of Jameson, which all three of them drank with relish.

At 1:00 a.m., as Sam was preparing to leave, Kelly said, "If you have the time, I'd like to buy another series of chess lessons."

Sam remembered how she had seduced him the last time. "We can talk about it the next time I come to the bar." *(I might have to start going to another bar.)*

On his way home, Sam decided to consult with Dr. Brown. He called him on Monday, and they set up an appointment for Thursday afternoon. He spent the intervening days reading the help-wanted ads and hanging out with Freddy.

AT DR. BROWN'S OFFICE, THE FIRST THING HE DID was to fill him in on the course his illness had taken since their last meeting. He talked about his paranoia, his hospital stay, and his treatment by Dr. Jackson. Then he turned to the topic of Kelly. "She's working as a bartender at my favorite bar, and she says that she only took the job because I'm a regular there."

"What are your thoughts about her?"

"I remember what you said— 'Kelly sounds like trouble—' and you may be right, but the physical attraction is becoming overwhelming, and if I keep going there, we'll probably wind up together."

"You think you'd be happy with her?"

"I don't know."

". . . Well, if you're ambivalent, I don't want to push you in one direction or the other. Ultimately, you'll have to decide for yourself." Dr. Brown stroked his chin for a few seconds, then said, "Let me ask you—what do you like about her besides her looks?"

"She's a gifted designer, she's very warm, she has a sense of humor. . . ."

"Is she a good person?"

"Actually, I don't know her that well, but I don't like the way she's stringing Aidan along. If she's tired of him, then why doesn't she break up with him?"

"It's very common for women to have overlapping relationships. Many of them just can't be alone."

"Well, maybe I'll give it a whirl."

During his Saturday shift at Mercer Books, he was so preoccupied that Dale noticed it.

"What's going on with you, Sam?" he asked. "Are you in love or something?"

"I'm always in love—that's my biggest problem."

"How about alphabetizing the psychology section to distract yourself?"

ON SUNDAY, AFTER TEACHING, SAM WENT to the Village Corner. Fortunately, he was the only customer there. He asked Kelly, "What are you doing tonight?"

"Anything you say."

"How about I meet you here at eight, and we can go somewhere for dinner?"

"I can't wait."

His next stop was The Chess Shop, to look for David.

"You ready for a drubbing?" David asked him.

"Yes, but there's something I have to tell you first."

They went to Washington Square Park and sat near the fountain.

" I've made up my mind," Sam said. "I'm going to give Kelly a chance."

"Are you sure you're doing the right thing?"

"I don't know if I'm doing the right thing, but I know how I feel."

"How's that?"

"Uh. . .I don't know." Sam laughed out loud.

"You seem a little giddy," David pointed out. "Are you sure you're not becoming manic again?"

"A psychiatrist once told me that the closest thing to a manic euphoria is being in love."

"Are you?"

"Uh. . . . No." Sam laughed again.

"You're certifiable," David said.

AT 8:00 P.M., SAM PICKED UP KELLY, and they went to eat Indian food on East 6th Street. When they were seated, she asked him, "What made you change your mind?"

"I don't know," Sam said.

After dinner, they took a cab to the West 4th station and hopped on the A train to Washington Heights.

Sam's room was a mess. "Are you going to be a slob when we live together?"

"Not if it bothers you." *(She's already talking about living together?)*

"Should I *look* for a place we can live together?" he asked her.

"You could do that."

"What's next?"

"Why don't we undress each other?"

Sam methodically took off her clothes until she was stark naked, then she did the same to him. The whole time, Kelly looked into his eyes without blinking. When they were both in their birthday clothes, she said, "Lay on the floor and put your hands above your head."

"Why?"

"I want you at my mercy."

"You're not into S and M, are you?"

"I'm *heavily* into S and M."

"That kind of thing doesn't turn me on," Sam said. "Besides, I don't know you well enough yet."

"What *would* turn you on?"

"I love to do it from behind."

They made love, if that's the right expression, for three hours. Then Kelly said, "I've got to go back to Queens, or Aidan will be suspicious."

"When are you going to break up with him?"

"Soon," she said. She quickly dressed, kissed Sam on the lips, and walked out the door.

On Tuesday night, Sam bought the *Village Voice* again and started looking for an apartment for Kelly and him to live in. There was nothing affordable being advertised. Besides, he wanted to avoid the broker's fee, so he decided to go from building to building talking to the superintendents. Rents in the East Village weren't that high at the time, so that's where he started.

To his surprise, he found an apartment on Avenue B after only three days of looking. Though he still hadn't found gainful employment aside from his one day at Mercer Books and a few private students, he impulsively put down a deposit on the apartment and told the super to give it to the landlord.

He resisted the urge to call Kelly at home, afraid that Aidan might suspect something. On Sunday, he went to the Village Corner to tell her the good news.

"Guess what?" he said. "I found us an apartment in the East Village. We can move in next month."

"Boy," she said. "When you say you're going to do something, you really do it."

"Why don't you break up with Aidan and stay with me in Washington Heights until the first of the month?"

"You know something? I've been thinking of finding my own place."

"But I already put a *deposit* down!" Sam exclaimed. "I can't afford the place by myself."

"Well, try to find a roommate. I'm not ready to live together yet."

"But I only have two weeks. What if I can't find a roommate?"

"Then let's discuss it again when we get there."

"But, Kelly, we planned to move in together."

"We just talked about it. We didn't make definite plans."

Sam was exasperated, but he tried to hide it. "I'll try to find a roommate, but if I don't. . . ."

"We'll talk about it then."

The next day, he went back to the building to speak to the super again. "Is the last tenant still living there now," he asked, "or is the apartment already vacant?"

"It's already vacant. Why do you ask?"

"Frankly, I'm going to need a roommate to cover expenses, and I want to be able to show the place."

"Strictly speaking, you're not allowed to sublet, but a lot of people do it, so I'll look the other way."

"Great. When can I show it?"

"Just give me a call the day before, and we'll set up a time."

"Terrific!"

That gave him two weeks. He immediately went to the *Village Voice* building and placed an ad in the "shares wanted" section. He went to the office of Roommate Finders and posted an ad there as well. Even with a roommate, he knew he'd need more money, so he decided to take a job driving a cab four days a week.

He copied the number of a cab company in Queens that was advertised in the *Daily News*. On Wednesday morning, he went to the office in Sunnyside and offered his services.

Manny, the manager, was a bearded guy in his fifties with two missing teeth. Sam told him that he wanted to work every week from Tuesday through Friday. Manny told him that was okay, as long as he was willing to work twelve-hour shifts. "You can start tomorrow at 7:00 a.m."

"That means I'll have to get up at 5:30 in the morning in order to be here on time."

"That's what I have to offer," Manny said.

Sam reluctantly agreed.

What with the cab, his shift at Mercer Books, and his private students, he was basically working fulltime. Monday was his only day off.

AFTER HE FINISHED TEACHING AT 3:00 P.M. on Sunday, he went to the Village Corner to see Kelly.

"Have you found a roommate yet?" she asked him.

"I've taken a job driving a cab, so I haven't had time to show the place, but have a couple of people coming tomorrow night."

"Well, do your best to find someone—but if you don't, I won't leave you in the lurch."

"Thank you. I'm so relieved. But if you don't move in with me, we'll only be able to spend Sunday nights and Monday afternoons together."

"That's okay," Kelly said. "I don't mind starting slowly."

"I thought you were so gung-ho."

"I am, but I know you need to work,"

"Yeah, well. . .I'll be looking for another job, and when I find one, we'll have more time together."

"How do you feel about driving a cab?"

"So far I don't mind it, but I'm working twelve-hour shifts, and that's a little too much. If I were working only eight hours like most people, I might have some time to play chess or to see my friend David occasionally. Now it's just going to be you and the taxi."

"You could do worse."

When she got off work, they went for Chinese food together, then took the subway to Washington Heights. As soon as they closed the door to Sam's room, they tore off their clothes and made love on the floor. Then Kelly said:

"I better be going."

Sam was despondent. "You're leaving already?"

"Don't worry. As soon as I find my own place, we won't have to sneak around."

She got dressed and left. Sam sat on the edge of the bed with his head in his hands for about ten minutes, turned off the lights, and lay down naked on the bed. *(What am I getting myself into?)*

CHAPTER 16

HE SLEPT SOUNDLY FOR TEN HOURS. When he awoke, he felt very depressed. *(Maybe I'll go back to sleep. . .no, you've slept long enough Sam! Today's the only day you have to find a roommate!)* He got out of bed, dressed without shaving or showering first, and turned on his answering machine. There were three messages from prospective roommates, all of them male. One had left his work number, the other two only their home numbers. He called the first right away.

"Can you come and look at the place tonight?"

"Definitely."

"Let me call the super and arrange a time, and I'll call you back."

They made an appointment for 6:00 that evening. Sam spent the afternoon at The Chess Shop, playing speed chess with Jim Smith for two dollars a game. He gave Jim five minutes for each game and took three for himself. After three hours, he was up by only four dollars. When they were finished, Sam bought a falafel at Mahmoun's on McDougal, ate it quickly, and headed over to Avenue B.

His prospective roommate was an Asian name Jong Li, who had just moved to the city from Philadelphia a month earlier and already landed a job with Lehman Brothers. He had been staying at his sister's apartment in Chelsea.

Jong and Sam hit it off right away. After only ten minutes, Sam offered him the room, and, the next instant, Jong brought out his checkbook and put down a deposit.

"Boy," Sam said. "I thought this was going to be a protracted process."

He immediately called his two other prospects and told them that the room had been taken.

Each evening, after Sam had dropped off his taxi at the garage, he headed straight back to the East Village. He didn't have the energy to play chess, so he started frequenting the bars on 1st Avenue and Avenue A. Like many barflies, he preferred to patronize those where the bartenders were female. Among his favorites were The International, the Sidewalk Café, and of course, the Village Idiot. Sometimes he'd visit two or three in one evening, drinking Guinness or Johnny Walker Black. He knew that mixing alcohol with his medication was potentially dangerous, and he had a slight hangover every morning. But once he got going, he felt all right.

After work on Saturday, he went to Café Reggio with David Rabinowitz. He filled him in on the new developments in his life—job, apartment, and lifestyle.

"I thought chess was your main addiction. Now it seems like alcohol is taking over."

"That's nothing new," Sam replied. "I've always been a drinker."

"What's new with Kelly?"

Sam sighed. "I only see her once a week."

"Is that enough?"

"No. No, it isn't, but I'm going to look for another job, and then. . . ."

David said, "You seem a bit depressed."

"Well, that's nothing new either," Sam pointed out.

"I'm a little worried about you."

"I'll be fine," Sam said emphatically.

On September 1st, Kelly moved into her own apartment in Astoria, not far from where she had lived with Aidan. The first Sunday evening in the month, Sam stayed over at her place. She had a king-size bed, a table, two chairs, and a large bookshelf. Apart from that, she had no furniture. She also had a little black cat named Thunder, who ran to hide under the bed as soon as they entered. Sam took a look around. "This has potential," he said.

When he took a look at her book collection, he was astonished to see that she had over thirty volumes about witchcraft.

"Goodness gracious! Are you a witch?"

"Yes, I am. And Thunder's my familiar."

Sam thought she was joking. "Now I know why I'm under your spell." His mind went blank for a few seconds, then he asked her, "So. . .how's Aidan taking this?"

"He seems okay."

"Have you broken up with him?"

"Not yet."

"When is that happening?"

As she had the last time he asked her that, she said, "Soon."

"Soon like days, or weeks, or—"

"Soon."

"But—"

"Shhh." She put her hand over his mouth and began unbuttoning his fly.

THAT NIGHT, SAM DREAMT HE WAS BACK in the Leonard Pavilion. His doctor was a ghoulish young man who had just completed his studies at Columbia Presbyterian. His patients referred to him as "Heathcliff."

Heathcliff wanted to try administering a new antipsychotic medication to Sam.

Sam said, "Before I take it, I want to consult with Dr. Berkun and see if he recommends it."

"If you make my life difficult, you're going to be here a long time."

He awoke in a cold sweat. While he was waiting for Kelly to arise, he went into the living room and started reading one of her books on witchcraft. At 10:00, she found him sitting on the floor in his underwear, surrounded by books.

"Why are you so interested in witchcraft?" he asked.

"I think it's an interesting religion."

"Religion?"

"Yes, I think it's a religion like any other."

"Really? Then why don't you have books on other religions?"

"I did, but right now I'm focusing on Wicca, so that's all I brought with me."

"Wicca?"

"White magic."

"Wow," Sam said.

"What would you like for breakfast?" she asked him.

"How about French toast?"

"Your wish is my command."

"Then my wish is that you call Aidan right away and break up with him."

"You'll get that wish when it's time. Right now I'm going to grant you your French toast wish. How many slices do you want?"

"Three would be fine."

After breakfast, she said, "I've got to work now. I'll see you next week."

"Okay." *(You can't even spend twenty-four hours with me?)*

He took the subway back to the Village and walked to his apartment, where he had an unread copy of the Sunday *New York Times*. He opened the newspaper to the help wanted section. Once again, nothing appealed to him. He asked his new roommate, "What would you do if you were in my position?"

"Have you considered temping?"

"That wouldn't be good. I'm the world's worst typist."

"What about paralegal?"

"I wouldn't be good at that either. I'm bad with details."

". . . What *are* you good at?"

"Uh. . . what about self-abuse?"

Yong laughed. "You might not find anyone to hire you for that. Supply greatly outweighs demand in that department."

IN MID-SEPTEMBER, A SHIPMENT OF BOOKS and wooden chess sets from India arrived at The Chess Shop. After carrying in the heavy books, Ahmed developed a sharp pain in his side. He asked David to carry the rest into the back room. When the pain wasn't gone by the end of his shift, he took a cab to St. Vincent's Hospital, where he was diagnosed as having a hernia. After the operation, he was told to rest.

While Ahmed was recuperating, Sylvia and Johanna agreed to cover his shifts, but neither of them was qualified to manage The Shop, so Naomi and Marcus had to take over Ahmed's responsibilities.

Johanna, Sylvia, Sam, and David all visited Ahmed several times while he was indisposed. One evening when Sam and Sylvia were in Ahmed's apartment, Sam and Ahmed had a heated argument about the Middle East. Sam was surprised to find out that Ahmed was very militant. He said, "I thought you were a moderate. Didn't you say that you were in favor of a two-state solution?"

"You have to understand," Ahmed told him. "I came from Lebanon, where, if you disagree with someone, they might shoot you."

"Well, *I'm* not going to shoot you, but I think Israel must survive. History has taught us that the Jews need a place of their own."

Ahmed blurted out, "That's their problem."

"Well, they solved it."

"They stole our land, and we won't stop fighting until we get all of it back."

"First of all," Sam said, "there's no way you can win. Israel has the strongest army in the region. They even have nuclear weapons."

"America had the strongest army in the world at the time of the Vietnam War, yet they failed to win because the Vietnamese people were determined to rule themselves."

"Yeah, well, it's very easy for you to support the Palestinians in a hopeless cause while you're safe here in New York."

"It's *not* a hopeless cause. We will prevail! And maybe I will go back at some point."

"Maybe you should."

While Ahmed was confined to his room, Naomi asked everyone when he would be coming back to work. Johanna told him, "That's all she seems to care about. She never asks about your health. It's just 'When is he coming back?' Over and over."

MEANWHILE, SAM WAS HAVING A DIFFICULT TIME trying to find another job, and it was killing him that he only had time to spend one night a week with Kelly. He decided to take Thursdays off so he could spend Wednesday nights with her. When he told her, she asked him, "Can you afford to take another day off?"

"No, but my craving for you is becoming overwhelming."

Kelly hesitated for a few seconds, then said, "All right, you can spend Wednesday nights here." She said this as if she were making a concession rather than being glad that they'd have more time together.

Sam stared at her silently for a few seconds, then asked her, "You're not still sleeping with Aidan, are you?"

"Of course not," she said, putting her arms around him. "Do you believe me?"

"Yes."

"Take your clothes off and lie down."

She put some oil on his back and gave him a massage. For a few hours, he felt at peace.

After breakfast the next morning, he took the subway back to the Village.

He wanted to read a novel to pass the time, so he went to Barnes & Noble on 6th Avenue, where he found a copy of *The Defense*, by Vladimir Nabokov; from there, he went to The Peacock Café on Greenwich Avenue.

When he entered, he noticed a cute young girl seated at a corner table, wearing a green-and-white Catholic school outfit. She had olive skin, dark brown eyes, and long brown hair in a ponytail. He sat down at the table next to hers, opened his book, and began to read. After a few minutes, she interrupted him. "Are you a fan of Nabokov?"

"Oh, definitely."

"The only thing of his I've read is *Lolita*."

Sam smiled at her.

"You *are* Lolita," he said.

"Are you Humbert Humbert?"

"Uh. . .potentially."

"I was just kidding," she said. "Actually, I'm not really underage. Besides, I have a boyfriend."

"Do you live in the neighborhood?"

"I live on Bedford Street."

"What do your parents do?"

"My dad's an economics professor, and my mom's a curator at Sotheby's."

"What about you?"

"I'm an aspiring opera singer and pianist. I'm going to apply to Juilliard in the spring."

"Why the outfit? Do you go to Catholic school?"

"Unfortunately, yes. I can't wait until it's over."

"Do the nuns spank you?"

"No, but my boyfriend does."

Sam rolled his eyes.

"What's your favorite opera?" he asked her.

"*The Marriage of Figaro*. And Susanna's my favorite part."

"I can see you in that part."

"Actually, I'm in the chorus at the Amato Opera, and I have a small part in *La Traviata*."

"What part are you doing?"

"Anina, Violetta's maid."

"When is it? I'd love to come hear you."

"I'm singing the role only once, on Saturday night."

"What time?"

"7:30 p.m."

"If I can get off work early, I'll definitely come. What's your name, by the way? I'm Sam."

"Inez."

On Wednesday, after he dropped off the cab, Sam went to Kelly's place. He decided not to tell her about Inez just yet, because he was afraid that she might be jealous. *(Do I have ulterior motives?)*

When he entered the apartment, she kissed him on the lips and said, "I have something to show you."

She led him to an easel covered by a sheet. "Close your eyes," she said. She uncovered the easel. "Now open your eyes."

He was surprised and pleased to see a portrait of himself. "Wow," he said. "That's a very good likeness." He threw his arms around her and gave her a big hug. "I love you, you witch," he said.

"Are you giving me a compliment?"

"No compliment, no insult. Just the goddamn truth."

"Let's play rape," she said.

"Do I rape you or do you rape me?"

"You rape me, dummy."

Without a word, he began ripping off her clothes, tearing her blouse and her bra, yanking off her skirt, and ripping her panties in half. Then he threw her on the floor and thrust himself inside her.

Afterwards, it took over five minutes for his breathing to return to normal. "You're going to kill me," he said.

ON SATURDAY NIGHT, AFTER WORK, SAM WENT to the Amato Opera. The theater, which had only 110 seats, was sold out, but they gave him a seat in the aisle. He was astonished by what Tony Amato had done with the small stage. The sets and costumes were beautiful, the chorus first-rate, the staging wonderful, and some of the singers seemed to be good enough to sing at Lincoln Center. Inez had a pretty voice and looked as titillating in her French maid outfit as she had in her Catholic school uniform.

Afterwards, she introduced Sam to her parents and her boyfriend. "It's a pleasure to meet you," he said to them. To Inez, he added, "Maybe we'll see each other at The Peacock."

It was a beautiful fall evening, so he went for a long walk before returning to his apartment. He strolled up to Irving Place, where he stopped to have a meal at The Cottage, a Chinese restaurant. He ordered Sesame Chicken and brown rice. Afterwards, he went to the Village Corner to see Valerie.

"Let me guess," she said. "Johnny Walker Black with one ice cube."

"Good memory."

"Many of the customers I know only by what they drink."

He told her about Kelly, that she only wanted to see him twice a week, and that she hadn't broken up with Aidan yet.

"You think she's still sleeping with him?"

"I asked her that, and she said no."

"Do you believe her?"

"I *have* to. Otherwise, I'll go nuts."

"I think you'd sense it if she were cheating."

"With my feminine intuition?"

"Women don't have a monopoly on that."

When the place closed at 2:00, Sam was still wide awake, so he walked over to Karavas Place, which was open until 4:00. Cindy was behind the bar. "Hey, kitty cat," Sam said to her.

"Hey, Fido. Where have you been?"

"You wouldn't believe it if I told you."

Aside from his mother and Johannah, David Rabinowitz was the only person who knew that he had been in the hospital.

"How's your love life?" Cindy asked him.

"You mean my sex life?"

"Same difference."

"Quality, but not enough quantity."

"Well, that's better than the opposite."

"I suppose. How's *your* love life?"

"I've got a few losers who are interested in me, but I'm not sleeping with any of them."

They bantered pleasantly for about half an hour before Sam said, "Well, I don't want to monopolize your time." By then, there were five other men in the bar.

"That's okay," she said, adding under her breath, "You're the only one here who can talk in complete sentences."

When the bar closed, Sam walked back to the East Village, reaching his apartment at 4:30 in the morning. On entering his room, he turned on the radio, which he kept next to his bed. On WQXR they were playing a recording of Shubert's "Wintereise." He slowly undressed, lay down, and pulled the covers over his head. As he listened to the music, he began to cry. *(Oh, what I'd do to get Megan back.)*

CHAPTER 17

THE FOLLOWING AFTERNOON, HIS FIRST STUDENT was scheduled for 4:00. Sam went to The Chess Shop an hour early, to look for David Rabinowitz. He found him there, giving a lesson to a businessman who once had been one of his own students. Sam couldn't resist making a sarcastic comment. To Ahmed, he said, "Look at the theoretician at work."

Ahmed laughed. David, who couldn't stand being laughed at, gave both of them an icy stare and continued with the lesson. After it was over, Sam approached David's table, but David abruptly stood up and left The Shop. To Ahmed, Sam added, "None of the strong players think David can teach." He didn't realize that David, who was standing right outside the door, had overheard his remark.

When Sam finished teaching, he went the Village Corner to pick up Kelly, and they took the E train back to Queens. On the way, he told her about the Amato Opera.

"Why did you decide to go there?" she asked him.

"I know one of the singers."

"Who?"

Sam changed his mind and told her about Inez.

"You're not thinking of cheating on me, are you?" she demanded.

"No, I wouldn't sleep with her even if I were single. She's only a child."

"I'm very possessive," Kelly said. "I don't like the fact that you have female friends. How am I going to know if you cheat on me?"

"You don't want me to have female friends, but you won't break up with Aidan?"

Kelly noticed some of the passengers on the train were watching them.

"Let's wait until we get home before we have a fight," she said.

They remained silent until they left the subway. Walking to the apartment, she said, "Woe unto you if you ever cheat on me."

"I'm not going to cheat," Sam said. "But if you don't want me to have female friends, you've got to break up with Aidan, and you've got to see me more than twice a week."

She didn't respond, but Sam could tell that she was very angry. When he entered the apartment, he tried to kiss her, but she pushed him away. Sam shrugged, sat down, and opened a magazine. *(She'll get over it.)*

Kelly started working on one of her abstract paintings, which was on an easel in her bedroom. After about fifteen minutes, Sam got up to take a look. Kelly's favorite painter was Miro, and he could see his influence on her work.

"This has potential," he said. *(I'd better flatter her or I might not get laid tonight.)*

". . .Do you think so?"

"Yes, I like the way you arrange things on the canvas— there's a lot of movement—and your colors are very strong."

"I'm glad you like it."

When Sam tried to kiss her again, she squirmed away. "Not so fast."

"Are you going to pussy-whip me tonight?"

"I'm going to make you beg for it."

He stuck out his tongue and began to pant like a St. Bernard. She giggled. "Give me a body massage," she said.

Sam began to undress her.

"Not the panties, Sam."

He massaged her from her scalp all the way down to her feet.

"Now what?" he asked her.

"Now get lost."

He tore off her panties, as he had earlier in the week. She fought him off for as long as she could, then surrendered completely. "You're very persistent," she said.

"You had me worried there," he admitted.

In the morning, she woke him up for more sex, then kicked him out of the apartment so she could focus on the jewelry she was making.

"Are you ever going to let me spend twenty-four hours with you?" he asked before he left.

"We'll live together eventually."

"I'll believe it when I see it."

He went back to the Village, where he stopped at the Strand and bought another novel, as much to serve as a conversation piece should he run into Inez again as for the pleasure of reading it. This time he chose *The Portrait of a Lady* by Henry James. He walked over to The Peacock, sat at the same table, and began to read. Surely enough, just after 3:00 p.m., Inez came in.

"Do you mind if I sit with you?" she asked him. "You don't have to stop reading if you don't want to."

"By all means, please do."

". . .Oh, you're reading Henry James? I just finished *The Ambassadors.*

"Wow," Sam said. "I couldn't have handled *The Ambassadors* when I was your age."

"I'm very precocious."

Sam smiled.

"So what do you do?" she asked him.

"I teach chess, and I drive a cab."

"How cool is that? Where do you teach?"

"At The Chess Shop, on Tompkins."

"I've always wanted to learn."

"Take some lessons. I'll give you big discount."

"I'd love to."

"When would you like to start?"

"How about this evening?"

Sam tried to hide his excitement. "Yeah, I guess that would be all right," he said.

"Say, about 8:00 p.m.?"

"Fine."

"Where should we meet?"

"Well, we could meet at The Chess Shop, or we could do it here. I'd just have to stop at home and pick up a set."

"Okay, let's do it here."

On his way to the East Village, he fantasized about her. He pictured her wearing nothing but her green and white Catholic school skirt. He saw himself fondling her firm young breasts, pulling up her skirt, taking off her white lace panties and—*(Lovelier thoughts, Sam).*

When he got to The Peacock, Inez was seated near the door with one of her school friends.

"This is my friend Vanessa," she said. "Is it okay if she sits in?"

"Certainly."

Vanessa was even prettier than Inez. She was almost six feet tall and had a freckled face, green eyes, and thick red hair.

"Okay, let's start," Sam said. "Do you know the rules?" They both did. "All right, then, let's play a game. Who wants to go first?"

"Inez can play," Vanessa said. "I'll just watch."

Inez was not a beginner by any means. She seemed to know the principles very well, so Sam decided to help her with her opening repertoire. "Since white moves first, it's more important to know your openings as black, or you can run into trouble very quickly."

He showed her how to answer 1.e4 with the Sicilian defense. They played three games with this opening system, which was a favorite of Gary Kasparov, the world champion. In each game, he showed her a few more nuances. The hour went by quickly.

"During your next lesson, I'll teach you defense to 1.d4. In the meantime, why don't the two of you play each other some games with the Sicilian, alternating between black and white?"

"Terrific," Inez said. "How much do I owe you?"

"Oh. . .let's say ten bucks."

He gave both of them his business card and told them to call him when they wanted another lesson.

Sam hadn't seen his mother in a while, so he took Tuesday off to visit her. When he got home on Monday night, he called her to say that he'd be coming out in the morning. He woke up at 9:00, had breakfast at Odessa, took a cab to the Port Authority, and hopped on a bus to Hackensack, arriving at 10:45. His mother greeted him with a big hug.

"I've got an idea," she said. "Why don't we drive up to Piermont for lunch?"

"Good idea."

Piermont is a beautiful town alongside the Hudson River, up in Rockland County, New York. On the way, Sam filled her in on the new developments in his life. "I'm driving a cab three days a week now, working Saturdays at Mercer Books, and teaching a few students at The Chess Shop on Sunday afternoons."

"I'm so glad," Mrs. Kanter said. "Working will keep you sane."

"I also have a new girlfriend."

"Wow, you're a fast worker."

"Well, I've known her for a long time. We've just recently heated things up."

"Is she a nice girl?"

Sam laughed. "Is she a nice girl? Uh, I guess I'd have to say no—she's not a nice girl. She's beautiful, she's talented, she's a very warm person, she says she loves me, but a nice girl? No, not at all." He laughed again.

"I worry about you, Sam. With your condition—"

"Never mind my condition," he said. "I'm a grown boy now."

"I know."

They parked the car by the river in Piermont and took a walk through the town. Many of the houses there are over a hundred years old. She took a photograph of him standing on a long pier that stretched out over the water, with the Tappan Zee Bridge in the background. They lunched at the Sidewalk Bistro, then got back into the car and took a slow drive up Piermont Avenue to Nyack, where they visited several antique stores. Then they took Route 9W back to New Jersey. On the way, she said, "Well, it seems like you don't have any symptoms now."

"How about that?" Sam replied.

In Hackensack, they had a coffee at her apartment; then Sam took the bus back into the city. When he got to his apartment, he found a message from Kelly on his answering machine: *Hi, Sam. I can't see you tomorrow night because it's Aidan's birthday.*

He didn't want to argue, but he was pissed off. *(I only get to see her twice a week. She can't celebrate Aidan's birthday on another day?)*

On Friday morning, he had trouble getting out of bed. He got to the garage three hours late. The dispatcher said, "Buddy, you can't come in this late. We need the cab on the road all day. If you're going to be late, you better get a medallion and drive your own cab."

"I'm sorry," Sam said. "It won't happen again." *(I hope I can keep that promise.)*

"If it happens again, I'm gonna have to tell the manager."

"It won't."

"And if you wanna take days off, you gotta tell us a few days in advance, so we can find someone to drive a cab that day. When the cab's not in use, we lose money."

"Okay, okay," Sam said impatiently.

The dispatcher stared at him. "Don't give me attitude buddy, or you're out of the job."

"Okay, I'm sorry."

After work, Sam had a Big Mac and some fries at McDonald's; then he went to the Village Gate to hear some jazz and chat with Raphael. He found Rafi at a table by the window, playing speed chess with Ben Lester. "Can I play the winner?" he asked them.

"Sure," Rafi said.

While he was waiting his turn to play, Sam closed his eyes and listened to the music. That night there was a quartet led by George Hargrove, a classy and soulful trumpet player. He enjoyed the music so much that, when his turn came to play, he said, "Why don't the two of you keep playing until the set is over? This music is doing me good."

After the music ended and most of the customers had left the club, Sam played a few games, but his mind was elsewhere, so he made several bad blunders. "What's with you?" Raphael asked him. "You seem so out of it."

"Marital problems," Sam said wryly.

Raphael locked up, and he and Ben went to the Washington Square Diner to continue playing. Sam walked them there, excused himself, and went to the Village Idiot. At the Idiot, there was a sexy new barmaid. Sam put five dollars in the jukebox and introduced himself. "Hi, I'm Sam. I'm a regular here. And if you're going to be working here, I'll be even more of a regular."

She laughed. "I'm Kristen," she said. "What'll it be?"

"I'll have a Johnny Walker Black with one ice cube."

"Want to buy me a drink?"

"Certainly."

There were only two other customers in the bar, so they had time for a long conversation. After about four drinks, Sam started telling her about Kelly. "I never get to see her more than twice a week, and she won't make a final break with her old boyfriend."

"Sounds like trouble."

"That's what everyone says."

He drank until he ran out of money, then stumbled home and went to bed. When he awoke, he had a big hangover, so he made a pot of coffee and drank a few cups. Since it was a beautiful day, he decided to go to Tompkins Square for a chess game.

The chess in Tompkins Square Park is much friendlier than in Washington Square Park, where it's all about money. He played a few slow games with Ted Gold, a painter he knew from the Marshall. Ted wasn't a book player, but he played very well for someone who was self-taught. After Sam beat him three games straight, Ted said, "I heard that you give lessons at The Chess Shop. What do you charge?"

"Thirty an hour."

"Maybe I'll take just one lesson to work on my openings."

"That's fine," Sam said. He thought for a minute, then asked, "Any chance I can see your artwork?"

"Sure. Why don't you come to my studio?"

"I'd love to. When can I come?"

"No time like the present."

Ted shared a studio with a friend in a building near Union Square. On the way over, Sam asked him, "Do you know a lot about art history? I love art, but I know virtually nothing about it."

"Well, it so happens that, every Saturday night, I go to The Met with a group of friends, and then we have dinner afterwards. You're welcome to join us whenever you want."

"That would be great," Sam said. "I'm sure I could learn a lot from your comments."

"I'm not that analytical, but some my friends are, so you'll learn some things if you come with us."

At the studio, Ted's friend was just leaving. "Bob, this is Sam," said Ted. "He's going to come to the museum with us."

"Then I'll see you soon," Bob said, giving Sam a firm handshake before leaving the studio.

"Bob's a man of few words," Ted said. "But when you get to know him, you'll find out how brilliant he is."

Ted's paintings were dark and tonal, with strong expression and thick paint. Most of them were cityscapes from around the five boroughs. Bob's work, on the other hand, consisted mostly of pleasant landscapes, very simple and evocative. Sam loved them. "Boy, you never know who you're going to meet in the city," he said.

They exchanged phone numbers, and Sam left Ted in the studio. He walked over to The Chess Shop to see if any of his friends were there. Ahmed was behind the counter. Sam asked him, "Has David been here today?"

"No, I haven't seen David for several days."

"That's strange," Sam said. "I thought he never misses a day, except on the Sabbath."

Jim Smith was playing an odds game with Costos, his favorite opponent, so Sam sat and watched for a while. "How are you, Master Sam?" Jim asked him.

"I'm overwhelmed with gratitude that a human being as elevated as yourself would deign to give me the time of day."

Jim gleefully rubbed his hands together and said, "And now for the mate."

At 4:00 p.m., Sam went to The Peacock. Inez was there, doing her homework. When she saw him, she smiled radiantly. "Hi," she said. "You're just in time to help me with my algebra."

"You're out of luck," Sam said. "I don't think I even remember how to do long division."

"Well, I think I know how you *can* help me. I have to write a paper for English class, and I have a list of six writers to choose from."

"Who are they?"

"Chaucer, Milton, Spencer, Wordsworth, Keats, and Dickens."

"No Shakespeare?"

"No, because everyone would pick Shakespeare."

"Then I'd probably choose Milton."

A woman seated at the next table, wearing a butch haircut and covered with tattoos, without even acknowledging Sam's presence, told Inez, "Milton was an old Puritan. You'd be better off reading Chaucer, and 'The Wife of Bath's Tale' is very good for gender studies."

With a smirk, Sam said, "I'm not going to break up this sisterhood."

"Let's talk about something else," Inez suggested.

"Okay. When are you having your next chess lesson?"

"Do you have a set with you?"

"No, but we can meet here later, or at The Shop."

"Let's meet here at eight, and I'll ask Vanessa if she can make it."

"Great."

Sam had Chinese food at Susie's, then went to The Chess Shop and read the periodical *New in Chess*, eagerly awaiting his appointment with Inez. When the time came, he borrowed an inexpensive set from Sylvia, who was working the evening shift, and sauntered over to The Peacock.

This time he showed Inez and Vanessa how to play the Benko gambit, an active defense to 1d4. Then he showed them some of the basic tactical motifs in chess: pinning, forking, discovered attack, and removing the defender.

"There's an excellent book they have at The Shop called *Chess Tactics for Champions*. All my students use that book."

"Great," Vanessa said. "I'll pick up a copy tomorrow."

When the lesson was over, Inez asked Sam, "What about what that woman said about Chaucer and Milton?"

"Chaucer's great! And the Wife of Bath's Tale is funny—gender *schmender*. And Milton *was* an old Puritan, but I think he's the greatest writer in the English language, aside from Shakespeare."

After work on Saturday night, Sam met Ted, Bob, and a couple of their friends at The Metropolitan Museum of Art. That month, there was a special exhibit of Manet and Velasquez. Sam listened to their comments with interest. After the museum closed, they all took a bus down to the Village, and had a late dinner at Panna, on East 6th Street.

On Sunday afternoon, Sam went to the Village Corner to see Kelly. For some reason, she seemed a bit distant. He decided not to say anything until they reached her apartment. When they were inside, he said, "You seem a little preoccupied today. Is anything wrong?"

"Listen," Kelly said. "I'm becoming very busy making the jewelry. I have enough orders to keep me working for the next two months. So. . .I hate to say this, but I'm only going to be able to see you once a week for now."

"That's not enough," Sam said.

"Take it or leave it."

"Take it or leave it?" He shoved her so hard that she fell on the floor, then stormed out of the apartment. He took the train back to Manhattan and headed straight for the Village Idiot. Kristen was behind the bar. "I'm surprised to see you," she said. "I thought this was your night with Kelly."

"How much do you charge for therapy?"

"It's part of my job. Just buy me enough drinks so that we both need to be carried out of here."

"It's a deal," Sam said.

He told her what had happened.

"She's only going to see you once a week now?"

"Yeah," Sam snarled.

"I think you should forget about Kelly. Let her old boyfriend put up with her shit."

"I'll drink to that."

He stayed in the bar until closing, then asked her, "Do you want to come home with me?"

"I can't," she said. ". . .But keep coming here. I enjoy your company immensely."

He stumbled home and slept for twelve hours. When he awoke, he decided to call Kelly and apologize for shoving her. When she picked up the phone, he said, "Kelly, I'm sorry I lost my temper last night."

"Fuck you," Kelly said. "I've been seeing Aidan for six years, and he's never laid a hand on me."

". . .I'm sorry."

"Go fuck yourself," she said, and hung up.

Sam had a splitting headache. He took three Tylenol caplets and lay down again. *(She'll get over it, and if she doesn't. . . .well, I'd be better off without her.)*

CHAPTER 18

When he awoke, it was four in the afternoon. He walked over to The Chess Shop to see if David was there. No one had seen him for weeks. Sam went to Washington Square Park to see if anyone there had. He got the same response. He hoped nothing was wrong.

He called Kelly again to see if her anger had subsided, but as soon as she heard his voice, she hung up the phone. Sam started to become agitated. *(Will she never speak to me again?)* As he often did when he was upset, he went for a long walk—up Fifth Avenue all the way to The Metropolitan Museum, a four-mile jaunt. On the way, he thought about what he would say to Kelly. He decided that, if she continued not to answer his calls, he would write her a letter.

When he reached the museum, Sam took another look at the Manet–Velasquez exhibit. As he looked at the paintings, his agitation subsided, but as soon as he left the museum, he began to worry about Kelly again. He took a bus back to the Village, bought a notebook at a stationery store, went to Café Dante and began to write.

Dear Kelly,

I'm sorry about what happened on Sunday. Even though you hurt me deeply, I had no right to become violent. If you can forgive me, I promise it will never happen again, no matter what you do. As for your 'take it or leave it,' I'm prepared to abide by your wishes. Even seeing you once a week is so much better than not seeing you at all. If you'll forgive me, I'll never complain. One day I hope we'll live together, and then, no matter how busy either of us is, at least we'll be near each other. Please call me or answer this letter as soon as possible. Don't keep me in suspense.

Love,
Sam

By the time he finished writing, the post office was closed, so he bought a stamp at a deli and dropped the letter in a mailbox near Washington Square. He was too agitated to play chess, so he went to the Village Idiot for the second night in a row. He was happy to see Kristen behind the bar. "I can only stay for an hour or two," he said. "I have to work tomorrow."

"That's fine. What'll it be?"

"Give me a Johnny Walker Black with one ice cube," he said. "Make it a double."

"So, did you talk to Kelly?"

"No, when I called her she hung up on me, so I wrote her a letter apologizing for what happened."

"Were you suitably contrite?"

"Yeah, but I have the feeling that I'm going to have to do a lot of groveling if I want to get her back."

"Women love it when men grovel," Kristen said.

"Should I practice on you?"

"Role-playing? Sure, why not. I'll be Kelly."

"Kelly, I'm truly sorry. It will never happen again."

"You're lucky I don't report you to the police, you bastard."

"I know, I know. If you take me back, I'll do anything you say."

"Anything?"

"Anything."

"All right. You've got to eat my pussy for an hour every time you come over, and I'm not going to do anything for you."

"If that's what you want. . . ."

"And now you're only going to see me at *my* convenience, even if it's only once every six weeks. And when I *do* want to see you, you've got to drop everything and come right away."

". . .Boy, you do Kelly better than she does herself."

"Forget about Kelly! There are other fish in the ocean."

"I suppose you're right," Sam said.

DRIVING A CAB THE NEXT DAY, he had trouble concentrating. In the middle of the afternoon, he had a fare from the Upper West Side to Canarsie in Brooklyn. He wanted to go via the Brooklyn Queens Expressway, but his fare, a young businesswoman, insisted on going through the streets because, she claimed, it was much cheaper that way. Somewhere in Flatbush, Sam took a wrong turn, and they got lost. He asked her, "Do you know where we are?"

"No," she said. "You're supposed to know the streets. You're the driver."

"Frankly, I'm lost," he said.

"All right, then turn off the meter and let's ask someone for directions."

Eventually, they found their way to Canarsie, but it took almost two hours.

On the way back, Sam, who could think about nothing but Kelly, got lost again. He decided to bring the cab back to the garage. *(If I keep driving in this state, I'm sure to have an accident.)*

When he got there, he told the dispatcher that he wasn't feeling well. "How come you didn't know that this morning?"

"Well, I felt bad this morning, but I thought I'd be okay. Now I feel much worse."

"You're not trying to pull one over on me, are you?"

"*No*."

"Well, are you going to be in tomorrow?"

"I think I need to take a few days off."

"If you must," the dispatcher said.

On the way back into the city, Sam started to feel very sleepy. *(Am I getting depressed again, or do I just need a nap?)* When he got home, it was already late in the afternoon, so he lay down on his bed. *(I guess I'm getting depressed.)* After a few hours, he forced himself to get up. *(If I stay in bed, it's only going to get worse.)* He sat in an armchair watching television, but he kept dozing off.

For the next several days, Sam spent most of his time in the apartment, getting up only to have a meal at the Odessa Diner once a day.

His roommate noticed the change in him. "Are you all right?" he asked.

"Frankly, I'm a little depressed."

"Is there any way I can help?"

"No, it'll go away sooner or later."

ON SATURDAY, SAM CALLED DALE AT MERCER BOOKS and told him he wasn't feeling well. Dale said, "Sam, you've missed work too many times. I'm going to have to let you go."

"I'm so disappointed!" Sam said.

"I'm sorry."

On Sunday, Sam called The Chess Shop and asked Richard Kelly to teach his students for him. On Monday, he called the taxi company and told his boss that he had pneumonia and would have to take at least a few weeks off.

"Okay, buddy," the dispatcher said.

Then he called Dr. Brown to set up an appointment. "Can you come and see me at 10:00 tomorrow morning?" the doctor asked.

"Is there any chance you could make it later? When I'm this depressed, I have terrible trouble getting up in the morning."

"Is it an emergency?"

"Uh, no. . . . Not really."

"Okay, then how about coming in on Wednesday afternoon at 4:00?"

"Fine."

He spent most of the next three days in bed. On Wednesday, he got out of bed just in time to keep his appointment. The doctor could see right away that he was ill. "What's been happening?" he asked.

Sam told him about Kelly. "I'd love to get her back," he said.

"From what you've told me, even though you want her now, I think that in the long run you'd be better off without her."

Sam did not answer.

"How long have you been depressed?" the doctor asked him.

"About a week."

"Well, if it goes on for another week, I would definitely call Dr. Berkun. He might want to make an adjustment in your medication."

"All right."

When he got home, Sam called his mother. "Mom," he said. "I've been very depressed all week."

"Is it a girl?"

"You know me all too well," he said.

"How serious is it?"

"I'm not sure. I've felt like this many times before, as you know, and sometimes I feel better in a week or two, but sometimes. . . ."

"I know. Sometimes it can go on for months."

"I'll keep you posted," he said. "I don't think we need to worry yet."

After another week spent mostly in bed, Sam decided to take Dr. Brown's advice and call his psychopharmacologist. As soon as Sam told him he was in a clinical depression, Dr. Berkun gave him an appointment right away. He quickly evaluated his patient, prescribed Zoloft, an antidepressant, and told him to continue taking Zyprexa.

"What should I do with my time?" Sam asked him.

"If you're too ill to work, try to remain as active as you can. If you spend all your time in bed, the depression could worsen."

Sam tried to get out of bed at noon every day, but he found it impossible. By about 4:00 or 5:00 p.m., however, he usually felt somewhat better. He avoided going to The Chess Shop or The Peacock Café, because he didn't want his friends to see him in the state he was in. He did want to confide in David Rabinowitz, so he called the player phone at The Shop.

Richard Kelly answered.

"Have you seen David?" Sam asked him.

"Not for a long time," Richard replied.

Sam got into a routine of waking up at about 4:00 p.m., having breakfast at Odessa, and then heading over to the Jefferson Market branch of the New York Public Library, where he stayed until closing time. His concentration was too poor to read a novel or even *The New York Times*, so he spent his hours at the library, reading the tabloids or looking at the models in *Cosmopolitan* and other women's magazines. He created a fantasy world in which he seduced the cover girls and brought them to his mansion in the Hamptons, where they swam naked in his swimming pool or had sex with him on the beach.

After the library closed, he made a habit of going to the Angelica Theater to see a movie. Sometimes his concentration was so poor that he had trouble following the plot. After midnight, he started going to French Roast on Sixth Avenue, which is open all night. It was a home for many Alcoholics Anonymous members who came there as a group after their midnight meeting. Sam found that many of the AAs, as Sam liked to call them, had problems similar to his, so he felt very much at home there.

One of them, a guy named Brad, was there every night. He had been on the wagon for years, but he was still barely functional. Sam enjoyed his company because he was a big film buff who knew all the important movies and directors like the back of his hand. He also knew who had won the Oscars for best film, best director, best actor, and best actress ever since they started giving out the awards. Brad made a long list of movies for Sam to see.

"Right now I want to stay out of my apartment as much as I can," Sam told him. "But eventually I'll buy a VCR and rent all the movies you recommended."

One of the AAs was a Dutch woman named Anike. Almost all the men in the late-night crowd had the hots for her, and she could be very obliging.

"I use sex to medicate myself," she was fond of saying.

One night after Sam had been coming to French Roast for about three weeks, Anike invited him to come home with her. Against his better judgment, he acquiesced. She lived in an SRO in the East Village, where she had a tiny room with only one window. There was one filthy bathroom on each floor. On the night that Sam joined her, there was no heat in the building.

"We'll keep each other warm," she said.

Before undressing, he sighed deeply. She looked into his eyes. "That was some sigh," she said.

"I'm a master sigher."

When she took off her pants, he saw that she had tattoos on both legs, and that she had shaved off all her pubic hair. He suddenly lost all attraction to her.

"I don't know if I'm ready for this," he said.

"What about oral sex?"

She promptly went down on him. After they were finished, Sam felt like he had to get out of there.

"I think I'm going to sleep at home," he said.

"I wish you'd stay."

He lied: "I have trouble sleeping when I'm in a bed with someone else."

"All right. I guess I'll see you tomorrow night."

When he left the building, Sam felt sick to his stomach. He stumbled home, stripped down to his underwear, went into the bathroom, and stared at his face in the mirror. His face was a study in misery. He went into his room, lay down on the bed, and began weeping. After a good cry, his mood improved somewhat, but he had developed a pounding headache, so he walked across the street and bought a box of Advil. Then he went back upstairs, took the Advil with a glass of orange juice, and lay down again. At about six in the morning, he finally fell asleep. When he woke up, he looked at the clock; he had slept for fourteen hours.

Outside, it was raining. He took a quick shower, pulled on his raincoat, and trudged over to East River Park. As he sat on a bench facing the river, the Simon and Garfunkel song about old friends sitting on a bench ran through his head.

He went back to Avenue A and the Odessa, where he ordered pirogies, kielbasa, and sauerkraut. Then he went to the Village Idiot to see Kristen. She was alone at the bar. "You look like death warmed over," she said.

"You mean death frozen solid."

"What'll it be?"

"A shot of Johnny Walker Black and a pint of Budweiser." His stomach was already somewhat upset from the Polish food. After a few drinks, he felt nauseous. "Excuse me," he said. "I need a little air."

He went around the corner, checked to see that no one was looking, and vomited on the sidewalk. Then he went back to the bar and ordered a coffee.

"I'm worried about you," Kristen said. "You look awful."

". . .I'm in a clinical depression," he said. "I haven't worked in over a month."

"Do you have a therapist?"

"Yeah, but I only go once in a while. Talking doesn't seem to help that much."

"Are you taking medication?"

"Yes, I'm taking an antipsychotic drug and an antidepressant."

"I hope you don't think I'm prying."

"No, I think you're one of those rare bartenders who actually cares about her customers."

She smiled warmly. "Why don't you go home and get some rest?" she asked him.

"I just woke up six hours ago."

"Oh."

At that point, two of the regulars came into the bar, so Kristen discreetly changed the subject. After a half an hour of small talk, Sam left and went to French Roast, where he talked to Brad for hours.

When he returned home that morning, there was a message on his answering machine: *Hey, Sam. This is Ted Gold. When are we going to have our lesson?*

Sam was conflicted. *(I don't know if I want him to see me like this, but maybe I'll be able to dissemble.)*

The next afternoon, he called Ted at his studio.

"Where've you been, stranger?" Ted asked him.

"I've been very busy lately, but I do want to find time for your lesson. What are you doing at 8:00 p.m. Thursday?"

"That's fine," Ted said. "Where should we do it?"

Sam thought for a moment. "How about my place?"

"Great."

Sam gave him his address. On Wednesday afternoon, Sam made a supreme effort and cleaned the apartment, which he hadn't done in weeks. The kitchen and bathroom weren't too bad, because Yong cleaned occasionally, but Sam's room was a pigsty. It took almost an hour before he finished.

Ted arrived Thursday evening at 8:10. Just from looking at Sam, he could tell that something was wrong. "Are you all right?" he asked.

"I'm just a little tired," Sam told him.

He didn't want to play a game with Ted, because the depression had made his concentration so poor that he was afraid he would lose. Instead, he showed Ted some Bobby Fischer games and helped him with his opening repertoire. Afterwards, they had dinner at Odessa. Ted was sure that something was seriously wrong with Sam, but he decided not to mention it.

After they said goodbye, Sam stopped by The Chess Shop to look once again for David Rabinowitz.

Ahmed was behind the counter. "Has anyone seen David?" Sam asked him.

"Jim Smith told me that he's seen him at the Marshall once or twice."

Sam promptly walked over to the Marshall, where he found David seated by himself at a corner table, methodically moving the pieces around the board.

"How come you never come to The Chess Shop anymore?" Sam asked him.

"Because I heard you and Ahmed laughing at me behind my back."

"That's all?" Sam asked him.

"Yeah, that's all. Get lost," he said.

Sam shrugged and left the building, but once he was outside, he sat on the front steps and cried. *(What am I going to do? He's my only friend.)*

Beside himself, he ran blindly through the West Village until he reached the Hudson. He ran out onto the pier at the end of Christopher Street and considered jumping in the river and drowning himself. *(No! No! No! Pull yourself together!)*

A gay man seated on the pier noticed his agitation and asked, "Are you all right?"

Sam clenched his teeth. "I've never been better."

He ran off the pier and onto the West Side Highway, where he narrowly missed being hit by taxicab. (Oh, God, oh, God, oh, God, oh, God, oh, God.)

CHAPTER 19

He found a pay phone and made a collect call to his mother. "Can I come over, Mom?" he said. "I-I'm afraid of hurting myself."

"What time is it?"

He looked at his watch. "It's 10:30."

"All right. You can sleep on the sofa, but don't wake me up unless you absolutely have to."

When Sam made it to the Port Authority, he had trouble finding the right platform—just as he had before his last hospitalization. He found the bus just seconds before it left, slumped onto a seat in the back, and drifted off to sleep, waking up just in time. At her building, he took the elevator up and crashed on the sofa, falling asleep almost as soon as his head touched the cushion.

When he awoke, it was just getting light outside. He couldn't go back to sleep. *(This is something different. Usually, when I'm like this, I can't stop sleeping.)* He went out on the terrace, where he remembered a poem by Coleridge he had studied in high school. He went back into the living room and found an anthology.

A grief without a pang, void, dark, and drear.
A stifled, drowsy, unimpassioned grief,
Which finds no natural outlet, no relief,
In word, or sigh, or tear. . .

(Is it worth experiencing depression if you can write about it like that? No, dammit, just let me be happy, and I'll willingly be a nobody.)

When his mother awoke at 8:00, she found him sitting at the kitchen table, trying to read *The New York Times.*

"How are you?" she asked. "You look terrible."

"I'm half dead," he replied grimly.

"Let me make you some breakfast. Would you like an omelet or French toast?"

"Whatever," he said.

When she served him, he was only able to take a few bites. "I'm sorry, Mom. I'm not really hungry."

"That's all right. Would you like some coffee?"

"Maybe later."

She sat down next to him, put her hand on his shoulder, and said, "Tell me what's been happening."

"My mind is in a fog," he said. "I can't even. . . ." He went blank.

"Have you spoken to Dr. Brown?"

"Yeah. He told me to go see Dr. Berkun."

"What did he say?"

"He gave me an antidepressant."

"Is it helping?"

"I don't think so."

After a long pause, she asked him, "Do you want to go into the hospital?"

"I don't know."

"If you're feeling suicidal—"

"I'm not going to *kill* myself. That would take more will power than I have right now."

She shuddered. "What's going on?"

"First, my girlfriend Kelly broke up with me, and now my best friend David isn't talking to me."

"That would make anyone depressed."

"Yeah, but when I get depressed—"

"I know. It's not the same thing." She thought for a minute, then added, "Listen. Why don't you stay here, where you're safe, for a few days, and if there's no improvement, then maybe you should consider going into the hospital."

"Okay."

"Do you want some coffee now? Maybe that'll pick you up a bit."

"I don't think even winning the lottery would pick me up right now."

"Well, I'll make you some coffee anyway."

While the coffee was brewing, Sam put his head on the table and promptly fell asleep.

"*Vey is mir*," Mrs. Kanter said under her breath.

Forty-five minutes later, she woke him up. "If you sleep all day, you won't be able to sleep tonight," she said.

"Believe me," he assured her, "that won't be a problem."

"Well, why don't you move to the sofa? Aren't you uncomfortable?"

He pulled himself up and collapsed on the sofa. She began to untie his shoelaces.

"Don't treat me like an *invalid!*" he barked. *(Even though that's what I am, I still have some pride left.)*

"I'm sorry," she said, and left the room.

FOR THE NEXT THREE DAYS, HE SLEPT ON AND OFF, getting up only once each evening for a meal. His mother unsuccessfully tried to engage him in conversation or get him to watch a little television. Finally, she said, "Sam, I think you should go into the hospital."

"Oh. . . ."

"Could you please call Dr. Berkun and tell him how you're doing?"

"Why don't you. . . ."

"Do you want me to call him?"

"Yes."

She left a message on the answering machine, asking Dr. Berkun to call her right away. Within an hour, he returned her call.

"Sam's severely depressed," she said. "I haven't seen him this bad in a long time."

"Can I talk to him?"

"Let's see if I can get him to come to the phone." She went into the living room and tried to awaken Sam.

"Leave me alone," he said.

"Dr. Berkun is on the phone."

"Oh, all right. . .give me a minute."

Somehow he sat himself up, went into the kitchen, and picked up the phone.

"Hello," he said.

"Hi, Sam. How are you doing?"

"Lousy."

"Can you come see me?"

"Honestly, I don't think I have the energy to leave the apartment."

"Then maybe you should go into the hospital."

"If you think so. . . ."

I'll call the Leonard Pavilion and make sure they have a bed for you."

"If you think that's best. . . ."

In her bedroom closet, Mrs. Kanter had a couple of pairs of Sam's socks and three pairs of his underwear. She put these in a plastic bag for him. "I'll bring you some more clothes when I come to visit you."

"I also need a razor and some quarters, so I can call you on the payphone."

She looked in her purse and found three quarters.

"I'll bring you more when I come."

"Thanks."

"Do you think you can get there by yourself, or should I call a cab?"

"I don't know if I can even get downstairs to wait for the cab."

"I'll go down with you."

She ordered a cab, and they went downstairs to wait. When the car arrived, Sam's mother gave him $40.00 to pay the driver with, then gave him a big hug.

"I'll come visit you soon," she said.

In the Leonard Pavilion, there were lots of familiar faces: Isabel, his favorite nurse; Edith, the OT lady; Margaret, the art therapist; and many of the same aides. Most of the patients were new, except Frank, whom he found playing solitaire, and Jill, the young anorexic girl. He was disappointed that Mary was no longer there.

He said hello to everyone, then headed straight to his room and got in bed. At dinnertime, Isabel came to wake him up.

"I'm not hungry," he said.

"Then why don't you come to the dining room and chat with the other patients?"

"Maybe tomorrow."

She decided not to insist. "Dr. Jackson will see you tomorrow," she said. "I'm sure she'll be able to help you."

"I'm not so sure," Sam replied glumly.

He stayed in bed for the next thirteen hours, sleeping on and off. At 7:00 a.m. Sandy, one of the aides, came to wake him up.

"Come to the dining room," he said. "It's time for you to have your vital signs taken."

Sam ignored him. Fifteen minutes later, the aide returned. "You have to get up," he said.

"I can't."

"If you don't come to have your blood pressure taken, you'll lose all your privileges."

"What privileges?"

"You won't be able to go for walks or leave the ward for any reason, and you might not be allowed to see any visitors."

Sam groaned but remained in bed.

Finally, Sandy brought the blood pressure machine and the thermometer to his room and took his vital signs in bed.

"I'm going to tell your doctor about this," he said.

At 1:00 p.m., Dr. Jackson came into the room and woke him up. "Let's go to the office and have a chat," she said.

"Can we talk here?"

"No, I want you to make the effort and come with me."

Sam sat up on the edge of the bed. "Give me a minute," he said. "I'll be there."

"I'll wait for you in the office."

After two minutes, he forced himself to stand and walked down the hall to the office, leaning one hand on the wall to keep from falling. When he reached the office, he found the doctor seated at her desk. He collapsed in a chair across from her.

"So what brings you here this time?" she asked.

"It's much less interesting than last time," he said. "I'm so depressed I can't function."

"What medications are you taking?"

"Zyprexa and Zoloft."

"Okay. I'd like to add another antidepressant. Have you heard of Welbutrin?"

"Yes, that's what Frank takes."

"Is that okay with you?"

"Sure."

"Now, you have to make an effort to stay up during the day. Even if you just sit in the chair in the day room, it would be better than staying in bed all day."

"I'll do what I can," he said.

"And little by little, I want you to become more active. In a few days, I'm going to start assigning you to some groups, and then I'll let you walk around the grounds with the nurses or the other patients. As the medication starts to kick in, you should be able to do those things."

"I hope you're right," he said.

He walked over to the day room and sat on the couch. After a few minutes, he was joined by a young Korean girl.

"Hey, couch potato!" she said to him. He didn't respond.

"Well, excuse me," she added.

"I'm sorry. . .I didn't mean to—"

"Oh, that's all right," she said. "My name is Kim."

"I'm Sam."

"What brings you to this country club?"

He groaned. "I don't want to—" he couldn't continue speaking.

"All right. I'll leave you alone."

He stayed in the day room, dozing on and off, until dinnertime, when he shuffled down to the dining room. He sat down next to Frank.

"Welcome back," Frank said. "What brings you here this time?"

"Ugh."

"You're supposed to wait until you taste the food before you say that."

"I'll say it again when the food arrives."

When the dinner cart arrived, he didn't have the energy to stand up and get his tray. Frank brought it for him. On his tray was a chicken pot pie, overcooked peas and carrots, a small carton of milk, and a few sliced peaches. All he could stomach was the milk and the peaches. One of the aides brought him a menu with the selections for the following day. He listlessly began to fill it out. The selections for breakfast looked okay, so Sam ordered scrambled eggs, whole wheat toast, orange juice and coffee, but he found the selections for lunch and dinner particularly unpalatable, so he asked for a tuna sandwich for lunch and a burger with fries for dinner. Then he went back to his room, where he stripped down to his underwear and got under the covers. Thinking of Kelly, he tried to masturbate, but he couldn't get an erection, so he just lay there staring at the ceiling until he fell asleep.

As was the case before his hospitalization, Sam had no energy in the morning; later in the afternoon he felt somewhat better. Every morning before breakfast, the aides fought with him to try to force him to get up and have his vital signs taken. After a few days, Dr. Jackson told him, "If you don't co-operate with the aides and nurses, you're going to be here for a long time. You must get your vital signs taken in the dining room every morning, even if you get back in bed afterwards."

"If you insist."

When Sandy woke him up the next morning, he got up and walked to the dining room in his pajamas. On the way there, he fainted and fell on the floor. He tried to get up but couldn't. He lay there for several minutes until Kim found him there. Alarmed, she ran to the dining room to get Sandy, who helped him up, took him by the arm, and brought him to the dining room.

While Sam was getting his vital signs taken, Sandy went to the nurse's station, where he found a cane, which he brought to the dining room and gave to Sam. "If this happens again, we'll get you a walker," he told him.

Sam felt like getting back in bed right away, but he forced himself to eat a bit first. Then, with the cane to help him, he made it back to his room and lay down again.

At about four in the afternoon, he finally felt energetic enough to go to the OT room. He asked Edith if he could sit there without working on a project.

"Of course," she said.

Frank, Kim, and Jill were there, along with Linda, an attractive black woman in her twenties. Edith, who was good-natured as always, asked Sam whether she could tell the new patients about his talent.

"My talent?"

"Sam is a first-rate chess player," she said. "He's even taught chess professionally."

"Oh, could you teach me?" Kim asked him.

"Maybe when I'm feeling a little bit better," he said.

FOUR DAYS AFTER HE WAS ADMITTED, SAM'S MOTHER came to visit him in the late afternoon. She found him seated by himself in the day room.

"How are you feeling, honey?" she asked. "Any better?"

"I'm not feeling anything but fatigue. If only I could cry, at least I'd feel human again."

"Would you like me to talk to your doctor?"

"If you think. . . ."

"Let me see if she's here today."

She walked down to the nurse's station to talk to Isabel, whom she had met during Sam's previous hospitalization. "Is Dr. Jackson here today? I'd like to have a talk with her."

"Have you asked Sam whether he'd like you to see her?"

"It seems to be okay with him."

"She'll be in tomorrow," Isabel said. "I'll have her call you to set up an appointment."

The following afternoon, Dr. Jackson called Mrs. Kanter at home, and they made an appointment for Friday afternoon. Before talking to the doctor that day, she stopped by Sam's room to say hello. She found him lying there listlessly.

"I feel like I'm lying in my grave," he said when she asked how he was.

"I'm going to talk to Dr. Jackson," she said. "We'll do everything in our power to make you well again."

"Thank you," he replied.

When she saw the doctor, she asked, "What are his prospects?"

"Well, it can take two weeks or more for the antidepressant to take effect. In the meantime, we should keep him as active as possible. Depression is a self-perpetuating illness—the more he stays in bed, the more depressed he may become. I'd like you to visit him as much as possible, and when you do, try to get him up. I'll tell the nurses that it's okay for you to take him for a walk around the grounds. You can even do that now, if he's willing."

"Thank you so much."

"You're welcome."

Mrs. Kanter went back to Sam's room. "The doctor suggested that I take you for a walk around the grounds," she said. "Do you think you're up for it? It's a beautiful day."

He opened his mouth, but nothing came out.

"Please try," she said.

He forced himself to get up. With the cane in one hand and the other hand in hers, they went outside and sat on a bench in the garden, a very well-maintained space with freshly cut grass, beautiful flowers, and elegant shrubbery.

"Doesn't it feel better to be out in the sun?" she asked.

"I suppose."

After twenty minutes, they went back inside. Sam's mother left him in the day room.

"I'll come to see you at least twice a week," she said.

Sam managed to give her a faint smile.

Shortly after she left, Kim came into the day room.

"Your mother seems like a very good woman," she said.

"She is."

"How about giving me a chess lesson? Maybe it will take your mind off your problems."

"Not right now," Sam said. ". . .But if you want to stay and chat a bit, I don't mind."

"Well, that's already an improvement," Kim exclaimed.

"Why are *you* here?" he asked her. "You seem so normal."

"My parents think I'm a nymphomaniac."

"Is that an *illness?"*

"According to them it is. If you ask me, I just enjoy sex."

"How old are you."

"I just turned sixteen."

"Sixteen going on thirty?"

"No, just sixteen."

"Well, I don't mean to pry, but just how many men have you slept with?"

"I'm not going to answer that."

Sam laughed. *(What a cutie.)*

"If the truth be told, I've also made it with a few women."

Sam rolled his eyes. "Let's talk about something else," he said.

"What should we talk about?"

"Do you have any other interests besides sex?"

"I'm also a kleptomaniac."

"I see. Anything else?"

"Yes. I also have phobias."

"Such as?"

"I'm afraid of heights, and I'm afraid of riding in elevators."

"Well, a lot of people are afraid of things like that, but it doesn't mean that they have to be hospitalized."

"I know. Like I said, I'm only here because of my parents."

"You said you're a kleptomaniac. Have you ever stolen anything valuable?"

"Not really."

CHAPTER 20

SAM AND KIM STARTED SPENDING A LOT OF TIME together. After a few days, their doctors let them take walks around the grounds together. Before they went on their first walk together, Isabel told them, "Remember: no touching, no kissing."

"Don't worry," Sam said. "I'm not a cradle robber."

"Don't worry," Kim added. "Sam's much too immature for me."

Little by little, the medicine started to work. Sam went on walks with his mother or Kim, started a project in the OT room, and began attending group therapy, where he was surprisingly articulate.

After he had been on the ward for five weeks, he went on a day pass with his mother, who took him to the Frick collection, her favorite museum. Three days later, Dr. Jackson released him, suggesting that he stay with his mother for a week before returning home or attempting to work. Sam and Kim exchanged phone numbers and promised to stay in touch.

After staying with his mother for three days, Sam started to feel very bored, so he ignored Dr. Jackson's advice and returned to his apartment in the East Village. When his roommate asked him where he had been, he lied. "I was visiting my sister on the West Coast. I'm sorry I didn't tell you before I left."

As he had before he was hospitalized, he spent most days in bars or at the library, and his nights at French Roast. He usually got to bed at around 6:00 a.m. and rose at three or four in the afternoon.

One of the first things he did was visit Cindy at Karavas Place. She was delighted to see him. "Where've you been?" she asked.

"Nowhere special. What's new with you?"

"Well, for one thing, I lost my virginity."

"Oh, yeah? How was it?"

"Oh, all right."

"Are you in love?"

"Uh. . .I guess not."

"I've got news for you, Cindy. You don't lose your virginity the first time you have sex. You lose your virginity the first time you fall in love."

She looked at him blankly for a few seconds, then said, "I guess I'll find out what you mean when that happens."

"So who's the lucky guy?"

"Some nonentity."

"Anyone I know?"

"I'm not going to tell you that right now," she said. "Maybe you'll find out eventually."

"Hmm. A mystery."

Sam stayed in the bar till 2:00 a.m. before heading to French Roast. Brad, the film buff, was seated at a table by the window with a heavyset man in his sixties. "Hey, stranger," Brad said. "Where've you been?"

"On the West Coast, visiting my sister."

"Welcome back. . . . Have you two met?"

"I don't think so," Sam said.

"Michael, Sam. Sam, Michael."

Michael was a retired philosophy professor and a very good painter. Unlike many academics, his knowledge wasn't confined to his area of specialization; he could talk with erudition about any subject imaginable. When Sam told him that he was friends with Ted Gold, he was surprised to discover that, not only had Michael and Ted known each other for over twenty years, but that they had been in group shows together many times.

Michael had what seemed to be an inexhaustible knowledge of art history. As a young man he had exhibited with some famous painters, like Arshile Gorky and Paul Klee. When Sam asked him if he would show him some of his work, Michael said, "You'll see it eventually."

Sam started sitting at Michael's table every night. During their conversations, Michael would suggest books on a variety of subjects for his new protégé to read.

Sam had never met anyone with Michael's intellectual prowess, so he greedily absorbed everything that he taught him. He started by brushing up on the history of psychoanalysis, from Freud to Eric Fromm and Carl Rogers. He was especially impressed by Carl Jung, whom he studied in depth. In the field of literature, Michael's favorites were Joyce, Mann, and Proust. Sam had already read most of Joyce's fiction, but he knew nothing of Proust, and among Mann's works he had only read *Death in Venice*. He devoured *The Magic Mountain, Dr. Faustus*, and *Swann's Way*. In philosophy, Michael was an expert on Heidegger and Husserl; he had done his doctoral dissertation on phenomenology.

Sam started spending four hours every day reading at the Jefferson Market Library; on nights when Michael was absent from French Roast, he sat in the restaurant and read all night.

When Michael was on his late-night schedule, he would wake up in the early evening and have a meal at The Sage Diner, which was near his apartment in Sunnyside, Queens. After that, he'd take a cab into the city and go to a multiplex theater in the downtown area, where he'd watch two, sometimes even three, movies, sneaking from theater to theater after seeing the movie he had paid for. He didn't seem to care whether the movie had any artistic merit, or indeed any merit whatsoever; he saw everything that was available. After leaving the multiplex, he would head to Vaselka in the East Village, where he'd spend an hour with Ted Gold and some of his other painter friends. After his colleagues had left to turn in, he'd take a leisurely walk over to French Roast, where he'd sit at a table with Sam, Brad, and sometimes some of the other AAs.

Although he knew that Sam was acquainted with Ted, Michael never invited him to Vaselka, or even mentioned that Ted was there; for some reason he wanted to keep his painter friends separate from his French Roast ones. The only one of his painter friends who occasionally came to French Roast was Angela, an elderly woman who, as a young girl, had been friends with William de Kooning and Richard Debenkorn. Angela thought that Michael's artwork was on the same level as the work of these luminaries. Michael, of course, agreed. One night he told Sam, "I like looking at my paintings better than looking at de Kooning's."

(But do you think you're a better painter than de Kooning?) Sam never asked that question out loud.

In the '50s, Michael had illustrated a magazine called *Jugin*, which had poems by the beat poets Allen Ginsberg, Gregory Corso, Lawrence Ferlinghetti, and others. One evening he brought one of the magazine issues as a present for Sam.

"Hold onto this," he said. "It's going to be worth something one day, if it isn't already."

After they'd been friends for about four months, Michael invited Sam to his apartment in Queens. Before they hailed a cab, they stopped at a deli near French Roast, where Michael bought ice cream, chocolate bars, and two half gallons of Coca-Cola. He was overweight to begin with, and a heavy smoker as well.

(You're going to kill yourself if you keep this up.)

Michael's apartment was a mess. There were hundreds of cigarette butts and dozens of Coke bottles on the floor. His paintings were all over the place in seeming disarray, although he claimed that he knew where everything was.

(Boy, if my apartment looked like this, I wouldn't show it to anyone.)

Michael's favorite subject, at least for the past several years, had been Lake George, as seen from Bolton Landing. He tried to go there at least once a year, usually accompanied by Seth Baumgarten, one of his former philosophy students. His Bolton Landing paintings had bright colors, with trees, islands, and boats, all with an anthropomorphic quality, surrounded by swirling blue water. Sam was impressed.

Little by little, Sam began to confide in him. Although Michael's dissertation had been in philosophy, he had earned enough credits for a second Ph.D. in psychology. He listened to Sam's story with interest. When he asked him whether he had ever been treated for depression, Sam said he occasionally visited Dr. Brown.

"What approach does he take?" Michael inquired.

"I guess you'd call it insight-oriented therapy."

"Do you find it helpful?"

"Somewhat."

"Tell me," Michael said, "have you ever heard of Albert Ellis?"

"No."

"Well, I've read several of his books, and I find them quite helpful when *I* get depressed. If you like, I'll lend you one of them."

The following night, Michael brought *The New Guide to Rational Living*, Ellis' most famous book. After reading the entire text on Monday, Sam told him, "I can see how this could be very useful. How can I find out more?"

"Actually, Ellis has his own Institute on East 65th. All his books are there, and if you want to join one of his groups or go for individual therapy, I think he has a sliding scale."

Sam decided to pay for one private session with Dr. Ellis to see how he worked. The doctor was quite a character. He sat in a comfortable armchair in his stocking feet for up to twelve hours a day while both his private patients and his groups filed in and out of his office. Sam told him what he'd been going through, and that he had read one of his books. After listening to his story, Ellis said, "I think there's some self-downing going on here."

"Well, I *am* very hard on myself."

"We need to cure you of that."

"Why? I think being tough on myself is a good thing. It makes me work harder, makes me treat others better, and makes me a better person in many ways."

"I think it contributes to your depression. You're making lots of demands on yourself, and every time you don't live up to those egotistical demands, you put yourself down. And putting yourself down isn't just bad because it makes you more depressed—it's also unethical."

"Unethical?"

"Well, it's unethical to put others down, isn't it?"

"Yes."

"Then it's equally unethical to put yourself down. It's exactly the same thing. Why should you treat yourself worse than you treat others?"

". . .I never thought of that."

Ellis recommended another book for Sam to read: *How to Stubbornly Refuse to Make Yourself Miserable About Anything, Yes Anything.* Sam purchased a copy and read it cover to cover; then he went over to French Roast to join the AAs.

Most of the AAs were a little bit off in one way or another, but one of them, Ned Diamond, was perhaps the strangest person Sam had ever met. He was full of self-pity; he thought that life had dealt him one bad blow after another. Michael seldom sat at the same table with him; he couldn't stand what he called Ned's "narcissism."

When Michael was in French Roast, Sam always sat at his table; but when his mentor was absent, he often interrupted his reading sessions to sit with Ned, whom he found fascinating, if only in a pathological way.

Ned was a rock guitarist and an amateur draftsman. He claimed that several of his compositions had been stolen by other artists, who had made a ton of money recording them. He also claimed that, whenever he auditioned at a rock club, he was inevitably rejected on the grounds that he was too weird.

(How is it possible to be too weird?)

Another story Ned told was that, when Son of Sam, the .44- caliber killer, was wanted for serial killings in the '70s, he had been arrested by the police and tortured until he confessed, while the real killer remained at large.

Sam found Ned's artwork to be very disturbing, too. His drawings were abstract, but they suggested knives, razor wire, and medieval armor.

(Boy, if you ever took a Rorschach test, they'd put you away for sure.)

Some of the AAs at French Roast were chess players. One of them, a bike messenger named Claude, challenged Sam to a game. Sam beat him so easily that, when they played again, he gave him rook-odds. Michael had played a bit as a young man; he enjoyed watching the game so much that, when he got up to go to the men's room, he said, "Wait! Don't move until I come back!"

When it came to chess, the roles were reversed; Sam became Michael's mentor. He recommended several books for him to read, among them Reuben Fine's *The Ideas Behind the Chess Openings*, Aron Nimzovich's *My System*, and *Pandolfini's Endgame Course*. He said, "This must be the only subject I know more about than you do."

Michael replied, "That could change." After a few seconds, he asked, "Have you ever been to college?"

"Yes, I have a degree in English Literature from Rutgers."

"Then why don't you get a master's degree and become a high school English teacher? The city is always looking for teachers, and I think they pay pretty well."

"Frankly, Michael, I don't know if I'll ever be stable enough to work full time."

"With Ellis's help and the right medication, I think you'd have a good chance. Besides, an education is an end in itself. As a philosophy professor, I only used a fraction of what I know."

"No matter how much I study, I'll never know more than a fraction of what you do."

"Well, think it over. You don't have to start right away."

At that point, Sam had only three private students at The Shop. Aside from that, he had no income. He reluctantly decided to apply for government assistance. Trudy, one of Ellis's assistants, had a master's in Social Work. He called her and asked her what kind of help might be available.

She said, "You have two possibilities. Either you could apply for Supplemental Social Security, which is available for people below the poverty level, or, alternatively, you'd probably be eligible for Social Security Disability, because you have a bona fide illness."

"It's funny," Sam said. "I never really think about myself as being ill."

"Oh, but you are. You'd better face it."

"Well, I'd better get something. I'm two months behind on my rent."

The following Monday, Sam called the Social Security office. He had to sit by the phone for twenty minutes before an operator picked up. She asked him, "What's your Social Security number?"

"I can't remember."

"Well, find out and call again."

He cursed under his breath. *(I have the feeling that this is going to be an ordeal.)*

He searched his apartment for half an hour and finally found his Social Security card in a dresser with his passport and his birth certificate. Then he called the office again. This time he waited half an hour before reaching an operator, who gave him an appointment for 1:00 p.m. on a Friday afternoon the following month. She told him to bring proof of residence, a rent receipt, proof of income, his tax receipts for the previous year, and a doctor's note. He told her that he had no income at that time—his chess lessons were off the books. He immediately called Dr. Berkun and asked him to put a letter in the mail, certifying that he was ill and under his care.

Three days before his appointment, he started going to bed at midnight, so that he'd be sure to get to his appointment on time. Because he had been staying up all night for months, he found it extremely difficult to turn his clock around; he lay in bed for hours before falling asleep.

On the appointed day, he got out of bed at noon and, without time to shower or shave, made it to his appointment at 12:55. His interviewer was a surly middle-aged woman who obviously hated her job. She made him feel like a criminal who was trying to rob the government. After he convinced her that he was really ill, she made copies of all his documents, returned the originals to him, and told him that it would take a month or two for a decision to be made. If he was approved, she told him, he'd receive a Social Security check once a month, and a Medicare card as well.

After his appointment, Sam went home and took a nap. When he awoke, he called his mother, told her what has transpired, and asked her if she could help him out with his back rent and lend him some money until the checks started coming. She asked him:

"Would you like to move in with me until you have some income? At least you wouldn't have to spend money on food."

He replied:

"I appreciate the offer, but right now I need the stimulation the city gives me. If I were in Jersey, I know I'd spend all my time in bed. I promise you—whatever you lend me, I'll pay you back in full as soon as I'm working again."

At two in the morning, he ambled over to French Roast to see Michael. This time the conversation turned to art history. In Michael's apartment there were hundreds of art books, most of which were about modern artists. He felt that the 20th century, or at least the first half, was one of the greatest eras in art history.

"As great as the Renaissance?"

"The Renaissance is overrated." Michael said.

(How could it be overrated?)

"What about the second half of the century?"

"Not as stellar as the first half, but there's some great painters in the second half as well."

"I think the arts are in a crisis," Sam said. "People like John Cage in music and Jackson Pollock in painting took things as far as they could go, and nobody's really sure what to do now."

"I disagree. I think artists like Mondrian and Malevich took things farther than Pollock did, and after them there were still great artists like Beckmann and Picasso."

"I guess you have a point," Sam said. "But I still think this is a confused time in art history. I like Jasper Johns, but after you mention him and a few others, it starts getting picky."

"It's funny that you should mention Jasper Johns. I like the way he handles paint, but aside from that, he doesn't do much for me."

"Well then, who do you like?"

"There are plenty of painters in the city just doing what they do. I could give you a list if you want—and if there's no Picasso right now, I wouldn't worry; there will be sooner or later."

"What about Pop Art?"

"Actually, people like Andy Warhol and Roy Lichtenstein weren't without talent, but the effect they had on the arts was devastating."

"You mean that you no longer have to be a cultured person to be an artist?"

"Precisely."

"What about conceptual art?"

Michael sidestepped the question. "I think that's in a separate arena."

"To me it's all art," Sam said. I just follow the layman's criteria: Do I like looking at it? Would I want it in my apartment?"

"Sometimes I like looking at Mickey Mouse," Michael said dryly, "but I don't consider it an art experience."

"There are some people who would disagree with you about that."

"Are you one of them?"

"Not really. I'm just playing the devil's advocate."

"The devil doesn't need another advocate. He already has the curators at the Whitney on his side."

CHAPTER 21

At The Chess Shop, Sam had a new student, a stunning young brunette named Lola who was an art student at Cooper Union. She lived in an apartment right above The Shop with her boyfriend Nigel, an aspiring poet in his twenties who worked as a film editor. Lola had very little money, so she asked Sam whether he would like to give her chess lessons in exchange for a painting. He took a look at her slides and immediately agreed. He chose a portrait of a slender woman with a disturbed expression on her face. To the left of her was a wagon wheel and, in the background, several dilapidated apartment buildings. The painting created a powerful psychological effect.

After her first lesson, she invited Sam up to her apartment. Both the living room and the bedroom were full of her paintings, most of them as strong as the one he'd chosen. He was astounded.

After he had known Lola for a few weeks, he invited her to French Roast to meet Michael, who looked at her slides and said, "I think you have a lot of potential." Didactic as always, he also made some suggestions right away. "I think you should work more into the negative space, and you need to hold surface better—some of the images seen pasted onto the canvas."

Lola didn't respond, but Sam could see that she wasn't happy about being lectured. She never spent much time at French Roast after that night.

Little by little, Sam started falling in love with her. She was very busy at school, so they only saw each other once a week when they met for her lesson. At first, he kept his feelings to himself. *(I'm almost old enough to be her father. Do I really want to rob the cradle? Besides, she's in love with Nigel; any attempt to win her over would be futile. Maybe in the long run. . . ?)*

One of the chess players was a homeless man named Scott, who spent countless hours at The Chess Shop. Looking at his troubled face, Lola could see into his soul. She asked him if he would sit for her in her apartment. She worked very quickly; within a week, she had done four portraits of him, all first rate. When she showed them to Sam, he was flabbergasted. After seeing them once, he never looked at Scott the same way. Or at Lola.

Although Sam was burning with desire for her, he tried to hide it, but of course she knew it as women usually do. One beautiful fall day, when the two of them were sitting in front of The Shop after her lesson, Jim Smith approached them and said, "You know he loves you, don't you?"

Lola smiled.

Jim continued, "He's just biding his time, waiting for you to get tired of Nigel."

Sam was incensed. "What do you know about love, you old lecher?" he demanded. "This little child's my heartstrings. I kiss her little foot. I don't care if she has a boyfriend or a husband or a harem, and I don't care if I never make it to first base. Of course the fact that she's beautiful is part of it, but that's all you'll ever understand, you creep!"

Jim raised his hands as if Sam were pointing a gun at him. "Touché, touché!" he exclaimed.

Sam abruptly left The Shop and strode to Washington Square Park. He was surprised and pleased to see Freddy there, playing speed chess with Dr. Li. There was a big crowd of kibitzers around the table, many of them making side bets.

In between games, Sam tapped Freddy on the shoulder. "Hey, *paysan*!" he said.

"Oh, it's you!" Freddy exclaimed. "I was going to call you. Listen, I'm going to play for an hour or two. Can we get together later?"

"Sure. Why don't you meet me at The Shop at ten tonight?"

"Solid."

Sam bought a falafel at Mahmoun's and made his way to the library, where he borrowed two books Michael had recommended—Van Gogh's letters and Gulot's *Life with Picasso*. He sat outside Café Reggio and read until ten, then headed over to The Shop to see his old friend. They strolled to the Café Borgia 2 on Prince Street, where they were served by a beautiful Danish girl. Naturally, Freddy came on to her. "Can I take you to dinner on Friday night?"

"Honestly, I don't think my boyfriend would like that."

"He doesn't have to know."

She looked into his eyes for a few seconds, then whispered, "Give me your phone number."

When she left their table, Freddy said, "I love Scandinavian women. They have no hang-ups about sex the way Italian women do."

"*Va subito*!" Sam said.

They went back to The Shop and played about ten speed games. Freddy gave Sam five minutes to two and still won every game.

"You're a sharp as ever," Sam said.

When The Shop closed, they went to The Continental Divide, ordered a pitcher of Budweiser, and sat at a table in the back.

"You know what grosses me out?" Freddy said. "A woman jerking off."

"Why?"

"Any woman can get laid any time she wants. The thought of a woman lying at home jerking off disgusts me."

"I never thought about it, but if I did, I think it might actually turn me on."

Freddy looked at him uncomprehendingly. "You're little weird, aren't you?"

"Aren't we all?"

Freddy shrugged. "In one way or another."

As usual, Sam went to French Roast late that night, hoping Michael would be there. He waited until 3:00 a.m. before deciding to call it a night. When he got home, he found a message on his answering machine from Kim, his friend from the Leonard Pavilion. The following afternoon, after having breakfast at the Odessa Diner, he returned her call. "How've you been doing?" he asked.

"Okay," she said. ". . .But I'm not getting along with my parents. I'm going to have to find my own place."

"What are you doing later?"

"Nothing," she said. "I have no life."

"Would you like to have dinner with me?"

"Just say where and when."

They met at Susie's on Bleecker Street, where they ordered Peking duck. She filled him in on what she'd been up to since being released from the Leonard Pavilion.

She had gotten together with an old boyfriend with whom she spent most of her time taking what she called "recreational drugs."

"Marijuana?"

"Yes."

"Cocaine?"

"Right again."

"Anything else?"

"Heroin."

"My, God, you're going to kill yourself!"

"That's what I'm hoping for."

"Kim, don't say that."

"My parents threw me out two weeks ago, and I've been staying with Peter ever since, basically being stoned non-stop."

"I don't think you should be living with him—he must be a bad influence on you."

"Sam, if I didn't have him to put me up, I'd be on the street."

"Well, why don't you stay with me until you can afford your own place?"

As soon as he heard himself speaking these words, he instantly regretted it.

"Do you mean it?" Kim asked him.

"Yeah, why not?" he said with a sigh.

"You're a lifesaver."

"But if you're going to stay with me, you've got to promise that you won't take anything stronger than marijuana."

She hesitated for a moment. "I promise."

They walked over to his apartment, where he told his roommate, "She's going to be staying with us for little while."

"No problem,"Yong said.

The first night, Sam told her to sleep on a futon in his room; he thought that, if he made a pass at her, she might think he was taking advantage of the situation. Full of desire, he watched her sleep for two hours before dropping off to sleep himself. When he awoke at 1:00 p.m., he found her in the kitchen, washing some dishes that Yong had left in the sink.

The two of them went to the Odessa for brunch; Sam paid, although he was almost as destitute as she was. While they ate, they filled each other in on what they had been doing since their hospital stay. He told her about Michael Schwartz and how much Albert Ellis was helping him. She told him that, after weeks of nonstop arguments between her and her parents, she had gone on a rampage and basically destroyed their house, smashing all the windows, overturning all the furniture, and breaking some of their favorite art objects. Sam was alarmed. *(You're not going to do the same thing to me, are you?)*

After they spent two hours together, he went to the library and she went to Tompkins Square Park to smoke a joint. They agreed to meet later at French Roast. At the library, Sam borrowed Einstein and Enfield's *The Evolution of Physics*, another recommendation of Michael's. Then he went around the corner to The Peacock Café and sat at a table by the window. He quickly read through the first two chapters on Newton's theories and some of the developments after Newton, but when he reached the chapters on relativity and quantum mechanics, he found them rough going. *(I'm going to have to ask Michael to explain this to me.)*

A few hours later, he gave up and walked over to Washington Square Park. He was surprised to find Lola there drawing Lovey Jenkins, his opponent, and a group of kibitzers watching the game. Her drawing, though realistic in part, made everyone look either depressed or anguished.

"Do you want to take a break?" Sam asked her.

"Just give me ten minutes, and I'll come have a coffee with you."

He joined the crowd watching the game. The position on the board was so complicated, he had no idea what was going on. Eventually things clarified, though, and he could see that Lovey was winning. When he checkmated his opponent, he had less than twenty seconds left on his clock.

Sam and Lola sat at a table in Café Reggio, where he told her about Kim. "I'd like to meet her," Lola said. "I used to take a lot of drugs myself, and I think I might be able to help her."

"Can you come to French Roast at two in the morning? She'll be there."

"No, because I don't want to see that pedant Michael."

"He's not a pedant. He used to be a college professor, and it just comes naturally for him to teach people things."

"Well, I don't like people telling me how to paint."

"I know. When I see Kim, I'll ask her if she wants to meet you."

He walked her home, then looked inside The Chess Shop to see who was there. There were only two players there, which didn't surprise him—it was such a lovely evening. He chatted with Ahmed for a while, telling him about Michael Schwartz and all the great books he had recommended.

Ahmed said, "You should get a master's. What future is there just teaching chess?"

"That's what Michael says."

At 2:00 a.m., when Sam got to French Roast, he saw neither Michael nor Kim, so he sat at a table with Rick Danger, a well-known comedian who was one of the AAs.

Rick greeted him with a flourish. "Hail, lofty chess player."

"Hail, lofty comedian."

"Have you seen my family crest? Penis rampant on a field of pussy."

"We must have the same lineage."

An hour later, Michael came in, but there was still no sight of Kim. Sam said to Rick, "I need to be alone with Michael, guys, so I'm going to move to another table."

After a few pleasantries, Sam told him about Kim, their hospital stay together, her problems with her parents, and her drug habit.

"Sounds like a hard case."

"I'm putting her up until she's back on her feet."

". . .Are you sure that's a good idea?"

"No, I'm not. I asked her without thinking about it first."

As these words were leaving his lips, Kim appeared. Sam introduced them.

"Hi, Michael," she said. "Sam told me all about you."

"So you know the worst?"

"He told me that you're one of the most brilliant men he's ever met."

"Only one of them?" Michael said. "Who are the others?"

They all laughed.

Sam decided not to talk about Kim's problems unless she brought them up herself. Instead, he mentioned the problems he was having with *The Evolution of Physics*. Michael said, "There's another book called *The Universe and Dr. Einstein* that might help you understand some of his ideas. I don't remember the author, but you should be able to find it at the library or in a bookstore."

Sam and Kim stayed at French Roast until dawn. On the way home, he said, "I thought you were going to confide in Michael."

"I think I'll wait until I know him better."

When they entered the apartment, she asked him, "Can I sleep in your bed tonight?"

Sam hesitated, then said, "I don't think we should—"

"I don't either, although I will if you want to. I just want to be held tonight."

They lay down together, and Kim put her head on his chest. "Will you sing to me?" she asked.

"You're such a child."

He gently sang Bob Dylan's "Lay Lady Lay" to her. She yawned deeply and fell asleep with a smile on her face.

When he awoke, there was no sign of her, so after eating breakfast at Odessa, he went to Tompkins Square to look for her. He found her sitting on a bench in the middle of the park, smoking a joint with a grungy young man in his twenties.

"Sam, this is my friend Peter," she said.

"Pleased to meet you."

"Thanks for putting her up," Peter said. He looked searchingly at Sam, evidently trying to ascertain whether he was sleeping with her.

"Don't worry," Sam reassured him. "She's in good hands."

When Peter offered him the joint, he declined with a wave of his hand. "I haven't smoked a reefer in ten years," he said.

"I've tried to quit a dozen times," Peter confessed. "I can't get through the day without it."

"I have a friend who used a lot of drugs when she was younger. I'd like both of you to meet her, because I think she might be able to help you." He didn't mention that he had already told Lola about her.

"To tell the truth, right now I don't want to discuss my problems with a stranger," said Peter. "Maybe down the road a bit."

"What about you?" Sam asked, turning to Kim.

"Yeah, I'd like to meet her," she said. "Then I'll decide if I want to talk to her."

"Just like with Michael?"

"Believe it or not, I'm a little shy."

"You certainly weren't shy with me when *we* first met."

"Well, that's different. We were in the hospital together."

"All right. I'll give you her phone number, and you can get in touch with her yourself."

"No, I want you to be there when I meet her."

"Okay, then we'll call her later."

"I've got to go to Avenue D to get my fix," Peter said. "I'll see you around."

"Do you have any plans for this afternoon?" Sam asked her.

"Well, you know what a busy social calendar I have. I'm having tea with Lady Astor at four."

He smiled. "Let's go for a walk."

They made their way to East River Park, where they sat near the water, watching the boats go by. Two women on the deck of a large sailboat waved to them.

"They must think you're cute," Kim said.

"Maybe they think *you're* cute."

"Oh they *know* I'm cute."

"You're cuter than Cindy Crawford."

"No way!"

"*Yes*, way."

"Then how come I'm not on the cover of *Vogue*?"

"I didn't say you're more *beautiful* than Cindy, just *cuter*."

"I see."

"To tell the truth, the supermodels don't really turn me on. They have beautiful faces, but most of them are too tall and skinny for me."

"Do I turn you on?"

Sam paused for a few seconds. "That's an understatement."

"Well, then, let's make out, Sam. What are we waiting for?"

He threw his arms around her neck, and they kissed as if their lives depended on it.

"Let's go home," Kim said. "I can't wait another minute."

"Neither can I." *(I know this won't be right.)*

They crossed the FDR Drive and ran to Sam's building. As soon as they were inside the apartment, they tore off their clothes and made love on the floor of the living room.

After they were finished, Kim began to sob. "Oh, Lord, please let me die now," she said.

"Live. Live and be happy." *(This may end in disaster.)*

Sam gently rocked her from side to side until she fell asleep, then quietly extricated himself from her embrace, lay down on his bed, and tried to sleep himself. He lay awake for hours, imagining scenarios of every kind. (Peter finds out about them and shoots him; Kim leaves him and goes back to Peter; Kim dies of a drug overdose; etc.)

CHAPTER 22

AT 3:00 A.M., HE WAS STILL AWAKE, so he quietly left the apartment and walked over to French Roast. He found Michael sitting at a table with Brad, the film buff, talking about Orson Welles, Brad's favorite director. He joined them, but he was so distracted that he had trouble following the conversation.

Michael sensed that something was wrong and tried to draw him in. "Who's *your* favorite director?"

Sam forced himself to talk. "I don't know if I could pick one."

"Well then, how about your top five?"

"That's a tough one too, but Hitchcock would certainly be a candidate. Of the foreign directors, Fellini would be a possibility. Aside from that. . . ." He closed his eyes. "Please excuse me for a minute."

He went to the men's room, where he sat down on the toilet, held his head in his hands, and cried until he felt somewhat better. *(As bad as it is, grief is better than depression.)*

He went back to the table, where the three of them talked about film until seven in the morning, then went their separate ways. At home, he found Kim in the kitchen, making french toast.

"From French Roast to french toast," he said.

"My, how eloquent."

Sam hugged her from behind and bit her on the neck. "I want to suck your blood," he murmured.

Kim giggled. "I've decided that I want to meet Lola."

"Alone or with me?"

"I don't know. . .I guess with you."

"It's too early to call her now. Let's wait a few hours."

"What should we do in the meantime?" Kim asked him.

"Let's go for a walk again."

"Where to?"

"Have you ever been to Riverside Park?"

"No."

"Then let's go there."

They walked over to Seventh Avenue, took the 1 train to 72nd Street, and crossed the park to the river, where they sat on a bench and watched the boats go by. He told her about David, how they used to walk everywhere together, and that David was no longer speaking to him.

"That's too bad," she said.

"Yeah," he muttered under his breath.

"That's happened to me. Sometimes you think you've bonded with someone, then all of a sudden they're out of your life."

Sam kissed her. "You're a wise old owl," he said.

"Everything I know, I've learned the hard way."

"That makes two of us."

They found a pay phone and called Lola. Sam told her, "Kim wants to meet you."

"Good. Why don't the two of you stop by my place at 11:00 tonight?"

"Terrific."

"What now?" Kim asked.

"Why don't we go to a museum?"

"That's a great idea. I've never been to a museum."

"You've never been to a *museum?*"

"I'm ashamed to say so, but it's true."

"Well, why don't we walk over to The Met?"

They crossed Central Park arm in arm. "Do you have a favorite painter?" he asked.

"I don't know that many of them, but my mom has a book of paintings by Monet, which I've loved since I was twelve."

"The Met has a great collection of Monets."

He took her straight to the Impressionist room.

"*Wow,*" she whispered when she saw the Monets.

"Which is your favorite?"

"I think I like the Rouen Cathedral the most."

"What else would you like to see?"

"Why don't you show me some of your favorites?"

He showed her Rembrandts, El Grecos, and Cézannes. "I think you're going to make an art lover out of me," she said.

"Even if that's all I do, it'll be a big accomplishment."

AFTER AN HOUR THERE, THEY CROSSED the park again, bought some bread, cheese, and wine at Zabar's, headed for the Sheep's Meadow, and had a picnic.

When they finished, he lay on his back and she put her head on his chest.

"I think I'm falling in love with you," she said.

Sam didn't answer. *(Oh, no.)*

"I'm going to the library for a few hours" he said. "Why don't we meet at The Chess Shop at 11:00? Then we can drop in on Lola."

When Sam arrived at The Shop, he found her sitting outside. "Are you ready?" he asked.

"I'm a little nervous."

"I can understand that. Opening up to people always makes me feel very vulnerable. But Lola is a good woman, and everything you say will be safe with her."

"Okay. Let's go."

Since her last lesson, Lola had dyed her hair blue. "You look cute," Sam said to her.

"I know."

"This is my friend Kim."

"What's cooking, Kim?"

"Oh, not much."

"Is Sam taking care of you?"

"Better than my parents ever did."

"So. . .he says you have a habit."

"Well, I did have more than one habit, but Sam's been giving me some tough love, and since I moved in with him, I haven't taken anything stronger than pot."

"That's great! Do you think you'll be able to keep it up?"

"I don't know."

"I'll tell you what. Whenever you have the urge to do some heavy drugs, call me, and I'll try to talk you out of it. And if you *do* take drugs, call me right away."

"Okay."

"Please. Because I've been near death more than once."

"Okay."

"So. . .what should we talk about?"

"Why don't you show Kim your slides?" Sam suggested. "She's becoming an art lover."

"To see all my slides would take more than three hours. I've been painting since I was eight."

"Then why don't you show us some of your most recent work?"

Lola showed them a series of paintings that she had done of her boyfriend, Nigel. "These are the ones that got me into Cooper Union."

"Amazing," Kim said.

"Isn't she a genius?"

"Flattery will get you everywhere."

"Everywhere?"

"Well, everywhere within reason."

SAM AND KIM TOOK THEIR TIME walking home. On the way, she said, "You're in love with Lola, aren't you?"

"Is it so obvious?" he asked.

"That's okay. What man in his right mind wouldn't fall in love with her?"

Sam gave her a big hug. "You're so generous," he said.

"Oh, I love you, and you love her, and she loves Nigel."

"And Nigel?"

"Does he deserve her?"

"I've only met him once or twice, but he seems like a good man."

"He'd better be."

When they got home, they went straight to bed. Kim fell asleep almost instantly. Sam lay awake for hours, mulling over their situation. *(Oh, what a mess this is.)*

When he woke up at 1:00 p.m., she wasn't in the apartment, so once again he went to Tompkins Square Park to look for her. She wasn't there either. *(I hope she isn't back with Peter.)*

Sam walked to the library, borrowed a Faulkner novel, and went to The

Peacock to read. He was pleased to find Inez there. "I haven't seen you in a long time," he said. "What have you been up to?"

"I'm at Julliard now, studying voice and piano."

"That's great! Are you still singing at the Amato Opera?"

"Yes, in fact I'm performing as Nanetta in *Falstaff* Saturday night."

"Wow! I'll be sure to buy a ticket."

"You're so supportive," she said.

"So what are you working on at Julliard?"

"Vocally, I'm focusing mostly on Mozart. My voice teacher doesn't think I'm ready for anything heavier than that."

"What about on piano?"

"I'm working on Beethoven's 'Appasionata,' Bach's *Italian Concerto*, and some *études* by Chopin."

"I'd love to hear you play sometime."

"Well, I don't really have anything prepared right now, but when I do a recital, I'll definitely invite you."

"I'd be honored."

"Right now I've got to go home and practice, but if you come on Saturday night, let's hang out afterwards."

"Solid."

Sam went to a phone booth and called home to see if Kim was there. No one answered. *(Don't be worried yet.)* Then he went to The Chess Shop, where he found his old friends Ben and Rafael playing speed chess. He joined them and they played three-way until The Shop closed at midnight, then they went to Rafi's apartment on Bleecker Street, sat on the floor, and continued to play until 3:00 a.m., when Sam left them and headed to French Roast. Michael Schwartz was there, smoking and reading the *New York Review of Books.* "Come and join me," he said.

"By all means."

This time the conversation turned to jazz.

"I don't really like jazz after the swing era," Michael said.

"You don't like Bebop?"

"No. I find it too cerebral."

"Cerebral? John Coltrane is cerebral? Miles Davis is cerebral?"

"Well, there are exceptions, but in general I don't like what was done in that era."

"What *do* you like?"

"Benny Goodman, Louis Armstrong, Ella Fitzgerald—but only when she sings the words, not when she scat sings."

"Hmm. What else?"

"Bing Crosby, Cole Porter, Frank Sinatra. . . ."

"Well, I like Crosby and Porter, but I think Frank Sinatra is nothing but white bread."

"*De gustibus non disputandum*," Michael said, but Sam could sense that his comment had angered him.

Suddenly, Lola ran into the restaurant, caught her breath, and said, "Kim overdosed on heroin!"

Sam shot up. "Oh, my God! Where is she?"

"She's at St. Vincent's, in a coma!"

"Oh, my God. Can I go visit her?"

"They don't want any visitors just yet."

"What are they going to do?"

"They're thinking of giving her shock therapy."

"Oh, my God! How—how did you find her?"

"She called me as she was starting to fade out. I called an ambulance, but by the time they got there, she was already unconscious."

"Oh, Lord. Please let her be all right," Sam said. "Please, please, Lord." He broke down and began to sob.

"Sam, pull yourself together," Lola told him. "You've got to be strong now."

"She's right," Michael said. "Why don't you go home and get some sleep?"

"I won't be able to sleep," Sam said flatly. "I'd rather just stay here with you."

"I'm going home," Lola said. "Call me in the morning, and we'll both go visit her."

Michael tried to distract Sam by talking about the current exhibits in New York's great museums. "At The Met, there's a Matisse exhibit."

"What else is worth seeing?"

"At the Modern, there's a Max Beckman exhibit."

"Wow. What else?"

"At the Guggenheim, they've got Kandinsky."

"Great. Maybe I'll see all of them."

Sam stayed with Michael until nine in the morning, then called Lola and ran over to St. Vincent's. He told the guard at the front desk that he was Kim's boyfriend, so that he could see her before visiting hours. He found her awake, but obviously she was severely depressed.

"How are you?" he asked her.

"Lousy," she whispered in a barely audible voice.

"Do your parents know you're here?"

"No."

"Can I tell them?"

Kim hesitated. "I guess so," she said weakly.

"What's their number?"

"I can't remember."

"Well, where do they live?"

"In Upper Saddle River."

"In Jersey?"

"Yes."

"I'll look them up in the phonebook."

Lola entered the room. "Hey, Super Kim," she said.

"Hey."

"We love you, Kim. Please don't ever do this again."

"Uh, I'll try. . . ."

"Do you want us to tell your parents that you're here?"

"I already told Sam—" she began to weep.

"Cry, honey," Lola said. "Everything will be all right."

"Stay with her," Sam told Lola. "I'm going to call her parents."

He went to the nurse's station and asked them if he could use their phone. He dialed information, found the number, and called.

A woman picked up. "Mrs. Park?"

". . . Yes?"

"I'm Sam, a friend of Kim's. She asked me to tell you that she's in St. Vincent's Hospital in Manhattan."

"My goodness. Why?"

Sam caught his breath. "She overdosed on heroin."

"Oh, my God!"

"Please try to stay calm, Mrs. Park. It looks like she's going to be okay."

"Can you stay with her until I arrive?"

"Of course."

"Just let me call my husband, and I'll be there soon as possible."

He went back to the room, where he found Lola singing a lullaby to her.

Kim had stopped crying, but she still looked miserable. They tried to cheer her up by telling her dirty jokes. They couldn't make her laugh, but after three or four jokes, they did elicit a faint smile.

"See, you're smiling," Lola said. "You're on your way back, and things can only get better."

"Thank you," the girl whispered.

When her mother got there, she found the three of them chatting pleasantly together.

"How are you, honey?" she asked her.

Kim started to cry again. "I'm sorry," she said. "I'm so sorry."

"It's okay, honey. Everything will be all right."

They hugged each other tightly. Then Mrs. Park said, "Let me go talk to the nurses."

She asked them whether she could take Kim home to Upper Saddle River.

The head nurse said, "Since it may have been a suicide attempt, she has to be evaluated by a psychiatrist before we can release her."

"When will that be?"

"Maybe as early as tomorrow morning."

When Mrs. Park returned to Kim's room, Sam asked, "Would you like us to leave you alone with her?"

"If you don't mind."

As they prepared to leave, she said, "I can't thank you enough for all that you've done for her."

"What else could we do?" Lola replied.

Sam walked Lola to her apartment on Tompkins Street, then stopped at the Village Corner to see if anyone he knew was there. A couple of the old regulars were, and they had a new barmaid as well. He asked her if Valerie was still an employee.

"No," she said. "Apparently I was hired to replace her."

"Well, what's your name? You're just as cute as she is."

" Lisa."

"I'm Sam. I used to come here all the time."

"Thou art most welcome, noble Sam."

He laughed. "What's with the Shakespearean language?"

"I'm a time traveler from Elizabethan England."

"Oh, I should've guessed."

AT TWO IN THE MORNING, HE CALLED FRENCH ROAST to see if Michael was there. The night manager answered the phone. "Is the professor there?" Sam asked.

"Who's the professor?"

"Michael Shwartz."

"Yes, he's here—earlier than usual."

"Please tell him I'll be right over."

He found Michael seated with Brad at a table by the window. He wanted to give Michael an update on Kim's condition, but not in front of Brad, so he sat quietly and listened to the conversation. He considered taking Michael aside and telling him but changed his mind. After an hour he left them and went to bed.

When he awoke at two in the afternoon, he headed straight for St. Vincent's. He was surprised to hear that Kim had been released that morning. He went outside, found a pay phone, and called her parents. Mrs. Park picked up. "How is she?" he asked.

"She's still very depressed."

"What did the psychiatrist say?"

"He recommended that she go into rehab at the Carrier Institute in Bellmeade, and they said a bed should be available in a day or two."

"Will I be able to visit her there?"

"We'll have to see what her doctor recommends."

"Well, please give her my love."

"I will, and thanks again for everything you've done for her."

CHAPTER 23

Sam went for a long walk down to the Lower East Side. When he crossed Delancey Street, he looked around. *(This is where David Rabinowitz lives.)* He stopped at several of the shops on Orchard Street. *(If I had more money, I might buy something.)* Then he drifted to the Bowery. When he passed the Amato Opera, he realized that it was Saturday. *(Inez is singing tonight!)* He stopped at the box office, bought a ticket with his Visa card, and went to the Village Idiot to spend the afternoon. At six o'clock he went to Phoebe's for dinner, then walked over to the theater.

Tony Amato's staging of *Falstaff* was magical, and Inez was charming as Nanetta. After the show, Sam went with Inez and her family to Cucina di Pesce, on East 4th. Her parents were both very cultured and erudite. She had an older sister who'd come down from her home in New Haven to hear Inez sing. Sam was a bit uncomfortable at first, because he thought her parents might consider him a cradle robber. But on the contrary, no one suspected that he was interested in seducing her. *(Am I?)* They all chatted pleasantly until the restaurant closed; then Inez and her family hopped in a cab, and Sam walked home.

He decided to go to bed early for a change, but he wasn't able to sleep. Two hours later, he got dressed and went to the Village Corner, which was open until 4:00 a.m. on weekends. Lisa was behind the bar. "How art thou?" she asked.

"Do you want the long or the short answer?"

"Let's go for the short."

"The short answer is. . .I'm bugging out."

"Well, you've come to the right place. The doctor is in."

"What do you prescribe?"

"How about a pint of Budweiser and a shot of Jack Daniels?"

"That might work."

They bantered back and forth until the bar closed, after which Sam went to French Roast. None of the regulars were there. He sat at the bar and tried to read the *Daily News*, but he found that he couldn't concentrate. *(My mind is racing—I hope I'm not becoming manic.)* He left the restaurant at 5:00 a.m. *(What should I do? I know I won't be able to sleep.)* He walked blindly through the West Village, composing rhymes in his head as he went along.

Lola, Lola, crunchy granola
Had a cup of chocolate milk and called it Coca-Cola.

Kim, Kim Cherubim,
I like you more than tiny Tim.

When it became light, he headed to Washington Square Park to look for an opponent. Pavel the Russian was already there, so he challenged him to a duel. "How much do you want to play for?" Pavel asked him.

"That depends on what odds you're going to give me."

"How about five minutes to two?"

"How about five dollars a game?"

"You're becoming brave in your old age," Pavel said. "I've never seen you play for more than three dollars a game."

Even though Sam was, as he put it himself, "bugging out," he played his best chess. Two hours later, he was ahead by four games. Since Pavel was one of the few hustlers who actually paid when he lost, Sam had $20.00 in his pocket. He crossed to the other end of the park, sat on a bench, and started talking to himself out loud. "It's a good thing I won, because if I had lost, I wouldn't have been able to pay, and things could've gotten ugly. Why didn't I think of that before we started?"

Once again, he returned to his apartment and tried unsuccessfully to sleep. At 11:00 a.m. he went downstairs, bought some challah, eggs, milk, and maple syrup, went back upstairs, and made French toast. He invited Yong, his roommate, to have breakfast with him.

"*This* is something new," Yong said.

Sam decided, for the first time, to tell his roommate what he was going through—that he suffered from bipolar disorder, and his concern that he might be becoming manic again.

Yong said, "I suspected, because of your irregular schedule, that you might have a problem. You can tell me anything you want—I won't breathe a word to anyone."

"You're a good man," Sam said.

"I have a first cousin who's bipolar, so I know all about it."

They talked for about two hours, after which Sam was finally able to get some sleep. When he awoke it was already dark. *(What now?)* He decided to give his mother a call. "How are you?" she wanted to know.

"I'm not sure," he said. "I've been kind of hyper the past couple of days, and I'm afraid I might be a little manic."

"Why don't you come out and visit?"

"Okay, maybe tomorrow."

He decided to stay up all night and visit his mother in the morning. He went barhopping until 3:00 a.m., then to French Roast, where he was pleased to find Michael sitting by himself. They spent the night talking about art history, Michael's favorite subject.

At 8:00, he took a bus to Hackensack. His mother gave him a big hug and asked, "Have you had breakfast?"

"Nope."

"Would you like some French toast?"

"Funny you should ask. I just made French toast for my roommate and myself yesterday."

"What about a bowl of oatmeal?"

"Terrific."

She gave him Quaker Oats, which he devoured. "You should eat more slowly," she said. "You'll digest your food better."

"Believe me, if indigestion were my biggest problem, I'd be elated."

He told her about Kim and her condition, without mentioning that he was dating her.

"How are you spending your time? Are you working at all?"

"Aside from a couple private students, no." He told her about Michael Schwartz, and how much he was learning from him.

"Did you ever consider going to graduate school? You have a very good mind."

"Michael suggested the same thing. Maybe I will eventually, but right now I don't think I could focus on schoolwork."

"I know I'm not your doctor, but I think that having a regular schedule would be good for you."

"I *have* a regular schedule. I go to the same bars religiously."

"Sam, I'm not joking. I worry about you."

"I know. I'll try to think of a healthy routine, but my mind is racing so much I can't sit still."

"Are you manic?"

"Maybe hypomanic."

"I know you're always the first one to know when you're ill. Promise me, if you start to become delusional, that you'll call Dr. Berkun and enter the hospital if he thinks it's appropriate."

"Okay."

After a few hours with his mom, he walked to the nearest bus stop and boarded the first bus that arrived. He dozed off for a few minutes and, upon awakening, realized that he didn't know where he was. He asked the driver, "Does this bus go to New York?"

"No, it goes to Union City."

"Uh-oh. Can I get a bus to New York from there?"

"Yes. I'll tell you where to catch it."

"All right, then. No harm done."

Sam went back to his seat. *(Watch what you're doing, dammit.)*

He decided to explore Union City a bit before going back into the city, so he checked out Bergenline Avenue, where he stopped for lunch in a Cuban restaurant. The menu was in Spanish, and none of the waiters knew a word of English, so he used his high school Spanish to order rice and beans and a bottle of Dos Equis. *(I didn't know a neighborhood like this existed in New Jersey!)*

When he had eaten his fill, he caught the next bus back into the city. Then he went directly home and slept for twelve hours.

When he got up, he went to the Village Corner to see Lisa and sat near the piano, away from the other customers.

"Welcome to our church," Lisa said to him.

"So now this is a church?"

"This is the church of the Latter Day Shakespearean Scholars."

"I see. And what will be the theme of today's sermon?"

"Today's sermon will address Shakespeare's contention that 'Life is a tale told by an idiot, full of sound and fury, signifying nothing.'"

"Who's the idiot? Anyone I know?"

"The idiots are legion."

"Well, if you're giving the sermon, doesn't it make you—"

"The idiot? I'm the idiot of the week. Your turn will be coming soon."

"I'm a perpetual idiot, at least when it comes to choosing women."

"I'll drink to that: one idiot to another."

Lisa mixed a container of "Sex on the Beach," and they had a couple of shots together. The alcohol gave Sam some courage, and he asked her, "Can I come home with you when the bar closes?"

"I can't bring you home. I have a boyfriend."

"Well, girls as cute as you usually do."

"Thank you."

He left for French Roast, to look for Michael Schwartz. Michael wasn't there, so Sam sat at a table near the door with Brad. "What's in the movie theaters that's worth seeing?" he asked.

"They're having a *film noir* series at the Film Forum. Tomorrow they're showing *Detour*."

"Do you recommend it?"

"Well, it's not my favorite movie, but it's a good genre piece."

"Good. Maybe I'll go see it tomorrow to take my mind off things."

After sleeping through the morning as usual, Sam called Kim's mom to ask, "How is she?"

"She's still extremely depressed."

"Can I see her?"

"She's in the Carrier Institute now, and the doctors won't allow any visitors except my husband and me."

"Please tell her that I'm praying for her, and I miss her a lot."

"Of course."

He called Lola to tell her.

"Oh, thank God you called, Sam. Can you come here right away?"

"I'll be there in fifteen minutes."

When he rang her doorbell, she buzzed him in. He found her lying in bed, sobbing.

"What's wrong, honey?"

"Nigel left me and went back to Nebraska."

"Oh, I'm so sorry."

"Stay with me tonight."

"Okay. But it's still early. Do you want to go for a walk? Would you like to eat something?"

"I don't know what I want. I want Nigel back."

"Let's go have a bite to eat. You'll feel better afterwards."

"I can't let people see me like this. Why don't we order some food and eat it here?"

Sam called Susie's and ordered eggrolls and Mu Shu Pork. Lola hardly touched it.

"I thought I wanted to eat, but now I have no appetite."

"Well. . . ."

"How about a chess game?"

"Okay," he said.

He gave her queen-odds, and she won easily.

"Where's Kim?" she asked.

"That's why I called you. She's in a rehab in New Jersey."

"Boy, when it rains, it pours."

"The rain will stop, and there will be a rainbow afterwards. You'll see."

Lola fell asleep then, but he remained wide awake. To pass the time, he made a mental list of all the women he had slept with. He counted forty-three of them. Then he tried to count the women he had desired but not attained, starting way back in junior high school. He counted 102. After lying perfectly still for two hours, he started to feel uncomfortable, so he went into the kitchen, where he found several boxes of slides she had made of her paintings. *(She's even better than I thought she was.)* Then he left a note on the kitchen table saying that he'd be at French Roast if she needed him.

When he got there, he sat at the table with Rick Danger, the comedian. "How are you?" Sam ventured.

"Miserable, as usual."

"It's a shame. You make so many people happy, and you're so unhappy yourself."

"Why should I be different from all the other comedians?"

"All of them?"

"Every one of them, from Woody Allen all the way down to the total beginner at an open mike."

THE NEXT DAY, SAM WALKED THROUGH CENTRAL PARK to Sheep's Meadow, where he lay down in the sunshine for a few minutes.

Suddenly he started to become paranoid. *(Kim's going to die, and it's all my fault.)* He got up and started rushing ahead. As he approached Central Park South, he ran into Kelly, his old girlfriend. When she saw him, she smiled. "Sam."

"Don't come near me. There's a curse on me."

"You're joking, right?"

"I'm not joking. Stay away from me."

Kelly looked bewildered. "Don't you want to have coffee with me?"

"No, no, *no!*"

He broke into a run. By the time he reached Times Square, he was exhausted. *(I've got to avoid everyone I know.)*

Usually his episodes developed much more slowly, but this time, within an hour of leaving the park, he was already quite psychotic. *(Should I call Dr. Berkun? No, then he'll become ill as well. I've got to avoid everyone. I can't even go home, or Yong will become ill.)*

In a panic, he concluded that he had to leave town. *(I've got to go somewhere where nobody knows me.)*

He went to the Greyhound ticket office at the Port Authority, where he used his credit card to buy a ticket to Iowa City. *(There I'll be a total stranger.)*

WHEN THE BUS STOPPED IN CHICAGO, he bought a slice of pizza and a Diet Coke, then returned to the bus. About halfway between Chicago and Iowa City, he started talking to himself. He remembered an argument his parents had had when he was ten years old. He recalled helplessly watching his father slap his mother in the face. He began to shout, "If you ever do that again, I'll kill you!"

A young boy sitting across the aisle from him became very frightened.

"Don't you dare touch my mother, you bastard!"

The child's mother moved him to another seat, and then told the driver what was happening.

"You motherfucker!" Sam shouted. "I'll kill you!"

The driver pulled the bus over and walked back to Sam's seat. "Come with me," he said.

When he and Sam were outside the bus, the driver said, "You'd better stop talking to yourself, or I'll take you off the bus."

"I'll do my best," Sam promised.

"Never mind your *best*. If you say *one more word*, I'll take you off the bus, and if you don't believe me, just try it."

"Okay, okay."

Sam went back to his seat and tried to meditate. He remembered having read in one of Dr. Ellis's books that a good mantra to use when meditating is the article: "the," because by itself "the" has no meaning. He closed his eyes and repeated "the, the, the. . ." hundreds of times, until he fell asleep.

When he awoke, the bus was crossing the Mississippi River. *(This will be the first time I've been west of the Mississippi!)*

In Iowa City, he left the terminal and asked a stranger, "Do you know if there's a cheap hotel in town?"

"Why don't you try the Bella Vista Bed and Breakfast?" The man gave him directions.

After checking in, Sam started exploring the city. He found several good bars, cafés, and restaurants, and planned to visit all of them while he was there. He stopped at a clothing store and bought three pairs of underwear and three pairs of socks. Then he sat by the window in a café and watched people walk by.

The first thing he noticed was that everyone seemed to be very down-to-earth. Most were casually dressed. There wasn't the variety that one sees in New York: the corporate look, the funky East Village look, the sexy club scene look, and so forth. Iowa City is a college town, and there were lots of students and professorial types reading, writing, and chatting about the arts in the café. *(I think I'm going to like it here.)*

Sam struck up a conversation with a woman named Susan who was in the Iowa State writer's workshop. She explained how she was using game theory in her poetry. *(That's a new one for me.)* Sam had written many poems as a young man; now, for the first time in years, he recited some of them. Within an hour, they were already good friends. He had always had the ability to keep his paranoid thoughts to himself, so Susan had no idea that he was delusional. They agreed to meet the following evening in the same café.

It was getting late, so he went back to the hotel to try and get some shut-eye. He lay awake for hours, his mind racing in every direction. *(Could Susan be an FBI agent? No, what would the FBI want with me? Still, I don't trust her. . . . But maybe I'll give her the benefit of the doubt. Kim's in the Carrier Institute; maybe I'll call her tomorrow. No, they'll trace the call and find out where I am. I'd better cover my tracks and keep on the move. My God, is this what it's like to be a fugitive? But who am I running from? Myself? Am I chasing my own tail? God, please save me from madness!)*

At seven in the morning, he finally fell asleep. He slept fitfully until 3:00 p.m., had a meal at a diner near the hotel, and continued to explore the city. He went to the museum, where he was surprised to see a Beckmann triptych in the front room. *(I'll have to tell Michael about this.)*

He still had a few hours to kill before his date with Susan, so he took a long walk by the Iowa River. When no one was in sight, he stripped down to his underwear and went wading in the river. *(Do I want to be baptized? No, my mom would never forgive me.)*

Twenty minutes later, he got dressed and headed back into town. He stopped at the hotel to put on dry underwear, then went to the café to wait for Susan.

Susan showed up with Beth, a young friend of hers who was also in the writer's workshop. *(I wonder if Susan's gay.)* The three of them took turns reciting their poetry. Susan's poems were very spontaneous, with lots of made-up words and clever linguistic play.

"I see what you mean about game theory," Sam said. "Yours is a poetry of chance."

Beth's poems were kind of prosy, but with very strong rhythms. When it was Sam's turn, he recited a couple of sonnets he had written when studying Shakespeare as a young man. He asked them who their favorite poets were. Beth's favorite was Emily Dickinson, and Susan's Dylan Thomas.

"Who's yours?" Susan asked him.

"Well, if you exclude Shakespeare and Milton, then I'd have to say that Wordsworth would be my first choice. I love his idea that there is a force for good in nature."

"I knew you'd pick a romantic," Susan said.

"Is it so obvious that I'm a romantic?"

"It's written all over you."

"Thank you," Sam said. *(If you only knew what a psycho I am. . . .)*

CHAPTER 24

THEY WENT TO THE LEMON, A BAR IN THE DOWNTOWN AREA. Susan and Beth knew everyone in the bar, none of whom had ever been to New York City. *(I'm totally safe here.)*

After introducing Sam to all the regulars, Susan bought a pitcher of Budweiser, and the three commenced a long night of drinking, noshing, and playing pool. Neither Susan nor Beth were unattractive, but the barmaid was a stunning blonde. *(I'll have to come here by myself.)*

When the bar closed at 2:00 a.m., Susan and Beth invited Sam to their place.

"It's still very early," she said. "And I have a case of Molson in my fridge."

The three of them stayed up until 5:00 a.m., when Sam left and hobbled back to the hotel. *(It's nice to know that there are people in this town who keep the same hours as I do.)*

He woke up at two in the afternoon with a terrible hangover, so he went downstairs and asked the lady at the desk for some Advil, then returned to his room and got back in bed. When he started feeling better after an hour or so, he went to a diner and had scrambled eggs and bacon, then continued exploring the town.

In a park not far from his hotel, he found several college students playing speed chess. *(Wow! Just like the Village!)*

He watched a few games, then asked the strongest players if he could play the winner. When Sam was hypomanic, he always had trouble sitting still for slow chess, but his speed game usually improved. He played in the park for two hours, winning every game. His toughest opponent said, "Wow, you're a great player. Where you from?"

"Some hick town called New York City." *(Should I be telling them this?)*

When he returned to The Lemon, he was delighted to see the same blonde behind the bar. "Welcome back," she said. "My name's Andrea. What's yours?"

"Sam."

"Where you from?"

"Some hick town called New York City."

"Oh, yeah? Well, if New York City is a hick town, what does that make Iowa City?"

"Uh, let me sleep on it, and I'll tell you tomorrow."

"What do you do?"

"I'm a chess instructor."

"How cool is that!"

"That's the reaction I usually get. Do you play?"

"No, I'm more of an outdoor type. I can play any water sport, though."

"How cool is *that*!"

"That's the reaction *I* usually get."

"Which sports? Swimming? Diving?"

"Swimming, diving, water skiing, water polo—you name it."

"Where do you do all this? Not in the Iowa River?"

"No. In the Mississippi."

"Wow."

"I'll be driving out there on Saturday. Would you like to come?"

"Sure."

"Why don't you meet me in front of the bar at 10:00 on Saturday morning?"

"Solid." *(I'll have to force myself to turn my schedule around.)*

After he left the bar, Sam decided to call Kim's parents. *(If I keep the call short enough, maybe they won't be able to trace it.)* He went to a deli, where he changed three dollars for twelve quarters. When he dialed the number, Mrs. Park picked up. "Sam!" she said. "I've been trying to reach you. Where've you been?"

He thought fast. "I've been hiking in the Catskills."

"Kim has been asking about you."

"How's she doing?"

"She's still in the Carrier Institute, but she's feeling much better, and they're thinking of releasing her in a few days."

"That's great!" Sam said.

"She'd like it if you'd visit her."

"Well, I'll still be away for a while, but as soon as I'm back in town, I'll definitely do that."

On Saturday morning, he met Andrea outside the bar as planned.

"My car's a block away," she said. It was a blue Corvette with the license plate *LUCKY. (Maybe* I'll *get lucky.)*

On the way to the waterfront, they got to know each other a little better. When he told her that this was the first time he had been west of the Mississippi, she was surprised. "I've been in every state with the exception of Alaska. Last year a friend of mine and I went to fifteen national parks."

"Wow. Have you ever been to New York City?"

"For a few days about four years ago."

"That's not enough," Sam said.

"I know, but I'm going to come and visit you, and you're going to show me everything."

Sam let out a low whistle. "Everyone in this town is so reticent," he said.

They drove to the waterfront, where Andrea worked as a lifeguard. She went to the boathouse to change into her bikini. *(What a body she has!)* Sam swam out to the rope and back ten times, then sat in a beach chair next to her.

"You're a good swimmer," she said.

Her shift lasted four hours, after which they borrowed a speed boat that belonged to a friend of hers.

"This is thrilling!" Sam said. "I've never been in so fast a boat."

"You're going to be even more thrilled later on."

(Does she mean what I think she does?)

They drove back to Iowa City, bought a pepperoni pizza and a half gallon of Coca-Cola, and went up to her apartment on the second floor of a two-family house. Her living room was tastefully decorated with comfortable white canvas furniture and photos of several national parks on the walls.

Sam posted himself on her loveseat and said, "Come sit on my lap."

"But the pizza will get cold."

"That's okay. We'll warm it up later."

They undressed in record time and made love for two hours, after which Andrea said, "Let's go out on the balcony and watch the sunset."

They did until the sun went down over the Iowa River.

"I feel like I could stay here forever," he said.

"Is that an option?"

He didn't answer. *(If only you knew. . . .)*

When he returned to his hotel, the concierge gave him a note from Susan: "Please meet me at the café at 8:00 p.m. tomorrow."

He slept until 2:30 p.m., had blueberry pancakes at the diner, and continued looking around. He found a wonderful bookstore near the center of town where he spent an hour browsing, bought Saul Bellow's *Herzog*, and went to the café to read. *(Wasn't it Saul Bellow who called madness a gift? Well, maybe it is, but it's a very double-edged gift. What I'd give just to be an ordinary Joe.)*

Sam wasn't surprised to discover that his concentration wasn't very good; after ten pages, his mind started drifting off, so he put down the novel and began writing a poem on a paper napkin.

NewYork City—it ain't pretty. Let's get out of here.
When a mind starts to unwind, it's time to have a beer.
Please avoid paranoid thoughts, which are worse than fear. Would you be poor Tom or the fool if you acted in King Lear?

Sam started laughing out loud, then noticed that everyone in the place was looking at him as they had on the bus, so he picked up the novel again and pretended to read. *(The last thing you want is to be committed to a mental hospital in Iowa, for God's sake.)*

At 8:00 p.m., Susan and Beth appeared at the café. This time Susan gave him one of her short stories to read. As was the case with her poetry, her prose was very stream-of- consciousness, in the manner of James Joyce or Virginia Woolf. She asked him, "Have you written any fiction?"

"No," he said. "But I'm planning to write a novel sometime in the near future."

"What about?" Beth asked.

"It's going to be about the chess subculture in Greenwich Village."

"Sounds fascinating," Susan said. "Be sure to send both of us signed copies."

"Naturally."

They went to The Lemon, where they found Andrea behind the bar. They ordered a pitcher of sangria and sat at a table near the jukebox. If Andrea was jealous, she didn't show it at all. Susan played some golden oldies on the jukebox: The Rolling Stones, The Doors, The Supremes, etc., along with some more modern artists like Nirvana and Melissa Etheridge. Sam felt right at home.

Susan got up from the table to play pool, leaving Sam together with Beth. Although she was much less talkative than Susan, he was able to get her to talk about herself. He was happy to hear that she had an apartment in San Francisco.

"I've always wanted to go there," he said.

"When you do, you'll be welcome to stay with me."

"I'll definitely take you up on that."

It turned out that Beth had a master's in English Literature from Stanford. "Wow," he said. "At some time in the near future I might go for a master's at Hunter."

"Then we can have an epistolary romance," Beth said.

(Do you swing both ways?)

When Susan and Beth left at 11:00 p.m., he took a seat at the bar. Andrea introduced him to some more of the regulars. Most interesting to Sam was a very cultured Irishman with a strong accent named Connor.

"How did you wind up in Iowa?" Sam asked.

"I was in jail in Belfast for giving material support to the IRA. When I got out, I wanted a complete change. A friend of mine and I rented a car and toured the United States. When he went back to Ireland, I decided to settle here, at least temporarily. How did *you* wind up here?"

"I was in a bar in New York where they had a big map of the states on the wall. I decided to throw a dart at the wall and go wherever it landed. Wouldn't you know it, the dart landed right on Iowa City?"

"You're pulling my leg, aren't you?"

Sam lied, "I came here for the writer's workshop."

He stayed in the bar until closing, then went home with Andrea. He undressed her slowly, kissing every part of her body as it appeared. When they finished making love, she said, "I think I'm starting to fall in love with you."

"You're so expansive," he said.

He held her in his arms and rocked her gently until both of them fell asleep. At 10:00 a.m., she woke him up and served him breakfast in bed.

"You make me feel like a king," he told her.

Andrea sang to him the lyrics from "Lavender Blue" about being a queen to his king.

"I really could. . . ."

"Stay here forever?"

"Yes. But I have to go back soon," he said.

She was due at the waterfront at 1:00 p.m. He decided to stay in town, went back to the café, and opened *Herzog* again. This time his concentration was much better. *(What a good woman can do for a man.)*

He read about seventy-five pages, then went to the park for more speed chess. Ron, the strongest of his opponents, asked him, "What's your rating, Sam?"

"About 2000."

"Really? I was sure that you were a master."

"Any expert in New York would be master anywhere else."

He played until it became dark, then went back to the café to look for Susan. She was at a corner table, reading *The Nation*. "If you read that," he said, "you must be very liberal."

"I'm beyond liberal. I'm almost a communist."

"Wow, there aren't too many of those around today now that the Soviet Union is gone."

"I was never a fan of the Soviet Union. I'm more a fan of Tito, who allowed small businesses to thrive while remaining socialist."

"Who did you vote for in the last election?"

"Nader, of course."

"If you didn't know Clinton would win, would you still have voted for Nader?"

"Yes, I would have. Frankly, I don't think there's much difference between the Democrats and the Republicans."

"I think there's a big difference."

"I don't think Clinton's really a liberal. I think Nixon was more liberal than Clinton."

"Actually, Nixon didn't seem to care much about domestic issues. He devoted most of his attention to foreign policy."

They went to dinner at a Thai restaurant near the river. "I feel like I'm in New York," he said. "Do you have Japanese food here?"

"Yes, there's a Japanese restaurant near here where they have very good sushi."

"What about Indian food?"

"We have that, too."

"Korean?"

"Korean? Not that I know of."

"Well, when I have a craving for a Korean barbecue, I'll have to get on a bus back to New York."

She invited him to her apartment for coffee. While she was in the kitchen, he looked at her bookshelf. She had a large collection of books on every subject imaginable, including several about New York City.

"How long have you lived here?" he asked.

"About three years. I came here mainly for the writer's workshop."

"Where were you from originally?"

"Wyoming."

"Well, anytime you want to come to New York, I'll show you around."

"That's a definite possibility."

Susan read a chapter of the book she was writing. It was a political novel, set in the Vietnam era.

"This reminds me of *The Quiet American*, the Graham Greene novel."

"That's a huge compliment. Graham Greene is one of my favorites."

"Mine, too. I think he should've won the Nobel Prize."

"Did you ever hear what Saul Bellow said? 'My mother would like me to be a little Graham Greene.'"

"What a condescending remark."

"Wasn't it? And I think that, at his best, Greene was a much better writer than Saul Bellow."

"I don't know if I'd go that far, but he's definitely underrated."

He told her about Michael Schwartz and their late-night conversations. "He can talk about any subject under the sun," he said.

"Who are some of his favorite writers?"

"His favorites are Joyce, Mann, and Proust."

"That's certainly not unusual, but of those three, I'd have to say that only Joyce is among my favorites."

"I like all three, but *my* favorites are Tolstoy and Dostoevsky."

Susan laughed. "From what I know about you, I think you should have been born in the nineteenth century."

"In my last incarnation, I was a Russian count."

"And I was a French courtesan."

After he left her apartment, he wanted to visit Andrea but he didn't know how she would react if he showed up unannounced, so he went back to his hotel and went to bed. As was so often the case, he couldn't sleep. *(One of the reasons I couldn't settle here is that there's no place like French Roast where I can go at any hour.)* He lay awake in bed until seven in the morning, when he went to the diner.

The waiter behind the counter said, "You're becoming a regular here."

"I'm a regular guy."

He went to the park after that to see if any of the chess players would be there at such an early hour but found no one. *(I'm going to have to go back to New York soon.)*

He lay on the grass and took a nap in the morning sunshine. When he awoke, two of the chess players were there, playing speed chess. Most of the time his illness didn't hurt his chess, but on that day he couldn't focus, so he lost most of the games.

At one in the afternoon, he went to The Lemon to see if Andrea was there and found a middle-aged man with a goatee behind the bar. When Sam asked him about her, he said, "She's at the waterfront today. She'll be behind the bar tonight."

Sam ordered a scotch on the rocks and struck up a conversation. "Are you a native here?"

"No, I grew up in Nebraska, but I've been here for ten years."

"What brought you here originally?"

"The writer's workshop."

"So you know Susan and Beth?"

"Of course."

"Are you still in the workshop?"

"No, but I was for four years."

"What did you write?"

"I finished two complete novels, but I couldn't find a publisher."

"Still writing?"

"No. I'm a professional bartender now. . . . What about you? What brought you here?"

"I was burning out in New York City, and I needed a change of pace."

"Wow! The Big Apple!"

"Have you ever taken a bite?"

"I think that might be more than I could chew."

Sam went back to the hotel, where he decided to call his mother. He used the hotel phone and dialed collect.

"My God!" Mrs. Kanter said. "Where *are* you? I've been desperately trying to reach you."

"I'm in Iowa City."

"Iowa City? Are you all right?"

"I'm not in perfect shape, but I'm all right."

"Even your roommate didn't know where you were."

"I'm sorry," Sam said. "I'll be back soon."

"Please, Sam, when you leave New York, let me know. I was about to call the police and report you missing."

"I'm sorry."

He slept all afternoon, and when he awoke he decided that he would head back to New York the following morning. He went to The Lemon to tell Andrea. She was philosophical about it. "I guess all things must pass," she said.

When the bar closed, they went to her apartment together for the last time. "Do you have a camera?" he asked her.

"Yes," she said.

"Do you have film?"

"Let me see."

She searched in her dresser and found a roll.

"Do a striptease for me," he said.

Just as he had kissed each part of her body as it appeared on his previous visit, this time he took a photo of her as each article of clothing came off.

"Make sure you leave enough film for me to take some pictures of you," Andrea said.

"I'll leave you half a roll."

When she finished her striptease, she said, "Now you do a striptease for me."

When there was no film left, they made love so passionately that it took ten minutes for their breathing to return to normal.

The bus was due to leave at 11:00 the following morning, so they lay awake all night in each other's arms. At 10:00, she made him a Spanish omelet and a cup of English breakfast tea; then she accompanied him to the bus station. While they were waiting for the bus, he gave her his address and phone number, and said, "You must come to New York as soon as possible."

"Oh, I will, I will," she promised.

Before the bus left, he called Susan to say goodbye, told her he was leaving, then added, "Say goodbye to Beth for me, and I'll see you both in New York."

CHAPTER 25

Back in New York, the first thing he did was to let his mother know that he was back. Then he called Kim's parents. "She's home now," her mother said. "I'll put her on."

"How are you, sweetheart?" he asked her.

"I'm much better."

"Are you ready to come into The City?"

"No, but I'd love it if you'd come visit me."

"I'll come tomorrow."

He went to Lola's apartment and rang the doorbell. She buzzed him in. "Where have you been, Sam? Everyone's been worried about you."

"I was feeling very stressed, so I needed to get out of The City."

"So? Where've you *been?*"

"Iowa City."

"Do you know someone there?"

"I didn't, but I made some friends there."

"How did you decide on Iowa City?"

"I don't know."

"Well, anyway, you're back and in one piece."

"Praise the Lord."

When he got home, he called Dr. Berkun to say, "I've been having some symptoms lately. I don't think it's anything to worry about, but you might want to make an adjustment in my medications."

They set up an appointment for that Friday.

Sam turned on the television and lay down on the sofa. A short while later, Yong came in. "Goodness!" he said. "Where have you been? I called The Chess

Shop and your mother, and no one knew where you were."

"I'm sorry," Sam said. "It was inconsiderate of me to leave without telling anyone."

"Well, all's well that ends well."

THE FOLLOWING AFTERNOON, SAM TOOK A BUS to Upper Saddle River. When Kim opened the door and saw who it was, she threw her arms around him. He kissed her gently on the forehead.

Her parents invited him to stay for dinner. He liked her father right away—a quiet, unassuming man who worked as a real estate agent in northern New Jersey. Her mother was more talkative, and equally charming. She told Sam, "You seem to understand Kim completely."

"Well, that's because I've had problems of my own."

He took the bus back to New York City. Before leaving, he said to Kim, "Come into The City at any time, and I'll make you feel at home."

On Friday, he told Dr. Berkun about the Iowa trip and mentioned some of the symptoms he was having. The doctor said, "I don't think we need to make any adjustments now, but keep me posted, and if things get worse, maybe we'll try something different."

AFTER NAPPING AT HOME FOR SEVERAL HOURS, Sam went to French Roast to see Michael. When he entered the restaurant, Michael exclaimed, "Hail, the conquering hero!"

Sam looked around. "What exactly have I conquered?"

"That's for you to tell me."

"Well, I've been to Iowa City. . . . And actually, I did conquer a beautiful barmaid."

"Congratulations, where is she?"

"She still in Iowa, but she'll be coming to visit soon."

Michael looked at him curiously, then asked, "If you don't mind my asking, Sam, what made you decide to go to Iowa City?"

"I needed a change."

"But why Iowa City? Why not San Francisco, or New Orleans?"

"You seem to forget that I'm mentally ill, Michael. You want logic in everything I say and do?"

"Of course not. And if you ask me, you're saner than a lot of people who've never had a single day in therapy."

"Thank you," Sam said. He told Michael about the museum in Iowa City and described the big Beckmann triptych.

"I know that painting," Michael said. "How about that? Out in the middle of nowhere, a masterpiece like that?"

"It's not the middle of nowhere," Sam pointed out. "It's a big college town with a thriving intellectual community."

"Boy, seeing that painting alone would make it worth the trip. I think I've told you that Beckmann's my favorite twentieth-century painter."

"You like him better than Picasso?"

"I like them equally, but Beckmann has always had a big influence on me, and another one of his triptychs—*Departure*—is probably my favorite twentieth-century painting."

"I'd have to say that my favorite is *Guernica*."

"That's a good choice."

A few days later, Kim came into The City to visit Sam. They went to see *Titanic* and spent the night together. Sam held her until she fell asleep, but he remained awake for hours. *(Is she getting in too deep with me? If I break up with her, what would she do? Would she become suicidal? I genuinely do care about her, but I'm starting to feel trapped.)*

He decided to talk about his situation with Michael.

Kim woke up just two hours after Sam fell asleep. She had the hardest time getting him out of bed. Somehow she succeeded, and they went to the Odessa for brunch. She looked at him adoringly. "Who loves you?" she said.

"The sweetest girl I've ever known."

She went back to New Jersey, and he went back to bed, where he dreamed that he was the defendant in a courtroom. Kim's father was the presiding judge, and Kim was his defense attorney. She was making a motion that the trial be moved out of New York City. "He can't get a fair trial here," she said.

"All right," her father said. "We'll move the proceedings to Iowa City."

When he awoke, he went to a gift shop on Bleecker Street and picked out a postcard to send to Andrea. On the front of the card was a photo of the Chrysler Building. On the back, he wrote, *Back in NYC and missing you already. Please come soon.*

It was a beautiful fall day, so after mailing the postcard, he bought a roast beef sandwich and a bottle of Heineken and went to Central Park to catch some rays. On the Great Lawn, several young men from the West Indies were playing soccer. After he finished his sandwich, he asked them if he could join the game. A thin man with dreadlocks said, "You can be our token white man."

"I'd be honored," he said.

After playing for forty minutes, he was exhausted, so he sat on the sidelines and watched the game. When it was over, he walked all the way from Central Park to the Jefferson Market Library, where he went to the literature section to pick out a novel. After browsing for half an hour, he selected *The Age of Iron* by J.M. Coetzee. He found the novel so riveting that he sat at a table reading it until the library closed, then moved to The Peacock Café to finish it.

When he was down to the last twenty pages, someone tapped him on the shoulder. "Inez!" he exclaimed as he looked up. "What have you been up to?"

"I just finished my first year at Juilliard."

"Have you been singing at the Amato Opera?"

"I haven't had time. I've put together two complete programs, one for piano and one for voice."

"Terrific! What's on the program?"

"My voice recital is all German *lieder*: Schubert, Schumann, Strauss, and Wolf. And for my piano program I'm preparing the Chopin ballades and four Schubert impromptus."

"That's fabulous! When can I hear you?"

"One evening I'll invite you to my parents' house and play piano for you. As for the *lieder*, I think you'll have to wait until the fall, when I can rehearse with an accompanist."

"I'll be waiting with bated breath."

Inez smiled. "What are you reading?" she asked him.

"Do you know J.M. Coetzee?"

"I've never read anything of his, but I've heard good things about him."

"I think he's one of the best writers in the English language right now."

At 2:00 a.m., Sam went to French Roast to tell Michael about the situation with Kim. "She's very unstable," he said. "I'm afraid that, if I reject her, she might hurt herself, but if I try to save her I might not succeed, and I'd be devastated. I don't know what to do."

"That's a tough one. Are you in love with her?"

"I'm not sure."

"Well, are you in love with your blond barmaid?"

"I think so."

"I don't know what to tell you, Sam, except to say that, if Andrea comes to stay with you and Kim finds out, it would be ten times worse for her than if you simply break up with her."

Sam shook his head. "I've never been this confused in my life."

"Well, you don't need to decide right away. Give it some thought, and whatever you decide to do, stick to your guns."

"I guess that's good advice."

THE FOLLOWING EVENING, HE WENT TO THE CHESS SHOP for the first time since his trip. Ahmed was behind the counter. They talked about Coetzee, whom Ahmed knew very well. After half an hour, Raphael and Ben came in. Sam played with them until The Shop closed, after which they went to the Village Gate, where Raphael and Ben continued to play while Sam bought a beer and listened to the jazz. When closing time arrived, Rafi said to Sam, "We have an opening for a full-time waiter here. Would you be interested?"

"Thanks, but, off the record, the hours I keep are too irregular for me to work full time."

A FEW DAYS LATER, KIM CAME INTO THE CITY AGAIN. Sam took her to Washington Square Park, where they listened to the musicians and watched the acrobats. Then they went to Susie's for Chinese food.

"What should I order?" she asked.

"Most of the specials are good."

Sam ordered Beef Jasper and Kim chose the Two-Flavor Shrimp. When they finished, they went to Café Dante for cappuccino.

As they made small talk, Sam's predicament was always in the back of his mind. Finally, he decided to raise the subject in an elliptical way.

"Kim, honey," he said, "what kind of future do you see for us?"

"I don't know. I'm pretty sure that I don't want any kids. I'd be afraid that they'd have my genes, and I wouldn't want my worst enemy to go through what I've been through, let alone my own children. As for marriage, I think it's almost meaningless without kids. I do believe in commitment."

Sam thought he saw a way out. "I think I want marriage and kids," he said.

Kim gazed at him silently. "Well, then, what should we do?" she asked.

"I love you very much," he said, "but if someone came along who wanted what I do. . . ."

After long pause, Kim said, "Then maybe we should break up."

Sam had a hard time hiding his relief. "I think that would be best," he said. He kissed her gently. *(What an asshole I am.)*

He accompanied her to the Port Authority and waited with her for her bus back to New Jersey. Before she boarded, he told her, "If you ever need someone to talk to, just give me a call."

When he got back to his apartment, there was a call from Ahmed on his answering machine: "I just got a call from the Children's Aid Society. They're looking for a chess instructor for their after-school program. If you're interested, stop by The Shop, and I'll give you their phone number."

Sam immediately walked over to The Shop, where Ahmed gave him the information. The following afternoon he called the Children's Aid Society and set up an appointment for an interview. *(Wouldn't it be nice if I didn't need Social Security?)*

Two days later, he showed up at Sullivan Street for his interview, which went very well. They hired him for two after-school classes, one for children five to seven, and another for those eight to ten. He called the Social Security office and told them that he'd found a job, then he went to The Shop to thank Ahmed, who said, "I'm glad I could be of help."

Since there were still two weeks before the fall semester began, Sam decided to play in a Labor Day weekend tournament at West Point. He stayed with his mother and borrowed her car to drive up. Having landed a new job, he was in a very good mood, so he played his best chess, winning $350.00 as the top player in his section. In between rounds, he explored the beautiful countryside nearby.

When he returned home after the tournament was over, he found a postcard from Andrea in his mailbox: *Dear Sam, I have two weeks off this fall. If I come to New York City, can you put me up?*

He immediately went to a gift shop and picked out a card with a picture of John Lennon on the front. On the back, in huge letters he wrote, *YES! LOVE, SAM!*

AT 2:00 A.M. THE FOLLOWING MORNING, he went to French Roast to see Michael, told him what had happened with Kim, and asked, "Am I an asshole?"

"Not at all," Michael said. "It's impossible to break up with a woman without hurting her at all. You did it in the nicest way possible. You have nothing to be ashamed of. If you asked Dr. Ellis, he'd say the same thing."

A WEEK AFTER LABOR DAY, THE AFTER-SCHOOL PROGRAM at the Children's Aid Society began. In his five-to-seven class, which met every Tuesday, he had three boys and two girls. One girl was a total beginner; the others knew the rules, but not much more than that. In his Wednesday class, he had a couple of students who were fairly talented. He started by teaching everyone the four-move "scholar's mate," and how to defend against it. He had an assistant who was a senior at Stuyvesant High School. He told her that she would be the disciplinarian, so that he could focus on teaching.

Now that he was working, Sam tried to turn his schedule around. He decided that he would go to bed at 2:00 a.m. except on Friday and Saturday nights, so he would meet with Michael only on weekends.

On Friday night, he told Michael that Andrea would be coming soon, and he mentioned some of his concerns: "What will happen when she discovers that I only work for five hours a week? Should I tell her about my illness?"

Michael thought for a moment. "Well, if she's only coming for two weeks, you could tell her a white lie and say that you took off two weeks so you could spend most of your time with her."

"Hm. And I guess I could say that I work in three or four places, and that Children's Aid is the only job where they wouldn't let me off."

"Something like that. But of course if it ever becomes serious, you'll have to tell her more of the truth."

"Well, if that happens, it'll be down the road a bit."

ON THE EVENING OF OCTOBER 12, ANDREA ARRIVED in New York. Sam went to meet her at the Port Authority. When she got off the bus, he gave her a big hug and a kiss. "I forgot how beautiful you are," he said.

"I forgot how romantic you are."

Sam used an old line of his: "Where does romantic end and corny begin?"

"Corny is fine with me," she said.

He grabbed her suitcase. "Well, let's go to Times Square."

"How far away is that?"

"Exactly one block."

As they walked on 42nd Street, he told her how the block used to be notorious for its pornographic movie houses before being rejuvenated, thanks largely to Disney. Entering Times Square, he showed her the building where the ball drops every New Year's Eve. He showed her the Times Square Toys "R" Us, and they went up to The View, the restaurant at the top of the Marriot.

In honor of her visit, Sam bought her a Manhattan.

"This is thrilling!" she said.

They stayed until closing; then he asked, "Do you want to turn in, or would you like to go to a nightclub or bar? I'm at your service."

"Let's go to a nightclub."

He took her to the Limelight, where they danced nonstop for an hour before she said, "Okay, I think I'm ready to hit the sack."

They hopped in a cab and went to Sam's apartment. *(I'm living way beyond my means.)* As soon as they were in the door, they stripped naked and made love like wild horses.

CHAPTER 26

THE NEXT AFTERNOON, SAM GAVE ANDREA a comprehensive tour of Greenwich Village—Washington Square Park and New York University, McDougal Street, Bleecker Street, Christopher Street, the Jefferson Market Courthouse, St. Mark's Place, and Tompkins Square. He also took her to The Chess Shop to show her off to his friends. Jim Smith was particularly impressed. "Blondes play here for free," he said.

In the evening, they went to Small's to listen to some jazz. After the principal performers were finished, they stayed for part of the after-hours jam session, where Sam's friend Raphael was sitting in on piano. Then he took her to French Roast to see Michael, who asked her, "How do you like New York?"

"It's the most amazing place I've ever been to."

"Then why don't you stay a while?"

"I was about to ask her the same question," Sam said.

"Well, relocating would be a big decision, but it's within the realm of possibility."

"You'd make New York a more beautiful place," Michael told her.

"I think I like you," she said.

Sam showed her the most anyone could possibly see in a two-week period. They went to his favorite museums: The Cloisters, The Met, The Modern, and The Frick, and to his favorite ethnic neighborhoods: Belmont, Chinatown, and Astoria. He even brought her to New Jersey to meet his mother—something he had done with very few of his previous girlfriends.

Her visit seemed to end just after it started. The night before she left, they made love from dusk until dawn. "I can't get enough of you," he said. "And you're leaving tomorrow."

"Don't worry. I'll be back soon."

Two days after she left, he was already sorely missing her. He confided in Michael, "I don't know if I can cope with the situation," he said. "I'm in pretty deep already."

"Well, no matter *how* deep you're in, just don't move to Iowa City. Your whole life is here."

"Half my life is there."

"Don't *move* there," Michael repeated. "Unless you're ready for marriage."

". . .I guess I'm not ready for that yet."

"One way to cool off your ardor would be to have an affair with someone else. Did you commit to one another?"

"We didn't talk about it."

"Wasn't there an old Crosby, Stills, and Nash song about loving the one you're with?"

"That's not funny."

"You've never cheated before?"

He thought about Megan and Kelly. "Yes, I have. But, boy, did I regret it."

"But Andrea's in Iowa. How's she going to know?"

"Mi-*chael!*"

"All right. I was just making a suggestion."

"I've got to be going," Sam said. "But before I leave, I wanted to let you know that, now that I'm working, I probably won't be coming here except on weekends."

"That's good," Michael replied. "You'll be much more productive if you're up during the day."

Sam decided that, for his eight-to-ten class, he would show them a famous chess game each week. He started with the "Evergreen" game, a nineteenth-century masterpiece by Adolph Anderson, which is known by all serious chess players. For his younger group, he reviewed the rules until they all knew them well, then he showed them some very simple tactical ideas, such as pins and forks, with just a few pieces on the board.

When Sam's credit card bill arrived, he was in for a shock. Between his bill and the back rent, he was in the red for about six thousand dollars. He paid the minimum, then he called his mother to tell her about his predicament.

"What have you been living on?" she asked him.

"On credit. And for cash I've been using my roommate's share of the rent. He doesn't know that I'm behind by three months."

"Well, I'll lend you enough money for your back rent because I don't want you to lose your apartment, but for the rest of your debt, you'll have to pay it off a little at a time."

"I'm so grateful," he said.

He decided to do a mailing to all the private schools in the Greenwich Village area, to see whether any of the principals would be interested in starting a chess program, either after school or during the school day. He also put up a big sign at The Chess Shop advertising chess lessons for beginners. *(I should've done this a long time ago.)*

Two weeks after he completed the mailing, he received a call from the director of the Little Red Schoolhouse, who said he'd be interested in starting a chess program in January. Sam was ecstatic. *(The next time Andrea comes, I'll have something more to show for myself.)*

Now that he was teaching chess again, he started studying the game as well, which he hadn't done in a while. He bought the latest edition of *Modern Chess Openings* and three of the most recent *Informants* to bring his openings up to date. He also bought Shereshevsky's *Endgame Strategy* and Jeremy Silman's *Reassess Your Chess*. He also started studying an hour of tactics every day. His goal was to attain a master rating so that he would have stronger credentials as a chess instructor. He began playing in the members-only tournament at the Marshall Chess Club every Thursday night.

Sam and Andrea sent letters back and forth every two weeks or so. She mailed him a big photo of herself in a bikini, which he put on the wall of his bedroom. In each letter he wrote to her, he gently suggested that she come to live with him in New York. He put together a big photo album, with pictures of all the sights he had shown her, and put it in the mail.

Whenever one of her letters took longer than usual to arrive, he became afraid that she might be dating someone else; then, when her letter arrived, he was somewhat reassured. Once again, he told Michael what was happening. "I'm so afraid of losing her," he said.

"Well, a little bit of anxiety is natural for someone in your situation, but if you think you're becoming paranoid, you'd better talk to Dr. Berkun right away."

"Okay."

When he had been studying hard for a few months, his improvement began to show. He played in an under 2200 tournament, finishing in second place, ahead of a few experts. He started taking one lesson every two weeks with Lev Barsky, an international grandmaster. They analyzed all his games together and expanded his opening repertoire.

He told Michael, "I've never had so much fun before."

Michael told him that there was an El Greco exhibit at The Metropolitan that was not to be missed, so Sam went there the following afternoon. He loved the exhibit, especially the *View of Toledo* and the portrait of Cardinal Don Fernando. After spending an hour in the museum, he took a bus down Fifth Avenue, past all the stores with their Christmas decorations, past St. Patrick's Cathedral, past the big tree at Rockefeller Center, past the main branch of the public library, past the Flatiron Building, and all the way down to Eighth Street, where the bus turned and headed east. *(I'll have to take Andrea on this bus the next time she comes.)*

When he got to his apartment, there was a message from Inez on his answering machine: *My voice recital at Juilliard will be on January 17th. I hope you can make it.*

He immediately called her back and said, "I'll definitely be coming on the 17th, and maybe I'll bring some friends with me."

He invited Lola and Rafael. On the program were some of his favorite *lieder*, among them "An Die Musik" and "Erlkonig" by Franz Schubert, "Widmung" by Robert Schumann, "Lebewohl" by Hugo Wolf, "Morgen" by Richard Strauss, and several songs he wasn't familiar with. After the recital, they joined Inez and her family for dinner at Bello Giardino, an Italian restaurant near Lincoln Center. He told Inez's mother Elisha about the El Greco exhibit and about Michael Schwartz's art.

"I'd love to meet him," she said.

"Well, he keeps very strange hours, but I'll try to arrange it. I'd be very interested to know what you think of his work."

Later that night, Sam went to French Roast, where he told Michael about Inez and her mother. "What's her full name? Maybe I know her."

"Elisha Birenbaum."

"I *do* know her. She's a curator at Sotheby's."

"Well, if she likes your work, maybe she can help you."

"Hm. If she can meet me in the evening, say at nine or ten o'clock, I'll force myself to be up. The two of you can pick the day and let me know when and where, and I'll make sure I get there."

When he woke up on Monday afternoon, Sam called Elisha right away. She invited Sam and Michael for a late dinner at her house on Friday.

Sam and Michael met at French Roast at 8:30 and strolled over to the Birenbaum house in the West Village. Michael brought some watercolors and some slides of his paintings.

During dinner they talked about the contemporary art world. Neither Michael nor Elisha were fans of the conceptual art that was so popular at the time. Michael said, "Once you get the idea, there's not much else you can say about it."

However, they differed about Jasper Johns and Robert Rauschenberg. Elisha liked most of their work; Michael wasn't impressed. "They do nothing for me," he said.

"Whom do you like?" she asked him.

"De Kooning, and maybe Francis Bacon, but after that it gets picky."

After dinner, everyone looked at Michael's slides and watercolors. Elisha liked them. "Do you have a gallery?" she asked.

"I haven't had a one-man show for a long time, but I show every fall with the street painters at the Cork Gallery in the basement of Avery Fisher Hall, and sometimes I have group shows at 55 Mercer with some my friends."

"Let me give it some thought," she said. "I might be able to find someone who would give you a one-man show."

Before they left, Sam asked Inez to play piano for them.

"I've been so busy with my song recital," she warned him, "that I haven't been working on my piano repertoire enough, but I'll see what I can do."

She played a Schubert sonata and Chopin's "Barcarolle."

Michael said, "Your playing reminds me of Dino Lipatti."

"That's a huge compliment," Inez said. "He's one of my heroes."

ON A SUNDAY AFTERNOON NEAR THE END OF JANUARY, Sam was in The Chess Shop, studying his openings, when a six-year-old boy named Jay Milton came in with his father, Marvin. Sam started watching him play. *(Maybe he's a potential student.)* He could see right away that Jay was incredibly talented. He was beating some of the best players in The Shop in speed chess, sacrificing pieces right and left. Sam challenged him to a match. They played a dozen games, nine of which Sam won, but every game was hard-fought. When they were finished, Ahmed told Marvin that Sam was a professional chess instructor.

"Do you think Jay could benefit from chess lessons?" Marvin asked Sam.

"Yes, he could, but frankly, he's too good for me to teach. Why don't you take him to Bruce Pandolfini?"

"Bruce Pandolfini. . .wasn't he the character played by Ben Kingsley in *Searching for Bobby Fischer*?"

"He's the one."

ALTHOUGH SAM'S LIFE WAS MUCH FULLER than it had been several months before, always, in the back of his mind, was the fear of losing Andrea. When he hadn't received a letter in a month, he called her. "Did you get my last letter?" he asked.

"Yeah, it seems like you're doing really well with your chess lessons."

"I am, and I'm also winning some money playing in tournaments."

"That's fabulous!" Andrea exclaimed.

Sam wanted to ask her whether she was seeing someone else, but he bit his tongue. Instead, he said, "Any chance you might be coming to New York anytime soon?"

"Sure, as soon as I get a vacation. What about you coming here?"

"Probably not until my after-school programs end in late June."

"I miss you," she said.

"I miss you, too. No matter what I throw at you, I always miss you."

For the time being, Sam was somewhat reassured.

Later that week, when he went home after teaching at the Children's Aid Society, he found a message on his answering machine: *Hi, Sam. This is Susan. Beth and I are in New York, and we'd like to hook up with you. We're staying at the Washington Square Hotel.*

Sam was thrilled. He immediately walked over to the hotel on Waverly Place. They weren't in their room, so he decided to play chess for several hours and come back after 10:00 p.m. He went to The Chess Shop, where he found Jim Smith playing with Costos "The Greek." He watched them play for an hour, then played speed chess with Marcus until 10:30, when he ran back to the hotel as fast as his feet could carry him. The concierge called their room, and the two girls immediately came downstairs and met Sam in the lobby. "Can you spare us a little of your time?" Susan asked.

"More than a little," he said. "How long do you plan on staying?"

"Only about a week, and while we're here we'd like to learn a little bit about literary New York."

"Well, then, the first thing you should see is the Chelsea Hotel. So many great writers have lived there—Dylan Thomas, Thomas Wolfe, and Brendan Behan, just to name a few. If you want, I'll take you there tomorrow."

"What about tonight?"

Sam laughed. "I guess you remember that I'm a late-night person."

"Why don't you take us to a nice bar or music club? If you're up to it, let's do both."

He took them to Arlene's Grocery on the Lower East Side, where Patty Rothberg was performing, then to the Village Idiot, which had become a popular bar in the meatpacking district, with country and western music on the jukebox and friendly barmaids who liked to dance on the bar. Susan and Beth got right into the act. After about three beers they were up on the bar themselves. They stayed until four in the morning, and then the three of them crashed at the hotel. Sam slept on the floor.

When he awoke at one in the afternoon, the girls had left the hotel. He found a note from them taped onto the inside of the door to the room: *We're going to explore the Village today. Why don't you meet us in front of the hotel at six, and the three of us can go out for dinner somewhere.*

At the Children's Aid Society that afternoon, Sam showed his students a famous game between Bobby Fischer and Boris Spassky from their match in 1972 that he had committed to memory. Then he played Zack, the strongest player in the class, a rook-odds game. When Zach beat him, he gave the boy a dollar. After the class ended at 5:00, he bought the *Daily News* and went to Café Reggio to read it. He showed up at the hotel promptly at six.

"What did you do today?" he asked the girls.

Susan answered for both of them: "We went to Washington Square, Bleecker Street, and the Café Figaro, and then we went to The Metropolitan Museum."

"Did you like it?"

"That's an understatement."

"Well, why don't we go to the Chelsea Hotel, then we can have a meal in that neighborhood."

"Great."

They took a leisurely walk up to 23rd Street, where Sam took a photo of them in front of the historic building; then they went for Thai food at Royal Siam on Eighth Avenue, where Sam and Beth ordered duck, and Susan ordered frogs legs. "I've never had them before," she said.

Sam and Susan did most of the talking. After twenty minutes, he turned to Beth and said, "Why don't you open up a bit? I'd love to hear some of your opinions."

"I'm not a big talker," Beth admitted. "But I like to listen."

Sam paused for a few seconds. "Can I ask you a personal question?"

"Shoot," Susan said.

"Are you two an item?"

"We are, but we're both bisexual, and we have an open relationship."

"I see." *(I wonder if they'd be up for a* ménage à trois*?)*

After dinner, he took them to the Village Corner. Lisa was behind the bar. "Holy cannoli, Batman!" she said. "Where've you been?"

"Cruising around in the Batmobile."

"Well, welcome back to Gotham City."

Sam smiled. "Lisa, this is Susan and Beth, two friends of mine from Iowa City."

"Any friend of Sam's, etc. Make yourselves at home."

They sat at a table near the bar. At the piano was Malcolm, with whom Sam had occasionally played chess in Washington Square Park years before. "Wow, I didn't know you were a musician," Sam said.

"Whatever you do, don't tell the chess players that."

"Okay, I promise."

"Do you have any requests?"

"How about 'The Girl from Ipanema'?"

"Oh, I *love* that one," Beth said.

"Do you know the recording by Stan Getz and Joao Gilberto?"

"I know it by heart."

They listened attentively. When Malcolm took a break, Sam asked the girls what was foremost in his mind: "Have you spoken to Andrea at all?"

"Yes," Susan said. "And she sends her love."

"Has she spoken at all about possibly moving to New York?"

"She's mulling it over."

"Good."

He walked them back to their hotel. When they were in front of the building, Susan whispered something in Beth's ear, and Beth nodded.

"Would you like to spend the night with us?" Susan asked him.

Sam considered it. *(If I did and Andrea found out. . . .)* He said, "I'm flattered, but right now I want to be faithful to Andrea."

"You're a good man," Susan said.

CHAPTER 27

On Friday night, Sam took the two girls to meet Michael Schwartz. They found him seated at a table with Brad. After he introduced them, Sam pulled over another table so the five of them could sit together. Naturally, the conversation turned to film.

"I'm sure you all know about Sarris's *auteur* theory," Michael said.

"Of course," Susan said, "although I didn't know he was the first critic to mention it.

"He wasn't the first, but he *was* the first to introduce it to this country."

"Well, what about it?" Sam asked him.

"I've been thinking about it, and I think it works better for the European directors than it does for the Americans. If you look at Humphrey Bogart's movies, for instance, he worked with so many directors, and it seems like every movie he was in was a good one. Maybe *Bogie* was the *auteur*."

Sam told Michael that Susan and Beth were in the Iowa Writer's workshop. Michael was impressed. "I know a lot of great writers came out of there."

"I've seen some of Susan and Beth's work," Sam said. "And I think they're both very talented."

"Thank you," Susan said.

"They both want to know about literary New York," Sam went on. "I already showed them the Chelsea Hotel. What else would you suggest?"

"You came to the right place. I knew most of the Beat writers back in the Fifties."

"Where were some of their hangouts?" Susan asked.

"Well, on the southwest corner of Bleecker and McDougal was the San Remo. Kerouac based *The Subterraneans* on people he met there, and further north on McDougal was the Provincetown Playhouse, where several of Eugene O'Neill's plays were premiered."

"Great. What else?" Susan asked him.

"Well, you could take them to the White Horse Tavern on Hudson, where Norman Mailer and some friends founded the *Village Voice* in the Fifties. You could go to Chumley's at 86 Bedford, which was a speakeasy during prohibition and was patronized by lots of great writers such as Dos Passos, Dreiser, and F. Scott Fitzgerald. . .um, you could go to McSorley's on East Seventh, where women weren't allowed until the Seventies. It was a favorite of John Lennon, Brendan Behan, and E.E. Cummings. What else. . . . Oh, you could take them to St. Mark's Church, where they have great poetry readings—both Allen Ginsberg and Gregory Corso read there. And you could stop by Minetta Lane, where Saul Bellow lived when he was in New York, and, of course, Washington Square, which was immortalized by Henry James, who wrote a novel with that name."

"And that's just in the Village!" Sam said.

"Wow!" Susan exclaimed. "We certainly did come to the right place."

"You know what?" Sam said. "I'm going to get a map of the Village and put stars in all the places you named."

"I have a map with me," Susan said.

"Do you have a pen?"

"Even better. I have a magic marker."

The girls' week in New York went by very quickly. When it was time for them to leave, Sam accompanied them to the bus terminal and told them to give Andrea his love. Then he went to Barnes & Noble on Astor Place to look at the chess books. There was a new book about the Sicilian Defense, Sam's favorite opening. He bought it, then went to The Chess Shop to study. The book had several games by Garry Kasparov, the world champion. Kasparov's games were so complicated that Sam had trouble understanding them; he could only marvel at their aesthetic beauty. He picked out one to show to his older class at the Children's Aid Society.

Although the winter was just ending, it was a beautiful day, so Sam went to Washington Square Park to watch the hustlers.

At a table near the park entrance, he found a game in progress with a lot of people watching. A teenage Filipino boy named Ferdinand was playing speed chess with a middle-aged tourist. Sam joined the spectators. The boy was giving his adversary time odds: five minutes for his opponent and only a minute for himself. Sam had never seen anyone play so fast. Ferdinand won game after game; once he had a winning position, he was able to finish a game in less than ten seconds. When Ferdinand's opponent gave up, Sam decided to try his luck.

"What's your rating?" the boy asked him.

"About 2000."

"Okay. I'll give you 5-2, five dollars a game."

Sam said, "I can't afford your prices."

"All right. We can play for two dollars a game, but if someone comes along who can play for more, I'm going to stop."

"Fair enough."

In the first two games, Sam blundered and Ferdinand won easily. Then Sam got into a rhythm and started playing better. They played for about two hours, and when they were finished Ferdinand was ahead by six games. They shook hands, and the boy said, "Next time we need to play for more. I've got to make a living wage."

"We'll work something out," Sam assured him.

When he returned to his apartment for the night, there was a message from Lola on his answering machine: *Hey, Sam, my new boyfriend Stan and I are doing a multimedia show together. Give me a call and I'll give you the details.*

It was too late for him to call her, but when he woke the following afternoon, he dialed her number right away. Stan answered.

"Hi," Sam said. "Are you Stan? Lola left me a message that you're doing a show together."

"That's right. Lola's been picked up by a gallery in Chelsea, and I'm going to read my poetry in the opening."

"Terrific. When is it?"

"It's going to be on Friday night at 6:00 p.m. Tell everyone you know."

"I definitely will," Sam said. "Where is it?"

"It's at the Gogosian gallery in Chelsea."

Sam invited Ahmed, Inez and her family, and Michael Schwartz. Michael said he couldn't make it, but everyone else promised to be there. On Friday evening, Sam and Ahmed went to pick up Inez and her parents at their home in the West Village, and they all walked to the gallery together, arriving at 6:30. Everyone availed themselves of the refreshments: wine, cheese, crackers, raw vegetables, and a variety of dips. On the walls were about thirty of Lola's paintings: portraits, landscapes, and still lifes. At 7:00, Stan began to read his poetry while Lola improvised on guitar.

They stayed at the gallery long after the entertainment was finished. Everyone loved Lola's work, especially Elisha. Sam bought a catalog to show Michael.

When he left the show, it was still too early to meet him, so Sam went to the Dante Café and composed a letter to Andrea:

My sweet adorable incomparable stunning love of my life: I had fun showing Susan and Beth around, but what they mostly did was remind me of you. In fact, everything reminds me of you. When are you coming? I'm having withdrawal symptoms. Love, love, love, Sam.

Two weeks later, Sam found a letter from Andrea in his mailbox:

Dear Sam. I have a couple of weeks off in April. Would you like to take a vacation together?

Sam immediately called her on the phone. "Hi. Andrea?"

"Yes."

"It's Sam. I got your letter, and I'd love to take a vacation with you, but I can only get one week off from my after-school programs."

"Okay, let's do a week then. Which week do you have off?"

"The third week in April. Why don't we go to Italy?"

"Well, I've never been to Italy, so I don't know if a week is enough."

"Then why don't we just go to one city and stay there for a week?"

"Which city should we go to?"

"Well, I've been to Venice and Rome, but I've never been to Florence, and it's supposed to be a jewel."

"Let's do that, then."

Sam wanted to write a letter to Freddy, telling him that they were coming, so on Saturday he went to the park to look for Dr. Li, Freddy's best friend in New York. He found him playing speed chess with Lovey Jenkins. In between games, Sam told the doctor, "I'm going to Italy in a few weeks. Do you have Freddy's address?"

"Yes, but I don't have it with me. Give me your phone number, and I'll call you."

Two days later, Dr. Li left Freddy's address and phone number on Sam's answering machine. He immediately drafted a letter to his old friend:

Dear Freddy, my girlfriend and I are coming to Florence in a few weeks. Can you come down from Milan for a day or two and hook up with us?

Freddy's reply came after only one week:

Dear Sam, I'd love to meet you and your friend. Give me a call when you arrive in Florence.

With two weeks to go before the trip, Sam taped a big calendar on his refrigerator and marked off the days until April 15th as if he were a young child waiting for Christmas. Ten days before their flight, Andrea called to tell him that she'd have twenty-four hours in the city between flights. He decided that a gourmet meal was in order, called the Four Seasons, and made reservations.

On April 14th, he met Andrea at LaGuardia Airport, and they caught a cab to his apartment, where they dropped off her luggage. It was a warm, sunny day, so he took her to Sheep's Meadow in Central Park, and they lay silently on the grass. *(I haven't been this happy since I was seeing Megan, and this time I'm not going to blow it.)*

After two hours in the park, they walked hand-in-hand to the restaurant. To go with dinner, they ordered a bottle of pinot noir. He proposed a toast: "May we never fall out of love with each other."

She said, "I'll drink to that."

The next day, they flew nonstop to Rome and then took a train to Florence. On the way, he taught her how to play chess, using a small portable set he had bought at The Chess Shop. They arrived at 5:00 p.m. local time, checked into a *pensione* their guidebook recommended, and had dinner in a nearby restaurant suggested by their hosts. Then they bought a bottle of Chianti and walked down to the Arno River, where they finished the whole bottle in half an hour, after which they went back to their hotel and crashed.

The next afternoon they spent three hours in the Uffizi Gallery. Sam was surprised to discover that Andrea knew a lot about art history. She knew the subject of every religious painting and all the mythology behind the paintings on Greek and Roman themes.

"Where did you learn all this?" he asked her.

"I had a minor in art history when I was in college."

"What was your major?"

"Recreation."

"Sound mind and sound body?"

"That's what they say."

One of the residents in their *pensione* was an elderly woman named Paola, who was in town to hear Alfredo Kraus sing. She was what they call in Italy an *appasionatta*; she traveled all over Europe to hear her favorite tenor. Paola took the lovers to the Opera to hear Kraus sing in Massanet's *Werter*, conducted by George Pretre. After the performance, the three of them went backstage to meet the star. Sam told him, "That was some of the best singing I've ever heard. Maybe the best."

"Thank you so much,"The tenor replied.

The next day, Sam and Andrea took a leisurely walk up to Fiesole, the hill town. On the way, he confided, "I want you to know, before we get too deeply involved, that I have bipolar disorder."

She shrugged. "I have no problem with that."

He gave her a big hug, then kissed her passionately. "You're so wonderful," he said.

On Friday night, Freddy came down from Milan for the weekend. Although he had a misogynistic streak, he could be very charming when he wanted to be. He took them to an excellent restaurant near the Duomo and insisted on paying the bill. On Saturday the three of them went to a chess club where Freddy and Sam played speed chess, just as they had so many times in New York City.

"How can you think so fast?" Andrea asked them.

The week went by quickly. Before they left, the lovers went to the jewelry shops on the Ponte Vecchio, where Sam bought a pearl necklace for Andrea and a silver brooch for his mother. Then they took the train to Rome and flew back to New York City.

BACK IN NEW YORK CITY, THEY TOOK A RIDE around Manhattan on the Circle Line. When the tour guide took a break from his lecture, Sam asked Andrea,

"Do you think we're ready to move in together?"

"Where would it be, in Iowa City or New York?"

"I don't know if I'd have enough stimulation in Iowa City. And with my lifestyle, being a late-night person, it might be too big a change for me."

"Well, I think it would be even more of a change for me," she said. "I've never lived in a big city."

"How about this?" Sam asked her. "Why don't you move to New York for three months. Then, if we're still in love, I'll live wherever you want me to."

"What about your roommate?"

"Let's give him a month to find another apartment. Until then, why don't you stay in Iowa City?"

"And what do I *do* when I come to New York?"

"With your experience, you'll have no trouble finding a bartending job."

"And what about my job at the waterfront?"

"Ask them if they can hold it for you for three months."

"All right."

Sam told Yong that he and Andrea wanted to live together, and asked him to start looking for another place to live.

"No problem," Yong assured him.

At two the following morning, Sam went to French Roast, where he informed Michael of the plans they had made. Michael stroked his chin. "That sounds very sensible," he said.

"It's going to be hard for me to be apart from her now, even if it's only for a month."

"Just try to keep busy, and the month will go by in a flash."

"You know what I found out in Florence?" Sam said. "Andrea has an extensive background in art history. I can't wait to bring her here and listen to the two of you discuss the subject."

"That'll be fun," Michael replied.

Sam thought out loud. "I wonder, if I move to Iowa City, whether I'll be able to find work as a chess instructor."

"Maybe you should start looking into that now."

"That's a good idea," Sam told him.

He called Andrea and asked her to bring a copy of the Iowa City phonebook to New York.

"You don't need to wait for me to bring it," she said. "I'll mail it to you right away."

"Good."

As soon as the phonebook arrived, Sam contacted the principals of several schools in Iowa City, told them he would be moving there in about four months, and asked them whether they would be interested in starting a chess program. The principal of the elementary school was enthusiastic about the idea. The others said they would think it over and get back to him. Sam also called the Dean of Iowa State University, who told him: "We already have an informal chess club, but I might be interested in putting together a team to compete with other colleges in the area."

"I'd love to do that," Sam told him.

When he got home after work the following day, he found a message from his mother on his answering machine. *Hi, Sam. I haven't seen you in a while. Would you like to have dinner with me this weekend?*

He called her back right away, and they made arrangements for him to visit her on Saturday night.

Instead of cooking a meal for him, she decided to take him out for dinner. They went to a Korean place in Leonia, where they ordered a traditional Korean barbecue. Sam told her about the plans he and Andrea had made. "She's the love of my life," he said.

As Michael had predicted, the month went by in a flash. When Yong moved out on May 15th, he gave Sam his new address and asked him to forward his mail.

"You've been a great roommate," Sam said. "Let's stay in touch."

"Definitely!"

CHAPTER 28

On the evening of June 1st, when Sam met Andrea at La Guardia, they locked lips, then took a cab to his apartment, silently holding each other with their eyes closed. They dropped off her suitcase, then went to East 6th Street to eat Indian food. Sam told her that he had found work in Iowa City.

"Great!"

Over dinner, she asked him, "Do you know any bars or clubs that might be interested in hiring me as a bartender?"

"Tomorrow evening we'll stop by all the bars where I'm a regular."

As soon as they entered his apartment, they tore off their clothes and made love until midnight. At 2:00 the following afternoon, she woke up and went to the nearest bodega, where she bought milk, eggs, and challah. Then she re-entered the apartment and cooked French toast, Sam's favorite breakfast. When it was ready, she woke him up.

"Breakfast is served," she said.

They went to the Village Idiot, the Village Corner, the Village Gate, and Karavas Place. At each bar, Andrea dropped off her resume, and they schmoozed with the employees.

Later, they went to French Roast to see Michael. One of the owners, Avner, was there. Sam introduced him to Andrea and asked him, "Do you need an experienced bartender?"

"Not right now, but we can always use a new waitress." He hired Andrea on the spot. "Come see Erin, the manager, tomorrow afternoon, and she'll put you on the schedule."

Since Andrea was new, Erin put her on the graveyard shift—midnight to

8:00 a.m.—which suited Sam fine, because many nights he was there with Michael. Michael, Sam, and Andrea had wide-ranging conversations about the arts. When the subject was painting, Sam did nothing but listen. After 3:00 a.m. or so, when Sam left, only Michael, Andrea, and the AAs, were there.

All the regulars loved Andrea. Brad called her "a breath of fresh air from the Midwest." But she made very little money at French Roast, because most of the AAs ordered nothing but coffee.

After three weeks, Erin switched Andrea to the evening shift, where she started making more money, but Sam was unhappy because he saw very little of her; when he came in on her shift, she was too busy to give him any attention.

At first, he kept his disappointment to himself, but after a week, he complained that he wasn't seeing enough of her. She said, "If you come into the restaurant at midnight, I'll stay for a couple of hours before I go home."

Since it was summer and Sam's after-school programs were off the agenda, the two fell into a routine. After she left French Roast, Sam stayed up talking to Michael until 4:00 a.m., when he walked back to the apartment and slipped into bed without waking her. He slept until 11:00, when she woke him up for sex. Then she went to work and he went to the Jefferson Market Library to look at the art books. When he joined her at French Roast, he peppered her with questions about art. Then, when Michael arrived, he told him what they had discussed, and the two delved deeper into the subject.

Sam asked him to suggest more books for him to read about art history and criticism. "I'd be glad to do that," Michael said. "You could start with Vasari's book on the Renaissance. Tatingin is very good on Expressionism. Let's see. . .Chipp's *Theories of Modern Art* is very good. . . ."

"What about a book on materials? I don't really know what an etching is."

"Okay. Mayer's book on materials is excellent."

"How about a general treatise on aesthetics?"

"For that I'd recommend Dewey's *Art as Experience*. You could also read Rollo May or Chiselin on the creative process."

"This is great," Sam said. "I'll buy all those books and bring them to Iowa."

In September, the time had come for Sam and Andrea to move to Iowa City. The night before they left, he called his mother to say goodbye. At 2:00 a.m., he stopped at French Roast briefly, where he and Michael promised to stay in touch by mail.

Before leaving his apartment, he called Dr. Berkun to tell him that he was moving. He asked him to find a doctor in Iowa City to write his prescriptions. "Call my mother when you find someone, and I'll get his phone number from her."

"Will do," the doctor said. "Best of luck with your new life."

THEY TOOK A GREYHOUND BUS TO CHICAGO, where they transferred to a bus to Iowa City. The entire trip took fifteen and a half hours.

As soon as they unpacked and settled into Andrea's place, Sam called Susan and Beth and announced his arrival. Susan was elated. "When can I see you?" she asked.

"Tonight I need to rest. I'll call you in a few days."

When he hung up, he tore off Andrea's clothes and jumped on her. When they were finished, he quoted from *Basic Instinct*: "You're the fuck of the century!"

"You're not bad yourself," she replied.

They lay awake for hours making small talk before falling asleep.

When he awoke the next afternoon, he found her in front of the television, watching the Oprah Winfrey show. He undressed her again and made love to her on the sofa. "Be more discreet," she said afterwards. "Oprah's watching."

She called the manager of The Lemon and told him that she was ready to go back to work.

He said, "Good. You can start on Friday."

She also called her boss at the waterfront and told him that she could start at any time. A few days later she was there. On her first day, Sam went there with her. He hadn't been waterskiing since he was thirteen, but he decided to give it a try. Somehow, he managed to stay on his feet for five minutes. Then he went for a swim in a roped-in area where Andrea was a lifeguard.

A FEW DAYS LATER, HE MET SUSAN AND BETH at the Fair Grounds Coffee House and asked them how things were going at the writer's workshop. Susan said, "I'm almost finished with my second novel."

"What's it about?"

"It's about the town where I grew up in central Wyoming."

"What was *that* like?"

"In a word, dismal."

"What about you?" he asked Beth.

"Right now I'm writing a series of Shakespearean sonnets."

"That's fabulous," Sam said. "I can't wait to read both of your works."

"I'll read you some selections from my novel," Susan said.

"And your poems?"

"I'd rather wait until they're finished," Beth replied.

Sam called Mr. Johnson, the principal of Lincoln Elementary School, and told him that he was in town.

"Why don't you come to my office tomorrow, and we can talk," Johnson suggested.

He also called the Dean of Iowa State, who said, "We can start at any time."

THE FOLLOWING AFTERNOON, SAM WENT TO MEET MR. JOHNSON. They hit it off right away. Johnson was enthusiastic about starting a chess program. Sam said, "I could either start one during school hours or after school."

"Let's start with after school, and if it goes well, maybe we'll make chess part of the curriculum."

On Friday night, Sam went to The Lemon, where Andrea introduced him to some more of her friends. He had a great conversation with an Irishman named Patrick who knew everything there was to know about James Joyce. When Sam told him that he was a chess instructor, Patrick said, "Maybe I'll take some lessons from you. I've always wanted to learn."

They shot a game of pool. The first time Sam missed a shot, Patrick cleared the table, and Sam said, "Maybe we could barter—chess lessons for pool lessons."

"That would be great."

Sam also met Shawn, one of Andrea's co-workers from the waterfront, who was a big sports fan. "I think the Yankees will win the World Series this year," he said.

"I haven't followed baseball for years," Sam admitted. "But maybe I'll start again."

"Now would be a good time."

On the way back to their apartment, Sam and Andrea went skinny dipping in the Iowa River. "I *love* it here!" Sam exclaimed.

AT THE BEGINNING OF OCTOBER, SAM STARTED the chess club at Iowa State. As the dean had suggested, he opened the club, not only to students at the University, but to anyone in the community who was interested. The club met every Thursday night, from 7:00 to 11:00. Sam got in touch with several other colleges and universities in the area too and set up a league for team competitions.

Their first match was at Grinnell. It was very hard- fought, with Iowa State winning by a score of 3½ to 2½. Sam was very pleased with the way his students played.

He advertised his new club in the local newspaper, and by the end of October he had thirty members. He also asked the editor, Mrs. Rose, if he could start a weekly chess column.

"What would be in it?"

"We could print up games by the world's top players, and I could give the reader some chess problems to solve."

"I'd love that!" she told him.

Sam called his mom every other week, and at the beginning of November he wrote a long letter to Michael Schwartz, telling him about all the good things that were happening in his life.

Michael sent a postcard in reply: *Freud said that success in love and work is the key to happiness. Congratulations!*

Once a week, Sam and Patrick played an hour of chess and an hour of pool. They were both fast learners. By the time Thanksgiving arrived, Patrick was competing almost evenly with the intermediate players in the club, and Sam was able to hold the pool table at the bar for an hour of 8-ball.

On Thanksgiving, Andrea and Sam went to her parents' house in Missouri for dinner. Andrea's father, William, was a farmer her mother a housewife. She had two younger sisters, Amy and Eve, both as beautiful as she was. Sam received a warm welcome from everyone.

Aside from Andrea, no one in her family had ever been to New York. Amy asked Sam, "Are New Yorkers really as cold as people say they are?"

"Am I the first New Yorker you've met?"

"No."

"Well, were the others cold?"

"Not really."

"Am I cold?"

"You're as warm as they come."

"Well, then, I think you should go to the city and find out for yourself."

"I might just do that," she said.

"If you come when I'm there, I'll give you the red-carpet treatment."

On the way back to Iowa City, Sam said, "Your family is wonderful."

IN HIS CHESS COLUMN EACH WEEK, SAM PRINTED UP games by the world champions and other great players. He started with Morphy vs. the Duke of Brunswick, a nineteenth-century masterpiece. He didn't feel strong enough to annotate the games by himself, so he relied on annotations by various grandmasters. He also gave his readers problems to solve, which he selected from a book of combinations. Each week he gave the solutions to the problems from the previous week.

By early December, Susan had finished her novel, and she gave it to Sam to read. Her work was mostly autobiographical. As a child, she had been beaten repeatedly by her father, an alcoholic who worked only sporadically doing odd jobs. Her mother was a weak woman who lived in constant terror of her husband's anger. Sam found the novel very gripping and very disturbing. Susan also showed Sam some photos she had taken of the house she grew up in. It was dilapidated, cluttered, and filthy. In the basement sat three broken refrigerators and two broken stoves. Sam asked her, "Do you still have issues with your parents?"

"Yes, but writing about my childhood is helping me work things out."

"I think your novel could reach a big audience if it gets published," Sam said. "So many people have had experiences like yours."

"That's what I'm hoping for."

DURING THE HOLIDAY SEASON, BOTH SAM AND ANDREA had two weeks off from work. For Christmas, they went to visit her parents again. Everyone treated him like one of the family. Then the two went on a road trip together to the Harry Truman historic site, where they saw the farm that he had worked on as a young man, and the Truman home, known as the "Summer White House" during his administration. Andrea surprised Sam once again with her knowledge of American history. They also went for a long hike in the Ozark Highlands.

Back in Iowa City in January, Sam decided to tell Susan about his illness. "Now that you've opened up to me about your childhood, I want to tell you something about myself. Can I rely on your discretion?"

"Certainly."

"I suffer from bipolar disorder," he said. "Right now I'm controlling it with medication, but there's always a chance that I might have an episode at some time in the future."

"I won't tell anyone, not even Beth. . . . And if you do have a problem, I'll help in any way I can."

"Thank you."

FOR THE SPRING SEMESTER, MR. JOHNSON DECIDED TO MAKE CHESS part of the regular curriculum at the school. So, in addition to his after-school program, Sam began to teach three classes during the school day, one each for the third, fourth, and fifth graders. Their homeroom teachers worked as his assistants.

Since he was working earlier in the day, he started going to bed at midnight—a big lifestyle change for him. Andrea told him, "You're not a vampire anymore."

He started preparing lesson plans for each of his classes. Each class began with a few simple tactical problems and some basic theoretical endgames, followed by showing his students an instructive grandmaster game, often the same one that he had published in his column. He focused on ideas rather than giving a lot of variations. He gave the weaker players queen-odds and played even with the stronger players. Whenever anyone beat him, he gave them a dollar.

By then, Sam was working more than he had in a long time and was more stable than ever. He told Andrea: "I don't feel like I'm ill anymore, and it's largely because of you."

"That's very gratifying," she said.

For the first time, Andrea told Sam that she was an amateur painter and showed him some of her work, which he liked a lot. With his encouragement, she started going to a drawing class at Iowa State once a week. When she got home, she showed him what she'd done. One weekend, she asked if he would pose for her.

"Certainly," he said.

She asked him to sit at a table, staring at a chess position. She set up her easel on the other side of the table, directly across from him, and painted him with an intense look of concentration on his face. After an hour, she gave him a break.

"Can I see what you've done?" he asked.

"I'd rather have you wait until I'm finished."

"How long will that be?"

"If we do an hour a day, about a week."

"A *week?*"

"At least. Do you know how many times Gertrude Stein posed for Picasso before he was finished?"

"No."

"Dozens of times."

Andrea covered up the easel and said, "No peeking, please."

Although Sam had never stopped playing, either in tournaments or in friendly games, he had stayed roughly at the same level for several years. Now that he was teaching more than ever, he continued to work towards a master rating. He bought the Smyslov-Levenfish book on rook endings, and studied the games of all the world champions, from Steinitz to Kasparov. He tried to study at least three hours a day, so that, between his teaching and his studying, he was working virtually full-time.

As she had predicted, Andrea's portrait of Sam was finished in about a week. When she showed it to him, he said, "Am I really so intense when I'm playing chess?"

"Definitely."

He took a few photos of the painting and sent copies to Michael Schwartz and to his mother. Michael wrote back, *Andrea seems to have a lot of talent.*

Sam asked her, "Have you ever had a one-woman show?"

"No."

"Why don't you make slides of your work and show them to some gallery owners?"

"I don't know if I have enough paintings that I'm satisfied with."

"Well, then, what about a group show?"

"That's a possibility."

CHAPTER 29

TO IMPROVE MORE RAPIDLY, SAM STARTED TAKING Lessons over the phone with Lev Barsky. Little by little, his hard work started paying off. During his spring break, he played in a big tournament in Chicago, tying for first place in his section. He knew it would be a lot of work to achieve a master rating, but he was determined to do it no matter how long it took.

For Sam's birthday on March 1st, Andrea threw a big party for him, inviting Susan, Beth, Shawn, Patrick, and a few of his chess friends. Amy drove all the way from Missouri to be there. Together they finished off five bottles of champagne. Sam drank a bottle and a half all by himself. At 1:00 a.m., he passed out on the living room floor. When he woke two hours later, all the guests had gone. Andrea scolded him, "You had way too much to drink tonight."

"I know," he said. "With the medication I'm taking, I really shouldn't drink at all."

"Well, if you know that, then you were foolish to drink so much."

"*Mea culpa*."

AT SAM'S SUGGESTION, ANDREA RENTED A STUDIO where she began to paint two hours a day, time permitting. She also continued going to the drawing class once a week. By early May, she had finished a dozen paintings and about twenty drawings. Sam gently tried to push her into having an exhibit, but she still felt that she wasn't ready.

When the spring semester at Iowa State was over, they went to New York for two weeks. He took her to see his mother again, who asked them, "When are the two of you getting married?"

Sam turned to Andrea and said, "Do you want to answer that, or should I?"

"It's certainly a possibility at some point," she said.

They stayed at the Washington Square Hotel on Waverly Place, as Susan and Beth had. Every night they went to French Roast to see Michael, staying up until about four in the morning. Andrea showed him several of her drawings, as well as slides of her paintings. He gave her very constructive criticism. Most of her drawings were studies of the male and female figure. Among her slides, in addition to her portrait of Sam, she had several landscapes of the countryside near Iowa City.

Sam went to The Chess Shop to say hello to Ahmed, Marcus and Naomi, Jim Smith, and the other regular customers. He also looked up Lola and Inez. Andrea was very impressed by Lola's art, and Lola had some nice things to say about Andrea's work as well. Inez invited Sam and Andrea to dinner, where her mother joined the chorus of praise. Andrea said, "It seems like everyone likes my work better than I do."

Inez gave everyone an impromptu concert, playing the Chopin "Berceuse" and Beethoven's *Waldstein Sonata*.

"You've improved noticeably," Sam told her.

"Then maybe all the money we're spending at Julliard isn't going to waste," she replied.

While they were in town, Sam and Andrea spent hours in New York's great museums again. By then, there were very few major sites in Manhattan that she hadn't seen on previous visits, so he decided to show her some of Brooklyn. He took her to the Brooklyn Museum and Prospect Park, then to Sheepshead Bay, where they ate fresh seafood and went fishing on a charter boat.

Sam said to her, "You know, I enjoy living in Iowa City, but I'd really like to move back here at some point."

She replied, "Let's talk about that down the road a bit."

WHEN THEY WERE BACK IN IOWA CITY, Sam suggested that she exhibit her work. "Look at all the positive feedback you got in New York. Michael and Lola are both first-rate painters, and Inez's mom is an art historian. What are you waiting for?"

She nodded. "I guess it's time."

There were six galleries in town. She showed her slides and drawings to the owners. Maxine, who ran the Iowa Artisan's Gallery, reacted with considerable interest and said, "I'd like to show your work when the summer is over."

"Surely," Andrea replied.

In addition to attending her weekly drawing class, she now painted two hours a day on days when she was working at the bar or the waterfront, and four hours a day on her days off.

Since it was summer, both the school and the university where Sam taught were closed, so all he had, chess-wise, was the club and his weekly column. He continued studying two or three hours a day, but he still had a lot of free time. For anyone else, that would've been a good thing, but Sam, when he wasn't busy, often became depressed and spent a lot of time in bed. This summer was no exception. He started spending twelve hours or more there; he had tremendous trouble getting out of bed in the morning, and he became listless and downcast.

Andrea noticed the difference. After couple of weeks, she asked, "Are you all right, Sam? You seem very depressed."

"I am," he said. "I need to find a way to keep myself busy."

"Why don't you take a part-time job until school starts again?"

He shrugged. "That's a good idea," he replied.

He started by going to all the bars in the city, but the owners all wanted someone with experience. Then he went to all the restaurants and cafés, but there was a lot of competition because many of the high school and college kids had taken summer jobs. Finally, he took a job driving a taxi for the local company. He worked eight hours a day, three days a week. Between fares, he waited at the taxi stand, studying chess combinations and chatting with the other drivers. Some of his co-workers were very interesting. Murray, a wizened old man in his seventies, had driven cabs in twelve different cities. Frank was a jazz pianist who drove during the week and performed in clubs every weekend. Bill was a Vietnam veteran with a prosthetic left leg who was a regular at Sam's Club. Diane was a professional midwife. All of them seemed to have an inexhaustible repertoire of stories to tell.

Sam continued taking lessons by phone. His teacher helped him with his opening repertoire, giving him dozens of games to study with positions that might occur in his games. He recommended the Sicilian Defense against 1e4 and the Nimzo-Indian Defense against 1d4. As white, Sam started studying the English opening. He asked his teacher, "Do you think I have the potential to be a master?"

"Definitely," Lev replied. "You're not that far away now."

"What do I need to work on most?"

"Your calculating ability. Your games are based too much on general principles. If you're going to be a master, you need to do concrete analysis."

"What's the best way to work on that?"

"First of all, analyze all your games in depth. You can also write down the moves of a well-annotated grandmaster game without looking at the analysis, do your *own* analysis, and then compare it with the variations mentioned by the annotator."

"What about studying combinations?"

"That can be very helpful, but the most important thing is to play in more tournaments, so you get in the habit of analyzing in depth."

Sam didn't mention that when he was depressed he had great difficulty analyzing in depth. He didn't feel he was in a clinical depression just yet, but just to be safe, he decided to call Dr. Stern, a psychopharmacologist recommended by Dr. Berkun. They met a few days later in his office.

"How can I help you?" the doctor asked him.

"Well, I have bipolar disorder, and I've been doing fine for a long time, but recently I've been feeling very depressed."

"Do you think we need to make an adjustment in your medical treatment, or is your problem more psychological?"

"Well, there may be a psychological component, but usually finding the right medication helps me the most."

"What are you taking now?"

"Zyprexa, Zoloft, and Welbutrin."

"Then why don't we add Trazodone?"

"What's Trazodone?"

"An antidepressant that's sometimes also prescribed as a sleep medication."

"What are the side effects?"

"Well, it can cause nausea, vomiting, or diarrhea, but only very rarely."

"All right. Let's try it."

"Now, I want to warn you," the doctor said. "It might take a few weeks before the medicine starts working, so I want you to promise me: If your condition worsens so that you can't function, and especially if you begin to feel suicidal, I want you to call me right away."

"Okay."

"Now, tell me—what do you do for a living?"

"Well, during the school year I work as a chess instructor, but in the summer there's not much work, so I've taken a job driving a cab."

"How's your concentration?"

"Not as good as it was a month ago."

"I'm concerned that, if your concentration worsens, you might have an accident."

"It's not that bad yet."

"Well, *if* it worsens, I want you to look for another job."

"Okay," Sam agreed.

ONE FRIDAY NIGHT IN LATE JULY, ANDREA AND SAM went to hear Frank perform. He was in a quartet with tenor saxophone, bass, and drums. The saxophone player reminded Sam of Stan Getz—very mellow and soulful. Frank was a competent accompanist, but no more than that. In between sets, he came to their table. Andrea was very complimentary, but Sam remained silent, not knowing what to say.

By the time the second set began, both of them had finished three martinis. When Sam ordered a fourth, Andrea said, "You've had enough."

"What? I've only had three drinks."

"Waiter, please bring us two Diet Cokes."

When the waiter left, Sam murmured, "Andrea, I'm a grown man. Don't treat me like a baby."

"Then don't act like one."

He was very angry, but he decided to hold it in. For the rest of the evening, they talked very little. When they got home, they went to bed without even kissing each other good night. Andrea fell asleep right away, but Sam lay awake for hours. *(All right, this isn't a big deal, but if we ever argue about something important, I'm not going to back down.)*

GRADUALLY, THE TRAZODONE STARTED WORKING. By mid-August, he was feeling much better. He decided to play in the U.S. Open, which was being held in Philadelphia that year. He stayed in a motel in nearby Cherry Hill, New Jersey. The tournament lasted nine days, with every round except the last held in the evening. During the afternoon, he explored the city, going to The Philadelphia Museum, the galleries in the old city, and the Barnes Collection.

Sam's play in the tournament was somewhat erratic. He did beat one expert, but he also lost to two weaker players. He finished the tournament with four points out of nine—not a good result for a player of his caliber.

Before taking the bus back to Iowa City, he stopped in New York to show his games to his teacher. Grandmaster Barsky could always find the critical position where Sam or his opponent had gone wrong. He also made some salient general comments. "Your openings are much better than they were, but you seem to get lost in tactical positions. Have you been analyzing your games as I suggested?"

"Yes, I have."

"I think you should read the book *Think like a Grandmaster*, by Kotov. He gives some good tips on how to calculate."

The book was out of print, but Sam found it at a used bookstore. He started reading it on the bus back to Iowa, setting up the positions on a small portable chess set.

Andrea was very relieved that Sam was feeling better because, although she didn't mention it, his illness had put a strain on the relationship.

FALL CAME, AND SAM RESUMED HIS WORK at the school and the university. It was also time for Andrea's one-woman show at the Iowa Artisan's Gallery. Sam helped her hang the work, and they invited everyone they knew in Iowa City. About fifty people showed up. The opening was a big success. Three collectors expressed interest in buying her work, and Mary, one of the curators at the local museum, told the director about her. She suggested that he purchase at least one of Andrea's paintings for their permanent collection. Between the museum and the private collectors, five paintings and seven drawings were sold.

Maxine told Andrea, "It's been a long time since we've had such a successful opening."

Sam started bringing his chess set to Andrea's studio and studied while she painted. Sometimes he'd take a break and peruse her work. "I think you're going to be famous one day," he told her.

By then his concentration was completely back to normal and his game improved at an exponential rate. Although his rating was still under 2100, in three tournaments he competed in that fall, he didn't lose to a single player rated under 2000. He also improved as a coach. The players on the university team won almost every match they played in. He taught them some openings he was studying himself. After each match, he analyzed the games of everyone on the team, and they started playing better, too.

Most importantly for his mood, he was having fun.

Bill, the taxi driver, started taking private lessons from him. Of all Sam's students, he was the most talented. In late October, they went to Cleveland to play in a tournament together. They both succeeded admirably. Sam won his section, and Bill won the under-1800 prize. After the tournament, they went to a strip club to celebrate. Sam ordered a Johnny Walker Black on the rocks with a pint of Budweiser. The barmaid repeatedly asked him to buy her drinks and kept pressuring him to buy more for himself. By 2:00 a.m., he was as drunk as a skunk. They took a late bus back to Iowa City and a cab back to Sam and Andrea's apartment, where Bill literally had to carry him up the stairs. He passed out with all his clothes on and slept for sixteen hours.

Sam and Bill showed all their games to the players at the club, using a big demonstration board. Everyone was impressed.

"I'm the best one-legged player in Iowa," Bill boasted.

Andrea asked Sam and Bill to pose for her. Instead of painting them at the chessboard, she had them sit at a table, playing cards. She consciously emulated Cézanne's *The Card Players*. When the session was over, she took a photo of them, so that she could work from the photo and they wouldn't have to pose for her repeatedly. When she had finished the painting after about two weeks, she brought it to the gallery to show to Maxine, who said, "I'd like to represent you on a regular basis, because I like everything you do."

Andrea assented immediately. They discussed how much they would charge for her work and what the gallery's cut would be. They decided on $600.00 for a drawing, $2,000.00 for a small painting, and $5,000.00 for a large one. Afterward, Andrea went home to tell Sam the good news.

"That's *phenomenal!*" he practically shouted. He threw his arms around her and kissed her on her hair, on her neck, and on her lips. "I adore you!" he exclaimed.

They went down to the Iowa River to watch the sunset and, when it got dark, watched the stars come out. Sam had a premonition: *I may never be this happy again,* but he forced himself to ignore it. At 1:00 a.m., it started getting chilly, so they returned to the apartment, where they made love again and again.

"I adore you!" he kept repeating.

"Ssh," was her only reply.

THE NEXT EVENING, HE RECEIVED A CALL FROM SUSAN. The two hadn't talked in a while, so they had a lot of things to tell each other. Sam said, "I was depressed for most of the summer."

"How come you never called me?"

"It's hard to explain. Sometimes when I'm depressed, I'm so down on myself that I don't want to impose on people."

"It wouldn't be an imposition. When my friends aren't doing well, I want to help them any way I can."

"Okay," he said. "Next time, I promise I'll call you."

On Saturday night, Sam, Susan, and Beth went to The Lemon to see Andrea. Both Shawn and Patrick were there. Everyone played eight ball for two hours, but no one was able to win a single game off Patrick.

At 2:00, the bar closed and most of the regulars left, but Andrea, Sam, Susan, and Beth remained there. They stayed until 4:30. As they were leaving, Sam told Beth, "Next time I see you, I want to read some of your poetry."

"Okay."

In early November, Sam tried to give Michael a call, but he couldn't get through. Two weeks later, he tried again, unsuccessfully. He began to worry. Since Andrea had said nothing about Sam visiting her family for Thanksgiving, as they had the previous year, he told her, "If I don't hear from Michael in a week, I'm going to New York to try and find him."

". . . What about your chess programs?"

"I'm sure they'll give me a week off if I tell them how urgent it is."

"Doesn't he have someone to take care of him if he becomes ill?"

"I don't know. For all I know, he could be lying dead in his apartment."

She frowned. "Don't panic. I'm sure there's an explanation."

The next week, he took a bus to New York. When he got there, the first thing he did was to go to French Roast, where he waited anxiously for the AAs to show up. At 1:00 a.m., Brad entered the restaurant. Sam asked him, "Have you seen Michael?"

"No, he hasn't been here in over a month."

The next day, Sam took a cab to Michael's building in Sunnyside. When he rang the buzzer, there was no reply, so he waited by the front door until Kathy, one of his neighbors, showed up.

"Do you know Michael Schwartz?" he asked her.

"Oh, the old professor? Sure."

"Have you seen him lately?"

"Now that you mention it, no, I haven't."

"Do you know anyone who's close to him?"

"Not really, but sometimes a woman named Angela comes to visit him."

"Oh, I know Angela. Do you know how I can get in touch with her?"

"I know she goes to the Vocal Record Collector's Club, which meets in a church on the third Friday of the month."

"Do you know the name of the church?"

"No, but it's on the corner of East 60th and Park."

"What time does it meet?"

"I think at 7:00 p.m."

It so happened that the third Friday in November was the following evening. Sam didn't sleep that night, and he was extremely restless in the morning. He didn't feel up to playing chess, and he didn't want to be alone, so he called Lola and asked her to keep him company. Fortunately, she had the day off. They met at The Peacock Café, where Sam told her what was on his mind. "I'm very worried," he said.

"Worrying doesn't help."

"It's hard not to—"

"I'll tell you what. Why don't we go to Coney Island together?"

"That's a great idea."

They took the D train all the way there. On the way, she told him some amusing stories. When they got there, they bought hot dogs and took a long walk on the beach, then rode back into town, where they had a bite at Karavas Place. When they were finished, they headed to the church.

"I'm so glad you're keeping me company," Sam said.

They got there fifteen minutes early and asked for Angela. Everyone knew who she was.

"She'll be here," the club president assured him.

When she came in, Sam recognized her right away. He took her aside and asked her, "Have you seen Michael Schwartz?"

"Yes, he's in the hospital."

"Oh, my God, what's wrong?"

"He has an infection in one of his legs."

"What hospital is he in?"

"St. Vincent's."

CHAPTER 30

SAM AND LOLA HURRIED OUT OF THE CHURCH, took a cab to the hospital, and showed up just before the end of visiting hours. They went straight to his room. "Michael! How are you?" Sam asked him. "I've been so worried about you."

"I've got a gimpy leg," Michael said.

"Why didn't you call or write?"

"I haven't felt well enough. . . ."

"Well, thank God you're alive. How are they treating you?"

"Like one of the family."

"Do you know how much longer you'll be here?"

"They said about five days or a week."

"I know that Angela's visited you. Has anyone else?"

"Yes, Ted Gold's been here a couple of times."

"Should I tell the AAs about you?"

"You can tell Brad that I'm here."

"Do you want me to bring you anything?"

"Yes—why don't you bring a chess set next time you come?"

"Can do," Sam said.

Sam and Lola walked over to the Washington Square Hotel, where he was staying again.

"Could you stay with me?" he asked.

"Okay, but I can't sleep with you."

"You don't have to."

They lay together with her hand in his. "You're the best," he said.

"Am I? Well, then, you're the second best."

He fell asleep promptly and didn't wake up for twelve hours. When he did, he found a note from Lola on the table: *I have three classes today so I can't stay with you, but I'll be thinking of you.*

In the afternoon, Sam went to The Chess Shop to say hello to Ahmed and the regulars. While he was there, he bought a small portable chess set to bring to Michael. He also picked up a copy of *The Life and Games of Mikhail Tal*, one of the most entertaining chess books ever written. Then he went to visit Michael. "I'm sure you'll enjoy this," he said.

They played a few quick games before Michael confessed, "I'm very tired. I need to rest a bit."

When Sam left the hospital, he called Andrea collect from a phone booth. "Michael has a bad leg," he said. "But it looks like he's going to be all right."

After saying goodbye to Andrea, he called his teacher and told him that he was in town but too busy to take a lesson.

"Call me when you're back in Iowa," Lev said, "and we'll continue our lessons over the phone."

"Great."

For the next four days, he visited Michael once a day. The day before Michael was due to be released, he went to Barnes & Noble at Union Square and bought *New in Chess* magazine, which he read on the way back to Iowa.

When he left the bus station there, he went straight to The Lemon.

"How's your mentor?" Andrea asked him.

"Much better."

Sam played pool with Patrick, losing every game as usual. After the bar closed, he and Andrea walked home together. She seemed very preoccupied, but Sam decided not to ask her why. *(If she wants to, she'll tell me herself.)*

When they reached their apartment, he tried to kiss her, but she recoiled. "I need to take a shower," she said.

When she was finished, she went to bed and lay down with her back to him and went to sleep right away.

(Something's wrong here.)

For the next few days, not only was she not interested in sex, she hardly spoke a word. Sam decided to give Susan a call. "Can you meet me at the café at 4:00 this afternoon?" he asked. "There's something I want to discuss with you."

She arrived promptly at that time. "What's up?"

"Andrea seems very distant," he said. "I don't know what to make of it."

"How long has this been going on?"

"Since I got back from New York four days ago."

"That's nothing," she assured him. "She might be having her period, or there could be any number of other simple explanations."

"So you don't think I should bring it up?"

"I'd wait at least another week."

"All right."

He continued teaching chess and running his club. In his spare time he studied fanatically. He read Bobby Fischer's *My 60 Memorable Games* from cover to cover. He also studied the games of two Soviet world champions, Botvinick and Smyslov. He deepened his knowledge of the openings he knew and learned some new variations as well. He did most of his studying in the café or the library, because he sensed that Andrea wanted some time to herself. Finally, he couldn't help asking her, "Are you okay? You've been so withdrawn lately."

"Well, I don't know why, but I haven't been happy lately."

"Can I help in any way?"

"I don't know."

He wanted to dig deeper but decided to let the matter rest for now. The next day he received a call from Susan. "I found a publisher for my novel!" she exclaimed.

"Congratulations! Let me take you out to celebrate."

"Can I bring Beth?"

"Certainly."

He stopped at a wine store and bought a bottle of champagne, then the three of them met at the café, where he asked the manager, "Is it okay if we drink champagne here?"

"Of course. You're all good customers. You can do whatever you want."

After they had about two glasses each, Sam asked Beth, "When am I going to see your poetry?"

Beth looked at Susan, then said, "Why don't we all go back to the apartment, and I'll read you some right now."

On the way to their place, Sam bought another bottle of champagne, which they killed off in half an hour. Beth read several of her poems, which Sam found to be quite witty. When she finished reading, she took out a bottle of white wine out of the refrigerator.

Sam started feeling drunk. "When Andrea sees how much I've been drinking, she's going to kill me."

Susan said, "Well, why don't you spend the night with us?"

"That would be even worse. She'll think I'm cheating."

"All right. What I'll do is make a big pot of coffee and give you a chance to sober up before you go home."

"Good idea."

He was feeling a bit nauseous, and the coffee didn't help. He stumbled home, where he vomited in the toilet and tried to clean it up but not enough to wholly eliminate the smell. When Andrea got up to go to the bathroom, she knew that he had been sick. She went back to the bedroom, where she exploded. "You've been drinking again, damn it. This has to *stop*. I'm warning you—if this happens again, I'm going to break up with you, and if you don't believe me, just try it."

"I'm sorry," he told her. "We were celebrating because Susan found a publisher for her novel."

"I don't care *what* your excuse is. I'm not going to be an enabler. Do this again and you're *history*."

"All right. I won't."

WITH THE CHRISTMAS BREAK APPROACHING, Andrea said nothing about him visiting her family, so he told her preemptively that he wanted to spend the holiday with his mom.

Instead of staying at a hotel in New York, he slept on his mother's living room sofa. "You don't need to cook dinner for me," he said. "Why don't we go to a good restaurant instead?"

They went to Stony Hill Inn, where Sam ordered a T-bone steak and his mother chose Chicken Milanese. Later that night, he took a bus into the city and went to French Roast to visit Michael. "How's your leg, Professor?" He asked him.

"Much better."

Several of the AAs were in the restaurant that night, including Brad, Ned Diamond, and Rick Danger. Sam told them, "I need to be alone with Michael."

The two of them moved to a quiet table, where Sam told Michael how Andrea had been behaving. "She's been very distant, and anytime I have too much to drink, she goes ballistic."

". . .Then you better not drink too much."

"I won't, but something else is bothering her, and I don't know what."

"Have you asked?"

"She says she's unhappy, but she doesn't know why."

Michael pondered this for a moment. "I would give her lots of space. It might just be a phase she's going through."

"I'm trying to play it as cool as possible, but inside it's tearing me apart."

"To hold onto a beautiful woman, a man needs to be strong," Michael said. "I know that from experience."

"I know how to give the impression of being strong, but inside I feel like mush."

"That's all right. How can you be something you're not?"

"That's what Albert Ellis would say."

"Dr. Ellis knows a thing or two. . . . In fact, maybe the best thing you could do would be to consult with him."

The following afternoon, Sam called the Ellis Institute and set up an appointment for a private consultation on Monday. He found Ellis seated in the big armchair in his office as usual. "Haven't seen you in a long time," the doctor said. "How can I be of help?"

"I've been living with a woman in Iowa City for over a year. Everything was going well for a long time, but recently she's been pulling away from me. I want to keep her if I possibly can, but I'm afraid of losing my mind."

"Do you know *why* she's been pulling away?"

"She says that she hasn't been happy, but she can't give me a reason. She gets upset when I have too much to drink, but I don't think that's all of it. Not nearly all of it."

"You've got to realize that, no matter what you do, there's a possibility that you might lose her."

"What should I do?"

"There are no 'shoulds.' Whatever you decide to do will be okay."

"Well, I want to keep her if possible, but if things stay the way they are for a long time, I'm afraid I might fall apart."

"Then you need to decide for yourself if it's worth the risk. Nobody can give you a crystal ball to see the future in. You've got to make up your mind—

and don't put yourself down no matter what happens."

"All right."

ON THE BUS BACK TO IOWA CITY, Sam sat next to a young woman who was reading the Folger Library edition of *Hamlet*. When she put the book down, he asked, "Are you reading this for a course or for pleasure?"

"Both."

"Are you in college?""

"Yes, I'm a graduate student at Iowa State."

"Majoring in. . . ?"

"English literature."

"Do you have a good professor in your Shakespeare class?"

"He's a *great* professor. He knows everything there is to know about Shakespeare."

"That's great. What other plays have you studied?"

"Well, we started with three history plays: *Henry IV Part One, Henry V,* and *Richard III*. Then we did some comedies, and now we're studying all the famous tragedies in detail."

"I'm green with envy."

She laughed. "I'm Marianne. What's your name?"

"Sam."

They shook hands.

"What brings you to Iowa City?" she asked him. "You look like such a New Yorker."

"Is it so obvious?"

"Yes."

"I'm living with a woman I met here when I was on vacation."

They had a wide-ranging conversation. When they were approaching Iowa City, Sam said, "Let's stay in touch. We have so much in common."

"Definitely."

They exchanged phone numbers and shook hands again. *(Che bella bambina!)*

HE FOUND ANDREA IN A BETTER MOOD. "How's your family?" he asked.

"Everyone's fine."

The two of them ate dinner at an Indian restaurant, then went home and tenderly made love. *(Maybe she's over whatever she was going through.)*

"I did some painting over the weekend," she said. "Would you like to see?"

"Of course."

She showed him two simple and lovely landscapes.

"Can I hang these up in our living room?" he asked her.

"Sure, why not?"

She was by then spending at least four hours a day in her studio. For the first time, she invited her dealer there to see her work in progress.

"You're improving exponentially," Maxine said. "Maybe you should have a show in New York or Chicago. I have some connections in both cities."

". . . You think I'm ready?"

"Oh, definitely."

Andrea came home that evening and told Sam what she had said. He threw his arms around her and gave her a big hug. "My girlfriend is a genius!" he exclaimed.

Andrea was much more affectionate than she'd been in over a month. Sam wrote a letter to Michael in which he told him that it seems like things were back to normal with her.

Maxine called three gallery owners in Chelsea and told them about Andrea. Sam decided to go to New York during February break to try and promote her work, too. The first place he visited was the Carver Gallery. The owner was on vacation, but Judy, her salesperson, liked the slides and said, "Why don't you leave them here, and I'll show them to my boss when she comes back."

"Right now I have only one set of slides, but I'll have some copies made and bring them or mail them to you."

"Awesome."

The second gallery owner, Paul Goodman, liked the landscapes but wasn't enthusiastic about her earlier work. "I'd like to exhibit her recent paintings in a group show in March," he said.

"That's a possibility," Sam said, "but if another gallery offers her a one-woman show, we'll have to go with them."

"Of course," said Mr. Goodman. "Let me know."

The owner of the Prichard Gallery liked the slides but said, "I can't represent her right now—I have too much on my plate."

When Sam visited Michael at French Roast, he showed him the slides and asked him whether there was any way *he* could help out.

"I don't have any connections right now, but I like what she does."

Sam was disappointed but kept it to himself.

Michael asked him, "How's she been treating you?"

"She's been *much* nicer, but she didn't invite me home for the holidays as she did last year."

"Maybe she's one of those women who runs hot and cold."

"I think I'd prefer someone who's consistently lukewarm."

"No you wouldn't."

WHILE IN NEW YORK, SAM PLAYED in a tournament at the Marshall. His performance was about par—he beat an A player, drew two experts, and lost to a master. Although he didn't finish in the money, he was relatively satisfied with his play. He showed the games to his teacher, who said, "You're becoming much more solid."

Because Sam was due back in Iowa City, he dropped off duplicate copies of the slides at the Carver Gallery before he left. He gave Judy their phone number and asked her to call them if the gallery owner liked them. "In fact, call us one way or the other."

"I will," she promised him.

When Sam got off the bus in Iowa City, Andrea was there to meet him. "What a nice surprise," he said, kissing her on the lips.

"You know what?" she said. "I missed you."

"It's good to be back."

"Come with me," she said. She took him by the hand and they walked to her studio together. On her easel was a big portrait of Sam. He was seated at a table with his chin resting on his hand. On his face was an expression of profound sorrow.

"Now look at this one." She showed him leaning against the wall, holding a large chess trophy. This time he had a triumphant expression on his face.

"You know me so well," he said.

He called Marianne and set up a lunch date. They met at the Fair Grounds Coffee House.

"How'd you do in your Shakespeare class?" he asked.

"I got an 'A'."

"Good for you. What classes are you taking this semester?"

"A course in Romantic poetry, one in English history, and a creative writing class."

"Maybe I should introduce you to my friends Susan and Beth. They're both in the Iowa Writers Workshop."

"Oh, I'd love that. I want to join that group after I graduate."

Sam was still working hard on his chess, but he was only improving gradually. He called Grandmaster Barsky and took a lesson over the phone. "Now that you know the ideas in your opening systems," Barsky told him, "I want you to memorize the main lines."

"That's going to be a lot of work," Sam said. "I don't have a very good memory."

"That's why I said memorize the *main* lines. If you had a good memory, I'd want you to learn every nuance."

Sam expanded his collegiate league to ten teams. His team was playing a match a week, either at home or away. He also continued teaching in the schools, writing his column, and coaching his private students. Bill was now rated about 1850, far above the theoretical average. Sam said, "Soon you'll be too good for me to teach."

"No I won't. You're such a good teacher, I'd rather have you than a grandmaster."

For Andrea's birthday on February 27th, Sam decided to throw a surprise party for her. He invited all the regulars at the bar, including Patrick and Shawn, his student Bill, Susan and Beth, and his new friend Marianne. He asked Susan if he could use her apartment, and she immediately assented. Susan called Andrea and told her she wanted her to look at a short story she had just finished. When Andrea entered the apartment, everyone shouted, *"Surprise!"*

"Oh, my God!" Andrea exclaimed.

Susan brought out a big birthday cake and a bottle of champagne. Sam said, "In honor of your birthday, I'm not going to have a drop."

He filled a glass of grape juice and proposed a toast: "To Andrea's career as a painter."

"Sam," Andrea whispered, "you're too good to me."

When they were back in their own apartment, they made love more passionately than they had in months. Andrea sang Madonna's "Like a Virgin."

Sam smiled. "I'm so happy," he declared.

As Grandmaster Barsky had suggested, Sam tried to memorize the main lines of all his opening systems. Each day, he looked in *Modern Chess Openings* and played over one variation until he knew it by heart. He started with the Sicilian Defense, because it was the sharpest and most theoretical opening in his repertoire. Against 1d4, he continued to study the Nimzo-Indian Defense. He also began to memorize the openings he played when he had the white pieces.

In the beginning of March, Andrea received a call from Judy at the Carver Gallery. "I showed your slides to the owner," she said. "She wants to give you a one-woman show."

When Andrea told Sam what she had said, he picked her up and twirled her around as if she were a child. Andrea decided to go to Missouri for a few days to celebrate with her family. This time she invited Sam to join them.

Everyone in her family was elated. Her sister Amy was especially impressed. "Small town girl takes the Big Apple!" she exclaimed.

On the way back to Iowa City, Sam said, "Now that you're becoming an established artist, why don't we move back to New York City?"

Andrea hesitated. "I don't know if I'm ready for that yet."

"I think it would be good for your career."

"I'll give it some thought. Nothing is written in stone."

In late March, they both took a leave of absence for a month and went to New York. Sam asked Bill to take over his teaching jobs and to run the club while he was away. Andrea brought several recent works with her, including her portraits of Sam. The opening was scheduled for April 1st.

Sam invited everyone he could think of—the chess players, the AAs, Inez, Lola, Ahmed, Michael, Angela, and others. Judy promoted the opening for the gallery, inviting the public, the press, and a few collectors she thought would look favorably on Andrea's work.

Altogether, more than sixty people showed up. One of the critics for the *New York Observer* gave her a positive write-up, which led to several more collectors coming to view the exhibit. By the time the show closed on April 30th, the gallery had sold twenty paintings. Once again, Sam brought up the possibility of relocating to New York. Andrea said, "Let me sleep on it."

The following evening she told him, "I'm going back to Iowa and give my bosses a month's notice. If you want, you can stay here and start looking for an apartment, but if you become ill, I'm going to leave you. I don't know what kind of person that makes me, but that's what I've decided."

Sam became very quiet and look at her searchingly. Finally, in a very faint voice, he said, "Okay."

CHAPTER 31

SAM STARTED GOING FROM BUILDING TO BUILDING in Alphabet City, asking the superintendents whether there were any apartments available. After about two weeks he found a one-bedroom on 11th Street and Avenue B. At first, he kept what Andrea had said to himself, but before paying the rent and security he told Michael: "Andrea says she's going to leave me if I become ill."

"Do you think she means it?"

"I think she does."

"My God. That would be like having an axe hanging over your head. If your mother dies and you have no one to take care of you, it would be a *death* sentence. If she's really serious about this, I think you should break up with her."

"I can't," Sam said. "I'm in too deep to do that."

Michael paused. "You know, it's kind of strange that she's willing to relocate and at the same time not committing to you. She seems to be very ambivalent."

"Well, I'm not. I'm totally in love with her."

"But if you become ill?"

"Then God have mercy on my soul."

He paid the rent and one month's security, told the landlord that he would be ready to move in on June 1st, then took the bus back to Iowa City.

The first thing he did when he entered their apartment was to call the dean at the university and the principal of the school and give them notice. He also called the editor of the newspaper that published his weekly column.

Then he went to Andrea's studio to see if she was there. He found her with her hair in pigtails, wearing an apron covered with paint. She gave him her cheek to kiss *(Not the lips?)* and said, "Let me work for an hour, and then we can have dinner together."

"Do you want to eat out or at home?"

"Let's eat at home. I'll make you a nice dinner."

"Maybe this time I'll make dinner," he said.

He stopped at the supermarket and bought everything he needed, came home, and prepared a classic Italian repast— linguine with clam sauce, salad with creamy Italian dressing, and chicken oreganata. He also brewed a pot of fresh Columbian coffee.

When she came home, she took a quick shower, and they ate heartily. "I didn't know you were such a good cook," she said.

"When I was in college, I had an Italian girlfriend who taught me a few things, but I only cook once in a blue moon. This meal is to celebrate your success in New York City."

She smiled but didn't reply.

The time passed quickly. On June 1st they took a bus to New York, where Sam took his furniture out of storage, and the two of them moved into their new quarters. The manager at French Roast rehired her immediately. Sam picked up a few students at The Chess Shop, but because the spring semester was still in session, there were no after-school programs for him to work in, so he decided to look for another job. He asked Andrea, "Should I drive a cab again?"

"No," she said. "The hours are too long. We'll have almost no time to spend together."

(She wants to spend a lot of time with me—that's a good sign.)

He found work in the music department at the Union Square Barnes & Noble. The pay wasn't good, but he liked what he was doing and found most of his coworkers friendly and interesting.

He and Andrea arranged their schedules so that they both worked the day shift. They also arranged to have the same days off, Monday and Tuesday.

Every afternoon when her shift ended, Andrea went to Central Park and painted until nightfall. When she got home, she showed Sam what she had done. He was genuinely enthusiastic. "Do you have any suggestions?" she asked.

"I love everything you do, but I know what Michael would say."

"What?"

"He wants to paint right on the borderline between representation and abstraction. I think he would say that your paintings are too literal."

She pondered that. "You know, that's a fair thing to say. Maybe I'll start pushing in a more abstract direction."

Andrea worked so feverishly that her paintings started filling up their living room. Fortunately, she'd saved a lot of money from her one-woman show. She decided to rent a small studio and share it with Michael's friend Angela. At first, she continued painting outdoors and only used the studio as a storage space. She told Sam, "I want to do a series of at least twenty Central Park pictures and exhibit them in my next show."

"That's a *beautiful* idea," Sam said. "I wonder if anyone's ever done that before."

"Well, even if they have, I'll do it better."

"You're finally starting to believe in yourself as much as I believe in you."

Every Monday night, Sam went to French Roast to visit Michael, whose leg had largely healed but who still smoked like a chimney and gorged himself on rich food. He was very overweight, bordering on obesity. "You're killing yourself," Sam told him.

"Let me worry about that. Tell me—how are things with Andrea now?"

"They seem as good as ever."

"Just don't forget what she said about leaving you if you become ill."

"I haven't forgotten, but I can't dwell on it or I'll go nuts."

BECAUSE HE WAS AN EMPLOYEE AT BARNES & NOBLE, Sam was entitled to discounts on all books. He decided to read at least one book by each Nobel prize-winning author. To save money, he took out books from the library if they were available; the rest he bought at the bookstore. Rather than going chronologically through the list, he skipped around, reading the most important writers first. Soon he was reading a book a week yet leaving time to study chess an hour each day. Everything he read, he discussed in detail with Michael.

Every Thursday night, he played in a four-round chess tournament at the Marshall. He never won the tournament, which attracted several masters and even a few grandmasters, but he often won the expert prize. His concentration had never been better.

He and Andrea enjoyed the city's cultural life, going to the opera, museums, foreign films, and occasionally to a dance recital. Their sex life was much better than it had been in a long time. Still, what she'd said about leaving him was always in the back of his mind, keeping him from being completely at ease.

Most of Sam's coworkers at Barnes & Noble were much younger than he was, yet he found that he had a lot in common with them. Ayla, a young Israeli girl, had been a fairly well-known photographer in her native country; she had come to New York to widen her horizons. Boris was a writer who'd published several short stories in *New Directions.* Richard, the store manager, was one of the most cultured people Sam had ever met—almost on the level of Michael Schwartz. Sam enjoyed gabbing with them.

Andrea invited Judy, from the gallery, to her studio to see her Central Park paintings. Judy was thrilled. "I've got to bring my boss here," she said. "I'm sure she'll want to give you another show."

After Judy left, Sam told Andrea, "I feel like an underachiever compared to you."

Andrea paused for a moment, then said, "You're the fourth person I've known with bipolar disorder, and you're by far the most productive of them. I think you're doing just fine."

(Is she saying this just to soothe my feelings?) "I guess, considering what I've been through. . . ."

"What's it like to have a nervous breakdown?" she asked him thoughtfully.

". . . Well, a lot of what I go through is similar to what any moody person goes through—it's just magnified a hundred times. Most people become depressed occasionally, but with me it's so severe that I stop functioning. And being hypomanic is kind of fun, too. The problem is that it always progresses until I become psychotic, and then it's hell. Believe me, there have been times when I almost completely lost touch with reality."

Andrea silently ran her fingers through his hair, then kissed him gently on the forehead. He was so touched that he almost began to cry. To hide his vulnerability, he said, "I'm tired. I'm going to turn in now."

"Let me take a shower, and I'll join you in a few minutes."

To empty his mind, he listened to the sound of the water falling in the bathroom. When she joined him, he was overwhelmed with passion. He kissed her again and again and buried his face in her hair. "I love you beyond reason," he exclaimed.

SAM'S SHIFT AT THE BOOKSTORE WAS 9-TO-5. As always, he had trouble getting up in the morning. About once a week he was a bit late, and occasionally, when he was feeling depressed, he called in sick. Early in July, Richard called him into his office. "You've got to stop coming in late," he said. "And when you call in sick, are you really sick?"

Sam decided that it was better to tell him the truth than to make something up. "No," he said. "It's just that sometimes I'm very depressed in the morning."

"Would you like to switch to the evening shift?"

(Then I'll have no time to spend with Andrea.) "Let me think about it," he said. "In the meantime I'll do the best I can."

A few weeks later, the gallery gave Andrea another show, where she exhibited twenty paintings and ten watercolors. Judy promoted the show again, advertising in all the local papers and inviting several art critics.

At the opening, the gallery was packed. Andrea looked radiant in a lovely blue sleeveless gown; Sam and Judy dressed up as well. The show was a big success. Andrea got write-ups in *New York* magazine, *Time Out,* the *Village Voice,* and the *New York Observer.*

"You've *made* it!" Sam told her afterwards. They hired a professional photographer to make slides of everything in the show. Michael, who was even more of a night person than Sam, didn't attend the opening, but he made some nice comments about the slides. As Sam had predicted, he said, "She's just a bit too literal for me, but she definitely has a lot of talent."

One Monday night, Michael brought a book of Cézanne's paintings to French Roast to show to Andrea and said, "Rather than criticizing your paintings directly, I'd like to analyze some of Cézanne's paintings with you, because he's influenced me more than any other artist. First, let's look at some of his landscapes. The first thing to see is how everything is knitted together: the brushstrokes, colors, and forms work together to form a coherent whole."

He showed her several landscapes, starting with *The Château at Medan.* "See how the diagonal brushstrokes are used throughout the painting—not only in the trees, but also in the clouds?" They went on to *The Bridge at Maincy, The Gulf of Marseille*, and several others.

"Now," she said, "how do I apply his principles to my own work?"

Michael laughed. "That's the hard part," he said. "I can't really make any suggestions based on your slides. I'd have to see the paintings themselves."

"Well, my show will be up for another five weeks. Do you think you can make it there?"

"I'll try, but with my sleep schedule, it might be hard."

"All right. When the show is over, the remaining paintings will be back in my studio, and you can come there at any time of the day or night."

"That's fine," Michael said.

Within a month after the opening, the gallery had sold half of Andrea's paintings and three of her watercolors. Encouraged by Sam, she quit her job in order to devote herself entirely to painting. She decided that, for her next project, she would paint some of the chess players, both in Washington Square Park and in The Chess Shop. In The Shop, she did drawings of Jim Smith, Raphael, Ben, and some of the others sitting at the tables, concentrating on their games. In Washington Square, she set up her easel and painted the hustlers, then focused on other subjects in the park: the fountain, the dog run, and a bocce game.

The summer went by quickly. On a Monday night in late August, Michael came to Andrea's studio. Sam came along to see what he would say. First, Andrea showed Michael her landscapes. He said, "I like the way you use light—you have a very sensitive touch, and a real empathy for your subjects."

"What would you change?"

"I'd like you to emphasize the formal qualities more." He pointed to one of her landscapes. "Here you could do more with the negative space, and you could make the background relate to the foreground, as Cézanne does."

Next, she showed him her Washington Square Park paintings. He said, "I'd like to see you put more of yourself into your paintings. Make the image you see subordinate to the abstraction you feel. Don't just copy nature—if you want to sell, that's okay, but if you want to create something beautiful and enduring, do what Cézanne did: Use the means of painting to make form."

Sam stopped by the Children's Aid Society to see if they could use his services, but in his absence they had hired somebody else, so he mailed his resumé and cover letter to over thirty schools throughout the city. No one offered to hire him right away, although the principals of two schools asked him to try again in November. Reluctantly, he decided to stay at the bookstore for the time being.

Inwardly, he was becoming somewhat jealous of Andrea's success, and he constantly worried about losing her. Without telling her, he decided to have another private session with Albert Ellis. "What have you been up to?" the doctor asked him.

"Nothing special."

"So how can I can help you?"

"Well, my girlfriend is becoming a successful painter while I'm working at a bookstore for just above minimum wage."

"Are you jealous?"

"In a word, yes."

"You don't *need* to be. Some men would be proud of her success and not a bit jealous. So you're doing this to yourself unnecessarily."

Sam sighed. "I guess."

"So every time you start feeling jealous, tell yourself: I don't need to be jealous."

"If only it were so easy. . . ."

"Nobody's *saying* it's easy. You've got to work hard on this. Every time you start feeling jealous, tell yourself: My jealousy is irrational. Tell yourself over and over, and tell yourself vigorously."

"Okay, but there's another problem. She says if I become ill, she's going to leave me."

". . .That's more serious. You need to decide whether you want to stay with her on those terms."

"What should I do?"

"How many times have I told you—'Thou shalt not should on thyself?' Make up your mind, and do it with your eyes open. But you've got to realize that, with your condition, you could become ill at any time"

"I think I should leave her."

"No *shoulds!"*

"Okay. I *want* to leave her, but I can't. I'm in too deep."

"Well, then, it seems to me that you've decided to stay with her, at least for the time being. That could always change later on."

"Thank you, Doctor."

On a Monday night in September, before going to French Roast, Sam stopped by The Chess Shop, where he found his old friends Raphael and Ben playing speed chess. He asked them, "Would you like to play three-way?"

They played until The Shop closed at midnight, then continued playing at the Washington Square Diner. The games were particularly hard-fought that evening, with very few blunders by any of them. By the time they were finished at 3:00 a.m., Sam was only ahead by two games.

After saying good night, he headed off to French Roast, where Michael and Andrea were studying Cézanne again. This time, Michael's book was open to the portrait *Madame Cézanne in the Conservatory*. "Do you see how the slant of her head works with the slant of the tree to unify the foreground with the background? Critics call that 'holding surface'."

Then Michael turned to *Woman with a Coffee Pot*. "See how the forms of the painting are just as important as the subject itself? That's what I tried to do in my paintings, and I think you should be aiming for the same thing."

"When can I see some of your paintings?" she asked him.

"Why don't the two of you come to my place next Monday night at midnight?"

"Okay," she agreed.

Andrea and Sam showed up on the following Monday at the stroke of midnight. They looked at his work until 1:30, when the three took a taxi to French Roast. When they got there, Andrea said, "Let's talk about something other than painting tonight. I need to digest what you've already taught me before we go any further."

"That's fine," Michael said. "Sam, what have you been reading lately?"

"Well, I'm taking a break from my Nobel Prize project. Right now I'm getting heavily into Graham Greene."

"That's a good choice. I assume you know the movie *The Third Man*?"

"Of course."

"Did you know that he also wrote a story called *The Tenth Man,* which was supposed to be made into a movie but never was?"

"No, I had no idea."

"Okay," Michael said. "Read *The Tenth Man*. That's your homework for this week."

Later, when they were in bed together, Sam asked Andrea, "Do you like Michael's work?"

"Yes. Don't you?"

"I *like* it, but he seems to be doing the same painting over and over. I'd like to see him paint something other than Lake George."

"I'm sure he's done other things in the past. He just showed us some of his latest work."

"He has done other things in the past, but that was a while ago."

"Maybe he'll do some other things in the future."

CHAPTER 32

THE FOLLOWING MONDAY, MICHAEL TOLD SAM, "I've good news! In October, I'll be showing several of my paintings with the Street Painters at the Cork Gallery again."

"Where's that again?"

"In the basement of Avery Fisher Hall at Lincoln Center. The opening's on Saturday, October 7th, at 2:30 in the afternoon."

"I'll be there, even if I have to take a day off from work," Sam said.

On the morning of the 7th, Sam called Richard and told him he needed to take a personal day. He and Andrea got to the gallery right on time. On the walls, there were about fifty paintings by the ten artists in the show, including three paintings and two watercolors by Michael. Andrea loved the show. Sam liked it, but with some reservations. Later he told her, "Just between you and me, I thought it was very retrograde. First of all, they're ignoring all the developments since World War II—Abstract Expressionism, Rauschenberg and Johns, Pop Art, Conceptual Art, and more. I'm not saying that any of these is necessarily the answer, but these paintings are clearly retrograde. And the other thing is, did you notice that we were the youngest ones there? Again, I'm not saying that they have to do something trendy that the kids would like, but if you don't have any fans younger than thirty, could you be missing the boat?"

"I think the Street Painters are on the boat," she replied. I think it's the art world that's missing the boat."

"Well, at least you're selling."

"Yeah, but that's because what I do is so easy to understand. If I follow Michael's advice and break things up more, I may not sell as much, but I'd be a much more interesting painter."

When Sam got to the bookstore on Sunday, Richard told him, "I'm sorry, but I'm going to have to let you go. You're just absent and late way too often."

Sam was quiet for a few seconds, sighed, then said, "Whatever. . . ."

"I'm sorry," Richard repeated.

That evening, Sam told Andrea what had happened. She said, "That's all right. You'll find something else."

Inwardly, however, she was angry with him.

Little by little, he started descending into a clinical depression. He spent most of his time in bed, getting up only at 4:00 or 5:00 in the afternoon. He was very subdued and hardly spoke. Five days later, Andrea said, "You seem very depressed. What's causing it?"

"I don't know."

"How could you not know?"

"Well, sometimes I have mood swings that are unrelated to events, and at other times they're caused by circumstances but then take on a life of their own."

"At least you seem to understand yourself."

"Believe me, it took a long time before I began to understand myself."

She started spending more and more time in her studio, arriving home only in the late evening. Neither of them was very interested in sex. The only joy in Sam's life then was his late-night meetings with Michael. He told him that he was depressed, but rather than using his friend as a therapist, he tried to distract himself by talking about intellectual matters. Always in the back of his mind was Andrea's threat to leave him. *(I've got to fight my way out of this, or her threat might become a reality.)*

Sam gave Dr. Berkun a call and made an appointment. He told him exactly what the situation was when he saw him. "Do you think we should make an adjustment in my medication?"

"Refresh my memory—what are you taking now?"

" Zyprexa, Wellbutrin, Zoloft, and Trazadone."

"In that case, I don't want to make any changes, but why don't you go to see Albert Ellis? Maybe he can help you."

"I saw him recently."

"Why not go again?"

"Maybe that's a good idea."

He called the Ellis Institute and asked the receptionist if he could see Dr. Ellis in the evening. "I have trouble getting up during the day," he said.

"Could you make it at five in the afternoon tomorrow?"

"I'll try to."

The following afternoon, Sam woke up just in time and took a cab to the Ellis Institute. When he entered the office, the doctor asked him, "What's the latest?"

"To begin with, I lost my job because I was absent or late too often. Andrea and I hardly have sex anymore, and we don't even talk very much. I'm terrified that, if she leaves me now, I might go into a tailspin. What should I do?"

"You're very worried?"

"Extremely."

"How does worrying help?"

". . . What?"

"How does worrying help?"

"It doesn't."

"That's right. Not only does worrying not help, it makes things worse. It intensifies your depression. You've got to talk yourself out of worrying, or your fears will become a self-fulfilling prophecy."

"How do I do that?"

"Just by telling yourself over and over that worrying doesn't help."

"Okay. What else?"

"Start by telling yourself, *'Que sera, sera.'* In the worst- case scenario, Andrea will leave you. That would be painful, but you'd get over it. Haven't you been hurt before?"

"Of course."

"And you lived to be happy again?"

"Yes."

"So, then, don't worry. Look for another job and hope for the best."

Sam smiled. "Okay, Candide," he said.

In his weekly chess tournament at the Marshall, he had more and more trouble concentrating. After losing to several weaker players, he stopped competing. Andrea objected. "But chess is the only thing you do now."

" I can still play at The Shop."

He didn't tell her, but he was having more trouble reading as well. After a few pages, his mind started wandering, and he couldn't focus. Even his conversations with Michael were affected. Michael did most of the talking now; he had trouble getting Sam to say more than a few words at a time.

On an evening in November, when Sam and Andrea were having dinner together, she told him, "Sam, I'm moving out."

"Are you breaking up with me?"

"I'm not just going to dump you precipitously, but I can't see you like this day after day. It's getting me down. I wish I could be stronger, but I can't."

Sam's face fell. "I understand," he said.

While Andrea was looking for an apartment, she slept on a futon in her studio. The two only met once a week for dinner and a movie, but he called her religiously twice a day.

Now he was spending even more time in bed. Except when he was seeing Andrea, he remained in bed until 6:00 p.m., then watched television until midnight, when he went to French Roast to get a bite to eat and to see Michael. Whenever he called Andrea's studio and she wasn't there, he was always afraid that she was with another guy. He even started contemplating suicide, but he didn't tell anyone because he was afraid of being committed to a mental hospital. He did call his mom, however, and told her what his situation was. She asked, "Would you like to come stay with me until you're feeling better?"

"Thank you," he replied, "but I'm afraid that, if I move to Jersey, I'll never leave the house. At least in New York I can go to French Roast at night."

SAM AND ANDREA DIDN'T CELEBRATE THANKSGIVING at all that year. In early December, when Andrea didn't answer his calls for three days, he started becoming frantic. He told Michael, "I think she's with another guy."

"Try not to worry," Michael said. "There might be a simple explanation."

When she finally answered his call, he started sobbing. "Where have you been?" he asked. "I've been worried about you."

"I just went to visit a friend of mine in Rockland County."

In a voice choked with emotion, he said, "I think we should break up, Andrea. I can't live like this."

"All right," she said. Inwardly, she was relieved.

As soon as he hung up the phone, he began to regret his decision. *(I've got to stick to my guns, or things will get even worse.)*

That night, when he told Michael what he had done, his mentor said, "I think you made the right decision. You don't want to live in constant fear."

"I feel like I'm dying."

"If you feel that bad, then maybe you should consider checking into a mental hospital for a couple weeks."

"Why?"

"Because you're spending almost eighteen hours a day in bed, and I'm sure that's contributing to your depression. In the hospital there will be things to do to keep you engaged, which could be very helpful."

"I'll think it over."

AFTER ANOTHER WEEK, HE DECIDED to ask both Dr. Brown and Dr. Berkun whether to follow Michael's advice. He told them what had been happening to him and how he was feeling. Dr. Berkun asked, "Are you thinking of hurting yourself?"

"No." *(If I say yes, he might commit me against my will.)*

Dr. Brown asked him the same question, and Sam gave him the same reply. The doctor knitted his brows and said, "If I call Dr. Berkun and we both agree that you should hospitalize yourself voluntarily, will you follow our advice?"

Sam took a deep breath, then quietly said, "Yes."

The next day, Dr. Berkun called Sam at home.

"Hi, Sam," he said. "How are you?"

"Lousy."

"I've been talking to Dr. Brown, and we both think it would be a good idea for you to go to the hospital for a few weeks."

Sam groaned. "Okay," he said, and asked, "If I check myself in, will you be my doctor?"

"Probably not, but I'll consult with whoever is."

"Good." Sam called his mother to tell her about his decision, but he didn't call Andrea. *(She mustn't know about this.)*

Two days later, he checked into the Leonard Pavilion again. Some of the same nurses and aides were still working in the same unit where he had been a few years before. Once again, he had trouble getting up in time for his vital signs to be taken. Helen, one of the nurses, told him, "If you don't get up in the morning, you'll be here a long time."

Each morning, Sam put on his clothes over his pajamas and had his vital signs taken, then took off his clothes and went back to bed, skipping breakfast.

In the afternoon he felt somewhat better, so he went to occupational therapy and some of the other activities. Unlike some of his previous hospitalizations, there were no attractive women for him to engage with. He did become friends with Jack, one of the older patients. Every afternoon they played a game of gin rummy and talked to each other about their problems. Jack had been a janitor in a city high school who, after being laid off, was without work for year. He told Sam, "I was addicted to marijuana, and I was addicted to sex."

"I'm addicted to love," Sam replied. "I *wish* I was only addicted to sex."

Jack always beat Sam when they played cards because he was a life master at bridge, and he remembered every card that was played. He offered to play chess, but Sam declined, explaining, "I need a break from chess."

Finally, they started playing Scrabble, a game in which they were approximately even. Sometimes some of the other patients joined in.

When he had been on the ward for three days, Sam's mother came to visit him.

He cordially introduced her to Jack and some of the nurses, but when they were alone in his room, he broke down and cried. "I'm never going to have an enduring relationship," he said. "My illness always ruins things."

She said, "I think there's someone out there for everyone. You'll feel better and live and be happy."

"My heart aches as if someone had stabbed me in the chest."

She rocked him gently in her arms and said, "I know it's hard. It would be hard for anyone, but time heals all wounds."

"I'm not so sure about that." He made a sound that was half sigh and half groan.

She said, "You sound like Hamlet in his scene with Ophelia."

Sam chuckled.

"See? You're laughing. That means you're on the road to recovery."

"To feel better and worse and better and worse ad infinitum."

She kissed him on the cheek and said, "I love you, kid."

Sam's psychiatrist on the ward was Jacob Stern, a friend of Dr. Berkun. He interviewed Sam every other day. At the first meeting, he said, "I've reviewed your case in detail with Dr. Berkun, and I'll continue to do so, because I know you think very highly of him."

"I do."

"Right now the two of us agree that we should make no immediate changes in your treatment. Let's wait a couple of weeks and see if your mood improves."

"Sounds like a plan."

When Sam was lying awake at night, he constantly thought about Andrea, but he refrained from calling her. *(She can't know I'm here, or she'll dump me. No! What am I saying? We already broke up. Still, I'd better not call her until I get out.)* He got on his knees and prayed, "Lord, please let me keep my sanity. That's all I ask. Please don't let me lose it. I'll be good. I promise."

Diane, Sam's nurse, had a talk with him every day. As Dr. Berkun and Dr. Brown had, she asked him: "Are you thinking about hurting yourself?"

"No," he said.

"Are you thinking about hurting Andrea?"

"No."

All the nurses and aides on the ward were in constant touch with the doctors. When there was any change for better or worse in the patients, everyone on the staff knew right away.

After about three weeks, Sam started showing up for breakfast and became much more animated in group therapy. Dr. Stern asked him: "Are you feeling better?"

"Much better."

"Do you think you're ready to be released?"

"I guess so."

"Okay, let's wait a few days, and if you're still feeling better, we'll release you."

"Thank you."

Three days later, they gave him the green light to leave. As soon as he got home, he called Andrea.

"What's been happening?" she asked him.

"Oh, nothing," he lied. "I've just been feeling a little blue, that's all."

As soon as he hung up, a dark cloud of misery descended on him. *(It seems like I can't even talk to her, let alone be friends with her.)*

At midnight, he went to French Roast to wait for Michael. While he was waiting, he read *The New York Times*. *(At least I can read again, even if it's only the newspaper.)*

Michael showed up at 2:00 a.m. "Welcome back to the land of the living," he said.

"I feel like the living dead."

"You must be feeling better if they released you."

"Am I feeling better? I guess so, because before I was depressed, now I'm only miserable."

"Misery is better than depression," Michael said, "because if you're miserable, at least you're in touch with your feelings. Depression is like a black hole that sucks your life force into it."

"How come you know so much about it?"

"This is off the record, but I've been there myself."

To keep busy in the afternoon, Sam started attending some of the lectures at the Metropolitan Museum. In the evening, he went to the Jefferson Market Library, where he read books on a variety of subjects, most of them recommended by Michael. He started looking for work as a chess instructor but received no offers. He felt very guilty that he wasn't working. He told Michael, "I feel like I'm a parasite."

"Don't beat up on yourself. It will only make things worse. Just keep looking. You'll find something."

CHAPTER 33

WHEN HE HADN'T FOUND ANYTHING BY LATE JANUARY, Sam took a job as a telemarketer for the New York City Opera. For four hours every afternoon, he called former customers to try to sell them subscriptions. He hated the work, but he was determined to hold the job until he found something better. Unlike his co-workers at the bookstore, who had been bright and interesting, the telemarketers were a motley crew, most of whom had taken the job out of desperation. Damien, who sat in the booth next to Sam, was a squatter who lived in Thompkins Square Park. Cynthia, an elderly black woman, was a member of the Communist Party. Jonathan was a retired sanitation worker who smoked foul-smelling cigars. Sam had felt more at home in the mental hospital.

Because he still needed eleven or twelve hours of sleep each night, now he only saw Michael on weekends. *(What kind of life is this?)*

One Friday night in February, Michael gave him a copy of the *New York Observer* in which there was a favorable review of a group show at Andrea's gallery, with several of her paintings on view. The following afternoon, Sam walked all the way from his apartment to the gallery in Chelsea. *(I hope she's not there, or I might drop dead on the spot.)* But, aside from Judy, there was no one there. *(What a relief.)*

Andrea's new paintings were very different from anything she had done before. They were much more abstract, with thick paint and more distortion of the subject matter, which included a self-portrait and five Coney Island paintings. On his way out of the gallery, he forced himself to smile at Judy, but as soon as he was outside, he sat down on the sidewalk and cried. *(She's on top of the world, and I'm in hell.)*

At work on Monday afternoon, Sam couldn't hide his misery.

"What's wrong?" Damien asked him.

"Oh, nothing. I'm just very tired."

"Are you sure?"

"Don't worry about me. I'll be fine."

Damien looked at him skeptically but decided not to pursue it further.

That evening, Sam called his mother. He told her where he was working and said, "I think this job isn't helping—it's only making things worse."

"Then why don't you quit? I'll pay your rent until you find something better."

"You're a good woman, Mom."

"You're a good son."

He laughed. "Let's not patronize each other. . .but I'm truly grateful."

He decided to call some of his friends. *(Being with people I love is the most productive thing I can do right now.)*

First, he called Inez, who was glad to hear from him. "Where have you been?" she asked.

" I was out in Iowa City for a while, but now I'm back. Are you still at Julliard?"

"As a matter of fact, next week I'll be performing in a master class with Vladimir Ashkenazy. Would you like to come?"

"Definitely."

No longer working, he fell into a new routine. He spent his afternoons at The Chess Shop, his evenings at the library, and late nights at French Roast. When he reached the library every evening, before starting his reading for pleasure, he looked at the help-wanted section of *The New York Times*. The only available jobs either required a lot of experience or didn't appeal to him.

He called Lola and invited her to join him at Inez's master class. Each of the six students in the class played one of Chopin's major works, either a sonata, a ballade, or a scherzo. Maestro Ashkenazy's comments were very insightful. After the class, Sam and Lola joined Inez and her family for coffee at Café La Fortuna. Sam told her, "I think you were the best."

"You're just biased," Inez replied.

At The Shop, Sam's favorite opponent was Jim Smith. The two sometimes played slow games, with Sam giving Jim knight- odds, or they played speed chess with five minutes for Jim and three minutes for Sam. By the end of the afternoon, they were usually more or less even.

At the library, Sam binged on James Joyce, rereading *The Dubliners*, *Portrait of the Artist as a Young Man,* and *Ulysses*. He tried to read *Finnegan's Wake* but couldn't get through it. He loved talking about Joyce with Michael, who had read, not only all his works, but also several biographies. Sam told him, "I've learned more from you than I did in four years of college."

"Now that you've read Joyce and Mann, maybe you're ready for Marcel Proust."

"Then I'll have read your three favorite writers."

"That's right."

"You know, I love Joyce and Mann, but most of my favorite novels were written in the nineteenth century—*The Brothers Karamazov*, *Anna Karenina*, *Great Expectations*, *The Betrothed*, Balzac's best novels—"

"What's *The Betrothed?* I'm not familiar with that one."

"Wow! You mean there's something I've read that you haven't?"

"There *are* gaps in my knowledge," Michael said.

"Okay. *The Betrothed* was written by Manzoni early in the nineteenth century."

"Manzoni? The writer that Verdi dedicated his *Requiem* to?"

"That's the one."

"I'm going to buy that novel tomorrow."

ON A FRIDAY NIGHT IN EARLY APRIL, Sam went to the Marshall to play in their weekly speed chess tournament. He was surprised to see David Rabinowitz there. Before the tournament began, Sam approached the table where David was sitting. "I just thought I'd say hello," he said. "Everyone misses you at The Chess Shop."

David averted his gaze and refused to answer. When the two played their game, which David won, he wouldn't shake Sam's hand. "You're a hard man," Sam told him.

On a Saturday night later in the month, he went to the Village Corner to visit Lisa. He struck up a conversation with Stuart, one of the regulars. At the other end of the bar was a new waitress, seated with her back to them. All of a sudden, she turned around quickly to see if they were looking at her. Sam decided to approach her, introduced himself, and asked her what her name was.

"Chantal," she said in a strong French accent. "Pleased to meet you."

Sam was thunderstruck. When he rejoined Stuart, he told him, "I think she's the sexiest woman I've ever seen."

After that, before going to French Roast each evening, Sam spent a few hours at the Village Corner. Little by little, he got to know Chantal better. Not only was she a knockout *(to die for!)*, she was also highly intelligent and a graduate student in Philosophy at Hunter College. Sam told Michael about her, and every night he dreamed about her. *(I must have her.)*

He thought of a way to spend some time alone with her. He asked, "Would you be interested in giving me French lessons? I can't afford to pay you much, but after each lesson, I'll take you out to dinner."

"*Mais certainment*," she said.

On her day off, he took her for Indian food, and they had a conversation in French. Although Sam had studied the language in high school, he was very rusty. "I don't know if once a week is enough," he said.

"That's all I have time for," she replied. "Why don't you start reading some French literature? That will increase your vocabulary, and it will give us something to talk about."

"What should I start with?"

"How about *Pere Goriot*, by Balzac? That's fairly straightforward and not difficult to understand."

"That's a good idea," Sam said, "especially since I've already read it in English."

At the Village Corner, Chantal flirted with all the male customers. She showed a special interest in Stephen Fall, the pianist. Sam was insanely jealous.

Chantal was dating Vincent, a Philosophy professor at Fordham University. "I'm getting tired of him," she told Sam. "Actually, the only thing I still like about him is that he's an expert on Heidegger."

"Then you should meet my friend Michael. He used to teach philosophy at Long Island University, and his specialty was phenomenology."

"I'd love to," she said.

So on Thursday night, after their French conversation, Sam took Chantal to French Roast. Michael and she talked about Heidegger for hours.

At 4:00 a.m., she took the A train to Washington Heights, where she lived by herself. As soon as she left the restaurant, Sam asked Michael, "Do you think she likes me?"

"I think she likes men."

"She told me that she's getting tired of her boyfriend. Do you think I should take that as an invitation?"

"I don't know. I have a feeling that she wants to attract everyone."

"I think I might be in over my head. . . . But if I have even the slightest chance of making her mine—"

"Well, to start with, I think you'd better find a good job. Women like her invariably go for successful men."

"I'll get on it right away."

He took *Pere Goriot* off the shelf at the library and started to read it, with the help of a dictionary. And every time they chatted at the bar, he addressed Chantal in French. Between their brief conversations at the bar and their longer conversations at dinner, his French started coming back. She was impressed. "I've met very few Americans who speak French as well as you do."

"In New York City, there are lots of people who speak French far better than I do."

"Still, you speak very well."

"My French will never be as good as your English."

"That's because I went to an international school in Paris, where all the classes were taught in English."

"So then you're totally bilingual," Sam said.

"I don't know—I have a lot of trouble reading Shakespeare in English."

"What if you read an edition with lots of notes?"

"Then I can get by."

"In that case, your English is better than most Americans'."

"Pas de tout."

Incredibly, within a month after meeting Chantal, Sam had almost completely gotten over Andrea. *(I'm so superficial.)* He and the French girl became good friends, which only made him crave her more. One evening when he entered the Village Corner, he found her sitting on the lap of one of the customers, a tall black man in his forties. Sam sat at the bar, where he ordered a Guinness and chatted with Lisa, but after twenty minutes he couldn't stand it and left the building.

Outside, he looked at his watch. It was 11:00 p.m. *(Too early for Michael.)* As he often did when he was agitated, he began to run. After about half an hour, he was exhausted. He looked around and realized that he was in the business district again. City Hall was dark, and all the businesses in the area were closed for the night. He started to worry that he might be mugged, so he ran back to French Roast and sat at the bar, waiting for Michael. He took out *Pere Goriot* and started to read, but he couldn't concentrate, so he laid his head on the bar and tried to sleep. Finally, at 3:00 a.m., Michael came into the restaurant.

"Thank God you're here," Sam said.

"What's the latest?"

"More of the same. Earlier tonight I stopped at the Village Corner, where I saw Chantal sitting on a customer's lap. I had to leave the building."

"That doesn't surprise me."

"I can't see her with another man, and I don't know if I can even be friends with her. What should I do?"

"As Albert Ellis would say, there are no 'shoulds.' If you want to be friends with her, you've got to realize that there will be ups and downs. If you can't be friends with her, maybe you should stop going to the bar."

"Aargh!"

The following afternoon, he met her at the Waverly Diner for a late lunch. He couldn't hide his agitation.

"Are you all right?" she asked him.

"In a word, no."

"What's wrong?"

"I don't want to go into that right now."

"All right. Let's talk French."

His concentration was so poor that he kept getting stuck in the middle of sentences. Finally, he said, "Let's speak English today. I'm having trouble focusing."

"Okay. By the way, I have good news. I have a new boyfriend."

(Good news indeed.) "Is it the man whose lap you were sitting on yesterday evening?"

"No, I was just flirting with him. My new boyfriend works as a security guard at the Metropolitan Museum. He is knock-dead gorgeous."

"Congratulations," Sam said. He was surprised that, rather than being devastated, he was somewhat relieved. At French Roast that evening, he told Michael, "Now that she's taken, I'm not going to pursue her anymore. She obviously likes me, but, just as obviously, she's not attracted to me."

"So you think you can be friends with her?"

"I don't know, but you know what? I'm going to try, because in between my fits of jealousy, I enjoy her company. And now that I know I'll never get to first base, maybe I'll settle for friendship."

"Good."

". . .By the way, do you speak French? I'm taking lessons from Chantal, but we only meet once a week, and I think that, if I really want to improve, I need more practice."

"I've done a lot of reading in French, including all of Proust, but I don't often get a chance to converse."

"Then speaking French will be good for both of us."

"Bien sûr."

In the bar the following evening, Chantal introduced Sam to Boris, her new boyfriend. They had a long conversation about art. Boris was very knowledgeable. "You seem to know a lot," Sam said. "Is that why you took a job at the Met?"

"Yes, I want to be near the art."

"Do you paint yourself?"

"I take a stab at it."

"My ex-girlfriend Andrea seems poised to have a big career as a painter."

"Where can I see her work?"

"She shows at the Carver Gallery in Chelsea."

"What's her last name?"

"Bryce. Andrea Bryce."

"Oh, I know about her. She's gotten some good reviews in the papers."

When Boris left the bar, Chantal asked Sam, "Isn't he gorgeous?"

"Well, to be honest, I think he has kind of generic good looks. I think my face has more character."

"Hm."

Sam finished *Pere Goriot* and discussed it with her.

"Très bien," she said. "For your next assignment I want you to read *Eugenie Grandet*."

Chantal was as much of a night person as Michael. After the bar closed, she liked to go to after-hours clubs when she didn't have classes in the morning. Since Boris worked during the day five days a week, he only joined her on weekends. During the week, she sometimes invited Sam.

Everywhere she went, Chantal attracted lots of attention. Every night at the after-hours clubs, at least two men asked for her phone number or gave her theirs. She had the knack of behaving in exactly the right way to drive any man crazy. At first, Sam found this irksome, but later he started to find it amusing. "You're a magnet," he told her, "and men are your iron filings."

"I know," she said.

After dating Boris for six weeks, she began to grow tired of him. She confided in Sam, "He has the looks I want, but not the brains."

"Would you settle for Bob Dylan?" Sam asked her.

"I'd consider it."

At the Village Corner, Chantal and Lisa began to dislike each other.

"She's a witch," Chantal told Sam.

"What makes you say that?"

"She's been giving me the cold shoulder on a regular basis. I think she's jealous of me."

"She's not that bad herself."

"No, she's not, but she can't compete with me. Besides, she's such a slut."

"That's just an act."

"Just an *act?* The way she acts, that's the way she is."

"No, that's just to entertain her regulars. If anything, she's the opposite of a slut—she's almost a prude. Do you know she's only slept with two men, and she's been married to both of them?"

Chantal bristled. "You don't know what you're talking about," she said.

Lisa wasn't exactly enamored of Chantal either. She told Sam, "I've never met anyone as conceited as she is."

"I like her," Sam replied. "Look. You both work in the same bar. I think you should try to be friends."

"Trying to be friends with her is futile," said Lisa.

CHAPTER 34

RYAN, THE OWNER OF THE VILLAGE CORNER, was a little bit weird. During the Eighties, his wife had been an economic advisor to President Regan. They were both disciples of Ayn Rand.

Chantal and Ryan often discussed politics and economics. She had very little respect for Ryan. She told Sam, "Ayn Rand can be dismissed, and his version of Ayn Rand is even worse than the original."

"I'm glad you feel that way," he replied, "because I'm allergic to Ayn Rand."

At French Roast, Chantal and Michael often discussed existentialism and phenomenology. Sam knew very little about philosophy, but when they discussed literature, he had more to say. Chantal told him, "You should go to Hunter and get a master's in English Literature. I think you'd make a very good English teacher. What future do you have just teaching chess?"

"That's what everyone says."

The next day he called his mother and told her, "I'm thinking of getting a degree in English Lit, with the idea of maybe teaching in the public schools."

"That's a wonderful idea."

"I want to go to Hunter College. Of course I'll apply for financial aid, but if I need some additional help, could you lend me the money?"

"Certainly."

AS SOON AS HE HAD DECIDED WHAT TO DO, his mood improved dramatically. Not only Michael and Chantal, but everyone he knew, noticed the difference. Michael said, "You look like a different person."

Sam quickly sent in his application and financial aid forms. He started to prepare by reading a book on English history. Then he read all the Shakespeare plays that he didn't already know and committed several of his sonnets to memory. He reread *The Canterbury Tales,* which he had studied in high school. Before reading Milton and Spencer, he decided to wait until he was in a classroom setting.

When the spring semester was approaching, he started to look for a bartending job, so he'd have some extra spending money. Since he had no experience, rather than hunt for a busy Friday or Saturday night shift, he took a Sunday afternoon job at a bar near Hunter.

At school, Chantal was always surrounded by men, so Sam had very little time alone with her, but he heard through the grapevine that she was having an affair with one of her professors. One Sunday she and her new boyfriend Andrew came into the bar. He was tall and slender, with short red hair and a beard. When Sam wasn't serving his other customers, the three chatted pleasantly. It turned out that he was the instructor in a course on Plato, and Chantal was his star pupil. He told Sam, "Chantal's paper on the *Crito* is one of the best essays I've ever read."

"Yes, she's very precocious," Sam replied. "If she doesn't get you with her looks, she'll get you with her brains."

Chantal began to sing Blondie's "One Way Or Another" and they all laughed.

On Saturday night, Sam told Michael about Chantal's new paramour. Michael said, "She's a big game hunter, isn't she?"

"She is. I'll bet she winds up with someone like Paul McCartney."

"*He* might be over his head," the professor remarked.

Unlike Chantal, Sam had trouble making friends at Hunter. He was much older than most of his classmates, and he didn't know what to say to them. Even when they came into the bar, he had trouble with anything more than small talk.

What he enjoyed most was the classes themselves. He participated actively in the classroom discussions, and everything he learned he discussed with Michael, who seemed to know more about each subject than Sam's professors did.

Sam and Andrew started to become good friends. Andrew often came to the bar by himself on Sunday afternoons. Sam called him "Barbarossa."

When Sam mentioned that he was friends with Michael Schwartz, Andrew said "I know him very well. I took a course on Heidegger with him at The

New School. He might be the most brilliant man I've ever met. In fact, none of my professors at Princeton was as erudite as he is."

"You should come join us at French Roast on Friday nights."

"So he's still a night person?"

"You seem to know him as well as I do."

THE FOLLOWING FRIDAY NIGHT, Chantal, Andrew, and Sam all joined the professor at French Roast. Sam said, "I feel like a mental midget compared with the three of you."

"Don't put yourself down," Michael told him.

"Okay, Dr. Ellis."

Andrew and Chantal started coming to French Roast every Friday night. They talked about every topic under the sun: philosophy, the history of science, art history, world literature, classical music, psychology, jazz, even military history.

Although Sam was enjoying himself immensely at Hunter, he was still very lonely. He told Michael, "Books aren't enough for me. I need to be in love."

"I'd imagine that Hunter would be an ideal place to meet young women."

"Well, there's plenty of them that I'm attracted to, but I haven't met even one who could possibly be a soulmate."

Michael thought for a minute. "Do you read the *New York Review of Books?"*

"I haven't lately."

"There's a singles organization called the Classical Music Lover's Exchange, which always has an ad in the magazine. You know a lot about music. Why don't you join?"

Sam shrugged. "Maybe I'll give it a try," he said.

"You don't sound very enthusiastic."

"I'll give it a try."

He bought a copy of the periodical, called the exchange, and put in an ad. He also contacted three women who had placed ads themselves. He set up a date with one of them, a radiologist who worked at St. Vincent's. She was bright and interesting, but nothing special to look at. Sam said, "I'm not ready for a relationship right now, but I'd like to remain friends."

"I have more than enough friends," she replied tersely.

Their date ended uncomfortably.

His next date was with a woman who was very attractive, but he could tell right away from the way she dressed that she was looking for a man with money. This time she was the one who wanted to be friends.

"That's a possibility," he said, although he had no intention of seeing her again.

One woman answered *his* ad. Before arranging a meeting with him, however, she interviewed him at length over the phone. He grew exasperated. "You're asking me things that I usually divulge only when I know someone very well."

"Well, I'd still like to talk on the phone one more time before we meet."

Sam hung up on her. He told Michael, "I'm giving up on the Classical Music Lover's Exchange."

In the middle of Sam's first term at Hunter, Heather, a woman from the neighborhood, started coming into the bar on a regular basis. She wasn't a great beauty, but Sam liked her a lot. She worked as a karate instructor in a gym in Chelsea. Sam said, "I've always wanted to learn karate."

"Why don't you join my class, then?"

"When does it meet?"

"Every Monday, Wednesday, and Friday night from 7:00 to 8:30."

"Do you ever give private lessons?"

"I never have, but with you I might give it a try."

"How much would you charge?"

"Why don't we barter? I'll teach you karate, and you can teach me chess."

"That's a great idea."

They started playing chess at the Hunter Student Center every Sunday night after Sam's shift at the bar, and after an hour of chess, they went to the gym for an hour of karate. Sam had never been much of an athlete and wasn't in very good shape, so they started each session with stretching, sit-ups, and push-ups. She told him, "I want you to do an hour of exercise at least three times a week."

"Fine."

Sam and Heather started having dinner and then going to a movie once a week. After about five weeks, she asked him: "Do you have a girlfriend?"

"Not right now."

"I'd be so interested."

Sam didn't reply.

"You don't have to answer right away," she said. "Think it over."

Later that night, as he lay awake, he did just that. *(Could I learn to love her?)* He decided to take a wait-and-see attitude.

One evening in May, he went to The Chess Shop to see who was there. None of his favorite opponents were, but Ahmed was behind the counter. When Sam told him that he was studying English Lit at Hunter, Ahmed said, "I guess you know that I have a master's in English Literature from NYU?"

"I think you told me that."

WHEN THE SEMESTER WAS OVER, Sam borrowed his mother's car to drive up to Woodstock and visit a friend he had gone to high school with. He invited Chantal to come with him. Mark, his friend, lived in a small commune outside the town, where he and his comrades ate vegetarian food and practiced Buddhism.. In the morning, everyone did an hour of yoga together, and they all meditated after each meal. Mark worked at a home for adolescents with behavioral problems.

Chantal loved it there. "I could live this way," she said.

"I couldn't," Sam replied. "I'm too much of a city person, and I like eating meat too much."

Mark was a very accomplished pianist. Sam told him about Inez. Mark said, "If she's at Juilliard, she must be very talented."

"She is."

The day before they returned to New York, Sam went for a long hike by himself. When he returned to the commune, he was stunned to find Chantal and Mark in bed together. *(I'm not surprised that Chantal would do this, but I wouldn't have expected it of Mark.)* Chantal said, "Whatever you do, don't tell Andrew about this."

"I won't."

Sam didn't know why, but he was extremely jealous. *(I've never been jealous of Andrew.)*

During the drive back to New Jersey, he hardly said a word.

"Is something bothering you?" she asked him.

"No."

"Are you sure?"

"Back off!" Sam exclaimed.

"Alright, alright."

Early in July, Sam saw a review in *The New York Times* of an exhibit of Andrea's work. One Saturday afternoon, he went to her gallery to see the show, which he loved. The next day he called her to tell her what he thought. "You keep getting better and better," he said.

"Thank you."

As soon as he hung up the phone, he started feeling miserable again. *(I thought I was completely over her.)*

The next day, after watching *Pulp Fiction* together, Sam and Heather went to the Village Corner for a nightcap. Steven Fall was at the piano. When the bar closed, Sam walked Heather back to her apartment on Hudson Street. She invited him in. When they were upstairs, she said, "Make yourself at home."

She took out a bottle of Chianti and put on a Bob Marley record. Then she sat down next to him on her loveseat.

"Are you trying to seduce me?" he asked her.

"Yes," she said. "Yes, I am."

"Well, I think you're succeeding."

He sat passively on the loveseat with a gentle smile on his face while she undressed him, then when he was completely naked, he undressed her. He kissed her tenderly, then picked her up and carried her to the bedroom.

When they were finished making love, he said, "I'm not really ready for a relationship."

"That doesn't matter."

They fell asleep in each other's arms.

On Saturday night Sam went to French Roast as usual, to see Michael, Chantal, and Andrew. He told them, "I have a new girlfriend." *(Didn't I say just the other night that I wasn't ready?)*

Andrew said, "Why don't you bring her here next week, so we can give her the once-over?"

"Why not?" Sam said.

After studying karate on Sunday night, he told Heather, "Some of my friends want to meet you."

She said, "I'd love to meet your friends."

When they met for dinner on Friday night, she said, "Why don't we skip the movie and go straight home?"

When they got in bed, Sam was surprised by how passionate he was. *(Usually only the most gorgeous women turn me on like this.)*

THE FOLLOWING SATURDAY NIGHT, HE BROUGHT HER to French Roast, where she met Michael, Chantal, and Andrew, as well as some of the AAs.

Everyone liked her. When she told them what she did, Chantal said, "Maybe I should study karate, so I can fight off all the men who are constantly pestering me."

As usual, they talked about philosophy, literature, and other intellectual matters. Heather wasn't as erudite as Sam's friends, but she was very socially adept. On the way back to her apartment, she told him, "I was amazed at the sophistication of the conversation."

AFTER THEY HAD BEEN DATING FOR A FEW MONTHS, Sam and Heather were spending the night together about four times a week. She asked, "Why don't you move in with me?"

After mulling it over, Sam replied, "Let's wait a few months first."

In September, she invited him to her parents' home in Forest Hills. Her father worked as a school superintendent in the neighborhood, and her mother as a nurse in the same town. Both of them made Sam feel right at home. Heather had a twelve-year-old brother named Rory. After dinner, Rory, Sam, and Heather played ping-pong in the basement of the house; then the two lovebirds took the train back to Manhattan. When they were in bed together, she said, "I love you, Sam."

In the morning, they went for a walk by the Hudson River, where he told her, "Before I move in with you, I want you to know that I have bipolar disorder."

She knitted her brows, then asked, "What should I do if you become ill?"

"Well, if I become depressed, just make sure that I stay out of bed and keep busy. If I become manic, remind me to take my medication, and if it becomes serious, try to convince me to check into the hospital. I might be resistant, but if you, my psychiatrist, and my mother all try to convince me, I'll probably go voluntarily. The rest of the time, just treat me like you would anyone else."

"So are you ready to move in?"

"How about if I do it during winter break?"

"I'm so excited!" she said.

Two days after Christmas, Sam finally moved in with Heather.

"You'll never regret this," she said.

A few days later, they went to her parents' house again. Sam brought a present for Rory—a handheld chess computer—and explained, "This has eight levels. When you beat level I, go to level II, and so forth. When you get to level V, you might even beat your sister."

"When will I be ready to play you?"

"For that you'd have to read some books or take some lessons, but if you apply yourself, there's no reason you couldn't beat me eventually."

On the way back into the city, Sam said, "You know what? I think I'm falling in love with you."

Heather closed her eyes, rested her head on his chest, and said: "I adore you, you beautiful man."

CHAPTER 35

On a Sunday afternoon in mid-January, Sam stopped by The Chess Shop to see who was there. He was surprised to find Freddy playing blitz chess with Jim Smith. Freddie was giving Jim incredible odds—ten minutes to one on the clock, yet he was winning most of the games. When he saw Sam, he said, "Stick around. Let's hang out later."

When Freddie was finished playing, he and Sam went to Karavas Place to have a beer and a bite to eat. Cindy was behind the bar. Freddy said, "You're not underage now, are you?"

"No, I'm not," she said.

"What are you doing later?"

"I'm going to be here until the bar closes at 4:00 a.m., and then I'm going to go home and sleep for twelve hours."

"Are you sure you don't want me to join you?"

"I don't think my boyfriend would like that."

"I'm not jealous."

"Well, I'm very flattered, but unfortunately, I live with him."

"I'm sure we can find a way."

"Down, boy," Sam said.

When Karavas closed, Sam and Freddy went to an after-hours bar on Barrow Street, where they stayed until dawn. Freddie insisted on paying for everything. Sam said, "You don't have to do that."

"Don't worry about it. I'm making more money than I know what to do with."

At 9:30 in the morning, Sam said, "I need some sleep."

"I'll be here for three weeks. Why don't you give me your phone number?"

"Can do."

When Sam got home, Heather asked him, "Where have you been? I was worried about you."

"Tell me honestly—did you think I was cheating on you?"

"No, I know you wouldn't do that."

(I wasn't always as good as I am now. If I were tempted. . . .) "I was at an after-hours club with my friend Freddy."

"Next time, please call."

"I'm sorry. I will."

At eight in the evening, he received a call from Freddy: "Can you meet me at The Shop?"

"Sure."

They sat at a table near the door. At the table next to them, Vim, one of the regulars, was reading Nimzovich's *My System*. Vim had a reputation for nastiness. He was also a chain smoker. Freddie asked him, "Would you mind putting out that cigarette?"

Vim ignored him and kept reading. Finally, Freddie lit a cigarette himself and said, "If you can't beat 'em, join 'em."

Vim said, "That's very clever. Do you want me to put this out on your neck?"

One of the players who was at The Shop every day was an ex-convict named Johnny. Since he had very little money, Ahmed had told him that if he cleaned The Shop every night after closing he could play for free. For whatever reason, Vim had taken an instant dislike to Johnny. Every time Johnny passed his table, Vim made some disparaging comment. Johnny told Ahmed, "Sometimes I feel like killing him."

"We all feel that way," Ahmed pointed out. "Just avoid him as much as possible."

"Okay."

When Sam went to the Jefferson Market Library on a cold afternoon in February to read, he was delighted to find Inez there. He said, "Why don't we go to The Peacock for a coffee?"

They walked to The Peacock and sat at a table near the window. After ten minutes of small talk, he asked her: "When can I hear you play or sing?"

"Why don't you come over right now?"

"Sure. Do you still live with your parents?"

"Unfortunately, yes."

They walked arm in arm to Inez's house. Her parents weren't home. "So let me run through a program I'm preparing."

She played three sonatas, one each by Mozart, Schubert, and Beethoven. When she was finished, Sam said, "Wow! Boy, have you improved! You sound better than Richard Goode."

"I wish."

SAM AND HEATHER DECIDED THAT, DURING SPRING BREAK, they would go to Paris for a week. He asked his mother to lend him the money for the flight and hotel. Heather said, "I'm a little nervous. I've never been in an airplane before."

"Don't worry. You're safer in an airplane then you are in a car."

"I know, but at least when I'm driving a car, I feel like I'm in control."

"Try not to worry. I'll be there with you."

In mid-April they flew to Paris, and she was much less nervous than she thought she'd be. "You're right," she confided. "Having you here makes it much better."

They checked into a cheap hotel near the train station and headed straight for the Latin Quarter, where they sat in an outdoor café on the Rue de Seine. They had a long conversation with a graduate student named Pascal, who was studying philosophy at the École Normal. Sam told him about Michael and Chantal. "I would love to meet them," he said.

"Sure," Sam replied. "Anytime you want to come to New York, you can stay with us, and I'll introduce you to both of them."

On their second day, they spent six hours in the Louvre. They particularly liked the room with the huge paintings by Delacroix and Gericault.

They did all the touristy things, going to the Champs Élysées, the Eiffel Tower, Notre Dame, Sacré-Coeur, and more. At the top of the Eiffel Tower, Heather got down on one knee and proposed to Sam.

"I don't know if I like this role reversal," he said. "But let me think about it. It might be a good idea."

They found a very good chess club on the Rue Saint-Antoine. Sam beat everyone in the room at speed chess. André, one of the players, invited them to come to his house for dinner. His wife was a gourmet cook. She prepared *coq au vin* and steamed vegetables. When they were finished eating, Heather remarked, "That was one of the best meals I've ever had."

Sam said, "I completely agree."

On the flight back to New York, he asked her, "Are you interested in having children?"

"Not really. Are you?"

"I love children. But with my illness, I don't know if I could take care of them properly."

"I'd still like to marry you anyway."

"If we're not going to have kids, I don't see the point of getting married."

"The point is, you're the love of my life."

"I love you too, but please let's wait a bit."

"You're a little skittish, aren't you?"

Sam frowned.

"I was just joking," she said.

IN NEW YORK AGAIN, SAM TOLD CHANTAL all about their trip and the people they had met in Paris. He also told her that Heather had proposed to him, and he asked, "What should I do?"

"Your instincts will tell you if and when it's time," she replied.

One evening in May, Sam stopped by The Chess Shop just before closing. Almost all the tables were full, and the room was full of smoke. Johnny was already starting to sweep the floor. When he brushed by Vim without apologizing, Vim said, "You better stay away from me, or I'll have to slap you around."

Johnny said, "What?" grabbed a glass ashtray, and smashed it onto Vim's head, then slapped him around. There was blood everywhere. Finally, some of the players pulled Johnny off Vim and calmed him down a bit. Ahmed took him aside and said, "I'm sorry, Johnny, but you can't come in here anymore. Nobody likes Vim, but we draw the line at violence."

Johnny said, "What? Am I supposed to ignore his threats?"

"I'm sorry," Ahmed repeated.

Johnny left without saying a word.

Ahmed came back inside and announced, "Everyone has to leave now. I want to clean up this mess."

Sam stayed behind to help him wipe the blood off the tables and the floor. Ahmed said, "Vim was stupid to mess with an ex-convict. He's lucky Johnny didn't kill him."

From time to time, Chantal would stop by The Chess Shop to see if Sam was there. She and Ahmed always chatted pleasantly. One day he told her, "I have an article by a French author that hasn't been translated into English yet. It's about Edgar Allen Poe's influence on Baudelaire and the other French romantics. Would you like to translate it for me?"

"Why do you need it?"

"I guess Sam never told you—I have a master's in English Literature. I want to show it to my old advisor. I'd even pay you something."

"Sure," said Chantal. "I'd love to do it."

When she told Sam about this, he said, "I'm sure it's just a ploy. He really wants to seduce you."

"Believe me, I'm in no danger of being seduced by him. He's not exactly a fashion plate."

They both laughed.

WHEN SAM FINISHED HIS SECOND YEAR AT HUNTER, he took a summer job as a chess instructor at a camp in Central Park. He had to be at work by 9:00 every morning from Monday to Friday. He found it very difficult to get up in time, but once he got there he enjoyed the work immensely. All his students were inner-city kids, and he was impressed by how well behaved they were.

He was with them every day from 9:00 until noon. Since most of them knew the rules, he spent the first morning teaching those who didn't while the others played. The second day he taught everyone how to record games. After that, he introduced them to basic chess tactics—pins, forks, discovered attacks, etc. He also showed them one game a day by Bobby Fischer and other world champions. He found his work in Central Park the most rewarding experience he'd had as a chess instructor. He told Heather, "You should talk to my boss, Dorian. Maybe she'll want to start a karate program there."

The next day, Heather came to the park, and Sam introduced her to Dorian. "Sam told me that he loves working here," Heather told her, "and he wanted to know if you'd like to start a karate program."

"That's a *great* idea. Why don't you print up a flyer for me to give to the parents, and if there's enough interest, maybe we can start in August."

"Great!" Heather said.

SAM WANTED TO CONTINUE SEEING MICHAEL at French Roast, so he got in the habit of taking a long nap every afternoon. He asked him, "Do you think you can get here earlier?"

Michael said, "I'll try to be here by midnight."

So Sam began to stay at French Roast from midnight to 3:00 a.m., when he took a cab home and slept until 8:00. After work, he napped from 12:30 until 5:30 in the evening, so he was getting about ten hours of sleep every day. But he was still always tired. Because of that, he and Heather were only having sex on weekends. She was frustrated but, for the time being, she decided to keep it to herself.

After three weeks with his new schedule, the fatigue started getting to Sam. He was often late for work, especially at the beginning the week. Dorian told him: "You *have* to be on time."

He told her, "I often suffer from depression in the morning."

"A lot of people do, but you've got to be on time."

"I'll try to force myself," he said. He told Heather, "Can you be sure to get me up by 7:00? I think Dorian's going to fire me if I keep showing up late."

"Certainly," she said.

So, every weekday at seven in the morning, she opened all the windows and turned the radio on high. When that wasn't enough, she literally pulled his leg and dragged him out of bed.

"I don't know what I'd do without you," he said.

NOT ENOUGH PARENTS ENROLLED THEIR KIDS in the karate class, so Dorian called Heather and said, "I think we'll have to try again next summer."

Sam started worrying about his future. He told Heather, "If I become a teacher, I won't *ever* be allowed to be late. And if I don't enjoy my job, it's going to be hard to get up."

"I'm sure you'll make it," she said. "And I'll always be there to help."

(Always? Will we always be together?)

IN EARLY AUGUST, SAM GOT A CALL FROM PASCAL, who told him, "I'm going to be in New York City in about three weeks. Would you be able to put me up?"

"With pleasure!"

With Heather's help, Sam was able to get to work on time. It was still an enormous struggle, though.

He borrowed his mother's car, and he and Heather went to JFK to meet

Pascal. The three had dinner at the Café Figaro. While Sam returned his mother's car, Heather gave Pascal a tour of Greenwich Village. He was surprised by how quiet it was in the area west of Seventh Avenue. "I could live here," he said.

When Sam was back in the city, he and Pascal went to French Roast to wait for Michael, who arrived promptly at midnight. Michael and Pascal had a long conversation about philosophy. Pascal was amazed by Michael's erudition. When Sam left at 3:00 a.m., Pascal asked him, "Is it okay if I stay here until Michael leaves?"

"Certainly," Sam said. "I'll leave you my extra key and you can let yourself in. You can sleep on the sofa bed in the living room."

Sam gave him directions to the apartment and said good night. Pascal stayed with Michael until 6:30 a.m. He entered the apartment just as Heather and Sam were getting up. Heather asked him, "Don't you have jet lag?"

"Yes, I do," he said. "But I think I could talk to Michael for seventy-two hours without going to sleep."

"Isn't he amazing?" Sam said.

WHILE SAM WAS NAPPING IN THE AFTERNOON, Heather showed Pascal the city. Then the three of them had dinner, sometimes in a restaurant, sometimes at home. After that, they went to a movie or a play, or went to the jazz clubs on Bleecker Street. At midnight, they always wound up at French Roast. Pascal stayed there all night and slept while Sam was at work. He only seemed to need about five hours of sleep.

A week after Pascal arrived, Chantal showed up at French Roast. Pascal was smitten. "I can't mince words," he told her. "You're simply the most beautiful woman I've ever seen. Can I take you out tomorrow night?"

"Certainment."

The following evening, they had dinner at Il Molino, then went to The Blue Note to hear Paquito di Rivera.

"How can you afford all this?" Chantal asked him.

"Money is not an object," he replied.

"Would you like to spend the night with me?"

"That's an understatement. I'd like to spend my life with you."

Pascal told Sam and Heather, "I don't know if I can go back to Paris," he said. "I'm head over heels in love."

Sam was tempted to tell him about Andrew, but he decided not to. *"Soit sage,"* was all he said.

When it was time for him to leave for France, Pascal begged Chantal to come with him.

"You can do anything you want," he said. "If you want to work, if you want to travel, if you want to raise kids, anything."

"I can't leave New York."

"If I move here, will you live with me?"

". . .I have to admit, I have a boyfriend."

"Oh, no." Pascal said. "Oh, no."

Once again, Pascal confided in Sam and Heather: "I'm obsessed with her, and she has another boyfriend. I'm at my wit's end. What should I do?"

Sam said, "I think you should try to forget Chantal. She's like a Carmen. I don't think she'll ever have an enduring relationship."

"Forgetting her would be impossible. Maybe I could find another woman in Paris. But forget about her? Impossible."

During his last night in New York, Pascal told Michael, "I'd like to correspond with you. I think you might be able to answer some of my questions about philosophy."

"That's fine."

Pascal and Chantal stayed at French Roast until 4:00 a.m., when they went back to Chantal's apartment and made love for six hours, finishing just in time for Pascal to pick up his things from Sam's place and catch a cab to JFK.

"I'll be back," he said.

CHAPTER 36

THAT EVENING, SAM AND HEATHER TOOK A SHOWER TOGETHER, then put on a Bruce Springsteen record and sang along. Sam decided not to go to French Roast, so they could spend the whole night together. They made love slowly and tenderly.

"You're so gentle," she said.

"You know something?" Sam said. "What are we waiting for? Let's go ahead and get married."

Heather broke down and cried. "I've never gotten what I wanted in life before," she said.

"You deserve to get everything you want, and more."

In the morning, Sam called his mother and told her that he was engaged.

"When can I meet her?" she asked.

"Why don't the three of us have dinner on Saturday night?"

"What's her favorite dish? I'll prepare it for her."

"Why don't you come into the city for a change, and we can all go out for Indian food?"

"Well, as you know, I don't really like coming into the city, but since this is a special occasion. . . ."

"Great. How about we meet in front of the Port Authority Bus Terminal at 7:00 on Saturday night?"

"That's fine."

Heather was a little nervous about meeting Sam's mother.

"Don't worry," he said. "She's not an intimidating person."

When Saturday arrived, she asked him, "What should I wear?"

"It doesn't matter."

"No, I want you to pick out something for me."

He chose a dress with a floral pattern, and white pumps. "You look lovely," he said.

"Really?"

"Don't worry, my mother will love you."

The three of them met at the bus terminal and took a cab to East 6th Street, where they went to Mitali, Sam's favorite Indian restaurant.

Mrs. Kanter said, "I don't know much about Indian food. Why don't you order for me?"

He ordered lamb masala, tandoori chicken, and green curry, and they shared everything. Sam and Heather both had Indian beer to drink, and Sam's mom ordered a mango lassi. For dessert, they ordered mango ice cream. When they were finished, they walked across town and had coffee at The Café Figaro; then Mrs. Kanter took a bus back to New Jersey, and Sam and Heather went home. On the way, she said, "You have to tell me whether she likes me or not."

DURING THE SUMMER, SAM HAD WORKED at the bar only on Sunday afternoons. When the new semester got underway, he asked Phil, his boss, if he could have a Friday or Saturday night shift.

"Well," said Phil, "I have someone for both shifts, but it's been so busy lately that I've been thinking about adding a second bartender. Friday's our busiest night, so let's try you out then. I assume that you want to continue working on Sunday afternoons?"

"Sure," Sam said. *(Not really.)*

His co-worker was a stunning blonde from Munich named Regina who worked off the books. She had the biggest following of anyone who worked in the bar. On his first Friday night, he said, "I feel a little bit guilty about pooling the tips with you. After all, you're the one who brings customers in."

"Don't worry about it," she said. "I can't handle the shift by myself."

Ahmed and Chantal started spending more time together. He continued giving her articles to translate, and, with his help, she started learning Arabic. She was a very quick study. After they had been friends for about four months, her Arabic was already good enough for conversation.

Across the street from The Chess Shop there was a small restaurant called Ben's Falafel. Chantal tried out her Arabic on the owner and his family. Ben had two adorable children, Imad and Delilah, whom she befriended. With Ben's permission, she brought them into The Chess Shop, where the three of them played backgammon.

Naturally, all the men in The Shop had a crush on Chantal. Ahmed tried not to show it, but he was very jealous. He was only happy when the two of them were seated alone together in a café or bar, where all the men were jealous of *him*.

SAM AND HEATHER DECIDED NOT TO HAVE a big wedding. In mid-October they had a civil union. Ahmed and Chantal were witnesses. They had a small reception at their apartment, inviting only family and close friends. After the guests left, Sam said, "Let's make love until dawn."

"You're the only man I've ever met who could last that long."

For their honeymoon, Sam took a week off from school, and the newlyweds went to Amsterdam, Sam's favorite European city. They stayed on a boat on the city's biggest canal. Next to them was a boat where heroin addicts were given free heroin and clean needles. Heather said, "I think this is a good thing. They don't have to rob people or sell their bodies like they do in New York."

They enjoyed going to Amsterdam's great museums, especially the Van Gogh. They took a tour of the Heineken brewery, where they were given all the beer they could drink at the end of the tour. Every night they went to Amsterdam's famous "brown bars." Heather smoked a lot of marijuana, but Sam abstained. "I'm afraid it might interact with my medicine," he told her.

Sam found a café frequented by Amsterdam's best chess players. He spent three hours playing speed chess, with mixed results. He and Heather befriended a ballet dancer from New York named Eileen, who was staying on the same boat with them. Eileen took dance classes every day during the day. At night, she went dancing in the city's most popular clubs. On their last day in the city, Sam and Heather joined her, and she danced with both of them. "You're the best dancer I've ever seen," Heather told her.

The three promised that they'd get together when they were all back in New York.

OVER THE THANKSGIVING BREAK, SAM DECIDED to play in a big chess tournament in Chicago. Heather came along to give him moral support. Although his rating was still well under 2200, instead of playing in his class, he decided to play in the open section. The tournament had eight games—two a day—over the long weekend. Sam got off to a good start, beating two experts. In the third round he faced Boris Koslovsky, a grandmaster from Moscow who had just moved to the U.S. the previous year. Sam defended the black side of a French defense, playing reasonably, but eventually Koslovsky outplayed him in an endgame. The game was exhausting, lasting over five hours, so Sam decided to skip the fourth round. The director awarded him half a point.

Since he had the afternoon off, Sam and Heather took a bus tour of Chicago. Sam had finished with an even score, which was a good result, because all but one of his opponents had a higher rating than he did. He told Heather, "I think I played well because you were with me."

On the bus back to New York, he played her in a blindfold game: She played the moves on a small portable set while he visualized the positions in his head. She tried to complicate the positions as much as possible, hoping that he would become confused and lose his way, but he was able to remember where everything was and eventually won.

"I'm impressed," Heather said.

"Don't be. Any good player can play a blindfold game. In fact, Miguel Najdorf, a grandmaster from Argentina, once played forty blindfold games simultaneously."

"That's incredible."

"Incredible, but true."

"The best chess players are geniuses, aren't they?"

"Oh, definitely. Bobby Fischer has an IQ of 180."

ON NEW YEAR'S EVE, PHIL, THE OWNER, THREW a big party at the bar. Sam invited everyone he knew. He found José and Bernardo, his old chess buddies, on the Internet. Both of them came down to New York from Providence, Rhode Island, where they had relocated. Raphael and Ben came as well, as did Inez, Ahmed, Lola, and Eileen, who was back in New York. Andrew and Chantal showed up too, and, to everyone's surprise, Michael Schwartz arrived at two in the morning. When the bar closed at four, everyone went to French Roast. The night manager put a tape of old Motown tunes on the stereo, and they all danced until dawn.

At seven in the morning, Phil bought breakfast for everyone in the restaurant, including the AAs, then the party finally broke up. Eileen invited José and Bernardo to stay at her place, so they wouldn't have to stay in a hotel. When Sam and Heather were back at home, Heather said, "I wonder if she's going to sleep with both of them."

About twice a month, Chantal received a love letter from Pascal, begging her to come and join him in Paris, and regaling her with poetry in French. She hardly ever wrote him back, but that didn't deter him in the slightest. In each letter, he reiterated that, if she would marry him, he'd relocate to New York. Although she was still attached to Andrew, she sometimes was tempted to pick up and go to Paris, at least for a while, because Andrew wasn't nearly as romantic as Pascal. She eventually told him, "You have a rival."

"Should I be worried?"

"Not as long as you treat me like a goddess."

She showed him some of Pascal's letters. "Boy, he's obsessed with you," Andrew concluded.

"Are you jealous?"

"Of course I am."

"Then why don't *you* write some poems for me?"

"I have many talents, but poetry isn't one of them."

Heather and Eileen started to become good friends. About twice a month, they went clubbing together. Sam occasionally joined them. Eileen was such a fabulous dancer that, when she and Heather danced together, they often cleared the floor. Naturally, after the clubs closed, the three of them went to French Roast. Eileen told everyone there that she had good news: "In June, I'll be dancing as a soloist with the Paul Taylor Dance Company at the Joyce Theatre."

"That's *wonderful!*" Michael exclaimed. "If I can get myself up early enough, I'd love to come watch." Some of the AAs promised to show up as well.

For Heather's birthday on February 19th, Sam made reservations at The Rainbow Room. As they took in the glorious view from the restaurant, Heather said, "Isn't New York the greatest city in the world?"

"It is."

When they left the restaurant, the temperature outside was below 20°F., so they took a cab back to their apartment, where they opened the windows, lay under a big comforter, and cuddled for hours before falling asleep. In the morning, they went back to Rockefeller Center, this time to go ice-skating.

"This is where I took my high school sweetheart for a first date," Sam said.

"What was her name?"

"Andrea Goldman."

"Was she beautiful?"

"I'll tell you what. When we get home, I'll show you my high school yearbook, and you can decide for yourself."

Back in their apartment, Sam found the yearbook and showed her Andrea's picture. "My God," Heather said. "She was stunning. If you can get a girl who looks like that, what are you doing with me?"

"First of all, you're beautiful to *me*—but, more importantly, you're beautiful *inside*."

The next day, when he returned to the apartment after his classes, he found a message from Freddy on the answering machine: *Hey, buddy, I'm back in town again. Leave me a message at The Chess Shop, and I'll meet you whenever you can make it.*

They met at The Shop after Sam got off work on Sunday. "How are things in Milan?" Sam asked him.

"Well, it's not New York, but there's enough going on to keep me busy."

"Is there a chess club there?"

"Yeah, there's a good one. I've been getting draws against some of the strongest players in Italy, but I almost never beat them."

"Maybe you should take some risks. Play the Sicilian Defense, for example. That's the best opening if you want to win with black."

"It doesn't suit my style."

They played chess for hours, with Freddy giving Sam five minutes to three on the clock. When The Shop closed at midnight, Freddy was ahead by ten games. Then they walked over to the Peculiar Pub on Bleecker Street for a beer.

"How's your love life?" Freddy asked him.

"I'm married," Sam replied.

"*Wow!* Can I meet her?"

"I think that could be arranged."

Sam called Heather and asked her to meet them at the bar. She was there in twenty minutes. When he introduced them, she said, "I've heard all about you."

Freddy took them for a late dinner at French Roast. As usual, he insisted on paying.

"Do you have a girlfriend?" Heather asked him.

"I'm playing the field."

After dinner, Heather left them to their own devices. Naturally, Freddy wanted to go to Karavas Place to try his luck with Cindy. "Every time I come here," he told her, "you look more beautiful."

"And every time you come, you're more charming."

"What are you doing after work?"

Cindy laughed. "I knew that was coming."

"Just give me a chance. Just once."

"You're nothing if not persistent."

"Well, how about it?"

"Not this time," she said.

Sam and Freddy stayed at the bar until closing, both getting plastered. After they left, Freddy told him, "I'm going to a whorehouse in Queens. Wanna join me?"

"I'll take a rain check."

Sam stumbled into his apartment at 5:00 a.m. When he awoke, he had a terrible hangover, so he missed all his classes on Monday. Heather admonished him, "You really overdo it sometimes. You should only drink on Friday or Saturday night, and you should *never* drink this much."

"Mea culpa," Sam said.

On Tuesday evening, Sam called a car service and accompanied Freddy to the airport. When he returned to the apartment, Heather told him, "You just got a call from Ahmed. He wants you to stop by The Shop."

When Sam got there, Ahmed said, "Let's go in the back. There's something I want to ask you."

When they couldn't be heard by the players, he said, "One of my assistants just quit, and I want you to work for me."

Sam chuckled. "Don't you remember that I worked here before you did, and that I didn't handle the job very well?"

"I want you because you're my friend, and I'm sure you'll do fine."

Sam decided to open up. "I guess I never told you. . .I have bipolar disorder, and poor organization is one of the symptoms."

Ahmed looked at him for a few seconds. "Oh, all right. Never mind, then."

Instantaneously, Ahmed's assessment of Sam changed completely. Instead of someone to be respected and treated as an equal, now he was someone to be despised or ignored.

Sam said, "I still want to teach here, though."

"That's fine."

IN EARLY MAY, SAM FOUND A MESSAGE from Inez on his answering machine: *Hi. I'm doing a recital at Juilliard on the 15th, and I'd love it if you could make it.*

He called her back right away. "I'll definitely come, and I'll bring my wife."

Inez played a very difficult program: Chopin's *Four Scherzi*, Beethoven's "Les Adieux" sonata, and the Schumann "Fantasy in C Minor." Heather was very impressed. "Your little friend is a genius," she said.

After the concert, a small reception was held in one of the classrooms in the Juilliard building. Sam introduced Heather to Inez's parents. Heather said, "I don't do anything as well as she plays the piano."

"What about your karate?" Sam pointed out.

"If my karate were as good as her piano, I'd be a fifth- degree black belt."

THE NEXT DAY, SAM RECEIVED A CALL FROM CHANTAL. "I need to talk to you. Can you come over right away?"

"I'll be there in no time."

When he reached her building, she buzzed him in. He was surprised by how miserable she looked. "What's the matter, honey? I've never seen you like this."

"Andrew and I just broke up."

"Oh, I'm sorry."

When they were seated on her sofa, he said, "Tell me what happened."

"We had a horrendous fight. He accused me of cheating on him with Pascal and several other men."

"May I ask if that's true?"

"I did have a brief fling with Pascal when he was in New York, but that's all."

(What about Mark in Woodstock?) "Do you think you can patch it up, or is it final?"

"It's final. He'll never stop being jealous. In his twisted mind, I'm sleeping with every man I meet."

"Don't worry," Sam said. "You'll find someone who will love you just the way you are."

"Every boyfriend I've ever had said that I was too much for him to handle." She started to cry.

Sam said, "Shh," and rocked her gently back and forth.

"You're so kind to me," she said.

Sam was overwhelmed with desire. He had to muster all his strength to keep from kissing her. "Everything will be all right," he said.

She closed her eyes and fell asleep in his arms. After about a half an hour, he woke her up and said, "I really should be going."

AT THE END OF MAY, SAM AND HEATHER WENT to see Eileen dance. "Of all the arts," Sam observed, "dance is the one I know the least about, but I can see how graceful she is."

"That's all you need to know," Heather told him.

When the performance was over, they went backstage to see Eileen. She introduced them to a sturdy young woman with a crew cut. "Heather and Sam—this is my girlfriend, Sandra." *(I had no idea she was gay.)*

The two couples went to Susie's for Chinese food, then to French Roast. Michael said, "Sorry I couldn't make it tonight."

"That's okay," Eileen said. "We make a video of every performance. If you want, I can get you one."

"Well, I don't have TV at home, but. . .you know what? Get me a video. I'll find somewhere to watch it."

Sam said, "You can watch it at our house."

"That's a possibility," Michael replied.

CHAPTER 37

A MONTH AFTER CHANTAL BROKE UP WITH ANDREW, Sam called her to see how she was. She invited him to visit her at home. He asked, "Should I bring anything?"

"Yeah, why don't you bring a six-pack of beer."

"Do you have a preference?"

"Stella Artois?"

"Good choice."

When he arrived, he could see right away that she was already a bit intoxicated. "Are you sure you want more?" he asked hesitantly.

"Of course I'm sure," she said. "I asked you to bring some, didn't I?"

"I just don't want you to have too much."

"Let me worry about how much I drink."

He decided not to press the issue. ". . .So how are you? Have you met a new guy?"

"I've met more than one, but none of them has a brain, which is okay with me, as long as they're tall, handsome, and well-hung."

Sam laughed. "How are things otherwise?"

"To tell the truth, I'm miserable."

"Can I help in any way?"

"Would you like to spend the night with me?"

Sam was shocked. "Chantal, you have never been interested in me in that way. Why all of a sudden. . . ?"

Chantal started sobbing. "I just don't want to be alone," she said.

Somehow, he mustered the strength to say: "I really can't. If Heather found out—"

"I won't tell her."

Sam's head was pounding. "I can't."

"Please."

"I have to go."

Once he was outside, he felt dizzy, so he sat down on the stoop in front of Chantel's building and began talking to God. "God," he said, "you owe me one for this."

He stumbled home. Heather could see that he was upset. "What's wrong?" she asked him.

"Nothing."

She looked at him dubiously. "Are you sure?"

He raised his voice. "Yes, I'm sure!"

It was only 9:00 p.m., but he went straight to bed. Heather stayed up reading a novel.

At 1:00, he woke up and said: "I'm going to French Roast. I'll see you tomorrow."

Heather wondered why he didn't invite her to join him but didn't ask.

Michael was seated at a table with Brad and some of the other AAs, discussing the films of Orson Welles again, when Sam got there. He tried to focus on the conversation, but he was very distracted. Finally, he asked Michael, "Can I talk to you in private?"

"Certainly."

They moved to another table out of earshot of the AAs. Sam sighed, "I was visiting Chantal earlier tonight, and she asked me to spend the night with her."

". . .And you refused?"

"Yes, somehow."

"You must be a strong person. I think Chantal is irresistible."

"I'm not a strong person. I just remember what happened whenever I cheated in the past, but if she asks me again, I might—"

"Then maybe you should stay away from her."

"But I want her as a friend."

"Are you sure that's *all* you want?"

"No, I'm not. That's the problem."

"Sam, you seem to have a good thing going with Heather."

"So don't blow it?"

"Not if you can help it."

Sam shrugged. "All right."

"I'm going to join the others," Michael said.

As he usually did when he was upset, Sam went for a long walk. For the first time in years, he started hallucinating. He heard Chantal sing in a seductive voice, *You want me. You know you want me.*

He forced himself to look at his surroundings. At first, he didn't know where he was; then he realized he had wandered into the meat-packing district. He entered a crowded bar called The Village Lady. There were about a hundred male customers and only ten women. He ordered a beer and a shot of Jack Daniels. The barmaid, a sexy brunette from Spain, asked him, "Do you want to buy me a drink?"

"Sure."

After an hour of heavy drinking, he left the bar. Outside, he became very disoriented. After stumbling blindly around the neighborhood for twenty minutes, he asked a prostitute, "Can you tell me how to get to the East Village?"

"Don't you want to go out with me?" she asked him.

"No, I can't," he said. ". . .I'm married."

"What's her name?"

"Chantal," he said.

"Okay. Two blocks up from here, you'll run into 14th Street. Just make a right, walk straight, and eventually you'll come to the East Village."

He did, but instead of going straight home, he found himself in front of Chantal's building. He couldn't bring himself to ring her doorbell, nor could he leave. He sat down on the stoop and began to cry. Again, he heard Chantal's voice: *Don't cry, baby. Everything will be fine.*

Half an hour later, he decided to head home, but once again he became disoriented. He walked around, not knowing where he was. An hour later, he turned up outside Chantal's building again. This time he rang the bell, and she buzzed him in. She could instantly see that something was wrong with him. "What's the matter?" she asked him.

"I'm flipping out."

"Did you have too much to drink?"

"I did, but that's only half of it."

"Let me make you some coffee," she said.

He sat down on her sofa. "Can I spend the night?" he heard himself saying.

She frowned. "Are you sure you want to?"

"I want to, and I don't want to."

She looked at him oddly. "Well, if you're really flipping out. . . ."

"Maybe I shouldn't?"

"It's strange—I always thought you were so stable."

"When I'm feeling all right, I can hide it, but I'm far from stable."

"In that case. . . ."

"I should go?"

". . . Well, you could stay, but won't Heather wonder where you are?"

"I guess I'd better go."

When he was in front of his building, he realized that he had misplaced his keys. He rang the doorbell repeatedly, but Heather didn't answer. *(What if she's cheating on* me?*)*

He took a handful of coins and threw them at their window. Still, Heather didn't answer. It was starting to become light, so Sam went to Washington Square Park to wait for the chess players. At 7:00 a.m., Lovey Jenkins showed up. They played speed chess for three dollars a game until noon, at which time Sam was behind by $39.00. If Lovey noticed Sam's condition, he didn't say so. Sam looked at his watch. "I have to quit," he said.

He went home and rang the bell again. This time Heather buzzed him in.

"Where were you?" she asked him.

"Where were *you?*"

"I've been here since 9:00 p.m. last night."

"You're lying!"

She stared at him. "What do you mean?"

"I rang the bell over and over, and even threw some coins against the window."

"I guess I was fast asleep."

"I don't believe you."

"Are you a little paranoid?"

"I don't know," he admitted.

"Honey, I would never cheat on you in a million years. You're the love of my life."

"Maybe I *am* a little paranoid."

"Why don't you call Dr. Berkun? Maybe he can prescribe something that could help you."

"I'm afraid that he might commit me to a mental hospital, and I might never get out."

"You've been hospitalized before, and they've always let you out. Why should this time be different?"

"I-I'm afraid."

"Call Dr. Berkun. If he thinks that you should be hospitalized, I'll come visit you. And if they keep you for more than a month, I'll get you a lawyer. I promise."

"I'm not ready."

HIS ILLNESS PROGRESSED TO A POINT where he couldn't read or play chess. He didn't know what to do with his time. He spent very little time in bed, and when he was in bed, he hardly slept. During the day he went for long walks. At night he spent hours with Michael at French Roast. He was full of delusional thoughts, which, at first, he kept largely to himself, afraid that Heather might call Dr. Berkun and have him hospitalized. In his mind, Michael was the head of the Israeli Mossad. *(I'd better be careful, or I might wind up in a mental hospital in Tel Aviv.)* He thought that Heather was a spy for Dr. Berkun. *(I can't tell her anything.)* Strangely, the only person he trusted was Chantal. He visited her at her apartment at least three times a week, mostly showing up unannounced. The first thing he told her was, "If I tell you what I'm going through, you have to promise not to tell Heather or Michael."

"Okay," she said.

"My condition is getting worse and worse. I don't want to go to my psychiatrist because I'm afraid that he might commit me. What should I do?"

"Goodness, I don't know what to say. I've never been in your situation."

"What do you *think* I should do?"

"I think you should ask your *doctor* that."

Sam gritted his teeth. "Dammit!" he said. "Everyone wants to put me away."

"No, I want you to be *treated.*"

Sam took a deep breath, then said, "I'll ask Michael what he thinks, and if he thinks I should go in, then maybe I'll call Dr. Berkun."

Later that night, Sam went to French Roast. He told Michael, "Both Heather and Chantal think that I should go to Dr. Berkun."

"How have you been doing?"

"I'm flipping out."

"What you mean by that?"

"I think I might be paranoid."

"Have you been severely depressed?"

"Not lately. If anything, I've been more manic than depressed."

"Have you been having delusions or hallucinations?"

Sam was about to ask him, *Are you the head of Mossad?* Then he thought better of it. All he said was, "I'm not sure."

"I think you should consult with Dr. Berkun, then."

"Oh, what the heck. . . ." Sam decided to go home and discuss the matter with Heather in the morning. But instead of walking towards the East Village, he started heading uptown. Before he knew it, he was at Columbus Circle. *(This means that I don't want to talk to Heather. No, I do!)* He tried to retrace his steps, but he wound up at Grand Central Station. *(Which train would get me to the East Village from here? What am I, nuts?)* He started laughing out loud. Everyone around him averted their gaze, which only made him laugh more. Then he broke into the song about everybody plays the fool sometime. Finally, a policeman approached him and said, "Are you alright, sir?"

"Frankly, no," Sam told him. "I am so not all right you have no idea."

"Have you been taking your medication?"

Sam looked at him suspiciously. "How do you know? . . ." He stopped in the middle of the sentence.

"Do you want me to take you to a hospital?"

"I—no, I have an appointment with my doctor tomorrow," Sam lied. "I'll let him decide whether I should be hospitalized."

"Alright," the policeman said. "But you can't stay here singing and laughing. How about I put you in a cab and let the driver take you home?"

"I don't have enough money to take a cab."

"Do you have someone at home who could pay?"

"I suppose my girlfriend could."

The policeman hailed a cab, and Sam got in but, instead of his own address, he gave Chantal's to the driver. When they got there, he asked the driver to wait while he went upstairs to get the money. He asked Chantal, "I just came from Grand Central Station. Could you lend me a twenty so I can pay the cabdriver?"

She was annoyed. "What would you have done if I didn't have the money?"

"I would have gone to an ATM."

"Alright," Chantal said. "But after you pay him, I want you to go to an ATM and pay me back right away."

He paid the driver and went to the corner deli to use the ATM, but he couldn't remember his pin number. When he told Chantal that, she said, "If you're so disoriented, I think you should go to your psychiatrist."

He looked at her searchingly. ". . .I suppose you're right."

Once he had made up his mind, he felt somewhat better. He had no trouble finding his building, where he went upstairs and got into bed without waking up Heather.

In the morning, he called Dr. Berkun. "I need to see you as soon as possible," he said.

"Is it an emergency?"

"No, I wouldn't say that."

"Why don't you come to my office at 4:00 p.m. on Monday?"

"Certainly."

He didn't know what day it was, so he went downstairs, bought a copy of the Daily News, and went to the Odessa Diner to read it. It was Saturday, July 1st. *(I don't want to spend July 4th in the hospital.)*

He ordered a coffee and began to read the paper. The front-page had the headline *Twister*. On pages two and three, there were photos and articles about a tornado in the Midwest that had destroyed many homes and killed four people. *(This is the wrath of God.)* As he flipped through the pages, he started becoming more and more paranoid. On page 6, there was a photo of Madonna. *(She'll be in the hospital with me, but I won't touch her, or I'll get AIDS.)*

After he finished reading the paper, he went home and found Heather in the kitchen, drinking tea. He told her that he had made an appointment with Dr. Berkun. She said, "I think you've made the right decision."

For the next two days, he didn't leave the apartment even once. *(If I go outside, the police will take me to Bellevue and I'll never get out.)*

At 3:00 p.m. on Monday, Sam went downstairs and took a cab to Dr. Berkun's office on the Upper West Side. Before entering the building, he walked around the block twice to make sure that no one was following him, then he rang the doctor's doorbell. It was still thirty minutes before his appointment. He sat in the waiting room, shivering with fear.

Finally, Dr. Berkun invited him into his office and asked, "What's been going on?"

"I don't know where to begin. I'm as paranoid as I've ever been, and all my friends think I need to be hospitalized."

"Do you agree with them?"

"I don't know. My friend Michael is the head of the Mossad, and he wants to put me on the payroll, but if he does, I am afraid that the FBI might arrest me."

"Sam, that's all in your mind," Dr. Berkun pointed out. "I think you should check into the Leonard Pavilion."

"How long are you going to keep me there?"

"Just until you're stabilized on appropriate medication."

"How long will that take?"

"About two weeks."

"And if the medicine doesn't work?"

"I can't make a prediction, but you'll almost certainly be out in a month or six weeks."

Sam put his head in his hands for a few seconds, then said, "Okay, just two things. Let me talk about it with my mother and let me wait until at least July 5th. I don't want to spend the Fourth of July in the hospital."

"That's fine."

He went outside, found a phone booth, and made a collect call to his mother. He told her, "Dr. Berkun thinks I should check myself into the Leonard Pavilion, but I'm not sure if I want to go."

"Have you talked about it with Heather?"

"I've talked about it with *everyone*, and they all think I should be put away."

"Well, then, I think you should go voluntarily, because if they commit you, you'll be there much longer."

Sam started crying. "Can you come with me when I check myself in, like you did before?"

"Certainly, sweetheart."

"All right. Let me see if Dr. Berkun can get me a bed, and I'll call you back."

He called the doctor and asked, "What time should I check into the hospital on the fifth?"

"I'll call and see if they have a bed. Where can I reach you?"

Sam gave him the number of the pay phone and said, "I'll wait here until you call me back."

Five minutes later, the phone rang, and Dr. Berkun said: "Why don't you check into the Leonard Pavilion at 3:00 p.m. on the fifth?"

"If you think that's best. . . ."

He called his mother back and told her what he had decided.

"I'll see you there," she said.

It was a beautiful day, so he walked all the way down to the apartment in the East Village, where he told Heather what he had decided.

ON THE EVENING OF JULY 4TH, HEATHER AND SAM went to East River Park to watch the fireworks. Afterwards, they went back to the apartment and tenderly made love.

At two in the afternoon the next day, they went hand-in-hand to the West 4th Street station, where they took the A train up to Inwood and walked over to the Leonard Pavilion. Mrs. Kanter was waiting outside the building.

When he saw her, he began to cry. "What have I done to deserve this?" he asked.

"You deserve to be happy, and you will be."

"I'm not so sure."

"So many people love you, and we all want you to be well. Maybe the doctors will find a medication that will cure you."

"You think so?"

"I think there's a good chance. They're coming out with better drugs all the time now."

She and Heather sat with him during his intake interview. Afterwards, he gave both of them a big hug and entered the ward.

Jillian, one of the nurses, showed him his room and introduced him to his roommate, Jethro, a thin, elderly man with thick eyeglasses. Then she told Sam, "I'll talk to you every day."

He walked into the lounge and perused the bookshelves, where he picked out a book of Robert Frost's poetry and began to read.

CHAPTER 38

AFTER A FEW MINUTES, A CUTE YOUNG BLONDE entered the room. "Hi, I'm Kitty," she said. "I'm Sam. Pleased to meet you." "What brings you here?" she asked.

"Just your basic case of paranoia. And you?"

"Just your basic suicide attempt."

"Ouch. How'd you do it?"

"I swallowed a bottle of Ativan."

"And survived?"

"My mom found me unconscious in my bedroom, saw the empty bottle, and immediately called an ambulance."

"What about now? Are you still suicidal?"

"I don't want to answer that."

"I don't mean to pry, but why did you do it?"

"My boyfriend dumped me," she said.

"You're still young. You'll find another boyfriend."

"I don't *want* another boyfriend," she said in a choked voice.

"Well, do you think you can get him back?"

She sighed deeply. "I guess not."

One of the nurses came into the lounge and announced, "Dinner is ready."

They followed her to the dining room. Sam took his tray and sat down next to Kitty. *(I wonder if she's above the age of consent.)*

There were eighteen people in the dining room, most of whom appeared to be very depressed. Jethro entered the room and sat down at Sam's left. "Why are you here?" Sam asked him.

"I'd be glad to tell you, but not here in front of everyone."

"Of course. My apologies."

Jethro turned out to be an interesting guy. They talked about the museums on Fifth Avenue, all of which they had both visited more than once. Sam told Jethro about Michael's art and that he had taught philosophy at Long Island University and The New School.

"Sounds like a fascinating guy."

"Beyond fascinating. He's my chief intellectual mentor." *(I'm not going to tell Jethro that Michael's the head of the Mossad.)*

While they talked, Kitty sat quietly pretending to follow the conversation. Actually, she was miffed that she didn't have Sam's undivided attention.

After dinner, Sam went to his room and lay down in bed. He started having delusional thinking. *(I'd better watch what I say; Michael might have spies here.)* Twenty minutes later, he dozed off and dreamt that he was in a straitjacket, totally unable to move, with Chantal standing in front of him and saying over and over, "You want me. You know you want me."

When he woke up, he had a huge erection, so he closed the door to his room and began to masturbate. When Jethro entered, he tactfully pretended not to notice. Even after ejaculating, Sam continued to masturbate. When the nurses turned off the lights in the hall, he changed into his pajamas and got back into bed.

In the morning, he got out of bed and went to the dining room. Miles, a heavy-set black man, took Sam's blood pressure and inserted a thermometer under his tongue. Once his vital signs had been taken, Sam skipped breakfast and got back into bed. At 11:00, Jillian entered his room and told him, "You have a visitor."

"Who?"

"A girl named Heather."

"Where is she?"

"She's waiting in the lounge."

Somehow Sam got himself up again and went to the lounge.

"Hey, baby!" Heather said.

"That's what I feel like, a baby. How are things in the real world?"

"Nothing much has changed."

"When does it ever? Anyway, thanks for coming."

He sat down next to her on the sofa.

"So," she asked, "have you met any of the other patients?"

"Just two. My roommate Jethro, and a little nymph named Kitty."

"Well, why don't you show me around?"

"Right now I'd rather sit. I'll show you around some other time."

Presently, Kitty entered the lounge.

"Hi, jailbait," Sam said.

"I'm not jailbait," she replied. "And I can show you my license to prove it."

"I was just joking. Kitty, this is my wife Heather."

"Pleased to meet you," the girl said, though she looked anything but pleased.

Heather stifled a laugh. "The pleasure is mine."

After an hour, Heather left. When she was out of earshot, Kitty remarked, "So that's your wife?"

"Yes."

"She's not much to look at."

"I think she's cute."

"Cuter than me?"

"Nobody's cuter than you."

"Then why not kiss me?"

"Whoa, Nelly. Slow down a bit," he said. *(Is she going to be another Kim?)*

"Okay, I'll slow down. You can kiss me in half an hour."

DESPITE KITTY'S ATTENTION, SAM FELT VERY BORED, except at mealtimes. Dr. Fletcher, Sam's psychiatrist, put him on a new medication named Clozaril, explaining, "It might take about two weeks to start working, but I'm very optimistic that this will help."

"I hope you're right," Sam told her.

A few days later, the doctor gave him the privilege of leaving the ward for an hour, accompanied by a nurse or another patient. He asked, "Is it okay if Kitty comes with me?"

"Sure, as long as it's okay with her doctor."

After obtaining the approval of her physician, Kitty joined Sam for a walk around the grounds. Before they left, Jillian told them, "Remember—no touching, no kissing."

They sat on a bench in the garden. "Sam," she murmured, "I think I'm falling in love with you."

"No, you aren't," he said. "Besides, you know I have a wife."

"I don't care." She snuggled up against him like a kitten. Finally, he broke down and kissed her. "This isn't right," he said, then kissed her again.

"I want to make it with you," she said in a throaty voice.

"No, no, no," he said, and kissed her a third time.

"You're acting like a woman," Kitty said. "Isn't the man supposed to be the seducer?"

Sam didn't answer. "Let's go inside," he said.

As Dr. Fletcher had predicted, the Clozaril started working very well. After Sam had been in the hospital for three weeks, most of his delusional thinking had vanished. Dr. Fletcher asked him, "Do you think you're ready to sign out?"

"Isn't that up to you?"

"No, the two of us can decide together."

"Okay, then I think I'm ready."

"I agree with you."

"So when should I leave?"

"How about tomorrow at one in the afternoon?"

"Great."

Sam immediately called Heather and told her the good news.

"Terrific!" she said. "What time are you being released?"

"One in the afternoon."

"Do you want me to come pick you up?"

"That won't be necessary."

"All right. Then how about we meet at the apartment at two, and I'll take you out for lunch?"

"Sounds good. See you then."

Sam also called his mother, who said, "I'm proud of you."

Then he went to look for Kitty, whom he found in the OT room. "Come to the lounge," he said. "There's something I want to tell you."

He sat on the sofa, and she sat next to him.

"I'm leaving tomorrow," he said.

She started to weep. "I'll be so bored without you."

Without thinking, he said, "I'll come and visit you." *(I wish I hadn't said that.)*

She told him, "When I get out, I'm going to make love to you."

Sam didn't respond. "I'm going to pick up my things," he said.

He ran to his room, where he pulled off his pants, got in bed, and started masturbating like a teenager. He was even hotter for Kitty than he had ever been for Chantal. *(Will I be able to resist?)*

He remembered what had happened when he cheated on Megan. *(I'd fucking better resist.)*

Two hours and three orgasms later he went to dinner, where he sat between Jethro and Kitty.

"Kitty told me that you're getting out tomorrow. Congratulations," Jethro said.

"Thank you."

He and Sam started talking about art again. "Who's your favorite painter?" Jethro asked him.

"I don't know if I have one favorite."

"How about your top five?"

"Well, Rembrandt and Vermeer among the Dutch painters, Titian and Rafael among the Italians, and maybe Cézanne among the French."

"Good choices," Jethro said.

Kitty was extremely upset that Sam was neglecting her. When they had finished eating, she said, "Let's go to the lounge." As soon as they were seated on the sofa, she said, "I don't think you should be talking to Jethro instead of me when it's your last day here."

". . .Kitty," he said, "you're not my girlfriend."

"But you know I love you, and it hurts when you ignore me."

He closed his eyes and put his face in his hands. "Kitty, you have to get over this. I'm married, and I'm not going to cheat on my wife."

She got up and stormed out of the room.

The next day, he left the ward on schedule, took the A train to West 4th Street, and walked across town. Heather was waiting on the stoop in front of their building. When she saw him coming, she ran to him and threw her arms around him. "Welcome home, sweetheart," she said.

"I'm back from the house of the dead," he replied.

"Was it as bad as that?"

"No, not really."

"Well, what kind of food are you in the mood for?"

"How about sushi?"

They went to a Japanese restaurant on Avenue A, where they both ordered miso soup and the sushi special. While they were eating, Sam told her, "I think this new drug I'm taking is going to help me a lot. I feel much better already."

"That's fabulous!"

"You know what?" he said. "I haven't been to The Chess Shop in a while. Would you mind if I went there for a game?"

"Not at all. Can I join you?"

At The Shop, Ahmed was behind the counter. He said, "Long time no see. Where have you been?"

"On the dark side of the moon."

As usual, Jim Smith was playing speed chess with a friend. When he saw Sam, he said, "There goes the neighborhood."

At a table in the corner, a young man was reading *Reassess Your Chess* by Jeremy Silman. Sam approached him and said, "Good book. Feel like a game?"

"Sure."

"I'm Sam, and this is my wife Heather."

"I'm Paul."

"Do you want to play speed or slow?"

"Let's play speed."

Sam won the first game; then Paul won five in a row.

"You're a great player," Sam said. "How old are you?"

"I just turned thirteen."

"*Wow.*"

They played for almost three hours, with Paul winning the vast majority of the games. Finally, Sam said, "I've had enough. Thanks for the lessons."

"Any time," Paul said.

Just after midnight, Heather and Sam went to French Roast to wait for Michael, who showed up at 1:30 a.m.

Sam told him about his hospital stay and the new medicine he was taking. Then he asked, "Have you seen any good movies lately? I know you see everything."

"Mostly junk," Michael said "But there's a good *film noir* series at the Film Forum. I have the schedule with me."

"What's playing tomorrow?"

"*Laura*, the Otto Preminger film."

"How about we see that tomorrow?" Sam asked Heather.

"Sure. I'm working at the dojo until six, but we can go any time after that."

"I'm psyched," Sam said.

While Heather was at work the next day, Sam went to The Chess Shop, where he told Marcus, "I'd like to pick up some students again, and if you hear about any after-school programs, please let me know. I could really use the money."

"Why don't you try Chess in the Schools?" Marcus said. "They're always looking for new people."

"I don't know if I'm ready to work full time," Sam said.

"You don't have to work every day. You can work three days a week if you want, and I'll give you a glowing recommendation."

"Maybe I'll do that, then."

SAM AND HEATHER WENT TO SEE *LAURA*, and later that night, they made their way to French Roast to compare notes with Michael.

"What did you think of it?" he asked them.

"We loved it," Sam said.

Sam got in touch with Chess in the Schools and set up an interview. He brought a letter of recommendation from Marcus with him. Carly, an attractive brunette in her twenties, conducted the interview. The first thing she asked him was, "What would be your approach if you were to teach a class of nine-year-olds?"

"I'd focus on the beginners and give a lot of attention to the students with some aptitude."

"Really? Usually a teacher focuses on the middle."

"I obviously have to start with the total beginners because they don't know the rules. But after that, if you prefer, I can focus on the middle."

Carly took Sam and two of her assistants into a small room with a demonstration board.

"Now, teach us how to checkmate with king and queen versus king."

"First let's introduce ourselves. I'm Sam."

"I'm Carly, and my two helpers are Grace and Fay."

"Okay. Now what you need to do in this endgame is to drive the king to the edge of the board, because you can't checkmate the king in the middle."

After he helped them solve the endgame, Carly asked him, "If we hire you, would you prefer to work full-time or part-time?"

"I'd prefer part-time."

"Okay. Part-time is three days a week. Would that work for you?"

"Definitely."

"All right. We'll call you in a few days and let you know what we decide."

AT THE BEGINNING OF THE NEXT WEEK, she called him and said, "Congratulations. You're hired."

"Thank you *so* much," he replied.

"What days do you want to work?"

"Well, I'm a full-time student," Sam said. "Let me see if I can schedule my classes so that I have three days off."

"Okay. Please let me know by the end of the week, because school starts in two weeks and I need to figure out which school to send you to."

"All right. I'll call you on Friday."

Sam set up his schedule at Hunter so that he had Mondays, Wednesdays, and Fridays off, and verified it with Carly.

Thanks to the Clozaril and the structure in his life, Sam felt better than he had in a long time. The only remaining symptom of his illness was hypersomnia—he needed a minimum of ten hours of sleep each night.

He was so busy with his new schedule that he had very little time to play chess. He tried to make it to The Chess Shop once a week to play speed chess, mostly against Paul.

One Saturday afternoon in September, he called the Leonard Pavilion to see if Kitty was still there. Jerry, one of the other patients, picked up the phone and said, "I'll see if I can get her."

He found her in the OT room and told her, "There's a call for you on the pay phone."

"Who is it?"

"I didn't ask."

"Well, you should have."

"Don't criticize me," Jerry said. "Just answer the phone if you want to."

Under her breath, Kitty muttered, "Asshole," and went to pick it up. "Who is it?" she asked.

"Sam."

"Where have you been?" she asked him.

"I'm sorry. I've been so busy. Would you like me to come and visit you?"

"Of course."

"I'm on my way," Sam said.

He took the A train to the last stop and walked to the hospital. Kitty was waiting for him in the lounge. "How are you?" he asked her.

"I wish I were dead," she replied. "If I ever get out of here, I think I'm going to kill myself."

"Sweetheart," Sam said, "you have so much to live for. You're young and beautiful and healthy—"

"Healthy? I'm *suicidal*, Sam."

"Yes, but that could change. Physically, you're fine. I could see if you had a terminal illness, but you don't. I'm sure your depression will lift eventually. It might just be a matter of their finding the right drug. That's what happened with me."

"I don't know how long I can wait," she said. "If I don't feel better soon, I'm going to kill myself."

"Don't. Please don't."

Before leaving the ward, he stopped by the nurse's station and told Jillian, "Please watch Kitty carefully. She's seriously contemplating suicide."

"I'll talk to her doctor and see if he wants to put her on constant observation."

"Good idea."

CHAPTER 39

CARLY ASSIGNED SAM TO A MIDDLE SCHOOL in East Harlem, where he taught five classes a day. Most of the children knew the rules, so after reviewing them for those who didn't, he taught everyone the elementary checkmates, basic tactics, and opening principles.

The next time Sam went to The Shop to play, Chantal was there, conversing with Ahmed. When she left, Ahmed said, "I'd love to go out with her."

"I wouldn't," Sam replied. "She's self-centered and egotistical, and she's been with so many men, I'd never be able to trust her."

The next evening, Chantal called Sam and told him, "I need to talk to you."

"Okay. I'll be right over."

When he was seated in her living room, she said, "Ahmed told me what you said about me. I don't appreciate you talking about me behind my back."

". . .I'm sorry," Sam said.

"You should be. You said you couldn't trust me because I've been with 'so many men.' How can *I* trust *you* if you're going to talk about it behind my back?"

"I'm *sorry*," he repeated. "It won't happen again."

Sam was furious with Ahmed for snitching on him. He went directly to The Shop in order to remonstrate with him, but he didn't want to raise the issue in front of everyone, so he asked him, "Could we go out for coffee when you get off?"

"I'm sorry, but I can't. I already have other plans."

"Okay, but I need to talk to you soon."

"That's fine," Ahmed replied, although, having guessed what Sam wanted to talk about, he had no intention of doing so.

Sam and Paul played speed chess at The Shop almost every week. Sam, who had a collection of over three hundred chess books, started giving the young man some books to read, among them Bobby Fischer's *My Sixty Memorable Games, Modern Chess Openings,* and *Power Chess* by Paul Keres.

Paul improved at an exponential rate. When they had known each other for about two months, he invited Sam to his bar mitzvah.

"Can I bring my wife?" Sam asked him.

"Certainly."

Benny Jackson, one of his sixth-grade students, was so talented that Sam asked Mr. Saunders, the principal of the school, "Can you give me the phone number of Benny's parents? I want to suggest that they start entering him in tournaments."

"I'll have to ask them if they want to give out their phone number."

"Please do, because Benny's very gifted."

"I'll tell you what," Saunders said. "Let me call them right now."

Beverly Jackson, Benny's mother, answered the call.

"Mrs. Jackson, this is Mr. Saunders, the principal of the Frederick Douglass Academy. The chess instructor would like to talk to you about your son. Is that okay?"

"Certainly. Put him on."

"Hi, Mrs. Jackson, this is Sam. The reason I'm calling is that Benny is one of the best students I've ever taught, and I think he could benefit from private lessons and tournament play."

"I've been thinking about that," she said. "Would you like to teach him yourself?"

"No, he's too good for me to teach. I think he should study with a grandmaster."

"Can you suggest someone?"

"Maybe if you call the Marshall Chess Club, they can suggest someone."

"Okay. I'll do that. And as for tournament play, he's already played in two tournaments at the Hunter School, and he won both of them."

"That doesn't surprise me. I think you should enroll him in the under-1600 tournament at the Marshall, which meets every Monday night. And if that goes past his bedtime, there are also weekend tournaments at the club."

"I'll look into it."

BY THEN, SAM WAS IN HIS LAST SEMESTER at Hunter College, which went by very quickly. After his classes ended, he went to pick up his diploma. He had graduated *magna cum laude*. To celebrate, Heather took him to Il Molino for Italian food. After dinner, they went dancing at the Limelight, where they stayed until closing. Then they went home and made love for hours.

The following evening, Sam got a call from Kitty. "Guess what?" she said. "They finally let me out of the loony bin."

"Congratulations."

"When can I see you?"

"Let me check with Heather. Maybe you can come over right now."

Kitty showed up at the building dressed to kill—in high- heeled shoes, fishnet stockings, a red blouse, and a black miniskirt. Heather graciously left the apartment so that Sam and Kitty could be alone together.

"So how are you?" he asked.

"I'm feeling much better. Just as you predicted, they gave me some pills that are helping."

"Good. Are you still having suicidal thoughts?"

"Now and then, but not in a serious way."

"That's wonderful. I'm so happy for you."

"Now all I need is a good fuck."

He raised an eyebrow. "Well, you can't get that here," he said.

"Too bad."

"Where are you staying?"

"For now, I'm with my parents on the Upper West Side, but as soon as I find a job, I'm going to look for my own place."

"What kind of job are you looking for?"

"I'll take anything that pays ten bucks an hour or more."

After they chatted for about an hour, Heather came back in. "Why don't the three of us go out for dinner?" she suggested.

"I have very little money," Kitty replied.

"It'll be my treat."

They all went to the Odessa, where they filled up on kielbasa, perogies, and borscht, then they walked over to the West Side and put Kitty in a cab back to her parents' house.

Paul's bar mitzvah was held at the Lincoln Square Synagogue. Afterward, everyone repaired to Paul's house, where they partied until midnight. Sam and Heather gave him a leather jacket and a gift certificate for a hundred dollars' worth of chess books.

When the party was over, Sam and Heather went to see Michael at French Roast, where Sam told him, "I just finished my degree at Hunter."

"Congratulations," Michael said.

"So what's new?" Sam asked him.

"Well, some friends of mine and I are going to have another exhibit at the Cork Gallery at Lincoln Center."

"That's fabulous," Sam replied. "When's the opening?"

"At 6:00 p.m. on Friday."

"We'll be there for sure."

On Friday, Sam and Heather got to the gallery promptly at 6:00. Michael introduced them to his fellow artists Richard Abrams, Ronnie de Silva, and Richard Parker. Although each of them had his own distinctive style, they complemented each other very well. Sam particularly liked the painting that Ronnie had done of the public library on 42nd Street. "I'd like to own that one," he said to Heather.

"Let's see what he wants for it. Maybe I'll buy it for you."

"You don't have to do that."

"I want to, if I can afford it."

De Silva told Heather he'd be willing to sell it for six hundred.

"It's a deal," Heather said.

"Let me just leave it here for the duration of the show, then you can come pick it up."

"Terrific."

After they left the gallery, Sam and Heather decided to go clubbing. First, they went to Webster Hall, then to The Tunnel, and finally to an after-hours bar in the East Village. Sam refused to let Heather spend a dime. When she demurred, he said, "Heather, you just bought me a painting. Don't argue."

By 6:00 a.m., they were back at their apartment. Although the temperature was below 30°F, they went up to the roof to watch the sunrise, then went back downstairs, and fell asleep in each other's arms.

MARCUS GRAF WAS ALMOST SEVENTY YEARS OLD, so he decided that it was time to retire. He and Naomi asked Ahmed if he would like to buy The Shop.

"What would it cost me?" Ahmed asked them.

Marcus gave him a price he couldn't afford, and the three haggled over the details for weeks. Finally, Ahmed, convinced that they'd never reach a deal, decided to open his own shop. Without telling them, he rented a property across the street and started furnishing it with chess tables. Since he had managed The Chess Shop for so long, he knew where to buy all the boards and pieces, both those with the traditional Staunton design and the other, less realistic sets. When everything was ready, he quit his job at The Chess Shop without giving any notice and settled in across the street. He called his new shop the Chess Emporium.

Both Naomi and Marcus were stunned by this new development. Naomi accused the players who went to the Emporium of disloyalty. She sat in front of The Chess Shop for hours, gazing at the enemy across the street. Most of the players chose sides and patronized one shop or the other, so there were a lot of bad feelings on both sides. Naomi couldn't even forgive the few players, such as Paul, who went to both shops. She asked him, "How can you call yourself a good Jew?"

He replied, "You just lost yourself a customer."

Since Sam had some friends who sided with Ahmed, he went to the Emporium to visit them. Ernie, one of the players, told him, "Don't you know that Naomi would fire you if she knew you were here?"

"I'll take that chance."

After he had been to the Emporium three or four times, Ahmed told him, "I think it would be in the interest of all concerned if you did not come here."

"You mean I can't come here to visit my friends?"

"I would prefer it."

"Now you're acting just like Naomi," Sam said.

"Don't compare me to Naomi."

After the Emporium had been open for about a month, Naomi told Sam, "Call the Emporium and find out what they charge for lessons."

"I'm not going to do that. Ask someone else."

Naomi shook her head. "You have to live in the real world," she said.

She hired Silvio, one of the chess players, to go to the Emporium. "Tell me who goes there," she said. "And let me know what Ahmed is up to."

She was so obsessed with the Emporium that, against her better judgment, she went there herself to take a look around. Ahmed shouted, "Get out of here, you spy." He followed her back to The Chess Shop and, in front of everyone, he spit in her face.

On a Saturday night in June, when Sam went to French Roast to visit Michael, he was surprised to find Kitty there, sitting at a table with a few of the AAs. "What a nice surprise," he said. "Have you been going to AA meetings?"

"No, I just came here to see you."

". . .How did you know that I would be here?"

"You told me yourself that you sometimes come here on weekends."

"Did you ever find a job?"

"Yeah, I'm working as a barmaid four nights a week."

"Great, which one?"

"The International, on 1st Avenue."

"I know that bar very well. They have a great jukebox. What nights are you there?"

"Tuesday to Friday, from eight at night to four in the morning."

"I'll definitely come see you there," Sam said.

"I was hoping you'd say that."

Sam told Heather about Kitty's new job. He said, "I'm going to the bar on Friday night. Would you like to join me?"

"No, I'm sure Kitty would prefer to see you alone."

"You're so trustful," Sam said.

"I know you'd never cheat on me."

"I never would, even if I were tempted. You mean too much to me." He told her what had happened when he cheated on Megan. "That will never happen again," he said.

On Friday night, Sam entered The International at 10:00. As soon as Kitty saw him, she ran up to him and gave him a big hug. "Thanks so much for coming," she said.

Kitty was dressed in a sexy red miniskirt. "You look fabulous," Sam said.

"So do you."

Most of the customers were men, and many of them were heavy drinkers. "What would you like to drink?" Kitty asked Sam.

"A Johnny Walker Black with one ice cube."

"How about a double?"

"Why not? Just give me a glass of water with it."

Kitty whispered in his ear, "I'd like to talk about our mental health," she said, "but not here in front of everyone."

"All right," Sam said. "We can wait until everyone leaves, or we could meet for coffee one afternoon this week."

Sam put some country and western music on the jukebox and chatted with his neighbor at the bar, an out-of-work construction worker name Steve. When Sam told him that he was a chess instructor, the man said, "Give me your card. Maybe I'll take some lessons if the price is right."

"I'll give you a big discount," Sam replied.

Kitty kept asking the customers to buy her drinks, as Will, the owner of the bar, had told her to. By 3:00 a.m., she could barely stand on her feet. Sam was very worried about her and said, "Kitty, I think you've had enough."

"Let me worry about that."

When the bar closed, she said, "Let's go get some coffee. I think if I get in a cab right now, I'll be sick."

They went to the Odessa. "So how are you?" Sam asked her.

"Well, I'm not suicidal anymore, but I'm certainly not happy."

"Life doesn't promise happiness. Just be thankful that you have your health."

She began to cry. "Sometimes I feel like I'd rather lose a leg then be this miserable."

Sam thought for a moment. "Are you seeing a therapist?" "No. Can you recommend someone?"

". . .Have you heard of Albert Ellis?"

"No."

"He's the founder of cognitive behavioral therapy. When I was feeling down, he helped me a lot. If you want, I'll bring you one of his books the next time I come here."

"I'd appreciate that."

Four days later, he stopped by the bar with a copy of *The New Guide to Rational Living*. "I can't stay here tonight," he said, "but let me know if you find this helpful."

The next time Sam went to The International, Kitty had the night off, but Ben Lester was there. He said: "I just turned twenty-one. How about buying me a beer?"

"Certainly," Sam said. He also gave him money to put in the jukebox.

Ben selected some tunes by the Velvet Underground and a few by Miles Davis. "What a great jukebox," he said.

Sam quickly finished his Johnny Walker, then downed two more. "Now," he suggested, "why don't you buy *me* a beer?"

Sam ordered a black-and-tan. By this time, Sam was pretty drunk, so he said to Ben, "Now how about buying me a coffee?" And when he'd finished that, he confessed, "I'd better go home now, while I can still walk."

Three days later, Sam was in The Shop playing speed chess with Jim Smith when Ben came in. In between games, Ben said, "You owe me money."

Sam asked Jim to excuse him for a few minutes while he went outside with Ben. "Why did you interrupt me when I'm playing?" he asked him.

"Well, you were in between games."

"You're a brat," Sam said. "And what's this shit about my owing you money? I don't owe you fuck-all."

Sam went back in The Shop and played for a few more hours, then he went to see Kitty at The International. "Did you read Ellis' book?" he asked her.

"Yes, I found it very helpful," she said. "Let's talk about it more when I get off."

"You mean I have to stay here until four in the morning?"

"Of course," she replied.

When the bar closed, they went to the Odessa again and sat at a booth in the back, away from the other customers.

"So, you liked the book?" he asked her.

"Immensely."

"Then why don't you go to him for therapy? I think you have a tendency to put yourself down, as I did when I first went there. Believe me, Ellis will cure you of that habit. He says that, except for the physiological component, self-downing is the biggest cause of depression. If you're anything like me, the pills will cure your medical problems and Ellis will cure your emotional problems."

"Alright, I'll give it a try."

CHAPTER 40

THE FOLLOWING EVENING, SAM RAN INTO INEZ, who was walking her dog on Sixth Avenue. "Hey," he said. "I didn't know you had a dog."

"Oh, I've had Caesar for three months now."

"What have you been up to?"

"I'm still at Julliard, and next year I'll be going for my master's."

"That's fabulous! When can I hear you play?"

"Want to come over now?"

"You bet," Sam said.

They walked to her house on Bedford Street, where her mother greeted them at the door.

"You remember Sam?" Inez asked her.

"Of course."

"I told him I'd like to play for him."

"Wait until he hears how much you've improved."

"Why don't you pick a composer?" Inez asked Sam.

"How about Chopin? Do you have anything by him prepared?"

"It so happens that I do."

She played an *etude*, the *Fantasy Impromptu*, and a nocturne. Sam was stunned. He told Elisha, "Boy, you're not kidding that she's improved."

Elisha was beaming with pride. "Would you like to stay for dinner?" she asked him.

"I'd be honored."

"Why don't the two of you relax and have a drink while I cook something."

"Sure thing."

"What would you like?"

"Do you have Campari?"

"Certainly."

"Then I'll have a Campari and soda."

Inez made a face. "I hate Campari," she said.

"I know," Elisha said. "What would you like?"

"Right now just a Diet Coke. I'll have a glass of wine with dinner."

Elisha prepared linguine with clam sauce, Wiener schnitzel, and an arugula salad. Sam said, Elisha, you cook almost as well as your daughter plays."

"Hardly," Elisha replied.

After dinner, Sam went to The Chess Shop. None of his favorite opponents was there, so he sat in the back room and opened a copy of *Chess Life Magazine*. He had only been seated for a minute when Ben Lester came in, threw a cup of hot coffee in his face, and ran out of The Shop.

Sam immediately called the police and told the dispatcher what had happened. Within minutes, three policemen showed up at The Chess Shop.

"He's probably over at the Emporium," Sam said. They all went across the street and, sure enough, Ben was there playing speed chess with Raphael.

Ahmed said, "You can't bring the police in here without asking first."

"Well, I just did," Sam replied.

One of the policemen brought Ben outside and put him in handcuffs. "Why did you throw coffee in his face?" he asked him.

"He owes me five dollars, and he refused to pay me back."

"Is that such a big deal?"

The police brought Ben to central booking, and Sam went back to The Chess Shop. Aroni, the new manager said, "Sam, your neck and chest are bright red."

"I'm alright."

"Even if you're alright, I think you should go to the hospital, if only to prove that Ben burned you, in case you want to press charges."

"Okay," Sam said.

Aroni called an ambulance, and the driver took Sam to St. Vincent's. The ER doctor examined him and said, "You have at least first-degree burns on your chest." He filled out a form proving that Sam had been burned, after which he released him.

A few days later, Michael brought one of his most recent paintings to show to Sam, who liked it a lot. "I think you should be at The Met," he said. "You're by far the best of the street painters, and you're not nearly as retro as the others. Still, I think you've gotten everything you possibly can out of Lake George. I'd like to see you paint a cityscape or a portrait, or even use some other medium, such as collage."

"I'll think it over," Michael said.

The following afternoon, Sam was in a deli near The Chess Shop when Ahmed walked in and said, "You'd better not bring the police in my shop again, or you'll regret it, Chess Shop trash."

Sam muttered, "Fuck you."

Enraged, Ahmed shouted, "Fuck *you! Motherfucker!"*

Sam quietly left the deli and walked to the 6th Precinct, where he told the sergeant on duty what had happened.

"Sounds like harassment," the sergeant said. "But it's going to be your word against his."

"So what should I do?"

"Why don't you fill out a report to start a paper trail, and if he continues to harass you, then you can press charges."

On his way back home from the station, Sam ran into Rafael. "I've been thinking," he said. "If Ben apologizes to me, I might be willing to drop the charges."

"I'll let him know," Rafi told him.

At French Roast later that night, Sam told Michael what had happened with Ahmed. "He thinks I'm a coward. Because when he cursed me out—"

"You didn't hit him?"

"I'm not a coward, I'm a wimp. I *should've* hit him."

"But then you go to jail, and he wins."

"Yeah, that's. . . ."

"That's the deterrent?"

At about 3:00 a.m. that night, Ben came into French Roast. "How did you know I was here?" Sam asked him.

"Rafi told me that you sometimes come here."

"So? What have you to say?"

"I want to apologize for throwing coffee at you, but I was so furious that you refused to pay me back that I overreacted."

"I honestly don't think I owe you a cent. I bought you a beer and gave you money for the jukebox. You bought me a beer and a coffee. We both spent exactly the same amount on each other."

". . .I guess I can see what you mean."

"Anyway, even if I *did* owe you money, you shouldn't have done what you did. You could've burned my face."

A tear ran down Ben's cheek. Sam said, "Well, either you're sorry or you're such a good actor that you deserve to get off on that basis alone."

The next day, Sam called the DA's office and dropped the charges. The lawyer who answered his call said, "Is he your best friend?"

"No. I just don't want to be responsible for giving the little jerk a record."

Sam never had much to do with Ahmed after their last meeting at the deli, so it never became necessary to press charges.

AFTER TEACHING CHESS IN THE SCHOOLS for about six months, Sam found a job as an English teacher in a high school in East Harlem, where he started a chess club in the afternoon to keep his kids off the streets. He penned thank you notes to Dr. Brown and Dr. Ellis, neither of whom he ever needed again. Now he just went to see Dr. Berkun every three months to give him an update on his condition.

Dr. Berkun told him: "You're my biggest success story."

Sam replied: "I'm sure you'll have plenty of others."

ADDENDUM

Chess Principles

1. Tactics

Fork—a fork is a move that uses one piece to attack two or more enemy pieces at the same time.

Pin—a pin is a move that forces an opponent's piece to stay in place because moving it would expose the king or another more valuable piece behind it.

Discovered Attack—a discovered attack occurs when a piece moves to uncover an attack by a piece behind it.

Removing the Defender—capturing a piece or a pawn, which fulfills a valuable defensive function.

2. Opening Principles

Development—putting the pieces in play, usually the knights and bishops first.

Central Control—controlling the central squares with pawns or pieces.

King Safety—usually castling.

3. ***Opening variations mentioned in this book (look at a board with numbers on the side and letters on the bottom):***

Sicilian Defense—1 1e4 c5

Queens Gambit Declined—1d4 d5 2c4 e6

Benko Gambit—1d4 Nf6 2c4 c5 3d5 b5

French Defense—1e4 e6 2d4 d5

Nimzo-Indian Defense—1d4 Nf6 2c4 e6 3Nc3 Bb4

English Opening—1c4

Open File—a vertical line with no pawns.

Semi-open File—a vertical line with only one pawn.

Scholar's Mate—a simple checkmate in four moves.

Books for Novices

Openings—*Ideas Behind the Chess Openings*, by Reuben Fine.

Tactics—*Chess Tactics for Champions*, by Susan Polgar.

Endgames—*Pandolfini's Endgame Course,* by Bruce Pandolfini.

Middlegame Strategy (for Intermediate Players)—*My System,* by Aron Nimzovich, and *Reassess Your Chess,* by Jeremy Silman.

www.ingramcontent.com/pod-product-compliance
Lightning Source LLC
LaVergne TN
LVHW050928080826
845145LV00001B/251

* 9 7 8 1 9 4 6 9 8 9 3 1 4 *